Second Sight

Books by George Szanto:

Fiction
THE CONQUESTS OF MEXICO:
The Underside of Stones
Second Sight
The Condesa of M.

LES CONQUÊTES DU MEXIQUE:
(translated by François Barcelo)
La face cachée des pierres
Double vue
La Condesa María Victoria

Friends & Marriages
Duets (with Per Brask)
Not Working.
Sixteen Ways to Skin a Cat

Essays
*Inside the Statues of Saints: Mexican Writers Talk About Culture
    and Corruption, Politics and Daily Life*
A MODEST PROPOSITION to the People of Canada
Narrative Taste and Social Perspective: The Matter of Quality
Theater and Propaganda
Narrative Consciousness

Second Sight

a novel by

George Szanto

Series Editor
Rhonda Bailey

National Library of Canada Cataloguing in Publication

Szanto, George, 1940-

Second sight: a novel

(Tidelines)

ISBN 1-894852-11-7

I. Title. II. Collection: Tidelines (Montréal, Québec).

PS8587.Z3S42 2004	C813'.54	C2004-941315-5
PS9587.Z3S42 2004		

Legal Deposit: Third quarter 2004
National Library of Canada
Bibliothèque nationale du Québec

XYZ Publishing acknowledges the financial support our publishing program receives from the Canada Council for the Arts, the Book Publishing Industry Development Program (BPIDP) of the Department of Canadian Heritage, the ministère de la Culture et des Communications du Québec, and the Société de développement des entreprises culturelles.

Layout: Édiscript enr.
Cover design: Zirval Design

Set in Bembo 12 on 14.
Printed and bound in Canada by Imprimerie Gauvin
(Gatineau, Québec, Canada) in September 2004.

XYZ Publishing	Distributed by: Fitzhenry & Whiteside
1781 Saint Hubert Street	195 Allstate Parkway
Montreal, Quebec H2L 3Z1	Markham, ON L3R 4T8
Tel: (514) 525-2170	Customer Service, tel: (905) 477-9700
Fax: (514) 525-7537	Toll free ordering, tel: 1-800-387-9776
E-mail: info@xyzedit.qc.ca	Fax: 1-800-260-9777
Website: www.xyzedit.qc.ca	E-mail: bookinfo@fitzhenry.ca

In memory of my father,
who taught me that water too has a language

Preliminary note

When *The Condesa of M.* appeared, a number of perceptive readers noted some comments I'd made about a trip to Mexico that would have happened before my 1993 visit, but after I was there in 1985. I did in fact spend several weeks in Michoácuaro at the end of 1990, but hadn't written about those misadventures. A couple of friends from the village had begged me not to, please—at least not right away. So I held off till now. I thought I was returning, in 1990, to a place I understood. As you'll see, I was wrong.

ONE

"Come celebrate my grand victory. You'll eat out of our garden." The telegram from Pepe, a good friend in Mexico, had arrived in late October. He'd been elected mayor of Michoácuaro. Not a role I'd have figured for him. Five years ago he'd just brought cable TV to the town.

The invitation did tempt me. A sun-drenched holiday, long talks with him and other old friends, fine tequila. Except my department here in Montreal was in the throes of a six-year review with me chairing the committee; of course I could resign my role— I wondered if I'd be able to cook up a new course for the January term while I was down there. No, if I did go away it should be a long-promised quick visit to Pieter and Katia in Amsterdam. And Mexico was becoming increasingly violent—I'd read about shootings and bombings during the elections.

The idea of Michoácuaro in December chipped away at my concentration. Going back to some of the magical places I'd discovered was appealing. Better than producing statistics about student-faculty ratios, costs per degree unit, comparative scholarly output. Would such a trip leave me refreshed to produce a well-documented review vital to the department's future? It was due February 1, 1991.

Since my year in Michoácuaro in the state of Michoacán, Pepe and I had been in contact off and on—six postcards, one serious letter. A lot of what he'd explained to me about his world I used in a book I'd published about my year in the town, the people I'd met, the many intriguing places. I didn't know what others there thought of the book; they were worse correspondents than Pepe.

Since it appeared, a few readers have tracked me down. Including some weird ones, like a couple of weeks after Pepe's telegram a phone call from a man in Germany, Hamburg. Gottfried Sommers he said his name was, and he'd read my book. His daughter now lived in Michoácuaro, "your little Mexican town." He was dying. Using my extra senses, I must insist to the daughter that she visit him one final time. He'd tried over and again to bring her home, but had failed. He refused to carry such a defeat to the grave.

"Look, I don't have extra senses—"

"I've just explained. I read your book. I know you." He offered me three thousand dollars.

"Three thousand? You're crazy."

"Very well. Five thousand. You will persuade her."

Five thousand dollars. If his daughter wouldn't go to him at his dying request, how could I convince her? Something was wrong here. No, the five thousand didn't tempt me. Yes, I'd been lusting after a new computer, I needed more memory, a colour monitor— An extravagance? Five thousand would buy a laser printer as well, eight pages a minute. "Call me back in a couple of days."

"You will hear from me," said Sommers.

That night I dreamt about Pepe. He was pleasantly drunk, though it didn't show—with Pepe it rarely does. He was telling a story to his friends; I was there too. He acted all the parts:

Miguel is furious. Every few nights something gets into his garden, trampling and eating his young peas and corn, his tomatillos, beans and beets. Twice he's seen it, fleeing into the shadows. One evening after a fourth glass of pulque he confides to his neighbour Alfonso, It's the nagual—the half-man half-beast monster. So as not to show Alfonso that he lacks in macho Miguel adds, But it doesn't scare me.

Alfonso, hiding his own fear, whispers, You sound terrified, and sips his pulque.

Miguel states, I'll set a trap. The plan: string a line of cans along the fence. As the monster's legs catch the string, these will rattle and wake him. With the rifle his grandfather carried while fighting beside Zapata he'll kill the nagual. Miguel asks, Can one kill a nagual?

Alfonso answers, I don't know. This late the pulque helps Alfonso know very little, a better way to slip toward morning.

In the middle of the darkest of nights, the can-trap rattles loud. Miguel wakes, grabs the rifle and a flashlight, runs to the garden. He hears thick breathing, shines the lamp— He sees the running legs of a brown nagual! He shoots at where its head must be. It gives a dreadful squeal and crashes to the ground.

Shining the lamp, Miguel approaches. There lies Evita, Alfonso's burro.

Dreadful. And even more terrible if Alfonso finds out. Quick, dispose of the evidence! So, all dark, he digs a large hole in the garden, buries Evita, and returns to bed.

He can't sleep. A hint of light in the sky, he gets up, slips out, stares at the grave. The ground above Evita is shifting. A quick thrust— One of Evita's hooves breaks through the dirt and sticks out in the air. Trying to escape! Miguel, frozen with fear, stares. More movement. Another hoof! Over minutes, a third. Then nothing.

He goes searching for a hatchet. Now two vultures are parading at the edge of the garden. He shoos them off. He works quickly, hacking away the burro's legs at the knees, reburying them.

Miguel complains to Alfonso, First a nagual, now vultures. Am I not cursed?

Alfonso says, I'm cursed, me! My Evita has disappeared from the face of Michoácuaro.

Soon Miguel's garden is producing the juiciest beets and tomatoes, the sweetest peas. All envy him. Alfonso says, Your bad luck has ended.

Pepe the one-man show, shooting the monster, burying it. Playing the monster, its rigored feet escaping the grave. We, Pepe's audience, laugh and laugh. We can't stop laughing. Though we've heard the story before, we keep on laughing. As long as we laugh, we're together.

My alarm woke me at seven and I had a feeling of well-being. I understood the dream very well; I'd been looking forward to seeing Pepe more than I knew. Then, later in the day, Gottfried Sommers called back. "You will accept my offer."

Dying men can make demands but this sounded like he was threatening me. "No. I won't."

Two seconds of silence. "You don't hear me, mein Herr. The five thousand is yours. You'll speak to my daughter. You will convince her. Understand?"

I wouldn't respond to the melodrama in his voice. "No."

"You will." The line went dead.

A crackpot. Unpleasant, too; just a bit creepy. Did he really call from Germany? More likely the phone booth down the street.

Some days later, Christmas over a month away, it snowed seven inches. Followed by ice rain. A slow melt. The slush froze. At a degree above freezing, it rained heavily. Puddles lay shallow over flat ice. A few feet from my door I slipped, tried to catch myself, landed hard on my shoulder. I was soaked and felt ridiculous. Nothing broken, but my headache throbbed for hours.

Was it just the damned report keeping me here? My wife Alaine had died over five years ago; it was her death that had sent me fleeing to Mexico the first time. I arrived the day before the great earthquake in Fall, 1985; my year there healed me. Since then I've had no steady woman in my life. In December maybe I'd get an invitation to somebody's Christmas dinner, or a New Year's party. How exciting. Amsterdam would be cold. I made up my mind, and phoned Mexico.

A woman's voice answered. "Sí?"

"Señor Pepe, por favor." I explained who I was.

"Ah, Señor Jorge!" Her throaty Spanish came out with a Michoácuaro lilt. "It's Vera, you remember? The daughter of Marta. Señor Pepe said you would call. Constanza said to greet you for her."

How flattering to be remembered, after more than four years. Constanza had been my housekeeper. Marta was her sister. "My very best to Constanza."

"Sí, señor. Un momentito."

Pepe came on. I said in English, "Congratulations, Mister Mayor."

"Have you lost your ability to speak? Amigo, estas hablando con el señor presidente municipal de Michoácuaro."

His English is way better than my Spanish; he only sometimes implies Spanish is the sole and true civilized language. We joked about this, but he won the language battle. I asked if there'd been any disturbances during the election.

"In Michoácuaro? Por favor, hombre! Little Michoácuaro?"

I accepted his invitation. "With great pleasure."

"Wonderful! Look for me at the airport in Mexico City."

"It's not necessary—"

"I know. But I'll be there."

Pepe is happiest when giving ease to his friends. He hardens if he thinks somebody's messing around with people he likes but he sparkles when he charms, as now, describing a low sun etching colours on his stone mountains. My woolly notion of returning took on edges and zing and for a moment I felt back there. More, as if part of me had never left. I'd call back with full flight information.

"The north will have changed you beyond recognition." He chuckled. "Wear a red carnation, so I can recognize you."

I laughed. There's a story about Pepe in the seminary from his mid-teens to early twenties studying for the priesthood, his mother's great hope. "This way I would forever be entrusted to the Virgin," he told me much later. "And the only human woman in my life? My mamá. As she would want." At the seminary he had proven himself a superior student. They sent him to Germany for five years, to study what he calls heavy theology. Time came for his return to Mexico. His mother's telegram read, Will meet you at the dock. Pin red carnation on cassock so I can recognize you.

In Veracruz he got off the boat wearing a linen suit with a flowered silk vest, a carnation on the lapel, his blonde German wife on his arm. Mamá fainted.

I spent hours choosing presents for a dozen people, and the pleasure of going back built on itself. I bought a large suitcase, packed it with my excellent selections to be given on The Day of the Three Kings—Twelfth Night—and borrowed a folding luggage cart. Playing the consumer usually brought on a headache, and this day was no exception.

I'd told a couple of colleagues about the man from Hamburg. Both said I should agree to try, since it was true-life Mission Impossible I'd certainly fail, but the money would be mine.

The morning of the flight I checked in at my office. The secretary handed me a brown envelope—a messenger had insisted it be given me personally. I did some slow paper-work and finally opened the envelope: five thousand dollars in hundred-dollar bills, U.S. currency. And a note, YOUR SUCCESS IS AWAITED. A phone number, a fax number. Both in Germany. I didn't even know his daughter's name. No return address. I called. No one, and no answering machine. An hour later, again nothing. At my bank, one more damn thing to do, I opened a special account, stuck the cash in and hustled to the airport.

In my shoulder bag I stowed three bottles of duty-free single malt, Glenmorangie; I boarded the flight and found my seat, on the aisle as reserved. The plane filled. The doors closed. I turned to stare through the window. Vast stretches of white, sub-zero elements made visible. The cloud cover was a porridgy mist.

We began to roll. I glanced up the aisle, and down. Every place was taken except the window seat beside me. Someone who missed the plane? I accepted my luck.

The captain announced take-off, the jets roared to full. I interlaced my fingers and held tight. We hurtled down the runway. Acceleration glued my back to the seat. The plane lifted, we banked, white fields fell away. No longer here, not yet there. My head ached. We rose above misty gruel. A low slant of light flashed on the clouds beneath. I glimpsed a still and ragged sea, and looked away.

I read for a while, a Mexican novel for kids. I felt a bit foolish but even that was hard going—the Spanish-vocabulary part of my brain had gone dry from inactivity. A steward offered drinks. I took a light-brown tequila with peppery lime-tomato chaser. He brought my meal, with wine. Then a digestif. I felt warm from the alcohol—precursor, I hoped, to boozy evenings with Pepe, Jaime, all of them. My eyelids drooped, my head dulled. I heard the fade of an announcement, the film would now be shown.

The film was ending as I woke. In the washroom I scrubbed the grit from my eyes. I tried my book again. Too many idioms. Michoácuaro suddenly felt like an immense distance away. I wanted, right now, to catch up on that life. I wished I had one of the senses another friend there, Ali Cran, claimed for himself, the ability to trace events left behind in time. I dozed some more.

The captain's voice announced our descent. The seat-belt sign flashed on. Ground temperature, sixteen Celsius. A light drizzle.

Rain in December? The plane dipped left and the city lay bright below—wet avenues and highways, blurred lines of street-lamps and cars. Smog equal to smoking two packs a day. I felt caught between vertigal queasiness and the delight of being here.

We touched ground, bounced once and roared along the runway. Several dozen hands broke into applause. My headache was gone. I checked my watch: 9:12. On time.

I can't explain this headache. I think I had it occasionally before I slipped on the ice. Now it came and went, sometimes with cause, sometimes for no known reason. A couple of weeks of warm weather would cure it. Maybe.

Immigration, which always makes me uncomfortable, went easily. I found my luggage and headed toward Customs, hoping I wouldn't have to unwrap the presents. They checked nothing and I was through. I looked about. No Pepe. Not wearing the suggested carnation, I suddenly counted this as bad luck. I lugged my bags and cart to the rear of the crowd. I waited ten minutes, twenty. I paced, scanned the arrival area, kept an eye on my bags. I did shoulder rolls. A neck exercise. I waited. My watch said 10:14. I took my bags and located Teléfonos de México, the long distance service, and gave the woman Pepe's number. She dialed and pointed to a booth. I picked up the phone. It rang fifteen-twenty times.

At last, "Sí, bueno?" Vera's voice.

"Is Señor Pepe there?"

"Señor Jorge, where are you?"

"Mexico City, at the airport. Is Pepe coming for me?"

"Oh señor, it's terrible, we're all so very frightened, we know nothing!"

"What?"

"It's Don Pepe, he—" Vera's voice caught a sob. "He's disappeared."

TWO

Four evenings ago Pepe had left the house to pick up a book from his Telecable office. Vera had begged him not to go out after dark, there were too many people around who feared he still might be inaugurated as mayor. "You know how he is, Señor Jorge, like a burro." He hadn't come back. The chief of police, Rubén Reyes Ponce, was investigating but had learned nothing.

So there had been serious opposition to Pepe during the election. He'd been plain cavalier over the phone—why hadn't he said anything? I like Pepe a great deal, but this side of him had already bothered me last time I'd been here. Now I heard the fear in Vera's voice. She spoke so quickly I couldn't get a full sense of what had happened. I tried to calm her; Pepe could be away for many reasons. I told her I'd be there as soon as possible, and put down the phone.

One day I had invited Pepe for comida, the main meal of the day, taken in mid-afternoon. He asked if he could bring a friend. Of course. Her name, he told me, was Raquel. Pepe, divorced twice, is firm against marrying again, and his description of Raquel, charming, lovely, was standard Pepe machismo. Raquel arrived without Pepe. She explained he'd said we should all meet at my place, he'd gone to Morelia, he'd be late. We waited an hour, then two. We were irritated,

we drank tequila, we worried. Well, Pepe was like that sometimes, and Raquel knew it. We got to know each other a little. We ate without him. We went looking for him. I was
angry enough for both of us. Two days later Pepe knocked
on my door. His first grinning words were, "Did you and
Raquel become lovers?"

Right here at the airport, should I be worried? Or again
just irked with him. There were two options—either, nothing to worry about, or, very much to worry about. What
kind of major turmoil had my splendid Michoácuaro gotten
caught up in? I made myself believe he'd no doubt be home
when I arrived, apologizing for my inconvenience. So I stood
in line for a local phone, a dial-it-yourself unit. I needed a
place for the night, and I hate hotels. My preferred host in
Mexico City is Jaime León, a journalist and photographer.
But, he'd told me, for Christmas he'd be in Xalapa with his
wife's too pretentious family. My second choice was another
friend, Cayetano.

I tried to decipher the telephone technology. Till 1982
calls had cost twenty centavos. Then with the inflation the
coin boxes needed to be changed. This proved so expensive,
for years public phones cost nothing. I find it civilized to
have an economy outstrip its technology and so provide free
communication. I read: a hundred pesos a call. I only had a
thousand peso piece, about thirty-five cents. The man behind
me tapped my arm, took my coin and dropped it down the
slot. A little screen lit up saying, 1,000. "Mil pesos credito." I
thanked the man.

A dozen rings, a female voice. No, Señor Cayetano was
away for the holidays. I started to hang up. My phone
instructor caught my arm and pushed a button halfway down
the machine. "Credito." I had nine hundred pesos worth of
time left.

Try Jaime? Remarkable patience from the line behind
me. I dialed. He answered. Well, Luisa had an ear infection,

they'd go to Xalapa later. Pepe hadn't met me? Of course I could stay with him. He'd be here in half an hour, maybe twenty-five minutes. No I mustn't take a cab. We agreed where to meet.

The screen showed eight hundred pesos. I pushed the credit button and handed the phone to my instructor. He grinned, as did two of the others. A woman said, "Bienvenido, señor."

I smiled back. "Gracias." It felt good to be here, despite not meeting Pepe.

It's scarily true that some who go missing in Mexico do disappear, are in fact done in. And too often one state authority or other is to blame. But surely Pepe's absence was a private matter. I could see he might have political enemies. But Pepe doesn't engage in antics that bring on real danger. Nothing to worry about, right? Get onto Mexican time. Wind down. Except I couldn't—how to be calm when a friend has maybe been kidnapped and I'm four hundred kilometres away?

Jaime's thirty minutes meant he'd be an hour. I needed to reserve a flight to Morelia, the nearest airport to Michoácuaro. It took twenty minutes to reach the counter. "To Morelia, late morning please."

The smooth-faced young man squinted at me. "Mañana?" I nodded. He scowled at his computer, shook his head, typed in information. He looked at me as if I were nine years old. "It's Navidad, señor. No seats until the twenty-seventh. In fact," and he clucked his tongue, "tomorrow we're overbooked."

"What about first class?"

His eyebrows rose. "Señor. We are a class-free airline."

"Any suggestions?" The humbled gringo in me spoke softly.

"Perhaps a car rental agency? But you know, it's Navidad."

Outside a thick whiff of diesel fuel caught my nose. Sweat trickled down my overdressed back. Six hours by bus to Morelia, two more to Michoácuaro. But the warm air on my face did feel good.

I've stayed with Jaime three times. Luisa was always sick, as if my pending arrivals made her so. "Her illness is an inconvenience," Jaime says, his irony lush. "Sometimes, a convenience."

He arrived. Fifty-five minutes. "Jorge!" A big man, round and bearded, he rushed from the car, took my hand, pulled me to his chest—a tight abrazo, a pat on the upper butt. "Ai, Jorge." This embrace, now formal affection, comes from an old ceremony, checking one's dear friend for a dagger on his belt. He grabbed me by the upper arms and studied my face with wonderful fondness. "Como estás, amigo?"

"Muy bien." Real affection. Except it should have been from Pepe. Jaime's warmth and generosity helped me overcome my worry for a few moments. Except Pepe, five years ago when I needed it, had breathed new life into me and right now, selfishly, I wanted more of that.

We got into the car. Jaime roared through the dark. The mist had become a drizzle and the road looked slick. "How's Luisa?"

He sniffed. "Like this city. Mexico has grown acutely unhealthy. Luisa takes the affliction into herself."

"The smog?"

He shook his head. "This rain. You see it?" He flipped his hand toward the windshield. "Perverse, Jorge. Four times in the last week. We have a pestilence here."

"A pestilence?"

"Jorge, I love this city more than any woman. But she is deeply infected."

I said in English, "Becoming an old fart, Jaime?"

He too shifted to English. "A fart, maybe. But old, not yet." He laughed, as if to stop aging he'd paid a usurious price.

"And what's her name?" Jaime was a longtime woman-izer; another explanation for Luisa's vapours, one that gave me a bit of sympathy for her.

He smiled. "Why aren't you asking just this of Pepe?"

I told him the little I'd got from Vera. "She sounded very worried."

Jaime turned onto a boulevard. "People disappear for many reasons."

"Probably."

He shrugged. "Every day a campesino from the hot country walks away from hunger or from the wife who can't bear children or who's made too many, he heads north, no forwarding address—"

"Except Pepe's no campesino."

"But all men have reasons to disappear for a while. Some reasons have radiant hair, warm lips, a soft bosom." He smiled to himself. "And so on down."

Yes, showing up late was more Pepe's style.

Now Jaime glanced at me, and scowled. "How well do you know Pepe?" A blast of horn and he swerved back into his lane.

Not well enough to imagine him running for mayor. "Pretty well."

"Maybe not being with a woman or heading to a woman. Maybe getting away from a woman."

"He said he'd come to the airport."

"What, you're so important? Maybe not from a woman, but from her husband and his knife. Or from the man the husband hired."

"Maybe."

"Jealousy doesn't wait for convenient times. If a man's life is at risk, he disappears for a while." He stopped the car.

I wondered if Pepe really had met up with some kind of danger, and whether it was sex or politics that had taken him there. "Hope you're right." A bit of worry crept into my stomach.

Jaime turned to the door. "Come on, let's say hello to Luisa."

We got out in front of a house on a quiet street in the Lomas de Chapultepec district. By the gate, thick attar of jasmine caught me up. "Wonderful."

He glowed. "Yes."

The scent was a fragrant barrier holding back the smog. Bougainvillea arched red and pink in the beam of a motion-detector lamp, all designed to keep one's glance off the leaden sky. We went inside. Soft light in the living room. From the radio a quiet guitar. Jaime gave me a tequila. We toasted each other's health, a too-formal gesture. He excused himself. I felt exhausted, but relieved to be here.

Jaime came back. Luisa, in bed, wanted to say hello. I went in. Yes, she felt a bit better. Soon they'd go to Xalapa. We chatted. Jaime and I returned to the living room. He poured more tequila. "And you, what plans?"

"To get to Michoácuaro." I despise favours bought with mordida, the bite, the bribe, but I let myself say, "However I can." Jaime had many contacts. "Can you find me a flight?"

"I have a friend." He shrugged. "Best to try in the morning."

I raised my glass. "Salud."

"And the best of health in Michoácuaro." He drank. "May the town be safer than other places."

A gloom to his toast. "Safer?"

"The damned elections. In Piedras Rojas, Santa Matilda, Tacámbaro, there's been trouble. In Jungapeo four people were killed." He put the glass down. "But people are killed even for non-political reasons." He smiled wryly. "In Michoácuaro also. A romantic place, yes? A place for lovers." The smile turned to a weak scowl. "But dangerous as well."

Dangerous wasn't my sense of Michoácuaro—at least no more than most small Mexican towns. I felt a bit insulted on behalf of a place I'd come to love. "Going to tell me?"

Jaime picked at the cuticle on his thumb. "I had a friend, Teófilo Através. A journalist. He went to Michoácuaro. He never returned." He bit at dead skin.

"What happened?"

A spot of blood appeared. "Two years— Yes, from October." He scratched his scalp. "Chinga, two years." He refilled his glass and topped mine off. "You don't like the tequila?"

"Very much. But I'll fall asleep."

He nodded, solemn now. "I loaned Teófilo a camera. A Leica III-f, a fine apparatus, made in 1923. Great clarity, and quite valuable. The Leica didn't return either."

"Is he dead?"

He sucked at a trace of the blood. "We travelled in Europe, Teófilo and I, in the sixties when the peso was strong. Teófilo is—was—a distant cousin of Luisa's." Jaime looked backward in time. "A good man. And a fat slob."

I waited.

"Teófilo called me. He was ecstatic. He'd gone to Michoácuaro on an assignment, very lucrative, for *Quest Magazine*. Know it?"

A glossy American travel monthly. I nodded. "He was researching?"

"Eighteenth-century Michoacán church architecture. Lovely basilicas and chapels. Why was he so pleased about this article? I don't know. His other reason for joy, he'd been joined by his mistress, a married señora from here, from the city."

"Lucky man." The response expected from me.

Jaime grinned. "They'd never before been together a whole night. She'd come back to Mexico City two days earlier. Teófilo was mailing me a package, she told me on the phone. To keep for him."

"What was it?"

"Love letters? A locket of her hair? He didn't say."

"So what happened?"

"He disappeared." Jaime rubbed at his thumb. "Why? I don't know. The señora's husband, seeking revenge? Here in the city a man will endure his horns in silence. Would he travel to the hot country, to kill his wife's lover?" Jaime shrugged. "I don't know the woman. Or the husband."

"You never saw your friend again?"

Jaime shook his head. "The chief of police there, he was once your landlord, no?"

I nodded. "Rubén Reyes Ponce. Yes."

"The federales too searched for Teófilo. They spoke to me. They knew he'd called me."

"Did they tell you anything?"

"Indirectly. The desk clerk swears Teófilo returned, about eleven. The next morning he didn't come down. The maid found no one. His papers and clothes were in disorder. Which is not unusual, at home too Teófilo lived like a pig."

"Maybe church architecture," I smiled, "is a dangerous subject in Michoacán."

"Don't joke. He could smell a story."

"Sorry. What about the package?"

"Maybe he never sent it. Maybe it was taken from the post office. I don't know."

Okay, one could disappear from Michoácuaro. I didn't want to admit it, not now, not tonight, but Jaime spoke about a town I'd had a few insightful glimmers of last time here. Now I wasn't sleepy—weariness had been overtaken by a perverse kind of excitement. Only momentarily, I hoped.

"And how much is it worth, a big story uncovered by a smart journalist? One life? Ten? A finger, an ear?" He glanced at my glass, still near full. "Ai, Jorge. So abstemious."

I felt far too sober. "Why are you telling me this, my friend?" Though I sensed what he would say: over a hundred journalists in Mexico kidnapped or killed in the last dozen years—

He rubbed his thumb. "A phone call comes: Meet me at such a place. The time is lonely, the place in darkness. I used to go. But now I feel fear. What happened to Teófilo? Quién sabe." He chuckled. "Maybe you're right, I am a fart, and old."

Not the voice of Jaime León the radical taunter who has fought decades long against newspapers that sell headline space to the ruling party. I ignored it. "How can you be sure Teófilo is dead?"

"Obvious, no? He never came back." He sighed. "Also, I felt his death."

Feeling a friend was dead. I'd been away too long, all that indirect awareness.

With a forefinger and the red-scabbed thumb he massaged his eyebrows. "Just that."

I felt a sudden exhaustion and let myself yawn visibly. "Jaime, I have to go to bed." Not sleepy, just dim and weary in the senses. "It's been a full day."

"Jorge." He grasped my forearm. "I'm worried about Luisa, very much. The doctors find nothing. But something is there."

"What are you suspecting?"

He shrugged his right shoulder. "She won't leave the city. This appalling splendid city. Our economists study at your universities, they say cities grow or they die. But if we grow more, we will surely die."

"Die?"

"Because you see, we ourselves, we are the growth. And it's malignant."

"You sure are sour." I sipped. "Worse. Metaphysical."

"Of course. What else?" He scowled. "Have you been reading, in Brownsville how many anencephalytic babies have been born? Twenty-eight in the last two years?"

"Sure, grisly—"

"Babies without brains, Jorge. Gruesome justice, no?"

"Justice for what?"

"Many things. Like the Finsa Industrial Park across the Rio Bravo from Brownsville. I've just written about it. I have some wonderful grisly photographs. My editor will publish none of them. The moment in our trade talks with the U.S. is sensitive, he says."

The Rio Grande, Rio Bravo to Mexicans, is filthy. Still, upriver there's been a serious effort to clean it up. "Can't you find another editor? Another paper?"

He stared into his glass. "I mean it this way." An explanation in the tequila: "If as she is now Luisa were born today, born as a baby, she'd be without a brain."

Then I'd had enough of concocted horrors. "Don't, Jaime." I needed to lie down.

He glared at me. "I must say harsh true things. Then I can feel better." He shook his head. "For the moment."

I nodded. "I do need to sleep."

"Yes, of course." He carried my small suitcase upstairs. His present would wait till tomorrow. "Thanks."

In the darkened room, sleep not yet there, I tried to picture fat Teófilo, with his likely string-bean mistress. In their bed in the hotel by the market they embrace all night, they fold into each other. In Jaime's guest bed I lay alone. As I had up north since my wife Alaine died. Oh, a couple of women, brief ventures of hope, but having reached fifty I was too set in my ways to start again. Or too busy. Which didn't keep me from glancing twice at a pretty face or slender long legs. But to envy a fat man and his skinny compañera? No, I'd not thought of Michoácuaro as a place for lovers. Nor, for that matter, as a place for political disappearances. That only happens in other places, right? The picture of Teófilo faded and a thick heavy sense of death took me over. The weight of the day's events finally drugged me out.

I awoke tired, momentarily unsure where I was, and with a shaky sense of loss. Jaime told me he couldn't reach his airline contact, anyone sane leaves the city at Navidad. A couple of cups of strong coffee helped. I called three car rental agencies; same story. I called Vera. Pepe hadn't returned. It'd be dark when the bus got me there.

My gift for Jaime, pirated software to speed up his word-processing, filled him with as much delight as a kid getting his first Nintendo package. He showed me pictures of the Finsa Industrial Park—shiny chemical canals, cardboard huts. "You see, Jorge? You're lucky, my pictures don't let you smell the stink. This is the drinking water. It glistens like a fluorescent bulb, very bright at the moment it dies."

We drove through drizzle to the bus terminal. Sorry, all first class buses booked for a week. Okay, second class unreserved—not a trip to look forward to. Jaime bought me a copy of *Proceso*, a kind of Mexican *Newsweek*, and waited with me. I got on, left my shoulder bag on a window seat, my pull cart in the rack. He stowed my suitcases in the luggage bin below and gave me the receipt.

A warm abrazo. "Jorge. A small favour."

"Of course."

"The camera I mentioned. Could you ask your police chief friend, does he know what happened to it? A Leica III-f." Jaime smiled, light. "I doubt he will."

"No problem. Thanks for the bed. See you on my way back." I climbed on, reached my seat, waved goodbye. A wide woman with a round face sat next to me. She smiled, I nodded. The bus backed out, people closed their windows, we were off. Quickly the air grew stale. My doctor friend in Michoácuaro, Felicio Ortíz, explains the Mexican cycle of the seasons: December is winter; winter is cold; here we catch cold easily so we keep the windows closed. Did that make sense, in some angular way? Five years ago I had often wanted to think so. Up north, no way.

Music blared, Mexican rock and roll aping a ranchero melody. My nasty friend the headache was back; clearly the music this time. I leafed through *Proceso*. I found an analysis of the mayoralty elections across the nation. Electoral reform, promised after the corruption-riddled presidential vote of 1988, hadn't happened. Around Michoacán, the Movimiento por un Michoacán Moderno insisted they'd been cheated out of seven mayoralties, supporters' names kept off voting rolls, stuffed ballot boxes. Like Chicago in the twenties.

Rain misted down. I spoke without thinking: "Strange, these rains."

The woman beside me said, "The city is cleaning itself."

I wondered about that, the self-cleaning city, and about Jaime's sense of Luisa, her internalizing the city. Neither made much sense. Or maybe I'd been away too long to understand. I returned to *Proceso*. I read about Piedras Rojas:

The municipal offices are besieged by supporters of both the party of the left and the party in power, the PRI, acronym for Institutional Revolutionary Party. Left supporters sit at the desks of the treasurer and the agricultural agent, PRI supporters at the desks of the tax man and the health officer. The left holds the men's washroom, PRI the women's—a source of significant shame to the PRI. The two groups, in daily life neighbours, compadres, trade jokes and friendly insults. Always prepared, they carry machetes, pistols, and rifles.

No candidate may enter the mayor's office. Going in presumes a legitimacy which neither side will concede to the other.

Out on the plaza the left's candidate Arturo Mendez Mendez addresses the crowd, campesinos carrying scythes or machetes. Mendez accuses the PRI of including on the rolls forty-two men and women who have long crossed over to the U.S., and fifty-nine who live only in the cemetery. The hundred-eleven dead and absent managed to show up for the election. "Prove it!" yells the PRI. Mendez demands the list of voters be made public. "It's been sent away for safety," cries a PRI organizer. Everyone knows where it is: locked in the safe in the mayor's office.

"Open it! Open it!" shouts the crowd.

"Yes we shall open it," proclaims Mendez. "Democracy will rule!" He jumps from the platform.

His aide catches his shoulder: "If you enter the office they'll kill you."

"I won't be the first corpse to be mayor of Piedras Rojas," jokes Mendez, "and if they're going to kill me, I should be there for the event!" He leads the crowd through, marches up the stairs and kicks in the door.

The trigger-itchy support groups begin shooting, more or less at each other. Mendez, ordering them to stop, is cut down in the crossfire. The safe remains closed two days later, as the *Proceso* article is being written. Mendez is dead. But, as one local wit notes, in the next election he'll surely be voting.

"Terrible." The woman beside me stared at the *Proceso* photo, a grizzled old man holding an ancient rifle, two bandoleras of bullets crossing his chest. I nodded.

We ground our way up from the Distrito Federal beside trucks belching toxins, autos with bumpers held in place by wire, a few new cars with tinted windows closed, buses of all classes. I closed my eyes. The music thundered.

We reached the top of the pass, wooded parkland on both sides, and descended to Toluca. Here was industry— refineries, beer bottling plants, chemical and electronic works, factories for clothing fashions with French, Italian, German, Japanese, and American names. Soft drinks. Auto parts.

We crossed the Rio Lerma, historically one of Mexico's seven great rivers, running saffron with streaks of luminous purple. It suddenly felt acutely absurd, riding a bus toward a friend who wasn't there. A poster read, Site of Toluca 2000, Biggest Industrial Park in Central Mexico, Space Available. Sheep grazed in the scrub beyond the sign.

An hour and a quarter from Mexico City the country-side opened up, fields and hills, some cattle, expanses of dry land.

We stopped in Heróica Villasucita. The town, in hills two thousand metres above sea level, sits high on a slope, its spires shining in the sun. Below is a lovely little oasis, the Hotel Rancho San Andreas. North lies the Parque Nacional Angangueo, winter home to millions of monarch butterflies, a magical world; amid flying monarchs the whisper of fifty thousand flapping wings tickles your ears. Pepe had brought me there.

"Señor, would you guard my seat?" The woman beside me stood. I nodded.

About Mexico I have an observation, corny and roman-tic: every town has an attractive plaza lined with four kinds of flowering trees and three kinds of palms, a central foun-tain where everyone gathers, beggars, car-guarders and shoeshine boys aged seven or forty-five or eighty, knots of girls giggling about boyfriends, old lady gossips, middle-aged men striking a minor business deal to the well-deserved detriment of some third party, couples parading amorously. It's the kind of public life that makes a community. To prove this true, an exception exists: Heróica Villasucita. The immense plaza is made of cement, a few scraggly trees sur-vive at one end, the main street is ochre-fume filthy.

When I used to wonder why, some would look at me oddly. Others muttered, "Quién sabe?"—more than, Who knows? here meaning, Forget it, no one can ever know. Quién sabe stops discussion, shrouding answers as in bus-exhaust.

The woman returned. A third of the bus's population was new. The driver revved the engine, its spewed jaundice-smoke contributing to Villasucita's image. He pulled the door closed and we chugged off.

I read my *Proceso*. Another stop, Hidalgo, another shift of passengers. Nearly 3:30. The sun dropped toward Mil Cumbres, the thousand peaks, a heavily wooded national park where logging is illegal but happens all the time.

I dozed. Then we were on the ring road around Morelia, and at the terminal—just a couple of hours from finding out what was going on with Pepe. We gathered to pick up our bags—suitcases, cardboard boxes, straw hampers. I found my small case and waited. More boxes. A crate full of bread. One of coconuts. I waited. I felt a creeping uneasiness, and waited. The luggage compartment was empty. My suitcase of presents wasn't there.

The driver walked away. I ran after him. "My suitcase, my friend in Mexico City put it in, it's gone!"

"What?"

"My other bag. It's not here." I showed him the receipt.

He came back to the bus, bent down, looked inside. He straightened. "You're right. Not there."

I was furious. "But what could have happened to it?"

He shrugged. "Quién sabe?"

THREE

In the terminal an old man in a work uniform was swabbing the floor, very slowly. People walked across soapy cement, leaving the patterns of their soles. "Where can I find the station manager?" He pointed to a door. My anger had dispersed into anxiety and a frustrated sense of loss. Wheeling my solitary suitcase, I followed two sets of shoe-tracks. A few steps from the door they vanished. I knocked.

The door opened a foot or so. A young woman with pale blue eyes said, "Sí?"

"Are you the manager?"

"No." She stepped halfway out. Behind her a man, his white shirt unbuttoned to the waist, sat on a desk.

"I want to speak with the manager."

"He'll return in the morning." She backed into the opening.

I put my foot on the door jamb. "Somebody has taken my bag."

She looked beyond me. "How did it happen?" I told her. She shook her head. "You should have been careful, señor."

"Wait a minute—"

"You want to fill out a form?"

I controlled myself. "Yes. Please." I moved past her, and turned. "But can you trace it?" She stepped up to me. I backed into the office.

The man slid off the desk and pushed up his sleeves. The woman shook her head. He glowered at me, then stared out the window.

All those gifts—a cashmere shawl for Constanza, four early John MacDonald novels for Pepe, a teddy bear and a panda for a couple of little kids, a bag of Lego blocks. "Can you maybe check with the police in Villasuscita? Or even here, and they could—" I could see by her face I was getting nowhere.

"As you wish." She looked unfazed.

Head-bashing-against-wall time. Tension level up above its Montreal version. I filled out a form and left. A phone booth. I could call the police myself. A Morelia directory. I dropped a hundred pesos into the slot and dialed.

After a dozen rings a male voice said, "Sí?"

I explained, giving my interlocutor gaps to help me along. No responses. My Spanish worsened with his silences. I ended.

At last he said, "Momentito, señor."

"Wait!" But he'd already set the phone down and gone away. No background noise. A quiet evening for the Morelia cops.

Momentito means, literally, a little moment. But it implies that before your problem gets dealt with a number of important events have to take place, including but not limited to half a dozen pointed exchanges with subordinates, an extended conference with the chief of section, and a series of random psychological classifications of the parties concerned, often based on the alleged sexual practices of their mothers.

Two minutes. I waited. Three, five. After eight I broke the connection. To look for help by proceeding directly was gringo-dumb. I knew one cop with maybe clout—my ex-landlord Rubén. I called his office in Michoácuaro.

In Michoácuaro the police station, across from the market and beside the cathedral, is attached to the jail. From the street you can see the inhabitants, mainly drunks, sometimes a murderer in transit to the prison in Uruapan. A prisoner can call out to the citizens passing by. They say the most comfortable position is to rest your chin on the level bar and let your arms hang out through the vertical bars. The sign above the jail door reads, Centro Preventivo de Readapcion Social.

Not only did I get through, Rubén himself answered. "Jorge. I heard you were returning."

Not a man for sentiment. "What news of Pepe?"

"We know nothing. It's not good. Michoácuaro has changed."

I explained about my missing bag. "There's even a present in it for you."

"Kind of you, Jorge." He sounded exhausted.

"Do you know anyone with the Morelia police to help me?"

"Where are you staying?"

"I'll be in Michoácuaro this evening, I—"

"Remain in Morelia. At the Posada de la Soledad. I'll try to reach my friend Enrique. He will call you."

A strange thing, hope; it abandons the body at the speed of a blink, then pops back in just as quickly. "Many thanks, Rubén."

"Be careful, amigo. Even in the bus."

I promised. "Adiós." In the growing dusk I found a cab to take me the four blocks to the hotel—converted from a sixteenth-century monastery, the driver said. The central patio, all grass and flowers, was gently lit. Evening birds sang. Yes, a room was available. Despite my dislike of hotels and the rankling last hour I felt a sense of release. I told the clerk I expected a call, a friend with the police. The clerk's deference increased. I was embarrassed to discover this pleased me.

I had a bath, read, waited for the phone to ring. I suddenly thought, the man from Hamburg, Sommers! ...you don't hear me... But a missing suitcase? Ridiculous. If

Sommers was responsible, he'd have left some kind of signal to remind me. I went down and told a new desk man I'd be in the dining room when my friend with the police phoned. After a dinner I barely tasted, my little revived hope draining away, I went for a walk. My state of anxiety was up there; even about Sommers. I made myself laugh at myself. It didn't much help.

An eminent cathedral, crenelated baroque highlighted by hundreds of sealed beams, dominated the main street. Across from it at a hundred sidewalk tables men and women laughed, drank, flirted and ate, untouched by the brilliance of the spiritual life. I saw them as through a picture window framing a party I wasn't invited to. Why the hell had I come back to Mexico.

"You know why." I spoke aloud. To be again with people who'd helped me understand the world and myself differently. Helped me too to bring my mourning to a close. It was now six years since Alaine had died. We'd been married nineteen years. She was ill a terrible long time. We'd been as close as two people could be, one of those loves that friends envied—all the more remarkable, they would comment, that you can have stayed so involved only with each other over the exciting sixties. We thought so too, and wondered at our luck. Even in the last four years, as she was dying, we were pretty nearly everything for each other—she needed me for the demands of her weakening daily life, I needed her for her wisdom—and for her grace. Even over those years it shone from her face.

I see her in the very last weeks before her death. Now she rarely smiles. But once as I come into the room her face is glowing, from a light upward curve of her lips to the soft pleasure in her eyes. I sit beside her, I try to smile too. "What?" I say.

"Appreciation," she says.

"For?"

"The privilege—" She breathes thinly. "The privilege…
of love."

Her skin is near transparent now. I see the small movements of her life under it. I take her hand, stroke her knuckles. They are cool.

"A kind of… thanksgiving." She coughs, shallow. "That
this—" Her breath catches. She waits. "That this love could
have—have happened…" A sniff, like laughter. "…to us…"

I have lived with memories so specific, so clear in out-
line, they seem corporeal. When I reach out, they dissipate.

I came for a year to Mexico. Alaine is lost to me, yes. But in
Michoácuaro I found ways to remake a large part of myself.
When I left I sensed a new ease. I came back to the north
with a greater range of ways to think and to feel. Another
kind of privilege.

That fine notion, mañana, changed me. Not everything
asked of me, not even the terror of my wife dying nor, more
mundanely, the bureaucracy of work, the patterns I'm tied
into, has to be dealt with today. One can do other things
today. But at home I live in a community of decent people.
Their, and my, ways of daily life go on inside me, reinforcing
northern patterns, large and small. In Mexico I had managed,
slowly, to forget some of the patterns. At home again the old
patterns were waiting for me, ever-present, ready to be re-
absorbed. Much of what I learned in Michoácuaro became
lost to me. A reason to go back to Michoácuaro.

The desk clerk was all discretion. "Your guest is in the bar."

The tiny bar held six stools, five tables, one bartender.
Two couples. And a man wearing a dark polo shirt.

He stood. "Lieutenant Rodrigo Ángel of the Morelia Police. Captain Enrique Malasombra, a colleague of the Michoácuaro jefe de policía, has asked me to meet with you." Contact with authority. We sat. "Thank you for coming." "It is our duty to deal with crime of every kind." On Lieutenant Ángel's right cheek a four-centimetre scar curved from his moustache toward his ear. "Describe what has occurred."

I told him about my suitcase.

"Perhaps not a crime. But Captain Malasombra believes every hint of crime must be investigated."

Hard to believe, and his irritation scraped at me. "And you don't?"

His mouth was a straight line. "Especially in the case of tourists." But his voice sneered. "Tourism is important to Morelia."

"Good."

"Especially tourist friends of influential citizens of Michoacán."

The repetition of "tourist" made me accept I'd never see the suitcase again. "Lieutenant. Call me when you find it." I stood.

Ángel looked up at me calmly. "You are very upset, señor. Because your suitcase is missing?"

"Everything seems to go missing in Michoacán."

"Ah." He leaned back in his chair. "What else have you lost, señor?"

"It doesn't matter."

"I believe it matters to you, very much."

I couldn't believe I heard a kind of psychologistic sympathy in his voice, but whatever it was cooled me out a bit. "Someone I know in Michoácuaro. He seems to have disappeared."

Now Ángel squinted, as if to see me more clearly. "And your friend's name is—?"

"Pepe Legarto. José Legarto Nitido."

He stared at me, not a flinch. "And what is Pepe Legarto to you?"

"He's my friend. There are important items for him in that suitcase." I felt the bartender's full attention.

Lieutenant Ángel took my wrist. "Señor, sit. I know Legarto. Twice he has been of help to me." A hard smile. "We will find him." His eyebrows rose. "And your suitcase."

"You're looking for Pepe?" He nodded. "Here in Morelia?" I sat. "What's happening?"

"I'm not at liberty to say, señor."

"Can one assume he's—" I shrugged, and forced some words out: "—maybe in trouble?"

"I'm searching for him, I assure you."

I sighed. The bartender had relaxed. Who was this Ángel? "How has Pepe been of help to you?"

His eyes narrowed, my question out of place—like telling him to hand over his pistol. "Why do you want to know?"

"Like I said, he's my friend."

Ángel thought a moment, then nodded. "One time, some months after I entered the Morelia police, there was a young woman." His sudden grin extended out to the scar and turned his face boyish. "I adored her, señor. Marilita."

I nodded. Rodrigo Ángel was transformed, a lad in love.

"Her family grows corn. And of course marijuana. You know the Americans, they insist there's marijuana in tierra caliente and they say, You, our Mexican friends, you have to destroy it. Then the federal police bring helicopters, for three days or a week they search, they burn one small field, another, then arrest a few campesinos. The Americans are satisfied, justice is done. Soon the charges are forgotten and the campesinos go home. The father of Marilita, one of these campesinos—" He stopped.

"The father?"

He shook his head and his smile went sad. "I have already said too much, señor. It is enough, that Pepe Legarto helped

me." He got up. "Forgive my brusqueness. My captain took
me from my investigation to meet with you." No smile at all
now. "I am Morelia's expert for Michoácuaro."
   I nodded and stood also. "My apologies."
   "They aren't necessary."
   "Then my thanks." We shook hands. He'd be in touch.
His professionalism was restorative. But the Morelia police
were concerned about Pepe so I was newly worried. Which
I expect was the cause of my returned headache. Nothing I
could do till morning. I took a pill and slept deeper than last
night.
   At the terminal I found the manager. Ángel had already
spoken with him. He was pleasant enough, but no luck yet.
A bus was leaving in five minutes nonstop to Michoácuaro.
I got on and again took a window seat.
   A campesino with a grizzled face sat beside me. In his lap
he cradled a machete. With each breath, he wheezed. The bus
drove out of the station, out of Morelia, down a road winding through hazy sunlight into the hills. We passed groves of
trees and fields of dry corn. After forty minutes we turned
onto hard-baked clay, an unfamiliar route. I turned to the
campesino. "Is this the road to Michoácuaro?"
   We were passing a shale wall. He glanced out the window. "It is the road."
   "We're taking a shortcut, then?"
   He smiled and nodded.
   The curving road was hacked out of a hillside. Rocky
soil crumbled into rusty powder. Water from an overnight
shower stood in red puddles. A thought, overdramatic but
shiny, came to me: little pools of blood.
   Now the edge on the oncoming side dropped straight
down, perhaps fifty feet. On the little bit of shoulder stood
three white crosses. My neighbour spotted them, muttered a
prayer and crossed himself three times.
   "Uh, friends of yours?"

"The Jiminez Molino brothers."

"You knew them?"

He sighed. "Their mother." He closed his eyes.

Behind me a man rapped on the window and a couple of kids cheered. I looked around. Despite the curves a pickup was pulling alongside. In its bed sat half a dozen men, all holding rifles, their shirts and pants muddy. The road dipped downhill toward a curve. The kids shouted. One of the men grinned up, a knife slash extending his open mouth an inch into his right cheek. Up ahead, a beer truck roared around the curve, lurching toward us. Our driver braked hard, some passengers gasped. The pickup pulled in with more than a second to spare. People cheered. I said a silent thank you.

Farther along we passed five crosses around a tiny shrine. I shook my head. My neighbour said, "Señor Oscar Mejía and his wife. Two daughters. And a friend of the older daughter."

"What happened?"

"It was deserved. For the señora also. Not for the children."

"Why for her?"

"Our Lord sees all." He nodded. "And takes as He wishes."

I remembered, but dimly, this sense of things. I had been away a long time. Some minutes later we passed yet another pair of crosses, one double the size of the other. "And that?"

"I can't tell you."

"Someone you don't know?"

"I know. I know."

"But?"

His eyelids closed again. "You mustn't ask."

Another story not told. We reached an intersection and were back on the old road. We passed three large avocado plantations and the village of Emiliano Zapata, one of nineteen by that name in Mexico, Pepe had told me. Then the paved road down to the house of a man who people say worked as a pistolero for a chemical plant in Morelia. Why the factory needed such an expert no one explained. I'd once quipped to Rubén how the chemicals likely killed more people than our local gunman. The jefe scowled; such gringo jokes were dangerous. Then the octagonal house, an evangelical church till the sect's priest was caught committing sins of the flesh with his male goat. On the patio of Las Rosas, a restaurant for roast meat and barbecued lamb, no one was dining.

By a showy tire dealership the bus rounded a curve. Ahead, spilling down the side of the hill, red roofs, adobe walls, dirt streets: Michoácuaro. A sudden sharp twinge told me, You know this place. Followed by another nearly as strong, Not as well as you thought.

Michoácuaro is basically the end of the road. To the west and south lies tierra caliente, hot country. A bit of hardtop heads into the valley, quickly becoming a dirt byway which branches into four-wheel-drive tracks. These peter into burro trails winding several hundred kilometres through the Sierra Madre del Sur down to the Pacific.

In the oncoming lane some road crew had dumped a pile of gravel. On top of it, four wheels off the ground, sat a sporty little Japanese car. We could see its plates: D.F., the Distrito Federal. My neighbour grinned. "Chilango." A resident of Mexico City. Smiles and guffaws from our busload of country cousins.

Halfway down the hill we passed Pepe's place, the gates shut. My chest tightened. On to the centre, the plaza as flowering-tree-shaded pretty as ever. A block beyond we reached the little terminal. I wished my seat companion a good day.

"Adiós," he answered.

I rolled my suitcase back to the plaza. A small carnival waited there, most of the stands and rides boarded closed. Only a tiny empty merry-go-round clanked away, circling, circling.

I passed the jail, a gloomy doorway with three guards in front. The cell bars now rose from a new waist-level cement wall. Two prisoners, arms hanging through, stared out. By the cathedral taco vendors tended their coals and the milagrito salesman offered his miniature tin legs, hearts, arms, eyes: buy one, present it to the Virgin, say a hundred-fifty Hail Marys and miraculously your arm or heart will be mended.

At Teléfonos de México, a bright blue sign: FAX available here. Also a miracle.

In front of Rubén's office, sandbags formed a four-metre semicircle. A half-dozen armed non-uniformed men lounged about—most unusual, at least compared to five years ago. A woman carrying a basket of lilies passed, deaf Gertrudis who owned a flower stall in the market. I started to wave, then held back.

Thirty metres farther on was the mayor's office, the palacio municipal, a concrete fortress with small round 1950s windows and a wide dark curving staircase to the second floor. How would Pepe manage to stay in good humour? In front of the door stood five men in black gabardine shirts without insignia; judiciales, I presumed. All pretty scary.

The judiciales are a division of police that comes out of the ground mainly to intimidate. They serve the governor of the state, here Michoacán, through the office of the Procuradora, the tax man, making the judicial a kind of treasury agent. They will charge suspected narco-traficantes with forgetting to pay taxes on their sale of drugs. Fines paid at the moment just before arrest cancel the charge. Doctor Felicio Ortíz who has done the necessary research believes that if, for protection, you have to choose between the judiciales and the narco-traficantes, choose the narcos—the odds of staying alive are four to one in their favour.

Two judiciales held what looked like the automatic rifles I'd read about in Proceso, each costing 3,500,000 pesos, about twelve hundred dollars. The others carried stubby black sub-machine guns. But shouldn't they be out in the hills, searching for Pepe? I felt their stares.

Beyond them stood a three-metre-high statue, Lieutenant Abelardo Núñez, tall in frock coat and Hessian boots, his long concrete hair flowing in the wind. He pointed a cement Colt .45 across the plaza. Off to the right lay Hotel Domicilio, the town brothel, a valuable asset; it made Michoácuaro a safer place for women.

I walked along the plaza in the shade of the arcade. At the far end stood a large truck with the logo of Televisa. Through its wide-open doors I saw piles of cables and electronic gear. National television, rendering Pepe's absence visible to the world. Suddenly in a very North American way Rubén's deputies and the judicial police all around made sense. Without TV, no one notices an elected mayoralty candidate who has, somehow, disappeared. With TV, you've got to present the image of order.

I started up the hill. On the curb sat the coffin seller, assistant to the undertaker. He'd been there five years ago and looked as if he hadn't moved. The skin of his cheeks, prune-dry and half a shade lighter, shrank against cheekbones and into eye-sockets. He wore wire-framed tinted granny glasses and a round-crowned straw hat with a six-inch brim. Behind him was an open shed of stacked coffins, each of which would put campesino families years into debt. The man's eyes followed me. I sensed he'd taken my measure and could offer me the deal of a lifetime.

I reached Pepe's gate. Instead of five hours from my airport to meeting Pepe it was forty to his home, and where the hell was he? I rang a bell, and waited.

Most Michoácuaro houses are eighteenth-century Spanish colonial, Mediterranean style. Their front walls begin at the sidewalk and an inner courtyard gives entry to all rooms. But Pepe's place is in a large compound behind a high stone fence. A similar kind of house, owned by Pepe but rented out, stands to the right. Dozens of chickens have the run of the gardens.

From behind the gate a voice, tentative, "Who is it?"

I announced myself. The gate opened a crack. A face I nearly remembered—

"Oh, Señor Jorge!" Vera's hands flew to her cheeks and she gave way to sobbing.

I put my bag down, reached for her elbow and she fell against my chest. I let her cry, wishing I had the good comforting words in Spanish. I felt awkward, this woman I didn't know claiming my support.

She stepped back, embarrassed now. Her cheeks shone wet. She blew her nose and wiped her face. "Oh señor—" We walked slowly to the big house, Pepe's casa.

FOUR

Inside the enclave grew impatiens in rows of white, pink, and purple. Three bird-of-paradise clumps, many blooms to each. Copa de ora trees, the golden trumpet flowers. Half a dozen tulipanos in full orange crown. Trimmed thick grass.

We went into the house. I quarter-expected Pepe to come around the corner, whooping "Surprise!" The kitchen was as I remembered, complete with fresh flowers in a large vase on the table. The only new item was a colour photo of a girl's face, maybe four years old, black hair, high forehead, big brown eyes, straight set mouth. Some godchild of Pepe's? I asked.

Vera blushed. "This is Alicia. My daughter."

"Beautiful." I didn't congratulate Vera on her marriage; likely there wasn't one. I looked around. Pepe's absence felt so palpable I pushed for Vera to tell me the full story right away.

She, calmer now, would answer no questions till I'd chosen among eight possible liquid refreshments. I asked for an agua fresca, water with fresh-crushed guavas. I couldn't stop glancing at the picture of Alicia. The face was familiar, beyond Vera's genetic contribution.

Vera's story came out convoluted, leaping ahead, doubling and tripling back: "Because Don Pepe ran for presidente municipal because it was his responsibility to

Michoácuaro, a battle against Señor Marranando of the PRI but many people wanted Don Pepe to challenge the PRI, you remember the PRI, the lying and bribes? Nothing's changed. They say Señora Emilia forced Señor Marranando to run, he didn't want to, she needed him. And because the PRI has all the money they threatened the voters, vote for Marranando or you'll lose your jobs at the sugar mills, without Marranando the textile factory won't be built. Everybody was afraid not to vote for Señor Marranando but Don Pepe was wonderful, everybody loves him, he was the candidate of the campesinos and the town-people, everybody knew we'd all vote for Don Pepe. Señora Emilia tried to influence people to vote against Don Pepe—"

"You mean Emilia Avéspare?" There was too much I didn't know, too many touchstones I'd lost contact with. "She's head of your PRI now?"

That flustered Vera. "How could such a thing be? Her son Ignacio is—you know Luís finally died. But Ignacio is a little boy, he'll always be a little boy. They say Señor Marranando paid Señora Emilia a hundred million pesos to be the PRI candidate. Everyone knows she doesn't need the money but she's a miser-woman, she controls Señor Marranando who is the nephew of her sister's mother-in-law."

"Stop. Señora Avéspare forced Marranando to run?"

She looked at me, and nodded. "That's what they say."

"And he paid her to become the PRI candidate?"

Another nod.

"Both?"

She nodded again. No contradiction here. I'd forgotten the Michoácuaran penchant for the simultaneity of contraries.

"Okay. And the election?"

More nods. "The ballots were counted in the presidente's office, for Don Pepe nine thousand five hundred and twenty-two. Against, six thousand and nine. Everybody agreed. The vote boxes were taped closed and the papers with the official numbers too, and the truck took the boxes to Morelia, and the official papers. We all watched, nine vote boxes, they locked them into the truck. But last week the announcement on the television said Señor Marranando of the PRI was elected by fifty-three percent."

"But what happened?"

"And when Señor Simón who ran Don Pepe's campaign went to Morelia the government said eleven vote boxes arrived, they showed him the boxes, and the official papers, except the papers never said these things when they left Michoácuaro. Many people said it was wrong but the governor said Don Pepe did well, he should be pleased with his good vote in a democratic election, Mexico needs good opposition candidates for the elections to be democratic."

"And Pepe accepted this?"

"He protested, they said they'd investigate, but in the D.F. they are the PRI also, no? And who else is there?" She shook her head. "The lawyers?" She giggled. "Our new bishop?"

"Then Marranando is presidente municipal?"

She scowled at me. "But how could he be? He ran away."

"What?" Her description was becoming fully baroque.

"Yes yes. The day to make him presidente he ran from the crowd. They say he's back in Uruapan where his family lives, or perhaps Morelia. Señora Avéspare is very angry."

"Can she be involved in Pepe's absence?" I spoke carefully.

Vera's eyes filled with tears. "The señora is not a good woman. But to—harm Don Pepe? No." She shook her head. "Now, Señor Jorge, you will rest." She got up, grabbed my bag—

"Wait. First, explain to me how Pepe disappeared."

She stopped moving. She breathed in deeply, as for a medical exam, and out jaggedly. Her eyes flowed over. "He went out. Four—no, now five days ago."

"Where to?"

"He believed that no one would dare—" She shivered. "That he was too important, too—strong."

"So. He left the house. And?"

She nodded. "In the evening. About nine. He needed a book from the Telecable office. I said I'd go. No, he'd be back in ten minutes, fifteen. Since then, no one has seen him."

That simple. Step into the night, and disappear. Pepe would act on impulse, but would he actively let someone suffer concern on his account?

Vera wiped her face in her sleeve. "We'll go to the casita." She marched out. "In one hour your comida will be ready, you'll be hungry."

No doubting her, soon I would be starving; she had decreed it. Alicia's picture— I saw it then, Alicia's father: Ali Cran? The line of mouth, same square forehead from hairline to eyebrows, and even at four a similar cheek shape, near straight from eye to chin. Had Alicito comforted Vera in an hour or a month of need? Or was she simply another conquest?

Vera led, a small stout young woman with power over Pepe's domain; she knew its boundaries. The casita thirty metres away lay behind the flowering trees and a stretch of bougainvillea. A rooster crowed. "What is this textile factory all about?"

We reached the door of the casita, on the side toward the big house. "There will be jobs, five hundred, a thousand."

"Here?"

She nodded, and unlocked the door. "Don Pepe opposed it." The casita is a solid little place, red brick, sitting on a slope. A large veranda facing east to the hills rises ten feet above a rose garden and the lawn. "I hope it's comfortable."

We came into a large room—first a kitchenette and a dining counter, then sitting space with comfortable chairs, and a bed in the far corner. Half the wall facing down the valley and across to the hills is glass, protected like the windows by white steel bars and screening, secure against thieves and bugs. Sliding glass doors open onto the veranda overlooking the garden. At the far end stands an old zapote tree. It's an altogether beautiful place. But for me, right then, Pepe's absence infected everything. I thanked Vera. "Now tell me, what's happening in town?"

She pulled back the bed cover. "Some say Señor Marranando will return. Others say Don Pepe is presidente, he won. Some say we need a new election, President Jimmy Carter will observe or at least Canada. But Don Pepe will win again, Señor Simón believes this, and I also. So we won't have another election."

Pepe is alive and well, he'll be back in a few minutes, he just forgot to tell Vera exactly when. Pepe has disappeared and is gone forever. Vera believes both. "Okay," I said, "with comida you can tell me more about Pepe."

"Good, señor. Oh—" Her dark skin lightened a little. "Señora Irini wants to speak with you."

"Who's Señora Irini?"

Her eyes narrowed. "But, the señora of the garden."

I started to say, What garden? but caught myself. I had a memory of Pepe mentioning a garden. In his telegram? Wait. Had he disappeared to set me up with this Irini, was it a ruse like with Raquel? "I'll be happy to meet Señora Irini." It was all in the cards.

Vera gave me keys to the casita, the big house and main gate. She left. Damn Pepe. What the hell was I supposed to do here, relax? Impossible. Worry? Sure, yes. Leave? It seemed foolish to be here without Pepe. What kind of game was he playing? But was he in fact playing a "game?" Or was someone else? A game with what kind of goal? Or was I just asking too many damn questions.

On a shelf by the window lay a pile of newspapers. I leafed through them. Stories about the campaign, speeches and arguments, the election, the results announced in Morelia; the last one, containing the story of Pepe's disappearance, was local. The prose was simpler than *Proceso*'s, sometimes as convoluted as Vera's and about as informative.

In the little refrigerator I found a dozen beers, six dark, six light. Clever Vera. In the side cabinet were some canned vegetables, preserved fruit, a bottle of brandy and a machete. I tested the shiny blade. Sharp. In the front cabinet, six bottles of honey and nine large clear plastic bags of white powder. In magic marker print on each bag, the word SAL. I poked one. Salt? No way would Pepe be mixed up with drugs. What was it not? Cocaine? Heroin? A strong desire: puncture the sacks. No. I untied one. Smelled, tasted it. Not salt. Sugar. A joke on those who don't sample first. Why mislabelled? By?

I slid the door open and stepped out on the veranda. Two panicked magpies fled down to the zapote tree.

To the right was Pepe's other house, rented to the retired teacher. Or did I hear he died? All new, a swimming pool! It sparkled blue. But it felt out of place, as if my plane had made a wrong turn above New Orleans and we'd ended up in Tampa Bay. And the hedge of scarlet bougainvillea separating the houses was gone, replaced by storm fencing topped by razor-wire like around a low-security prison. Why? How could the chickens go back and forth? On the grass by the house a dog, mostly German shepherd, rose to sniff the air. It wobbled on skinny legs, whimpered, and sank to the grass.

Along the neighbour drive by a ledge of rocks stood a huge Mexican cypress, an ahuehuete, growing out of rocky earth and a little stream. The trunk is like a dozen trunks melted into each other. Pepe said it expanded like this, more than twenty-five metres around and growing. It rises to less than thirty-five metres but is of venerable stock, a survivor of twelve hundred cycles of seasons. Pepe built the house in its shade.

Along the back of the house facing the pool ran a terrace. From this to the garden was a wide brick staircase. Around the terrace and along the stairs sat dozens of geranium-filled clay masetas, serried ranks of crimson flowers. Some masetas had geometric designs, some were shaped like frogs or burros, some were painted green and black. A brown and white cat pawed at a maseta on the second step down.

Below me a dash of water gushed out along a sluice, the casita built above it to avoid diverting the little stream. I sat, put my feet up on the rail, looked out at fifteen trees in bloom and four flitting butterflies. The rosebush area had tripled in size. Was this the garden of the unknown Señora Irini? Water burble and soft wind tickled my ears.

Where was Pepe? Jaime's notion, Pepe in hiding from some mistress's husband, seemed plausible. But the Morelia police lieutenant was taking his absence seriously. I didn't know what to think. More than ever I yearned for Ali Cran's sense of tracing. Had Alicito tried to trace Pepe's movements?

For Ali Cran tracing is a true sense, a common human property. He claims he sees a pattern of events after they occur: people leave their traces wherever they go and, something like dogs, others can later trace mood and movement. A developed sense of tracing is a basic way of understanding, similar to hearing or smell. "You have many senses, Jorge," he maintained, "more than the five your habits limit you to. You have to learn to use the others."

"Tracing? Come on." I said this, skeptical, not to Ali Cran but a week later after, several tequilas, to Rubén Reyes Ponce, chief of police and a good drinking companion.

"Sí." Rubén nodded slowly. "Ali Cran developed this skill when he was young, to survive. From his sexual adventures." Rubén's tone fell between envy and disgust. "What Alicito does with his tail, for much less are other men killed. By the woman's father or husband." He drained his drink. "Alicito absorbs a woman's smell, her movements, he traces her desire to a past moment. You understand? To when the man kept her from her satisfaction, or her hope." He reads the doubt on my face and scowls. "Fill my glass, Jorge." I did. Rubén said, "It's a curious thing, to trace a need to its source."

"Que milagro! Bienvenido Don Jorge!" The deep voice of Flaco, Pepe's blind gardener. Que milagro!—what a miracle!—is one of my favorite expressions. People say this when someone returns from the distant world. Flaco, a big grin, glazed eyeballs, straw hat shoved back, reached a bouquet of three perfect roses, white, yellow, carmine, over to me.

"Flaco! Gracias, muchas gracias."

I took the flowers and gave him a gentle abrazo. He'd been working hard all morning, I could smell it. We discerned we were both well, his family was well, the weather cold for December. I put the roses in water. I told him about the snow and sleet I'd left behind. A strange world to live in, he said.

He lowered his voice. "Do you believe, señor, Don Pepe will come back?" A question draped in faith but tinged with misgiving.

"I'm sure of it." My northern empirical authority.

"If the Lord wills it." He smiled a little. "As the Lord willed it last time."

"What do you mean?"

His sightless eyes met mine. "We were worried then also."

"For how long?"

"Maybe, one week."

"Where'd he go?"

"He didn't say, señor."

"But why?"

Irony tempered his smile. "He said, a secret mission."

"I don't understand."

Flaco dropped his glance. "He didn't share her name, señor." The smile for his macho boss Pepe, lover of beautiful women, held on his face.

"I see." So that was likely it. I felt a sense of gentle relief. "A beer, Flaco?"

"When it's warmer, señor. Gracias." He went back to work. He trims bushes by feel of height and thickness. He cuts the grass with his short-handled sickle, crawl-walking over terrain he knows every bump of. He deadheads roses and camellias as they start to brown. He can smell faded petals metres away. He lost his sight seventeen years ago, spraying mangoes. The wind blew the insecticide into his eyes and burned the irises. He was rushed to the hospital. Too late, in five hours he was blind. Pepe hired him. They've been loyal to each other since.

I poured myself a beer. A rich tan head formed on the bronze liquid. "Salud, Pepe, wherever you are." I sipped, and lay on the bed. Flaco and Jaime agreed, Pepe was off screwing around. He'd be back. I dozed.

And woke sharply. The Morelia cop, for one, had taken Pepe's absence seriously. I needed to talk to Rubén right away.

At the casa, Vera introduced me to her cousin Chaba. He shook my hand warmly. "It's good you're here, señor. To have the famous professor back, it was ordained so."

"Chaba." Vera looked peeved.

I'm not famous. Last time here I appeared on Pepe's local Telecable Michoácuaro to talk about a shooting in front of the cathedral. I made an amusing case for a strange explanation: a ghost in the statue on the plaza had shot the man in question. Some people believed me.

"Chaba wants to know if he can look around in the casita."

"Sure. For what?"

"His father's bed."

I started to laugh but Vera's face said, No no— "There's only one bed in there."

"Muchas gracias, señor." Chaba bowed, straightened, backed away. "Muchas gracias."

"Would you like to look now?"

"Please, later." He smiled, sad.

Vera said, "You are comfortable in the casita, señor."

"Oh yes." Then I asked about the bags of sugar, labelled salt.

Vera twitched. "You say, in the bags, there's only sugar?"

"Yes, I opened one. What're they all about?"

The right side of her mouth smiled. "Not important."

"Vera—"

"Sugar." Chaba shook his head. "Only sugar. Goodbye, señor. Vera." He left.

"Is he—?" I tapped my temple.

"No no. He has a good job at the hospital, he's an orderly. He was away a few years."

"What's this about the sugar? And his father's bed?"

She stared out the door after Chaba. "His father, my uncle Bartolomeo, died while he was gone. Now he wants to marry. He believes he'll conceive children only in his father's bed, his father promised it to him. But the bed is gone from his family's house. He looks for it everywhere."

"Hope he finds it." I didn't ask, Why doesn't he look now? or, Only in his father's bed? These weren't Michoácuaro questions. So I asked what she knew about Rubén's investigation.

She took a moment. "Jefe Rubén asked many questions. And all his deputies search also. Señor Simón too, and the campaign people, everyone looks for Don Pepe. Señora Irini, she's very worried, she comes here and we talk."

"But nobody's learned anything?"

"I think—" The tears started again. "No, they haven't."

I checked my watch. Rubén would be at his own comida now; I'd eat and find him afterwards. Vera brought the meal she'd prepared, chicken with green tomato and chile sauce, and rice and tortillas. Delicious. I asked about old friends. Yes, Doctor Felicio kept on practising, he'd come twice in the five days since Pepe disappeared, he was kind. And Constanza was still connected to my old house, she cleaned for three priests living there now. Vera giggled—one of the priests was a bigger gossip than Constanza herself, and he wrote poetry! Constanza prayed for Don Pepe's safe return. Oh, and Señora Irini had called, she'd stop by.

Vera didn't mention Ali Cran. I asked.

A trace of smile from Vera. A dismissive wave of her hand. "All he thinks about is getting richer."

Ali Cran, who allegedly satisfied the needs of a hundred women and survived, concerned with making money? "I can't believe it."

"Oh yes. At his two ranches. He grows plants that Don Pepe experiments with."

"Pepe's experimenting with plants?" I grinned.

She looked at me harshly. "Don't laugh at me, Señor Jorge."

"I'm not laughing." What was this garden? "Please, go on."

She shrugged. "Ali Cran and Don Pepe, in the old days they told many stories, funny stories, sad stories. Now they speak of the price of cherimoyas. And how to make better fertilizer. Fertilizer!" Her head shook in disgust.

I didn't get it. These weren't the same people I'd left behind. I couldn't get my mind to reconcile this agricultural picture of Pepe and Ali Cran with the men I thought I knew. Nine years ago Pepe brought telecommunications to Michoácuaro, investing his energy into the cable station. Farming, Ali Cran's devotion to ranching, these were throwbacks to the lives of their parents. I had to assume Vera was exaggerating. Anyway, no sense challenging her. "So. Much is different, is it?"

Vera nodded a vigorous yes. And, she went on, the biggest change was next door. The old maestro had died. The house was rented now to a Chilango, a terrible mistake. "He hates me, he wants me dead. He is one of those who want to build the textile factory."

"Hates you? What did you do to him?"

"Señor, nothing. My friend Laura, she worked for the maestro eleven years. The Chilango fired her. She too did nothing. Only her job."

Occasionally a house changes occupants. What happens to the criada is often a problem. Most houses middle middle-class and up have a criada, partly the maid but more a house-and-people-carer. She cooks, cleans, is part of the family, attends to the aging parents, can be closer to the children than the mother. If the family moves, the criada may go too. Or she might stay with the house if that's her choice and the new inhabitants want her. Or she ends up with a small pension; or nothing. I probed a little: "But why is the Chilango so angry with you?"

She shrugged. "I told him—what I thought of him."

"What did you say?"

"He's a terrible man. He drove away Señora Irini. She came here with him. They lived without the blessing of the Church. The Church would condemn a marriage to such a man."

I could hear Pepe's laughter: The Church relishes sanctifying any old marriage! It's sin or sacrament, no middle way! "And Pepe's relation to Señora Irini?"

"She's kind." Vera cleared my plate. "She's his assistant."

"Why does she want to meet me?"

Vera frowned. "You're Pepe's friend."

So. If Pepe was off with a woman, it wasn't Irini. Back in the casita I unpacked my bag—

"Hey, señor!"

I went out on the veranda. Beyond the wire fence stood a man, fortyish, black moustache, wide shoulders. He wore a straw hat, white shirt and chinos. "Howdy." He spoke English.

"Hello."

Still in English: "You're the professor?"

"Yes."

"Okay, you'll testify for me. Pass through there." He pointed to the back of the casita and headed off.

On the side away from the big house the ground sloped up to veranda level. The fence was pulled apart, a half-metre gap.

"I'm Ernie Montemayor. Those two witches made it, this passage. Come on over." He pulled the wire mesh wide. "The witches' passage." He roared a laugh.

I stepped through. "What d'you mean, testify?"

"This way."

I followed him around and past the dog, sleeping now. "What's his name?"

Ernie stopped. "That? It's useless." He laughed again. "Called Blaze." He cackled.

We walked by the ahuehuete and along the gravel driveway. Well-pruned trees, but fruit rotted on the ground. The grass and bushes were overgrown. In a far corner, crates, broken lengths of crenelated plastic, an automobile fender, piles of brush. We reached the gate, a sheet of reinforced steel. He pulled it open. "There." He pointed to his lock. Its arm was sliced through, clean. "She did it. The bruja, the witch."

I didn't say, Which witch? "Who?"

"Pepe's witch!" He handed the lock to me. "Or the witch who worked in my house. They're both witches."

I examined it. A clean cut. "Strange."

"She did it. With her eyes."

"Hnnnhh. It's like a laser cut."

"Laser eyes." A superior smile. "Be careful."

"Of?" I gave him the lock back.

"You saw what she did." He started down the drive. "You can testify about it."

I followed. "Why would anyone cut your lock?"

"To frighten me, make me leave." A cold chuckle. "They'll have to carry me out."

"Who?"

"Her, that one, Laura, she wants to run the place like she used to. Know why?"

"Why?"

We passed the dog. He growled. "Fuck you, Blaze." Ernie punched air toward the dog. Blaze shrank back. "She wants to build the shrine again."

"I'm sorry?"

"The old asshole teacher who died here, know what she did? Got this plastic dummy from a department store, brought it on the bus from Morelia. You imagine that?"

Strange goods arriving on the bus from Morelia... "Why?"

"She dressed it in his clothes and lay it on the bed. Staring up at the ceiling. Covered him with all his degrees and certificates. Black curtains, windows nailed shut, incense, it stank to high heaven. Burned-down candles, wax all over the floor. Know what it cost to fumigate this place?"

"No."

"Don't ask."

I didn't. "The maestro was good to her."

"Screwed her every night and twice on Sunday—hell, he liked fucking witches. She casts a spell on me again, she's gonna get hurt."

"Why would she?"

"See that swimming pool? Beautiful, right? I put it in."

We reached the fence. "You're saying Vera cast a spell?"

"Damn right. For her witch friend."

I shook my head. "What kind of spell?"

"What do you care?"

"I don't." And I didn't.

He sighed dramatically. "I'm telling you this, man to man. She spooked me. I couldn't get it up. For two months nearly. Hoodoo."

"So—what'd you do?"

A hard smile. "Found myself another witch. An honest one."

"Yeah?"

"She made a barrier, an old witches' obstruction, the oldest."

"What's that?"

"Think I'm going to tell you?" He sniffed a laugh. "I'm safe now."

"Good for you."

"Bastard Pepe, getting himself killed." He handed me the lock again. "You keep this."

"You think he's dead?"

"You see him here, scrambling to be Mister Mayor?" He stuck out his hand. I took it, automatically. "Hey, and thanks, pal."

I stepped back through the fence. I wasn't about to take Ernie's analysis of anything seriously. But his sense that Pepe was dead left me newly worried.

FIVE

I watched a large-winged fly zag around the casita. It settled on the drawn curtain across from the bed, lingered, explored, took off. On the ceiling it found a crevice, crawled in and disappeared.

I wrote a note for Vera: Gone to Rubén Reyes Ponce's office, if Señora Irini comes please telephone me there. I put a bottle of scotch in my bag, locked the casita, unlocked the gate, locked it from outside and walked down the hill past the Chilango's gate.

Ernie, convinced Pepe was dead; alive he'd be in town. The argument made a simple but solid kind of sense.

The coffin seller watched as I approached, as I passed. I felt his eyes till I turned the corner, and after too. In the plaza, wind-tattered election placards hung from strung wires. "PRI And Marranando, The Future Of Michoácuaro!" "Pepe Legarto, An Honest Presidente!" "Legarto Brings Clean Government!" "For The Continuing Development Of Michoácuaro, Juan Marranando!" Townsfolk sat on shaded benches. Three boys on the fountain rim took turns falling backward into the water. The Televisa truck was parked in place. The visible judiciales, the governor's constabulary, patrolled in pairs and in slow-rolling cars.

I swept through the gaggle of deputies in front of the Rubén's office. As I reached the door, one jumped up. "What do you want, gringo?" A scruffy mid-twenties tough sporting a few long beard hairs. Scabbed cuts on his chin and right cheek proved he could take a beating. He wore a vest, no shirt. Brown hairless skin shone through.

"To speak with Rubén Reyes Ponce."

"Nobody goes in."

In Mexico taking on any kind of police is a bad idea. But the little bully had pushed my lousy mood too hard. I gave him my next-to-meanest grim smile. "Out of my way, muchacho, or Rubén will have your balls."

The fellow's eyelids flickered. I advanced. He backed off. I opened the door and went in. I could have had a litre of explosive in my bag.

Rubén sat behind his desk, feet up on an open drawer, staring at a file. His face broke into a grin. "Jorge! Que milagro!" He stood and marched toward me, broad in chest and belly, black hair greying and receding. His abrazo felt real. "Back at last."

"I promised, no?"

"Ah, to promise, even a woman can promise. You're well? Welcome to Michoácuaro, centre of our nation's attention."

"You enjoy this attention, my friend?"

"Disaster brings its benefits." He pointed to five wooden crates in the corner. "We just received the rifles and ammunition we requested thirty-one months ago. Also twenty-six blankets for prisoners, and three pillows."

"Congratulations."

"You'll be pleased with me. At a seminar in Monterrey I learned a theory. In visible crises, our government locates material requested long ago. I always assumed this principle to be a fact. No no, they said in Monterrey, this is theory. Now, here in Michoácuaro, theory and fact are one. Since Thursday."

"Welcome to the twentieth century, hombre. Here." I opened my satchel and handed him the bottle. "To happier times."

He looked at the label. "A strange gringo habit, import-ing spirits from Scotland, so far away." He shrugged. "True, the maguey doesn't grow beneath the snow." He broke the seal.

"It's for the quiet of your home."

"Jorge, trust no one. What did I teach you? Perhaps you've been paid large sums to heighten the flavour of this fine scotch with strychnine? Yes, it may be in the interest of certain powers to eliminate a man with a near-impossible task, to control the peace of his town." Two narrow glasses appeared in his hand. He poured us each half an inch, parsi-mony his compromise.

Rubén had been a regular drinker, heavy even, in the year I'd known him. But never in his office. "To the return of Pepe."

Rubén nodded, and we sipped. Five years ago he tossed his liquor back, flushing it past the palate before taste could happen—in part because he bought the rawest tequila. He spoke slowly. "Pepe is such a pain in the eggs."

"I'm relieved you're assuming he's alive."

"I deal only in fact. I haven't seen his corpse. Therefore he's alive."

"And are you investigating? Searching for him?"

"For four days my deputies searched. Some are back only this morning. They found no one. And he has many friends, they have made themselves into small posses, they ride about calling, Pepe! Pepe!" He shrugged. "It is all very well, but no one has found him."

"Have you stopped looking?"

"Of course not. Eight new deputies are still out in the low hills, out in tierra caliente. But we cannot search Morelia, Mexico City, there others are looking."

I nodded. "Yes. But still—"

"Understand me, I'm worried. We have our differences but Pepe is my friend. We'll find him. But it was unnecessary."

"What?"

Rubén glared a Don't-norteamericanos-grasp-anything? scowl. "To run for presidente municipal."

"I hear lots of people wanted him to."

"Pfeghgh—" a head-shaking whistle-grunt. "His god-damn garden."

"Yeah, what is this garden?"

"I thought you wrote to each other. That's what you people do, no? reveal your important projects in your letters?"

I imagined Rubén, wakeful midnight to dawn, powerless to cope as Pepe and I sent clandestine epistles back, forth, back, hatching cabals. "He hasn't told me anything."

He didn't believe me. "Everything is for his garden." He smoothed his moustache flat. "He wanted city money for it, that was the problem."

"But what is it?"

"You see the result? A town full of reporters, judiciales, television. The fucking election upset the whole economy."

Except Rubén's personal economy was likely just fine. It centred on the tenants in his half-dozen houses, and whatever they paid in rent. He bought houses cheap, for back taxes. "Who sent in the judiciales, the Procuradora in Morelia?"

A weary nod. "They think they're judge and executioner. If they act as they think—" He glared at me. "Mobs come, mobs go. Bring in the judiciales, you can bet the mob will stay."

I understood that; Rubén would be powerless to cope. I couldn't disagree so tried to salve. "Mobs are people too."

"Not in Michoácuaro."

The phone rang. Rubén grabbed it. "Sí?" He listened, and nodded. "Gracias." He hung up. "No one has seen him, heard of him, nothing."

"Tell me what's happening."

He finished his scotch. "Emilia Avéspare said it best. Remember Luís Avéspare? Eighteen years he ran the PRI. The PRI ran everything. We had a quiet town."

Pepe had explained to me many aspects of life in Michoacán—its psychology, its social patterns, its history; and especially, its governance, specifically the PRI: Do you need a kidney operation for your sister's husband? Speak to the PRI. A bus ticket to Mexico, your son is taking the engineering entrance exam? Check in with the PRI. Crocheting lessons for your daughter, she with six thumbs, so she'll be marriageable? See the PRI. And by the way, a licence to practise your new business? Certainly the PRI, and for a small or larger consideration, many things can happen...

"A fine peaceful town." Rubén shook his head. "Then Luís died. They made his boy Ignacio head. They thought he'd keep the old man's contacts with Morelia and Mexico. But for favours, for strategy, Ignacio was useless. But guess what." Rubén poured us each another finger. "The contacts? All the time they were Emilia's, she ran Luís. Like she runs Ignacio now." He laughed through his nose.

"I met her once." Luís too. Ali Cran held a party for Felicio Ortíz, his eighty-fifth birthday. Rubén wasn't invited. Emilia Avéspare's husband was a bluff good-fellow, tall, everyone his friend, everyone a vote. Señora Avéspare mixed easily but preferred intimate groups. In her late thirties then, she must have been darkly beautiful once. She still retained a modicum of conventional allure, a bit unusual in provincial Mexico where normative bourgeois traits of feminine beauty peak early, win a husband, over several pregnancies are recast as somber, plump, familial. "We didn't really talk."

"You see, if Pepe doesn't return, others may take on his cause. And with Pepe as martyr, ay, he would be more insufferable away than right here."

I wondered about this: If Rubén is right about Avéspare's concern, then she can't be responsible for his disappearance. But if he's wrong, if no one else is interested in Pepe's cause, then it just might suit her well if Pepe never returns. I needed more.

"She knows how things happen in Michoácuaro."
Rubén smiled. "She makes them come about, important
things. And she'll do much. Soon as we find Pepe."
"What do you think, what happened to him?"
"Some say he's dead, some say he's alive."
"And Rubén Reyes Ponce who drinks good scotch and
rotgut tequila, what do you say?"
"Pepe doesn't run from a battle. That means someone
removed him." He sipped. "Who? I can say who didn't. I've
eliminated his own party, by which I mean that fox Simón
who runs it." Rubén grinned. "Or tries to. At first I thought,
maybe Simón took Pepe to a safe place. The judiciales have
no love for Three-M people—"
"Three-M?"
"The Movement for a Modern Michoacán. No, MMM
worried Pepe would get killed, murdered by someone who,
we'd later learn, was definitively in Morelia at that hour."
"So, not Three-M?"
"No, they need a very visible Pepe. And not our
Michoácuaro PRI. They're helping bring an important project here, a textile factory. From the taxes we'll build a new
high school and hire nine teachers. And for the clinic, two
new doctors, clean the place up, it's full of roaches and
incompetence. But first we need calm. A disappeared candidate doesn't bring calm."
"A factory to produce what?"
"Important work. Sweatshirts, work clothes. Inex-
pensive."
"And the money for this?"
He smiled, smug. "Michoácuaro money. American technology."
Michoácuaro's own maquiladora. "And who else didn't
make Pepe vanish?"
"Also not the federal government, a case like Pepe's
could provoke those human-rights Americans, Mexico is

crawling with them." He scowled. "And not the governor, he can't afford the money to keep judiciales here. Or the Morelia police, seven of their officers are seconded to the search. My friend Enrique complains, his best men— Ah! And your suitcase?"

I told him. He sympathized. And returned to the details of all he'd done to find Pepe.

Rubén's categories were telling; all the groups eliminated were political. But what of Jaime's notion, a love affair? "Maybe a woman, a last private moment before his duties begin?"

"He'd have let Vera know. He has before. She's deeply upset now."

I nodded. "And what's Ali Cran done to find him?"

Rubén flicked a crumb from his desk. "He's useless."

"A man of the countryside—"

"I know the countryside. Alicito knows nothing and tells me less."

"He's becoming a rich fruit rancher?"

"He'll never be rich." Disgust on Rubén's face. "True, he's afraid of dying poor."

"Aren't we all?"

Rubén shook his head. "Once, we lived, we died. In between we enjoyed what we had." Rubén stared into his small reservoir of scotch. "Ali Cran sells his produce to the gringos. They say Pepe has instructed him."

"And Alicito wants this?"

"Maybe he's getting smart." Rubén shrugged. "As we grow older, Jorge, we do not get any younger."

I laughed. But little of Rubén's old whimsy remained.

"Don't laugh. Ali Cran fears financial uncertainty."

"Ali Cran the seducer?" I shook my head in mock-awe.

"Today when he plows, it's only in the earth. Land, a good business investment, these produce richly."

I said, "Like, of course, houses."

My ex-landlord grinned.

"What about Marranando? Maybe Pepe's hiding from him."

"Marranando's an ass. He's in the hospital, a broken leg."

"Oh?"

"Jorge, a mob is a monster, ten thousand feet and no head. It stopped the inauguration." He noted my glass. I'd barely sipped. "So. The liquid is poisoned."

"Very mildly."

"I shall be heroic." He filled his own glass. "The governor has the touch of a master. He decided, the inauguration should be early. Mark me, he will become president of the nation."

"But his tactic backfired, no?"

"It nearly worked. Except two blocks from the plaza the mob spotted Marranando and Basilio Naranjo, you remember him, the old mayor? So the mob chased them. Some followed Basilio. Marranando ran to the house of the oral surgeon Matos-Lobos." Rubén grimaced. "They tried to break the door. And Marranando stood on the roof waving a pistol, 'Get back! Get back!' Jorge, never point a pistol at a mob."

"I promise."

"The door gave, the mob rushed into the surgery. Many had machetes. When they left they carried dental drills."

"With you in the middle?"

"I to my shame stayed with Basilio, to protect him."

"Ah. And Marranando?"

"Yes, he jumped down to the patio of the house next door, and his leg cracked." Rubén chuckled. "They dressed him like a woman, thick powder, he shaves twice a day. A dress, a rebozo around his head. They drove him through the crowd. Too late one of the mob decided the moustache of the woman in the car was as thick as his grandfather's. Marranando is now in the Morelia hospital." Rubén took a sip. "Two days later the judiciales came."

"I don't understand. When did they arrive?"

He thought. "Ten-eleven days ago."

"Then they were here before Pepe disappeared?"

"Of course. Maybe five days."

"But I thought they came to search for Pepe."

Rubén's heavy scowl. "They're here to keep order."

"You work with them?"

"They pay me no attention."

The phone had rung only the one time. Rubén wasn't in charge in Michoácuaro these days. "So they're not looking for Pepe?"

Rubén's scowl darkened. "It's best they don't find him."

A distasteful notion took me. "Rubén. Do you have him locked up somewhere?"

"If only I did." A sad shaking of his head.

I sighed and felt a kind of reinforced relief. He believed that Pepe, though likely not free to leave, was alive somewhere. As, conversely, Jaime felt his journalist friend was dead. I remembered the camera. "Amigo. Jaime León in Mexico City, you know of him?" Rubén shook his head. "Two years ago a friend of his was here, a journalist, Teófilo Através. To write about church architecture. He disappeared."

Rubén's eyes closed tight. "A fat man. Brash. Sneaky."

I shrugged. "I didn't know him. But Jaime loaned him a camera. The camera wasn't returned with his effects. A very good Leica." I raised my eyebrows. "There may be a reward."

Rubén allowed a small smile. "In two years, a camera can travel far. Yes, I'll inquire."

It wouldn't be found. "Através himself never turned up, I understand."

Rubén shook his head, slowly.

"Any connection between the journalist and Pepe disappearing?"

"I see none."

"Did Pepe know him?"

He shrugged. "Quién sabe?"

Enough. I stood. "We'll talk again soon, my friend."

"We'll have comida at my home."

"I'd like to." But this was unlike Rubén, his house was his sanctuary. A whole new man.

He shook his head. "We should make all politicians run for office in Michoácuaro. Then they'd all disappear."

"A good project, for the new year."

He nodded. "Avoid the judiciales, my friend. They watch everyone. They have nothing better to do."

I left. Walking away I felt Naked-Chest's scowl on my back.

The judiciales had come well before Pepe disappeared. Did he leave because of them? Were they holding him somewhere? Or someone else? MMM? The PRI? Emilia Avéspare? Or someone I'd never met so couldn't consider. I passed the coffin seller. His dry face was motionless. But I felt an unexpected elation now— Rubén believed Pepe was alive, and I trusted his sense of that.

Back at the casita I slid open the veranda door and stepped out. From the zapote tree two birds, black and gold in the afternoon sunlight, dove toward the porch. A few feet from me they veered off to the cottonwood, chattering and scolding. Water burbled down the stream. Clouds to the southeast hung thick and wet. A storm in the mountains, six months from official rainy season.

A new sound, unnatural inside the compound, an internal combustion engine. The Señora of the garden, at last?

SIX

A dark blue VW bug, early sixties vintage, parked at the end of the drive. Doctor Felicio Ortíz climbed out. Felicio stands five feet one inch, his height for over seventy-five years. His thick hair is white. He regularly wears short-sleeved white shirts, cream pants, black military boots to a couple of centimetres below his knees. Where he treats people in tierra caliente, he explains, the rattlesnakes and scorpions play their games. It's not healthy, an old man bitten by one of these. Today he was dressed as ever. Not many rattlers in town; el doctorcito knew he cut a dramatic figure in black and white.

"Ai, Felicio." We embraced. Very little meat there.

"My friend, you're a miserable replacement for Pepe." The dapper old gent spoke Spanish. His grin was pure Michoácuaro. "But I delight to see you."

"Que milagro, eh?"

He pulled back. "Milagro? Where do you learn such ignorance? You sound like a campesino. Come, tell me about your trip. And your country's recession, the desperate northern unemployment? Truly you live in the Third World."

We walked back to the casita. "You look well, Felicio."

"Another minute without beer and I'll look dried out. A dark, please."

"Do I have any?"

"Vera understands a man's thirst."

Like she understands spells? In the kitchen I opened two
frosty Negras and handed him one.

"A glass?"

He'd always drunk from the bottle. In his eyes I saw a
new tiredness—ruddy veins in the whites, his gaze tighter. At
ninety, maybe eyeglasses at last. He shook his head. "Your
health," he said in English.

"And yours."

Felicio added, "And Pepe's." We drank.

"What about his disappearance, Felicio? What do you
think is going on?"

He held up his hand. "First, tell me of you."

So we sat out on the veranda and spent twenty minutes
on my work, my state of mind, why I hadn't found myself a
woman. "Hard to replace the very best," I said.

"Ai, a dead lady lives in your brain, she's clinging to you.
She'll drag you to her side, down below the ground."

My throat had tightened. "You didn't know Alaine." I like
Felicio a lot but wasn't sure he'd earned the right to say this.

"I say what I see." He grunted, and asked for another
beer.

I went inside. Just what did he see? I returned with the
chilled bottles and changed the subject. "Tell me something.
Is Vera a bruja?"

"She's a curandera, yes." His face remained placid. "Why
do you ask?"

"Oh, stories. Like, she cast a spell on the guy in the maestro's place." I thumbed toward next door. "The Chilango."

"I doubt it. But he could use a spell—of improvement."
He giggled. "We don't like him."

"Why not?"

"Chilango supremacy." More titters.

"So is Vera a bruja or not?"

"But you know, to cure a disease you have to understand
the pathways, where it travels." An opaque smile. "A curan-

dera is a double agent, yes? One who cures illness can also cause it."

"I guess." With Felicio I used to think I understood him, then realized I didn't, at all. More important right now was Pepe. "And Pepe? Tell me what you know."

Felicio frowned. "People here tell me what they see, what is said. About Pepe they know nothing." He shook his head. "Not even in tierra caliente, where friends say the ground murmurs in a different way when a stranger walks across it." With his fingers he combed his hair back. "I tell you, I know Michoácuaro less well. Each week. Pepe believes this also, that the town is becoming something else."

"What?"

"If I could identify that." A frown took his face. "Irini, you've met her?"

I shook my head. "Who is she?"

His eyebrows rose, and quickly dropped. "But the custodian of the garden. No, she came after you left. Her face is calm but she worries very much about Pepe." He stared at his beer.

"Tell me this. You think there's a political reason for his disappearance?"

"That grand political party the PRI? Or Emilia Avéspare?"

"Whichever. Or the MMM."

"Emilia won't speak with me." A dim little grin. "I think something she has done might be—" he searched, "causative."

"How?"

"You understand, what I fear is, Pepe is hurt. Or that some force we don't know—" He grimaced. "But of course that makes no sense. The forces in Michoácuaro are finite, we know them all." He sighed. "And if he is being held somewhere, by one of these—"

This sounded like the oncoming consensus. A finite problem is solvable; I hoped. "And Avéspare?"

"In some way, she's involved. How—?" He shrugged.

He seemed a bit frightened. "What if I talk to her, someone not from here?"

"Talk is a transaction. Be careful what she takes in exchange."

I grinned. "Seductive, is she?"

"In her way. The sexual is least interesting."

I tried to tease: "You speak from experience?"

"Experience takes many contours."

"A new maxim, doctorcito?" Avéspare as cause. Pepe, held somewhere. Did Felicio know anything at all? Did he have any reason for these guesses?

"I hope Pepe will—" he chose carefully: "reappear. Maybe after January first if the new presidente takes office on this day. Ballots exist, you see. They 'prove' Marranando won this election. Pepe may not even know who removed him but—"

"Removed?"

"Pepe tried to block new industry from coming to us."

"This textile plant?"

He nodded. "It comes to Michoácuaro for our notable location." A few drops of rain splattered on the tiles.

"Rain in December, Felicio?"

"It'll stop."

"Michoácuaro's location?"

"We're at the edge of civilization. In tierra caliente live a hundred thousand campesinos. Some would kill their compadres to earn seven dollars for a ten-hour day, cutting waistbands for jogging suits." The rain stopped.

"Not minimum wage, I presume." A joke.

No smile.

"The argument, at least that they'll have some work—"

"Oh yes, five hundred jobs. We'll be a frontier town. I'll become rich treating those who drink from the river. Or eat the lettuce anywhere downstream. Including from Pepe's garden."

"No treatment of the outflow?"

His dry eyes looked redder. "At the border hundreds of maquiladoras pay mordida to inspectors every month and poison gushes into the river. Here for a single sweatshirt factory the inspectors will pass once a year for payment." He raised his empty glass.

He could wait for his next beer. "This garden, what is it?"

"A grand concept." He waited. "You truly don't know?"

I shook my head.

"Simple. Pepe is experimenting with food-plants that grew before the Spanish came."

The rain fell in earnest now, a thin slanting sheet of grey like a scrim across the valley. We pushed our chairs farther back beneath the overhang.

Felicio said in English, "Long as you're up, a beer please."

I went for a pee. Talking with Felicio made me hungry for Pepe's conversation. This older Felicio was increasingly obscure. I brought back the last two Negras. How did Felicio keep so much liquid in that little bladder? "And what does Pepe's garden grow?"

"Ah." He sipped. "Many things. Fruits, vegetables. Arracacha, yuca, cherimoya, pacay. He experiments with quinoa, have you tasted it? All fibre, you know, and amino acids." He made a sour face. "Very healthy."

I shook my head. "I tried yuca once."

"There's a great demand. In New York cherimoyas sell for ten dollars a pound."

"What are cherimoyas?"

He cackled. "It tastes like banana and coconut together and the texture is like custard. Go to the farm, they'll sell you cherimoyas. I detest custard."

I laughed. "They?"

"Seventeen people work there." He was cheerier now. "In his campaign Pepe promised to enlarge the farm."

"And his Telecable business? Does he still run it?"

Felicio shrugged. "It brings the world into Michoá-cuaro. Which is good, and a problem, yes? But the garden is for the town. He directs it, with Irini. The artist of the garden."

"Okay, who is this woman?"

He sipped beer. "Now there's a story." Back to Spanish. "She came a few years ago with," he gestured toward the Chilango's pool, "Don Ernesto. As he likes to be called. You know he'll be jefe of the textile factory?"

"Everything's interconnected, right?"

A diluted chuckle. "Sooner or later everybody here consorts with everyone else. Or refuses to." He looked along the valley toward town. "Or so it used to be."

"Tell me about Ernesto and Irini."

"She left him, of course. He was furious, crazy." A stream of sun angled through a cloud. "He went back to Mexico City. She stayed."

"You know her pretty well?"

"At times I believe she is truly wise." He grinned. "Often I know she's banal."

In the rain-washed air each leaf on the zapote looked magnified. "She and Pepe are a couple?"

"No." He considered it again. "I don't think so." He shrugged. "Pepe's too smart."

"Why'd she and Ernie split up?"

"He hurts people. Out of stupidity. Including himself." Felicio gave me a nasty smile. "See his pool?"

"Looks inviting." A breeze rustled the surface, horizontal sunlight broken into yellow splotches.

"Wait ten days. The blue will turn dark green."

I stood for a better angle. "Why?"

"Algae. He'll let the water out, to clean it. Every two weeks. There's no filter. When they fill it, it takes five days. Why? Because he put in no pump. He fills the pool with two garden hoses."

"Why no pump or filter?"

"He came here on weekends. 'Who needs them?' he said." His gardeners did the work. 'I can pay three men twelve years for the cost of a pump,' he insisted. Now he's here five days a week, in Mexico two. Often he can't use the pool." A gloat coated Felicio's face.

"Don Ernesto, bringing ever more employment to Michoácuaro."

"Just so." Slowly he stood. "You have no more beer, Jorge. Walk with me."

"I do have more beer."

"The blond only." He turned. I kept myself from asking how he knew.

We headed to his car. "And when did you last see Ali Cran?" The two of them used to keep at least a couple of arguments running, dispute being the basis of their friendship. "How is he?"

"A son of a bitch."

"What did you do to him now?"

"What he did. Nothing. The whole time of Pepe's campaign, nothing. Many in town, powerful ones, they were for Marranando."

"But Pepe won by a huge majority, didn't he?"

"Who could know this before? The new bishop, every Sunday his sermon lashed out at Pepe."

"Do I understand he's less corrupt than his predecessor what's-his-name?"

"And so more dangerous. Delcoz is a cleanser of the Church. Every day he conducts a celebratory mass. To thank his Lord that Pepe Legarto is no longer here."

"Could he have—removed Pepe?"

"It's not his way." Felicio shook his head. "But my point is Ali Cran. He didn't oppose Marranando. Ali Cran is now an agro-capitalist."

"So I'm discovering." Though not yet believing.

Felicio shrugged. "Still, he agrees with me, that Pepe is—" he swept his arm southward, "out there." He got into his VW, stared at the wheel, then turned back. "Jorge, I should be able to figure out what happened to Pepe. I can't. We need your help."

Self-reliant Felicito, asking help from an outsider. "I'll do whatever I can. But, Felicio, I'll be damned if I know what that might be."

"Thank you." He switched on the engine and released his brake. He reached his hand through the window. His old eyes glistened. "Come visit me. We'll speak."

I squeezed his fingers, and went to open the gate. He drove away. I stood a while beside the wall. My research in criminology grows from other people's reports, from newspapers, from my own interviews, all set against a world I know, a history I know. But, it was becoming increasingly and irritatingly clear, Michoácuaro wasn't my world. Still, some of those who knew the town best believed Pepe to be alive, and that was very good to know.

To reach Ali Cran I needed Pepe's Jeep. In the casa by a window, Vera, ironing a shirt, started to smile. Then she couldn't. "Don Pepe will need it, when he—soon."

"On the second or third of January, Vera."

"What?" She looked over to me. "You know where he is?"

"I've learned this could happen." I held her glance. "Just as I've learned, he went away before, just disappeared."

She set the iron down. "It's true, Don Pepe can be rash. But this is different."

"Where is he, Vera?"

She bit her lower lip. "Last time, after one day, he called me. I must not tell anyone where he is, he said." She sniffed back tears. "Now, he hasn't called."

"You should've told me he'd gone away before."

She nodded, and picked up the iron. "Sí, señor."

"I believe he'll return." I did, I believed it. And if I was wrong, Vera could mourn later. "You mustn't be frightened."

"No no." Her head shook. "Oh! Señora Irini called again, she'll come tomorrow morning." She smiled, brave now.

I took the chance to ask, "Vera, tell me, do you practise the bruja art?"

A tic froze on her face. She set the iron down and stared at it. The tic passed. "Why do you ask this?"

I said gently, "I've heard stories. About your power."

"From my grandmother—" A sudden shyness. "I learned some potions. For healing."

"Your grandmother knew a great deal?"

"Sí, señor." She found my eye then, and spoke two of the proudest words: "Muchas cosas." Many things.

"And you? What sorts of things do you know?"

"It—isn't easy to describe." She worked the iron's tip around the shirt cuff.

"Vera?"

She concentrated on the shirt-sleeve. "I know very little, Señor Jorge."

I let it be and asked to borrow the Jeep.

She nodded, put down the iron and found me the keys. "Be careful."

No doubt certain herbs and potions can bring about both cures and diseases. And I take seriously Felicio's sense of the double agent—the curandera heals, the bruja using the same crafts can bring on bad times. Depending, too, on one's point of view; the despair of some is the joy of others.

Flaco's blindness wasn't caused, Felicio claims that the local story goes, by a shift in the wind. A bruja's curse blew the spray into his eyes. The bruja was paid a month's wages for this. Flaco has proof.

The bruja, a short skinny woman, comes to him. "You must pay me two months wages," she says. "Or I carry out the curse Gloria has paid me for."

Flaco says no, he doesn't have the money. This Gloria, it seems, is infatuated with Flaco. And Flaco is mightily attracted to Gloria. But Flaco's desire to receive Gloria's glory is held in check by two forces—he fears the scourges of hell so he accepts the commandment against adultery; and he loves his wife.

He tells Gloria, "No woman is so beautiful as you. But I won't commit adultery."

Gloria is furious. It's said she's never needed to ask a man to lie with her. Rejected by Flaco! Her pouting lips whisper, "Come to the lower gate when the sun is setting. Or you'll never see such beauty again."

Flaco shakes his head. "With all my heart I wish I could."

They speak of Gloria slapping Flaco, and hissing.

The bruja comes to Flaco with her offer. He sends her away. In the following week he sprays the fruit trees, the wind shifts, and he's blind.

In despair he consults with his friends. If he wants it, they swear to him, they'll kill Gloria. "But that won't bring my sight back!" he cries. The best advice is from his brother Nicandro: if one bruja can cause blindness, maybe another can make his eyes good again.

With fury in his gut and led by his young son, Flaco searches for a bruja with great powers. Deep in tierra caliente he finds Señora Carmela. She gives him an unguent to place on his eyes. "This," she says, "will travel from your eyes to your heart, and still its fire, and bring you light."

"What do you mean?"

"Go."

Flaco returns. He does as she's told him. Pepe hears the story, he understands it. He hires Flaco to be his gardener. There is no looking back for either.

In the low light I drove south toward tierra caliente along the old cracked road on the far side of Cerro Madre and turned off by an adobe restaurant offering hot food day and night. It had been closed when I came by five years ago and it was closed now. One new item—a weathered sign on the front door said, Open Tomorrow.

The road, dirt, bare rock and shadowed potholes, wound through the hills to Ali Cran's near ranch, Dos Arroyos. Lomas Secas, his distant one, was reachable only on horse-back. I passed along a gully, up a sharp rise, at last a level stretch. I recognized a grove where Ali Cran had left his truck when we rode out to Lomas Secas. A couple more kilometres and Dos Arroyos lay ahead on a broad spit of land between two streams that met two kilometres south of the house. The bridge, rebuilt, felt sturdy. The track followed an uphill curve to the side of the house.

I got out. On the porch, her hands on the railing, stood Gitana, Ali Cran's wife. Her mouth smiled as I remembered. The cheeks and eyes of her oval face did not. Her ebony hair was pulled back. "Welcome, Jorge." She held out a hand.

I took it. "Glad to be here."

She squeezed my hand, brought her face to mine and kissed my cheek. "We were expecting you."

"Good. Ali Cran is here, then?"

"I'm waiting for him."

I'd wait too. She offered coffee, her own beans. I accepted. She went in to brew a pot. I sat in a chair built of rough-hewn planks softened by stuffed goat-hide cushions.

I'd spent a good evening here once. In the living room one wall is covered with hanging masks that depict a range of human states—masks of anger and friendship, of docility and for wooing, the horned face of Malo the Evil One and the faces of pink cherubs, a human face covered by a mon-ster scorpion, old man masks and scarlet woman masks.

How is it, I wondered, that Ali Cran has settled on, and down with, Gitana? Her doe-brown irises are set in ivory, her smooth skin shines brown from brow to throat, her wrists are slender, her fingers long. But physical beauty isn't dominant for Alicito. Rubén's explanation, that Ali Cran lives to ease a woman's needs, any woman's, is generally accepted. Then what does Gitana need from Ali Cran? Some women need to bear children. Gitana has not made her husband a father. Ali Cran, sire to dozens of illegitimate kids, has none running around his own ranchos.

"The coffee will be ready in four minutes." Gitana sat in the other chair. She wore a yellow blouse with a front embroidered in red flowers and yellow xxxxxxx patterns, and loose black buffed-polyester slacks that shimmered. "You're comfortable in Pepe's casita."

"It's a great little place."

"We're all distressed."

A wary distance to her words. "And where do you think Pepe is?"

She sniffed a sad laugh. "Sometimes it feels as if he'll be back this evening." She stared into the distance as if he'd soon appear from beyond the last ridge.

"Did he ever talk about something like, say, going away for a while?"

She shook her head. "You see, it's more than our friend that's gone. It's the man who won our election. Though for Pepe, being presidente municipal would be only a role. He believed—" she caught herself, "he believes there are many ways to make the town honest again." She got up. "The coffee will be ready." She walked into the house. The synthetic pants gave her shape a fine sway but it seemed wrong for a working rancho. Like her tone; as if she were pretty sure Pepe was dead and she could say nothing. I didn't like that sense from her, not at all.

To the south the fields spread into the distance. I remembered the bright green of cane. To the southwest, trees. A small cloud of fireflies sparked ten feet in front of me. I didn't think fireflies hatched in the winter.

She came back. "Gitana. Do you think Pepe is held somewhere, against his will?"

"Kidnapped?"

"Or just hiding out?"

She shrugged; then her head shook.

"You think he's alive?"

She stared at me. She didn't see me. "We must assume he is, Jorge." She poured coffee.

"Yeah." Fair enough. "And when he comes back, how will he make Michoácuaro honest?"

"One day perhaps you'll ask him." Meant to comfort.

"I'd like to."

We waited for Ali Cran. No, they no longer grew cane. Yes, more bananas. Cherimoyas were a valuable crop. Antonio, once assistant here at Dos Arroyos, now was foreman at Lomas Secas. Two new men helped. Yes, she still worked with medicinal herbs, balm for the inner or the outer body. She sold them packaged now. Pepe's garden linked her to distributors and so to regional and international markets.

I told her my stories and kept my patience by Mexican time. The sky had gone from dying gold to dim to black. Small stars multiplied. "When do you expect him?"

"Alicito? Tomorrow, possibly."

Damn them! "Gitana—I thought he'd be here any minute."

"I don't think so."

"Where is he now? At Lomas Secas?"

Her right hand grasped her left. "He's out in tierra caliente."

"Why there?"

"Searching. Always."

"For Pepe?" Not Rubén's version, or Felicio's.

She turned to me. "Have you seen Pepe's garden, his great experiment?"

"No."

"It's a model. For many gardens. Still, for each the site has to be correct. Maybe Pepe went in search of other sites. But often strangers aren't welcome in tierra caliente."

"Pepe knows his way around, no?"

She played with her fingers. "These are guesses."

"Where out there?"

"Gardens need water. Ali Cran has sent two of our men down along the river. But they've found nothing."

More oblique information. At least from my northern perspective. I had to say, "What can I do to help?"

"If I knew this, I would tell you."

On the way back the dark gullied road held my attention. At the hardtop I stopped by the closed restaurant, killed the lights, got out, stared at the huge sky. And down here, immense stretches of country to hide a man in. Or a corpse. I said aloud, "Shit."

I drove back slowly, turned in, parked, locked. Scented breezes drifted through the compound, swept the leaves and shuffled westward. A single light shone down from the corner of Ernie's house. At its edge lay the old dog, asleep.

In the casita I had a beer. Dark, replaced by Vera. Do my exercises? It took an act of will. I had the sensation, foolishly, of some other presence here. In bed I stared at the ceiling, my own sleep elsewhere. My books were stowed in the lost suitcase. But Pepe's study held all kinds of treasures.

I took the flashlight, pulled my pants on and went outside. The casa was dark. I had another sudden flash of not being alone. I walked quietly. I listened. The stream gurgled away.

The house was locked but I had my key. I stepped inside. All was silent. And uninviting.

My lamp found the steps to the study upstairs—the crow's-nest, Pepe called it, an all-inclusive chaos. I followed the beam and opened the door. Vera wasn't allowed to clean here. Two rooms, this and one behind. The back room held

Pepe's papers, a space he keeps in control. On three sides, shelves; on the shelves, blue file boxes. Each is neatly labelled: 1982. 1983. 1984. Invoices. Conferences. I asked once, why didn't he neaten up the front too? He laughed and explained that back there he had deposited the past but, in front where he worked, this was the messy present.

The couch was a clutter of books and papers. On his desk a dozen pamphlets, paperbacks, four face-down open, many notes—the desk of a man who'll be back tomorrow morning. Most dealt in some way with agriculture. I flicked the light on and opened the door to the back room. The neatness was unchanged.

Somewhere here, information to explain Pepe's disappearance? I glanced over the chaos. How could I ever know.

Tomorrow I'd try. Tonight I needed escape reading. I located three shelves of mystery novels, including several by his beloved John MacDonald. The titles I'd brought weren't there. Great. Now if only I had my suitcase. For when he came back.

My eye caught a paperback in large format, *La Condesa de Michoácuaro*. The cover showed an elegant woman in an eighteenth-century gown, high on a magnificent horse; a romance of some sort, I assumed. I chose a mystery writer whose name I knew vaguely, went downstairs, locked up behind me, crossed to the casita. Clearly no one else here. I read a while and put out my lamp.

Up at the ceiling, a flashing light. The Chilango's beam through a hole in the roof? The angle was wrong. Some reflection from the window—I turned my bedside light on. Nothing. Off. Again the twinkling. I shone the flashlight at the flicker. A lightning bug. Blown in with the wind? I lay back and marvelled at it.

Then, etched on the retina, a trace memory. Lights again. Where wall met ceiling over the bathroom door, a scorpion—alacrán, as they're called here—a handsome beast, the long tail arched elegantly over its back. Its venom numbs the nerves, causing local paralysis and constriction, particularly of the throat. For old people and babies it can be deadly.

Shoes on. A weapon, a broomstick. I reached up and knocked it down. It scurried for safety. I ran after it, stepped on it, felt it squish to juice. I rubbed the floor dry and flushed the flat corpse down the toilet.

I read, the novel tense enough to soothe my nerves. I put out my lamp, thanked the lightning bug, fell asleep and dreamed of Pepe visiting me in the north, in the snow, far from here.

"Aaaaaayeeeee-aaaaaahh!" A scream full-pitched and bloodthirsty. A mighty splash—

SEVEN

I yanked the blanket away, grabbed my robe and shoved open the veranda door. Murmuring water, thin new light. The hills across to the east, masses of stone, lay dim brown.

I heard machine-regular splashing. In his pool, Ernie the Chilango, swimming laps. Butterfly up. Crawl back. A lap of backstroke. Dull as a pendulum, but impressive energy. And determination—the water would be chilly. Well, good for him.

At the rear of my skull my headache thumped lightly. I lay down for a while and let my lids slide closed. I'm not sure if I slept again but when I opened my eyes the headache had lessened. Still, I needed coffee. I washed, dressed and headed to the casa. Night-damp coated leaves and grass, but the cloudless sky promised a hot day. That sense last night of someone in here— A sliver of sun broke over the mesa-top, lifting colour from each flower and tile. An intruder? Sure, one scorpion. An analogy: as these colours come back with the sun, so too Pepe will return. Or maybe he was here and we couldn't see him because the light was wrong.

Bullshit. Coffee.

I heard a radio crackle. Surges of Oxbridge rasped from the kitchen. Through the glass I watched Vera, playing with the shortwave, finding and losing the BBC. I saw Pepe, over daily breakfast, listening to the world news. For Vera, English was simply noise. She was bringing Pepe back however she could.

I stood still and let the sun warm me. The static stopped. I waited a minute and walked in. Vera sat on a stool, a cup in her hand, eyes glazed. I said, "Buenos días," and she twitched as if I'd caught her casting a spell. Black liquid crested her cup and sloshed to the floor. Coffee.

"Oh, Señor Jorge—"

"I hope there's more of that. For both of us."

"There is, yes, I'll get it, sit, please."

She fussed with milk, sugar, how would I like my eggs? She squeezed me a glass of orange juice. "Thank you, Vera. But tomorrow I'll make my own breakfast."

"My breakfast isn't so good, I understand—"

"It's wonderful. But you mustn't arrive so early to serve me."

We argued, we compromised. She'd make my comida and supper. I ate her excellent huevos rancheros, chiliquilas and beans, and sipped fine coffee. Maybe a mistake, refusing her breakfasts. Besides, feeding me likely helped shape her worried mornings. I headed back. I'd give Señora Irini an hour.

A high wail... I glanced out the windows. No sound, only the stream. I made my bed. The wail again. A visit to Emilia Avéspare. The wail, loud, broken as with whispers. I stepped out on the veranda.

Small yips. A splintered howl. The old dog, still tied, wobbled by the edge of the house, soaking wet. His eyes gleamed of fear. Ernie a few metres away was bare to the waist. He gripped a pool-filling hose two handed, like a machine gun. Its nozzle was a clasp-and-release spring device; squeeze it— He did and water spurted, thin under sharp pressure. The blast hit the dog neck and shoulder. The dog howled in pain. His chain, a short line to a ring pin, kept him from running away. He bared his gums. Very few teeth left. His mouth opened wide, the wail a set of broken gasps. Ernie the bastard shot water down the dog's throat. The dog retreated, his head sagging. He sniffled, half-turned and dropped to his front knees. But Don Ernesto was ready for the dog's cowardly ways. He angled to the dog's rear, knelt, aimed and sprayed a hard blast at the dog's testicles. The dog yowled, whimpered, lunged toward the spray. His collar aborted the feeble leap in mid-thrust. Ernie shouted, "Son of a whore, you won't attack me!"

I stood locked in place. Ernie grabbed the hose six-seven feet from the nozzle end and swung it at the dog, a whip with a knob on the lash. He thrashed wildly, swiping laterally. As the spring-nozzle hit the dog or slammed the ground, water sprayed in all directions, including on Ernie. He made contact every three or four tries. Missing infuriated him. He swore at the dog, his curses harsh versions of chinga!

I had to react. At the rail I leaned forward—

He spotted me. His grin said, Want a turn with the whip, gringo? "Hey, Jorge!"

I shouted, "What the fuck you think you're doing?"

He walked away, to the far side of his house. The dog crept into the shade, licked his thigh and knee, then his balls. A feeble tongue stroked at the hair, trying to soothe the bruised flesh underneath. No, it wasn't fear in the poor beast's eyes. The dog was blind. Many here agree, animals have to be beaten regularly, show them who's in control. Some men speak about, and handle, their women this way.

I was back in the casita for ten minutes when the howling began again. Ernie, hose in one hand, broom handle in the other, blasted the dog with water. The dog crawled forward yowling his misery. Ernie, just out of reach, smashed the animal across the snout with the broom handle.

I sped outside. "What the hell's the matter with you?"

He sprayed, he slammed. I was furious, I ran to the witches' gateway— What, wrestle the hose from him? I stood

there, couldn't stop him, couldn't look away. He over-
extended, a bad swing, hit the dog's far flank and the ground
at the same time. The broomstick broke. He stormed to the
shed, rushed back with a bamboo pole maybe an inch and a
half thick. He stared at the hose, kicked it, with two hands
swung the bamboo at the dog. He missed twice, then caught
the animal on the back leg. A thin scream—

I ran to the passageway and pulled the wires apart. A car
rumbled down Ernie's drive. A man I didn't know got out
and called, "Don Ernesto!" Ernie said something and pointed
at the dog. The two men laughed and went inside.

The dog licked its wounds and lay still. I'd seen violence
in Michoácuaro, and angry passion, but not sick brutality like
this.

Ten minutes later a door slammed. The visitor, holding
some files, left. The Chilango came out, marched down past
the dog, found the pieces of broomstick and hurled them as
far as he could—specifically, over the fence and into my garden. Then he went back in.

I knew well enough that there are greater calamities in
the world than the beating of an old blind dog. I'm powerless in the face of most of these. Which now increased my
outrage. My headache pounded. I marched over to the casa.
"Vera?" No answer. "Vera!"

She came round the corner. Holding her hand and
squeezed against her thigh, a girl of about five. The child
wore a blue dress, ironed shiny, and a little white apron.
Straight black hair glowing in the light fell to her shoulders.
She saw me, turned and giggled into her mother's leg.

"Alicia, say buenos días to Tío Jorge." Vera, trying to
sound strict, managed to produce only affection and pride.
She turned Alicia to face me.

I squatted, and reached out my hand. "Buenos días, Alicia."

Alicia looked my way, giggled and spoke into Vera's dress:
"Buenos días, Tío Jorge."

Vera again tried to turn her about. "Alicia, please."

Alicia reached out her hand. I caught a couple of small fingers and moved them up and down once before she pulled away. My outrage had evaporated.

But not the memory. Vera sat and Alicia scrambled onto her lap. "Vera, this Ernie Montemayor, he's dangerous. Don't make him more angry. I just saw him beat his dog."

She nodded. "He beat Laura too."

"He's a pig."

She nodded harder. "Two times he tried." Alicia buried her face in her mother's bosom. "The second time it didn't happen."

"And when it did?"

"You see, the maestro was paying a hundred fifty thousand pesos a month"—about fifty dollars—"and the Chilango said she'd get four thousand pesos a day. She was part of that house for eleven years! She was furious. He hit her very hard, her head and shoulders."

Alicia twisted about to see if I was watching. She caught my eye, giggled, again hid.

"So Laura went to the palacio municipal, the treasurer is her cousin. She told him what the Chilango did. But the cousin could do nothing, not if he wanted to keep his job. But Laura can't live with a hundred thousand pesos, she's the only support for her mother and— Alicia, please!"

Alicia had again turned my way, giggled, swung back against Vera. Vera set her down. Alicia climbed right back up.

"So what did Laura do?"

"She said he had to pay more. She was cooking his soup. He said it was impossible. She cried, she told him her mother would starve. He got furious, he picked up the soup and threw the pot at her. It burned her face and her eye, it was bandaged for weeks. They said she wouldn't see from it again but it's okay now except when the light is bad. So she cursed him and—"

"I thought you did that."

Vera smiled. "Yes. Also."

I nodded. Alicia had grown quiet. "What did he do?"

"He fired her. If she went away, maybe the curse would too." Vera giggled, malicious.

"Vera, this curse—"

The phone rang. Alicia jumped from her mother's lap. It rang again. Alicia bounded around the corner.

"I mean, taking a man who is—" Spanish for superstitious? "A man who believes you can make him experience—"

Alicia came back, whispered to Vera, Vera whispered back and pointed to me. Alicia shook her head. From Vera a stern, "Sí."

Alicia took a small step my way. "It's for you, Tío Jorge."

Lousy timing. I went to the phone. Felicio, in English: "Jorge. How did you sleep?"

"Fine." I told him about the firefly and the scorpion.

"A fable from Aesop." He laughed. "Listen, tomorrow you must take the Christmas meal with me. It had been planned for us to indulge ourselves at Pepe's. So give Vera the day off. She'll object but she'll be pleased."

I thought for a moment. "Okay. Thanks." My poor Spanish, coping at a dinner party… "Who else'll be there?"

A couple I didn't know. Irini. The group Pepe had invited.

"So I'll meet the lady at last."

"She didn't come yesterday?" Concern in his voice.

"She did telephone. Vera said she'd be here this morning."

"Good. Tomorrow she'll drive you. Save me a trip." He laughed. "Who knows what will happen by tomorrow in Michoácuaro."

"What do you mean?"

"Go down to the plaza. Michoácuaro politics in action. There's a rally this evening, speeches and much incitement."

"Real *Proceso* material, is it?"

"Rubén and his deputies will be there so you can count on shooting." Felicio clucked his tongue. "The bishop will speak, you'll hear our demagogue in person. The rabble will rise."

"He's that good?"

"Oh yes. He knows everyone in power is evil. The law is corrupt—he means how Rubén once was, since now the bishop courts the jefe's wife. Oh, in a most religious fashion. Most villainous is Pepe Legarto who brings the evil of television to our innocent town. Pepe and his pagan vegetable patch. Do you not know, Jorge, what grows in this garden? The very fruit of Satan's cesspool! Bring past your lips and onto your tongue an arracacha, the brands of hell will sear your flesh with agonies far fiercer than Eve suffered for accepting the apple from the serpent fiend. A direct quote, Jorge. At least a paraphrase. Our Delcoz. With his Ramus Dei."

My Latin was long gone but this I could figure. "Branch of God? What's that?"

"I could be a member, or Pepe. You, even." Felicio sighed. "They are lay people, a secret group. And some priests from Hermosillo. Like Opus Dei when it started in Barcelona."

"A kind of conservative Catholicism?"

"Arch-reactionary. You have to hear him first hand. After, you're allowed to puke. Or if you can, during. The immediate purge is valuable."

I laughed. "A man not to be missed."

"We do not live in funny times, Jorge."

We said goodbye. Bishop Delcoz. Enough arrogance there to kidnap Pepe? Or to complain before a faithful congregant, Oh that my world were free of this Legarto...

Vera was washing dishes. Alicia had gone. "You never answered my question, Vera."

"Question, Señor?"

"About casting spells and curses."

"This is nothing, señor."

"Can you do such things?"

She put her hand over her mouth. "Only when necessary."

"And when is that?"

She pulled her hand away. A smile remained. She turned back to the sink.

I waited. "Vera?" One day I'd get her to answer. Maybe. "Vera. Tell me. What kind of man is Bishop Delcoz?"

She scrubbed a frying pan, and spoke evenly. "Very strict."

"How do you mean?"

She stopped washing. "I'm happy a different priest baptized Alicia." She turned the scouring cloth and worked at some resistant baked-on egg.

Why couldn't she be a real gossip, like her aunt Constanza. Yes, I'd hear Delcoz tonight first-hand. Right now I needed coffee, butter, rolls. "I'm going shopping."

"Take Don Pepe's Jeep."

"I'll walk, I think."

"Señor Jorge. Be careful."

"About?"

She hesitated. "If Don Pepe can disappear…"

"I'll be fine. If Señora Irini comes, tell her to wait."

"Go safely with God, señor."

I borrowed a shopping bag, headed to the casita, and thought about the curse business. It could be seductive. If one believes he's cursed, let's say Ernie the Chilango, the curse or spell can have a powerful effect. If one doesn't believe in spells, can one then be hexed? Or, conversely, protected from spells by one's private gods?

The buzzer at the gate rasped. Señora Irini, at last? I went to unlock. A dark sedan drove in and parked. A tall short-haired man in a light shirt, dark tie in place, maybe late thirties, got out. "You are the North American professor?"

I introduced myself. "And you?"

"Lieutenant Estaban Blanco, Judicial Police of Michoacán." A small salute. The sides of his mouth rose. "We will speak."

"About?"

"Pepe Legarto." He blinked hard.

"Of course. Will you come in?"

"There is peace in this enclosure. We can speak here." More blinks. "Your friend is missing." The smile fell away. "Do you know where he might be?"

"I wish I did. I'm worried." I wouldn't share my little bit of hope which, I realized, was slowly dissipating.

His smiley-face mouth looked ready to bite. "And why?"

I turned his way. "This absence isn't like him."

"You know him well?"

"Very well."

A nod from the lieutenant. "Señor. If you hear from him, you'll inform me immediately."

"Of course."

Two blinks. "We too are concerned." Again the little salute. He turned, got into his car, and backed out.

And what was that all about? Hardly an interrogation. In the casita I changed from shorts to slacks and locked my door. An old black pickup turned into the drive. I glimpsed a woman get out the far side, turn and walk to the casa. Señora Irini? Hell with her. I started off. No, she was Pepe's friend and garden-partner. I unlocked again, withdrew to the veranda and waited. The old dog lay curled up, his breath shallow draws and little vibrating exhalations.

A knock. I grabbed my shopping bag and opened the door.

"Hello. I'm Irini Farolla."

I saw a tall woman, mid-thirties, straight black hair to her shoulders, wide opal-green eyes. Stunning.

EIGHT

"You received my message." Irini Farolla spoke an English correct in detail but as if learned in schools with good teachers, a high-school year in Madison, an exchange in Bristol. She looked at the bag in my hand. "May I come in?"

"Of course." She did. "Would you like some tea?"

"Only to speak with you." Her eyes, large, green flecked with black, searched my face.

"Look, what can you tell me about Pepe's disappearance?" A kind of blurt— "Everything you're thinking." I had the sense she could see my mind. "I'm very concerned."

"It's good you're here." She dropped her gaze. "Vera trusts you. She's frightened."

"I've tried to calm her."

We stepped out on the veranda and she went to the rail. "From my house I can watch the sunset. But this view is my favourite."

Her eyes surveyed the valley and she owned it. She was slender, stood maybe five foot six, wore a short-sleeved white blouse, a long flared black skirt with small white dots, and sandals. Her tanned skin was smooth, like a bed sheet tucked in tight. I found it very hard to take my eyes from her.

She turned, leaned sideways, and pointed to the huge tree. "You like my ahuehuete?" She stepped away from the rail, and sat. "I owned it once." She sniffed a laugh. "Now he does."

I suddenly felt angry on Pepe's behalf—right now he wasn't Irini's primary concern. "Can a tree belong to someone, really?" I sat in the other chair.

She leaned my way. "I was speaking of intimacy."

"Look, about Pepe."

"We're all very worried." She touched my arm. "But what shall we do, look under each rock? Rubén and his deputies have searched. Our friends search. No one has found him."

"An accident?"

She shrugged.

"Kidnapped?"

"There's been no note." She drew her hand away.

"Sent to someone else. Rubén?"

"He assuredly would tell me."

"Or somebody's locked him up till Marranando is sworn in?"

"But Marranando's gone too."

"He'd come back, wouldn't he?"

She shrugged. "I don't know Señor Marranando. But I believe Pepe is alive. I do believe this. Yes, truly I do. And he'll return soon. I believe that."

I was glad to hear her say this and wanted to feel her hope. And yet— "But you just sit around?" Did she know anything at all? "And wait?"

"I'm at the garden, all day. A garden needs work." She scowled and swung about to face the hills. "Pepe fears Ernesto will cut the ahuehuete down."

This flitting from subject to subject chafed at me. But yes, Ernie just might. "Aren't there laws to protect old trees?"

"Mexico has many laws. Trees can't enforce them. Do you know what a cosmic tree is?"

"A Mayan notion, no?" Why were we talking about trees?

"This ahuehuete was a cosmic tree of the Aztecs. They took it from the Maya. They transformed it, of course." Her eyes caught mine again, held, and dared me to contradict her. I didn't. "Of course?"

"They eliminated Mah K'ina. The Great Lord of the Sun? You remember him, the tree came from his seed. He warmed the seed, then the sapling, and the tree grew huge." She closed her eyes and breathed, flat and deep. "After, the tree gave Mah K'ina its own seed to eat, and his life renewed itself perpetually." Her eyelids opened. She smiled. "But the Aztecs had their own sun god and didn't need Mah K'ina."

Lancing eyes. "I see." Speared by a woman's eyes— Bullcrap! I was thick-skinned, I could handle anything. Even new-age rhetoric.

"The Aztecs kept the part about roots, the trunk, the high branches." She stared at the tree. "I ran my hands up his bark. I talked to him, he understood. Roots in the under-world, branches in the upper, I beside him in the middle world."

Now I was pissed off. We should be figuring out how to find Pepe, not babbling about cosmic trees. She seemed so uninterested in looking— I calmed myself down. Maybe she was right, what else to do besides talk about cosmic trees. Except where the hell was Pepe?

"I'm still beside him." Again that smile. "But at a distance."

My friend Pepe's friend, gone archaeologically spiritual. Remarkable eyes and a weird gambol through cosmology. "What do you mean, distance?"

"About three kilometres away." She laughed. "Naturally you'll come. To the garden. We're reviving the ancient plants."

"Doctor Ortíz mentioned—"

"Ai, Felicio is impossible. He doesn't even visit."

"No?"

"He approves. So why bother, he says, to see each new catch-ditch. He bought the land for us, you know. Twenty-five million." She saw my face. "Oh, twenty-five million pesos."

"Still a nice chunk of cash."

"Eleven hectares. On the river." She stared toward the river. "You're going shopping and I'm keeping you."

"No—"

"Come. I'll take you. I have to go anyway." Her sideways-darted glance held me, and it burned my neck. "You know which stalls to buy from?"

I broke away. "Let's go." I got up, she followed me out the door. I opened the gate, she drove the pickup through, I closed, locked, and got in beside her.

Except she whispered, "Damn," and turned up the hill.

I gave her a grin. "Kidnapping me?"

"I forgot money."

Where the Morelia road turned left, we headed right. A couple of hundred metres on she stopped the truck at gates in a brick wall, got out, unlocked, pushed the gates open and drove in. A small compound—many trees and four little houses. Two kids raced through the landscaping. She rented her place from a Mexico City family, she said. "I'll be back."

I watched her walk away, her long black skirt swinging. An elegant face. Eyes that made demands. A bit skinny. Pepe's partner in more than the garden? And with her truck, why wasn't she out there somewhere, looking for him? Yes, yes, under which rock…

The wall enclosed a hectare or so of lush lawn and trees, some fruited, some in bloom. The enclosure ended at a steep cliff, and down it a thin waterfall maybe four metres high splashed into a stream. At the base of the cliff grew tall white calla lilies, in Michoacán called alcatraz. The stream, flowing through diagonally, sent water down narrow irrigation canals into every corner.

Irini returned wearing wrap-around sunglasses. "Please shut the gate."

She drove out, I closed and jumped in. Her eyes were hidden now, a disappointment. I asked, "When did you come to Michoácuaro?"

"I? First, four years ago. With your neighbour."

I grinned my naivest. "How could you live with him?"

She nodded. "Pepe was right, you'll ask anything."

We didn't speak further. The silence felt okay. Nearing the plaza, trucks blocked our way. Women with shopping bags, campesinos with sickles. The television vans, closed tight, hinted of news events to come. Irini parked four blocks before the market. At the plaza three men were erecting a speaker's platform and eight shouted advice. Apparent turmoil but I felt a sense of order. I said, "You didn't answer my question."

She took her glasses off. Our eyes held. "Ernie can act Mexican, or American. He believes macho in American means tough." She shrugged. "He can also be charming."

Notices everywhere announced the rally, PRI and MMM both calling on concerned citizens to be present. The posters were headed, What Is To Be Done? "A charming dog-beater," I said.

"I'm sorry?"

We made our way to the market stalls. I told her about the beating. She drew stares from many men, glances from women.

"Poor Blaze." She stopped at the third vegetable stall and helped herself to some tiny potatoes. "Everyone beats a dog. To be beaten is why dogs exist, no?" She smiled, grim. "Ernesto beats his women." She tested several avocados, and selected two. "The woman doesn't object, to hit her means he knows she's there. So it's a relationship. You want none of these vegetables?"

"I need breakfast things." I held Irini's bag. Shopping together felt like a small conspiracy. "That's how he treated you?"

She sighed. "A long story." We walked by a dozen kinds of peppers. "Most of what you see here comes from far away. But the little peasant ladies on the ground, they sell their own radishes, and cilantro, and nopalitos. This is the freshest."

"You sell some of your farm produce here?"

She turned, and her eyes again found mine. The right side of her mouth smiled. "It's one thing to teach our workers to grow new vegetables." She sniffed a laugh. "To eat them too? Please!" We stopped at the stall of a dark-skinned woman. "The best place for eggs." She said in Spanish, "My friend Irís," and introduced us, telling Irís to provide me with her freshest eggs. At moments Irini's Spanish took on a lithp. I bought half a kilo of eggs.

"You learned Castilian Spanish?"

"My mother's language. To my shame." She walked on.

We found tea, milk, butter. Instant coffee. Some avocados, I couldn't resist. A small papaya, some mangos, peaches. Bread. I wanted sardines too, in case I had to make myself a meal. I located a small shop I remembered. "You have sardines?"

The bald young storekeeper thought for a moment. "No, señor."

I spotted a can of tuna, reached— Directly beside it, one tin of sardines. Triumphant, I picked it up. "Look."

He studied it. "I'm sorry. If you take it, I won't have any."

"I can't buy it?"

"No, señor." His head shook. He looked very sad.

I nodded, bought the tuna, and we left. I realized I accepted his sadness, and it made sense.

Irini said, "You've returned to Michoácuaro."

In the flower section we found deaf Gertrudis. "Qué milagro, Señor Jorge!" A powerful handshake. She chose a perfect yellow rose and gave it to me. I bought three bird of paradise stalks for Vera.

"Gracias, Gertrudis." I moved my lips carefully. "And three of those, also." I pointed to some long-stemmed canela flowers.

She laughed. "Your accent is still terrible, señor."

Gertrudis's deafness results from a firecracker rocket shot off by the priests to announce early mass at four in the morning of the feast of the Virgin of Guadalupe, Mexico's patron saint. One rocket, falling on its side, travelled eight metres and struck Gertrudis bull's-eye in the left ear. She was fifteen. The rocket took out tympanum, anvil, stirrup; the works. It deafened her on the right side too. The inner workings there are intact but she hears nothing with either ear. The will of the Virgin, they say in Michoácuaro.

Back at the pickup I handed Irini the three canela blossoms. "Thanks for taking me shopping."

"Thank you." She took the flowers as her due. "And tomorrow you can see the garden."

"Yes, good. But I'm going to Felicio's for Christmas dinner. Oh, and so are you."

"He hasn't spoken to me." She sounded annoyed. "First, tomorrow come to the farm. Early when everything's fresh."

"Close enough to walk?"

"Yes." She gave me directions. We agreed on eight-thirty. "Hasta mañana." She drove off, waving, not looking back. She'd barely mentioned Pepe. What was going on in her mind, regarding him? After her insistence, I was more optimistic again.

But my churned-up responses—I mean my responses from ignorance, from the beliefs of others—were like those of a yoyo chameleon. I'd been jerked from hope to fear, and back and back, taking on the emotive colouration of the last person I'd talked to. I'm a theoretical criminologist, for pitysake, versed in victims' rights and responsibilities, and bureaucratic reports. I should know better, I should be thinking better. The allure of Michoácuaro had somehow blinded me—the allure both of the town I'd known five years ago, and my memories of it up north. Time for some practical research.

I walked up the hill. People nodded to me in greeting. Did they remember me from my brief television appearance? Behind the casita Flaco was digging a hole with a man who looked like him but had half again the bulk. "What's it for?" I asked

"Orange trees, señor. Very good for the health." Flaco introduced his brother Nicandro.

"A pleasure, señor. I've heard many things about you."

"Good things, I hope."

Nicandro nodded. "From Flaco, and from Ali Cran."

"Ah. You'll see him again soon?"

"I'm helping to build a new corral for him at his rancho."

"Tell him I send an abrazo. I'd like to welcome him here."

"I'll say these things, señor."

I unpacked my purchases, went out and sat on the veranda. From below I heard Flaco and Nicandro. Less what they said, mostly the melodic Michoácuaro accents. Then they were laughing. I looked. Nicandro pointed over to the Chilango's garden, to the old dog. Blaze was trying to pee. Nicandro explained, "He does not lift his leg, look he is strrrretching his legs in the back, wide wide." Laughter from both. Nicandro said, "Like a woman!" Roars of laughter.

I went inside and lay down. Damn their pleasure! Back to the square, see Avéspare… Tomorrow the famous garden… Irini Farolla… I dozed off.

Three sharp raps woke me. I opened the door. A woman stood there, a rebozo draping her hair and shoulders, wrinkled cheeks, lines at the corners of her eyes. She wore a dirty yellow dress covered with a patched blue-checkered apron. In her left hand she held two purple shopping bags, grubby and filled with bulky things wrapped in newspaper. In her right was a red woven sack, synthetic, worn, nearly empty. How'd she get into the compound? "Yes, señora?"

"I'm very poor. Please, you can help me. I'm hungry. What can you give me?" The rebozo came down to her eyebrows. Her eyes stared out from under saggy lids, beseeching.

"I'll see what I have. Come in."

She stepped into the doorway. I felt her eyes. "Would you like some mangos?"

"Sí."

"Or some bread and cheese?"

"Sí."

No, I'd need these. "Some money, to buy what you wish."

"Sí."

I gave her two mangos and a thousand pesos. "For tortillas."

She dropped the mangos into her bag. "Muchas gracias, señor, muchas gracias." The coin went into an apron pocket. She pointed to my handy little flashlight. "This."

Why that? But I could borrow Vera's big one. This little señora, doubtful she had electricity— I gave it to her. "I hope it lights your way."

No smile. "Gracias, señor. Gracias." Same intonation. A phrase from a recording.

"De nada."

Her lingering stare moved across my face. "Ai, so far away."

"What is, señora?"

"Tarpaulin." Her head bobbed again. "For shade." A quick turn and she was out the door.

I watched her go. And what was she about? I did my exercises. Something fluttered about the room. A butterfly, all black except for white spots on the rear wings. At the window it bashed its body against the glass. I opened both doors wide and shooed it toward them. It lit on the fruit bowl.

A glass. A sheet of paper. The mangos would be sweet, the butterfly was all over them. Its tail was nearly as long as its body. The white dots looked like eyes. I moved slowly, brought the glass quickly down, and caught it. With so little room in the glass it couldn't injure itself.

I slid the paper under to cover the opening. On the veranda I turned the glass on its side. The butterfly crawled out, perched at the brim, fluttered to the railing. It balanced there, wings trembling in the light wind. It took flight, clumsier than before but making headway toward the zapote tree.

From the bougainvillea a yellow-beaked magpie swooped across the garden, plucked the butterfly in midair, crushed it tight and darted back to cover.

NINE

Silver knife and fork from Santa Anna de la Plata, blown wine and water goblets from Tlaqueplaque. A starched cotton Pátzcuaro napkin. Rococo-patterned Puebla plates, copper undersettings from Santa Clara del Cobre. And roast turkey thigh with red mole sauce, nopalitos and chapotes, made for me by Vera. My view to the mountains was pristine, the feather breezes warm and cooling at the same time.

I sat alone at the table in the dining room, Vera serving my comida with devoted insistence, performing the ritual in full. One part of life must remain normal.

In the kitchen Flaco and Nicandro ate the same meal. I heard male laughter, Vera's snicker, giggles from Alicia. I'd have joined them—their eating with me in the dining room was beyond Vera's sense of propriety—but the brothers' relish at watching Blaze pee still made me angry. I ate with little joy.

Vera returned. "Something is wrong with the turkey?"

"It's delicious." I shrugged. "My appetite."

"I understand." She scowled. "They shouldn't laugh so, Flaco and Nicandro. But, you know, they're frightened for Don Pepe. They laugh so I won't see their fear."

Clever Vera. And so Flaco won't see Nicandro's fear, and vice versa. Complicated stuff, macho. I nodded. "I'll eat the mole this evening. Now I need to meet with Señora Avéspare."

"Señor. Pleasc. Do not upset things here. Be careful."

"You keep saying that. About what?"

She shivered. "You watch, you understand, you explain. This is enough."

"Vera. This morning you hoped I'd help find Pepe."

"He'll be back. You said so, in January. Please?"

I smiled. "I'll go to visit Constanza."

"She'd like that, Señor Jorge."

I borrowed a flashlight, left it at the casita, and walked down into town. Vera's fear bothered me. Why does she think my presence here could lead to danger? The speaker's platform was set in place. The Avéspare house stood directly on the plaza, the north side. Beneath a portico a cement sidewalk ran the length of the block.

The facades of all the buildings along here were similar—adobe walls rising from the sidewalk, broken by high tight-shuttered windows, painted red to a metre and half above the ground, then white to the portico beams four metres overhead. Two wooden gates each a metre wide and three high, the old carriage-entry, separated the house from the plaza's bustle. A front door was cut into the left gate. I knocked.

No answer. I tried again, harder. The house had a large frontage. One can measure breadth from the age of the paint—where it contrasts in freshness, the next house begins. A last knock. Still no answer. I turned to go, heard the door open, looked back.

"Sí?" A muscular gent, late thirties, stood in the doorway. He wore jeans and a white tee-shirt with a pack of cigarettes rolled into the sleeve below his right shoulder. A southpaw. I hadn't seen the butt-bulge since high school when the toughboys came on like James Dean.

"I'm looking for Señora Avéspare."

"She's expecting you?"

"No." I gave him my name, and credentials: friend of Pepe Legarto.

"Wait here." He closed the door. I watched campesinos milling in the plaza. The benches were full—men, some women, a few kids. The gatekeeper returned. "Come in."

"Thank you." I stepped through the doorway. Five metres of passageway led to an open courtyard. To the right, a parked car, a large Nissan. Ahead easily a hundred masetas, each holding a dwarf bougainvillea. Rich and cluttered, a lot of colour but without focus.

My guide led me around the maze of pots to the back. Under a thatched canopy stood a low table, some wicker chairs, a couch, and a fine roll-top desk. Emilia Avéspare at the desk turned as we approached and smiled at the man. "Gracias, Toni."

I too said gracias. Toni left but stayed within eyesight. And hearing distance. "Señora, it's good of you to see me."

She gestured to where I should sit. She picked up a pen and leaned over her desk. She wore a light-blue wide-skirted dress. Her face was sterner than I remembered and there was more of her, as if the skirt gave her greater breadth. From somewhere I heard the sounds of a kitchen.

She turned. "We've met before. I can't recall when."

"A birthday party for Doctor Ortíz."

Her eyes narrowed. "Perhaps. How can I help you?"

"First, my condolences on the loss of your husband."

She waved my courtesy away. "The mourning time is over."

I nodded. "Life continues." Her widowhood looked to be proceeding well. "My concern, señora, is with the disappearance of my friend Pepe Legarto."

"We in Michoácuaro are deeply concerned."

"Where do you think he might be, señora?"

A thin smile. "If I knew, would I not tell the police?"

"Not if you feel your ideas are only guesses, unfounded."

"If I had such ideas, should I share them with you?"

The moment to bring out my usual research tools. I pushed on. "Partial ideas from several people, taken together," I smiled back, "could give us a more complete picture."

She nodded. "Pepe's return would be good for us all. But I will tell you, señor, it would even serve us well to know that he has died. Only lack of certainty is dangerous."

"Dangerous?" I shuddered invisibly at her pragmatism.

"Pepe Legarto was a responsible man. Responsible men don't turn a thriving city into an armed camp. What did your friend Pepe tell you?"

"But I haven't seen him."

She waved my answer away. "Before you arrived." She shook her head. "There's been great confusion here, distrust. For too long."

"No, Pepe told me nothing." I suddenly found the conversation muddily frustrating. As if I hadn't done my homework, my legwork, so had no points of reference. I'd been irresponsible, hadn't researched what I was getting into before I stood in the middle of it. Except in my own defence, the question, What could I have done? turned out to be no better than, What was I doing now? Northern research methods didn't work in Michoácuaro. So why bother? Indirection, the only way left to go. And what did she mean, distrust? "What distrust?"

Her eyes narrowed, as if she didn't grasp why I didn't understand. "But because of our ex-presidente municipal." She took a pack of cigarettes from her desk and tapped it. Four filter-tips stuck out their butts. She reached them toward me. I shook my head. She took one, set it between her lips and struck a match, inhaled. Smoke drifted from her nose. "Two cases of petty corruption came to my husband's attention. He died too soon to deal with them. We delayed further action till the new presidente arrived." More smoke.

Arrived. "I see." Not, was elected.

A chilly smile. "All will be resolved soon."

Time to see what a prod would bring out. "I hear the election was stolen from Pepe."

"Nothing was stolen." A grey-blue cloud gathering about her shoulders gave her yet greater substance.

"But weren't the ballot boxes altered?"

"Lies have been spread. Many by Legarto's manager."

"In Mexico City there are stories about—"

"In Mexico?" Her eyebrows rose. "There are always stories. They cannot know the truth about our city." In her voice, a double sense—fear and hope for Michoácuaro's future. Perhaps, for Señora Avéspare, anything she does to and for the city is permitted. She knew the web of her power, and the geography it stretched across. She sat still, a wide-skirted spider, spinning for Michoácuaro its political texture, concealing her web in puffy smoke. The brawn of her intentions was impressive. She leaned forward. "They cannot know, right now, how much we worry about violence."

"Maybe tonight's rally can relieve some anxiety."

"The rally is a mistake."

I'd figured her for being in favour. "Why?"

"In times of crisis, to bring large groups of people together is foolhardy."

"But the PRI is sponsoring this too, no?"

"The organizers use our name. Some members, idealists, cry, 'PRI and MMM together for peace in Michoácuaro!' Naive, señor."

A little more of a nudge. "Do the idealists back your textile plant?"

She sat back and studied me. From university politics I've learned, when you deal with a spider, retain advantage by avoiding the parlour. I suspected Señora Avéspare would right now have preferred to be a bullfrog with a long prehensile tongue. "Most of us here want the plant."

"Pepe Legarto doesn't."

"Have you spoken to him about it?"

"No. How could I? But—are you saying Pepe would?"

She took a drag on her cigarette. "Tell me, how do you view the economy of this city?"

I conceded her the lead. "I'd say, mixed. Too much cane. Avocadoes, some corn, a little fruit—"

"One cement factory. A lumber mill. Two construction firms, the only businesses employing more than twenty. Sheep and pigs. Too much marijuana." Her head shook. "Fifty-six percent unemployment."

Is a campesino, scratching away on a hectare of dirt, employed? Unemployment, it suddenly struck me, is a concept borrowed by Mexican bankers from our anglo north. "Is your textile mill going to eliminate unemployment?"

She shrugged. "It'll mean more work than today. A hundred men to build it. Three hundred employees in the first year."

I heard Jaime León:

The employee returns home after a day at the mill. An armchair, a good meal? He reads to his daughters? No.

He sits on the earth floor of the cardboard and rough-plank hut on the side of Cerro Gordo. The rain pours in, across the mud. He thanks the Virgin that much of the water flows out the lower side. His four children are angry with hunger.

The mother asks again, We must go back to the village. At least adobe keeps out rain.

The employee curses her. He sold their adobe and the two hectares for money for the trip to Michoácuaro. They can't give up his salary, nearly seventy-five thousand pesos a week, twenty-five dollars. He goes out into the rain, to where he's hidden a bottle of cane liquor. It cost him six thousand pesos. It'll help him sleep beside his sniffling kids.

I heard Pepe:

Does the industrial city of Michoácuaro have the infrastructure to support a textile maquiladora? Housing, water, sewage system? What schools and teachers? Health facilities?

Avéspare smiled. "With new money in the economy, money being spent, spent many times, you call it—" she switched to English, "'trickle-down,' we will be the envy of all Michoacán."

"Your English is impressive. You've lived up north."

A bitter smile. "For some years."

I placed her gaze: partner to the undertaker's associate, taking measurements. Coffin seller and spider, an industrious team. Trap. Desiccate. Bury. A woman who made things happen in Michoácuaro, claimed Rubén. Now she ran the PRI. Need a favour? See the PRI. Throw gasoline on tinder, see it flash. "Señora. I would like to ask a favour of your son."

She tilted her head to look at me. "What?"

"For a friend. He lent his camera to a man who disappeared here two years ago, a journalist, Teófilo Através. It was an expensive camera, a Leica III-f."

Her stare was unblinking. I was unsavoury prey.

"Through the PRI, could you inquire? So the camera can be returned to my friend."

Still no blink. "Why should the PRI know about a camera?"

I shrugged. "The influence of the PRI is wide."

She said at last, "I doubt my son can learn anything."

"I appreciate your help." I got up.

She remained seated. "Is that why you came to talk with me? Or was it Legarto?"

"Both, señora."

"Pepe Legarto was a good man, brave, when he ran against the PRI. If he returned today he'd agree, the city needs the factory." She was certain.

I had to obliterate that past tense reference to Pepe. "You know what Pepe is thinking today?" Movement behind her, a man. He nodded and passed. A face contoured like Emilia Avéspare's, a muted shadow of it. The son?

"Toni will show you out." She raised one finger.

"Adiós," I said. Toni led me to the front door. I turned. Avéspare was watching. I said in English to Toni, "And adiós to you too." He, silent, closed the door behind me.

On the plaza men in knots argued and smoked. Small groups of women sat chatting. Nobody at home, preparing for Navidad? Across from the cathedral a man on a flower-tub harangued a dozen campesinos and three dogs. The dogs took irregular turns nosing each other's anus. I'd learned something, talking to Emilia Avéspare. What? It hovered, beyond reach.

Someone grabbed my arm. "Señor!"

I turned. Chaba, Vera's cousin. "Hello. How are you?"

"Very well, I thank you for asking. Señor—" He glanced about, then pulled me against the wall. "Señor, I have news. I've located my bed." A large three-toothed smile.

"Aha!" And who would be the lucky bride? "In time for Navidad."

"The mattress. Assuredly the rest of the bed is nearby."

Such pleasure on his face. "I'm certain of it."

"The compadre of my sister's husband has seen it. He'll take me where it is."

"You're a lucky man."

"No. But I have faith." He hung his head. "Thank you."

I answered with an honest, "De nada."

I walked up the hill. The mood away from the plaza seemed muted, uneasy. The coffin seller was away from his post. What, nobody dies on Christmas Eve? Maybe he was over at the plaza, sizing up likely clients.

I closed the gate to Pepe's compound. Soft air, hushed colours. What had I learned from Avéspare? At the neighbour

house, no Chilango. Blaze, asleep. A gleam of crystalline light
on the hills. A dark beer. Normally a time for talking. Politics,
music; stories. I suddenly doubted Pepe was alive. Had I
taken on the sense of loss emanating from Avéspare?

No, damn it, I was the chameleon again, accepting the
latest stance I heard. Pepe, held captive in tierra caliente.
Pepe, dead. Pepe, off gallivanting with a lady friend. Pepe,
victim of some accident. Damn it, I had so few touchstones.

I sat on the veranda. The ahuehuete tree sparkled green,
backlit by low beams of light, home to birds and insects.
When a thing has lived so long, yes, one could saturate it
with larger purpose. But Irini's quick shifts from a practical
to a cosmic realm smacked of intentions I didn't get. Behind
my eyes she walked away, her skirt swaying.

My one-time sweeper Moisés de Jesús used to talk of patterns, invisible daily structures—dogs knowing they're slaves
to humans, air currents keeping birds aloft. Ali Cran, in
speaking of senses he's developed beyond the five favoured
by our civilization, claims the human organism has an ability
called direccionando—the best I can do in English is thrusting. He compares it to speaking: a way of making an interlocutor feel a certain way—ease, hate, affection, but without
using words. He maintains one can thrust, say, the fear of getting on a too-full bus—he thrusts the sense that the bus is
due for an accident. The thrusted sensation brings on a feeling of discomfort, uncertainty, to others in line. They won't
get on the bus. Leaving space for Ali Cran.

And tracing. Rubén spoke of it in relation to señoras in
need. But for Ali Cran it's much larger. He demonstrated it
for me several times. He stands in my courtyard. He tells me
he's sorry that a half hour before I had a such an unpleasant
disagreement with my criada Constanza.

"Did we shout so loud?"

"No. But the traces of the argument are everywhere."

"All right, what did we argue about?"

He walks around the courtyard. "Money."

"What about money."

He paces. "It's a cool day," he says. "The breeze has blown away some of the traces."

"Sure, right."

"Constanza believes you pay Rubén too much in rent."

I'm impressed. Stunned, actually.

"You believe it doesn't matter, it's only for a year."

I shrug. Nod.

"A place so beautiful would cost much more in the north."

He's right. I'd said just that to Constanza.

"The argument traces are still in you. And out here, its pattern."

I went north confused. Among my colleagues the more direct ones said I was bats. Gentler ones smiled: You look way better than when you went away, but hey, get back to reality.

An anthropology colleague thought some of this should be explored further. If I applied for a grant to investigate tracing she'd be pleased to join my team.

I stopped speaking about Ali Cran's extra senses long ago.

But I did try to train myself. How would Ali Cran do this thrusting and tracing? I began by assuming most of us generate our abilities and develop our talents—a carpenter his eye, an intellectual his mind. A wine taster distinguishes annual vintages from the same fields, a Bedouin reads different kinds of wind, sand and sunlight to survive. Ali Cran develops his senses out of the stuff of daily living. How to use his sense of sense as a guide?

I noted a real sense of balance as it exists within a person, and between people. On the surface this is a cliché—we use the phrase "sense of balance" all the time. But it's not one of the so-called five senses. Below the surface I felt a more complex kind of balance—a sense that tells us when, say in a room, a gathering is out of balance:

I walk into a committee meeting. I'm late. I sit down. Everyone shifts position slightly. We don't realize we do this, let alone why. A new balance is established.

I've learned to use balancing to advantage. By physical placement, by gestures I construct, I can turn a discussion around, undermine a colleague spouting nonsense, best of all make it clear the meeting has now come to an end. Some call me a fidgety bastard, others simply think I'm rude. But it works.

A tactic borrowed from Ali Cran; which he never taught.

The sun was gone from the hills. From the ahuehuete tree, flight. In front of me a slice of black through the air, and another. Bats. Some of the big branches had to be hollow. Not good news for the old tree.

I heard whimpering. Blaze, but I couldn't see him.

Michoácuaro without Pepe was deeply out of balance. I could sense that even if I wasn't sure what I meant. I felt a chill. I knew what I'd felt leaving the Avéspare house: maybe Ali Cran was trying to find Pepe, maybe the Morelia police, maybe some scraggly posse of campesinos, but no one else was. Not Rubén and his deputies—I couldn't believe those hangers-on could find a horse in a stable—nor Irini or Felicio. Nor the judiciales who arrived before Pepe disappeared. What in fact should they be doing? And what should I do? Talk to more people, get some pieces of information to send me down the right path. Except that sounded too sensible. Pepe, gone, wasn't sensible. In what way not? Maybe I should try avoiding the sensible side of thinking. The notion of indirection came back. Great. Except what did indirection mean, here, today?

TEN

Sunset, Christmas Eve. The bishop would be speaking soon. I pulled on a sweater and jogging shoes, and went over to say goodnight to Vera. She'd already left. It didn't feel like Christmas, I wasn't bundled against a northern wind, no ice to crash down on. And I felt cheated, no cleverly chosen gifts to give. I walked to the plaza with a hundred others and joined the thousand already there. No familiar faces. I realized I was looking for Irini.

A metallic voice brayed from the loudspeakers. I couldn't understand a word. Electric beams blazed down to the stage, highlighting the speaker and a row of seated men. I knew one of them by sight, Simón, Pepe's campaign organizer—Avéspare's perpetrator of the "lie" of the altered ballot boxes. Most imposing was the glowing man at the centre, his skullcap silver on thick black hair. The new bishop, I assumed. The light caught his vestments. They sucked in the glare and expelled it as radiance.

I skirted the crowd. Emilia Avéspare and the shadow of her I'd seen earlier, her son Ignacio I guessed, sat on chairs in front of her door. Behind them hovered Toni. An eerie presence.

Under the statue's outstretched arm, Rubén spoke into a two-way radio. In front of the presidencia stood six judiciales. At the corner of the street to Marranando's house four more, rifles ready, scanned the crowd. All of us were equally suspect—I at least no more than others.

Vendors sold tacos, gordos, roast meats. Half a dozen balloon salesmen. Several women were seated on the ground, ceramic bowls and plates spread before them. Two young men sold straw Christmas ornaments—stars, braided candles, dangling bells, bright red and green balls. I bought a selection, a gesture of presents for Vera and Constanza. I'd give them tomorrow, small tokens of the day, then try to find something appropriate for them for The Day of the Kings.

Below the platform at the Avéspare end stood a large van, the Televisa logo on its side. Half a dozen men and a couple of women, a group to themselves, sat scribbling—the press reporting on strife, here deep in the provinces. Two men with portable cameras shot footage.

"Buenas noches, Señor Jorge."

I turned. Gertrudis, her arms folded tight. "Gertrudis. Enjoying the excitement?"

"Our great disarray."

"People expressing their concerns, no?"

She shook her head. "What they fear stays inside them."

"I'm not following you."

She pulled her brows together. "You can't hear it?"

I shook my head.

"So now my ears are better than yours." She smiled.

"Your pleasure is you can't hear the electric screeching."

"Or the words. I don't read the lips of loudspeakers."

"I can't make out a single phrase."

"You don't need words to know brutality."

"What do you mean?"

"The new violence. It's not ours. It's so alien."

Applause broke out. Without thinking, I tried to speak above it. Someone took Gertrudis's arm, Gertrudis gave me a smile, a wave, and left. Did alien violence mean the judiciales?

The next speaker was a Voice of Reason. I caught the drift. Call on the federal government, he begged, put in an interim leader— This was shouted down by two men on the platform. From where they sat, now stood, their voices didn't reach the microphone. They acted as in pantomime. The Voice of Reason finished. Scattered applause; bad news? One of the mimes rushed to the microphone. Simón the organizer, a large man, blocked his way. An argument reached the mike, angry remarks I didn't get.

I climbed a few steps to see the plaza better. About two-thirds men, one-third women, maybe two thousand total my estimate. It looked like neighbourhood democracy, people gathered to determine the fate of their community. Many men wore white shirts. Light mirrored from these, a sea of political neatness. I hoped.

The moon had risen, new white light washing the plaza. On three sides the straight roof-lines separated walls of adobe from the beginning of sky. I had the sense of a box, or a pit, and we were toy people in it. The best viewing angle was from my left, up high. Someone else had the same idea—a man in profile, broad, wearing a hat, stood on the roof above the Avéspare entrance, taking us all in.

A new oration. I understood it, the speaker insisting we consider the power in our hands. Bring democracy and prosperity to Michoácuaro! And this power was? To pay no taxes! To pay no rents! If we refused to give money to corrupt governments, corruption would disappear! The crowd yelled back with pleasure.

Rubén's notion of a headless mob came to me. I didn't want to buy it but my sense of noble democracy was slipping. The speaker finished. The tight crowd swayed. More applause.

The thought of left-over turkey urged me back to the casita. I passed by the bank. An armed guard. Somehow familiar—? I thought I heard him say, Señor Jorge? I turned. "Yes?"

"Buenas noches, Señor Jorge."

The guard's arm was extended, pointing the rifle my way in salute. "You remember me?"

I walked over to him. "Eliseo?"

"Sí, señor. I heard you were here."

"Yes." Eliseo used to be one of Rubén's deputies. "And how are you?"

"We survive, señor. It's not easy, but we survive."

A thunderous cheer went up from the crowd. People stamped and applauded. The new speaker was less clear. He went on, on, to increasing applause. "What's he saying?"

"He says... a new election... Legarto and Marranando... even if Don Pepe is dead... we need a real winner."

More applause, and cheers. I stepped higher. Eliseo had grown a moustache. "You no longer work for Rubén?"

He gestured with his rifle toward the police office. "Who can work with those deputies?"

I joked, "And besides, the bank pays better."

"Yes." All solemnity. "I have seven little ones now."

"A great responsibility." Eliseo was maybe thirty-five. I produced my offering to population control: "You should stop having children." The platform speaker left the mike.

A sincere grin. "Another arrives in April."

"My sympathies."

"The burden is great. But a man must fulfill his duties."

The crowd had grown quiet. At the microphone, the white bishop. He began, a whisper honed clear, all gravity and zeal. He too spoke of corruption. There were many wicked towns in Mexico. Of all these dissolute places the greatest shame ran from the hillsides of Michoácuaro. The walls of houses echoed with the sins of their inhabitants. Debauchery, dissipation and perfidy stank from this very plaza. Ignominious Michoácuaro, a town devoid of leadership, no one to govern its people, not in the hallowed ways of heaven, not even in ways befitting the terrestrial children of Jesus Christ. "Of course you have no secular guide! Of course you have no presidente municipal! Because the office itself has been warped, it is degenerate, it is befouled. Your last presidente was a miscreant. Today, of your two candidates, the one is a runaway coward in the eyes of Our Lord, a traitor, a wearer of women's clothing. The other, far worse, poisons our immortal soul. With fancy television cables he seduces our women and our children. He slips into our living rooms with rancid tales of evil and dissipation. The slime oozes even into the sacred marriage bed!"

The bishop made use of the speaker system as if he'd studied its limitations, found viable decibel ranges and slipped his voice into their sound-troughs. The crowd was silent, and still. Ninety-five percent would be Catholics, most of them believing. Or at least untroubled by doubt.

"Not only does this man pollute your minds and hearts, now he seeks to befoul your bodies with heathen forage, fruits fit only for the infidel, he the purveyor of Satan's weeds! Do you not fear your Lord? Do you not fear His only Son Jesus Christ who left His Mother's womb in torment to cleanse you of your contemptible sins? For you are corrupt, your leaders are corrupt, your town is corrupt!"

I understood every word. Eliseo was mesmerized. The bishop was a scary man.

His voice dropped again. "I have been sent to you by my Archbishop, by His Eminence the Cardinal of Mexico, and by the Earthly Father of us all, our exalted Papa. Through my presence your Holy Church has come to help you. But you must desire help. You will desire it with all your heart. You will shout for help with all the breath in your lungs! You will suffer the anguish of penance. Men of Christ, show your repentance! Not only with a hundred, a thousand Hail Marys! Not only with the tithe, even the double tithe you bring to the cathedral! Show your repentance with your body, the house of your soul. I speak to each of you, alone."

His silent eyes searched out this person here, that one—
"Are you a man, truly? Scourge your limbs and torso
daily, at your rising, at your bedding. Are you a man, truly?
Scourge your skin with thorns, and with nettles, and with
cactus spines. Are you a man, truly? Show, in your pain, your
expiation for the sake of Lord Jesus your Christ. Show, in
your anguish, your remorse, the grace of Jesus your Christ!"

A long searching silence. Then: "And you, women caught
in Satan's snare—" his glance brushed his listeners—"but are
you women, truly? Return to Jesus Christ, return to the perfect virtue of Our Lady. And you—" He caught an eye,
another, "are you a woman, truly? Only in the travail of
childbirth will you recreate your purity, each child you bear
in your womb brings you into the presence of Our Lord.
And you," another eye, another, "are you a woman, truly? In
your pain, cry out for the benison of your Virgin Lady! Each
of you, are you children of Our Lord Jesus Christ? Then
meet Him in your torment, for He, impaled on His cross, has
died for you! And you will die for Him!"

Silence. The bishop glared across the sea of faces. Slowly
he glided toward his seat. He turned, all eyes still on him. By
the fountain a cry rang out: "Viva Cristo Rey! Viva Cristo
Rey!"

A shudder took me. Long Live Christ The King! This was
the battle cry of the Cristeros, militant Catholics in the twenties who had warred with the new post-revolutionary government. Words not used publicly in half a century. Again,
again, and from other parts of the crowd: "Viva Cristo Rey!"

I turned to Eliseo. On his face, a small smile. "Eliseo?"

"Very powerful, no?"

"Doesn't he frighten you?"

Eliseo's smile broadened, and he nodded.

The cameramen, now on the platform, were videoing
the crowd with their machines of evil. The Cristo Rey shout
came in waves. At the mike Simón shouted for quiet.

Another group yelled, "Del-coz! Del-coz! Del-coz! Del-coz! Del-coz!" Repelling. But, despite repulsion, I too was fascinated.

Suddenly above the rumble of the crowd a sharp retort, like a gunshot. One of the lamps fizzled to black. Another shot, another lamp, and a third. Screams, people too tightly packed to run, Simón screaming through the microphone, "Stay where you are!" People broke at the edges and stampeded down the side streets. A man in a dark shirt grabbed the microphone and yelled, his voice cutting all other sound, "The statue! It's the statue!!"

This announcement, the absurdity of it, created an instant lull. The speaker took advantage: "All is well! The gun is dead! There's no more danger! The pistol exploded!"

I stared at the statue. The pistol as well as the hand were blown away. Only an inner iron bar protruded. Old stories in town claimed the Núñez memorial was more than a block of cement, that it held ghosts. But for it to shoot out lights at a political rally? Not part of the statue's patterning, as Ali Cran might say.

The speaker in calming the crowd had likely saved people from being trampled, a heroic act. But then an old campesino with a machete climbed the stage and grabbed the microphone. "It's a statue of the PRI!" He waved his machete high. "The PRI wants to kill us all!"

A younger man in a white shirt and red bandanna replaced him. "Kill the PRI statue! Before it kills us! Tear it down!"

The hero grabbed the mike back. "It's not PRI! It isn't dangerous! It's disarmed!"

"Tear it down! Tear it down!"

A new person at the mike. "It's against the PRI! Only the PRI can save us, tear down the statue that shoots at us!"

A couple of men were beseeching the bishop, pointing to the microphone. Delcoz shook his head, and again.

The old campesino: "Tear it down! Tear it down!"

The crowd took up the chant: "Tear it down! Tear it down! Tear it down! Tear it down! Tear it down! Tear it down!"

The whole thing was nuts, from a statue taking potshots to the mad argument to the sudden unity of the crowd: tear down the image of Abelardo Núñez and bring peace to Michoácuaro. Loco. But the outrageousness of the moment made it all the more scary.

Rubén and his deputies, a dozen men, ringed the statue. And, crazier now, the crowd rushed the statue, a thousand men and women surrounded it. Rubén and his deputies faded into the crowd. Already someone had found chains, someone backed a pickup through the bedlam, ropes and chains were wound about the statue. Cheers, chants, horse-power, manpower—

They toppled the figure of Abelardo. Some people didn't get out of the way; broken bones and mashed fingers, I assumed. The shards of Abelardo were thrown around. Cheers, more cheers.

Eliseo said to me, "Incredible."

I shook my head. Did the statue deserve such an end? I clutched my sack of straw presents tight, as if I had to pro-tect them.

"A statue shooting the lights." Eliseo's head shook, all-admiring.

Across the plaza Señora Avéspare and her son had van-ished. Toni, I think it was Toni, was gone from the rooftop.

The crowd dispersed. I needed someone to talk to. I wouldn't find anyone tonight. I walked up the hill, alone inside and unsettled. People turned off to their houses. Well before Pepe's, I was alone in reality. I passed a truck parked near Ernie's gate. Two men came out of the shadow and stood in my path. The taller one said, "Señor Jorge?"

"Yes?"

"We have a message for you."

I looked from one to the other. Tall's face was thin; his nose, broken and healed, pointed right. The other had a thick moustache. Both wore hats, jackets, loose pants. The second, shorter, stocky, moved to my left. I said, "A message from—?"

"Ali Cran."

They were close, both of them. "And? What's he say?"

"You should come with us. We'll take you to him."

"Now?"

"Sí, señor."

My message via Nicandro? "Tell Ali Cran to visit tomorrow." I backed away.

Tall shifted slightly and was behind me. "He says, this evening."

Maybe they really were from Ali Cran? "Does this have to do with Pepe Legarto?"

Tall said, "Ali Cran Ocampo, señor. Will you come now?"

"No," I said. "No, I don't think so."

Stocky said, "Señor, we'll bring you there." He reached for my forearm—

I shouted, in English, "Keep your fucking hand away from me!" and swung my bag of Christmas straw. It hit his head and broke open, ornaments flew everywhere, Tall so distracted he tried to catch one— I ran to Ernie's gate, gate without lock? and pushed. It opened. In, slam, and I slid the bolt. Fear followed me down the driveway. To the Chilango casa? I heard them climbing the gate. To the left, the rose bushes. I slipped behind them. To the storm fence, slow, slow. One crashed over the gate, and cursed. I found the witches' passage and pulled the opening wide. One leg through— My sweater caught on a snag and I panicked. On the driveway both of them, looking about, cool, no doubt certain they'd find me. I tried to tear lose, couldn't—calm, calm—twisted back to the Chilango's side, unhooked. They stood by the edge of the house, clear in the moonlight. Suddenly a terrible wail. Blaze on his feet gave a muffled bark. I lowered my back, pulled myself through, squeezed the wire together. A tiny thin wail. Slowly I edged to the casita. Stocky and Tall approached the fence. They walked its length, down, back up. Passing by the witches' passage, not seeing it.

A pounding from outside Ernie's gate, and shouted curses. Tall and Stocky crept behind overgrown bushes. More swearing, kicking sounds, silence, then the roar of an engine and the gates smashed open. Ernie's truck ground down the drive, braked, the man himself sprang out. He ran to the fence eight metres from me, grabbed the wire and screamed through, "Fucking witch! Fucking witch!"

He walked back to the gates and kicked them closed. In the house he turned on all the inside lights. The outside ones too.

To the gate crawled two figures. It took them long minutes. They stood and ran.

On Pepe's veranda I sat a little while and watched the moon. Large, yellow. I unlocked the door, went in, relocked. I ate some fine cold turkey mole. In the dark.

I'd evaded two muggers. I was safe. Northern exercise, paying off. I waited an hour. I went outside. No sense of anyone in the compound. I unlocked the casita door, found the flashlight, shone it about. Undisturbed, and no scorpions. I lay on the bed fully dressed. Did Tall and Stocky have anything to do with Pepe being gone? Had they kidnapped him? Why come after me? I sensed I'd see them again. My mind-images slid down along softer lines, Irini Farolla, green eyes, black hair. Her face slipped in and out of focus. Sleep came slowly.

ELEVEN

"Aaay-aaay-ayeeeee-aaaaaahh!"

I pushed myself up— The splash. I collapsed sideways, and closed my eyes… Tall and Stocky, who were they? Acting on their own? Or the muscle. For? Somebody who knows I know Ali Cran. So, anyone.

No knives or guns visible. Take me without hassle? Ha!

And if Ali Cran did send them? Late at night? Come right now? Unlikely. Unless Ali Cran had located Pepe. They'd have said. I'd have gone.

From here on I'd be looking over my shoulder and watching my back. I'm not trained for this.

Off to Irini's garden. I washed, breakfasted, locked and left. Except for Ernie's crashed-in gates, Stocky and Tall seemed far away. Then I spotted a straw candle and a star, squashed on the road.

Down at the plaza, posters announced the new election, set for New Year's Day. The rubble of Lieutenant Abelardo Núñez lay about.

Four boys and a girl played a new game, Tumble the Statue. The girl climbed the pedestal, the others reached up shards, an upper arm, the top of the lieutenant's head, a knee, a high boot. She piled them in a heap, passed cord around, with stentorian aggression and much glee yelled, "Tear it down! Tear it down!"

On by the market, the fruit and vegetable colours an eye-feast. I saluted Gertrudis opening her shop. She waved back. At the garden I'd at least get a sense of what Pepe had been up to over the last months.

In ten minutes I was walking between fields. Shoots of dull green slanted in the furrows between dead corn stalks. A few trucks passed, heading into town. Low water in the river splashed down little chutes. The road swung right, the river left. It was getting hot. Along the field beside me ran a new storm fence, a strand of razor-wire at the top. Soon it angled down to the river. I glanced back. Nobody following. Foolish. Nothing could happen, here in daylight.

Now in the field I saw regular flat-topped mounds—island shelves of land, with water-filled ditches between them. Two women on a green plateau, bent over, hacked with hoes; neither were Irini.

Ahead, open steel gates. Above the gates a sign: JARDÍN DE LOS VIEJOS. Garden of the Old Ones; or, the Ancients. Pepe's kind of irony.

I walked through. On both sides rose more mounds, a metre and a half wide, about fifteen metres long. The ditches around the mounds, as wide, were filled with barely moving water. A couple of hundred metres along by a small cement-block building and an open shed stood two stake trucks and Irini's pickup. Off to the right, three palapas. I checked the block house; locked. I tried the horn of the pickup. A shriek cracked the stillness.

Well-vegetated mounds rose in all directions. Beyond by the river grew fruit trees. From behind me came a call, "I'm coming."

Irini and another woman hurried my way. I walked toward them. Irini in jeans and plaid long-sleeved shirt, looking simultaneously innocent of the world and in control if it, carried a bamboo pole maybe eight feet long. In Spanish she introduced María-Luz. "She is responsible for our jewellery collection." María-Luz, holding a red plastic bucket covered with a checkered cloth, giggled.

"Is your jewellery valuable?"

"Very, señor." María-Luz lifted the cloth. I saw a dozen tubers, red, yellow, purple, shaped like short thick shiny carrots. "Have one."

I took a purple tuber. It felt waxy. "What are they?"

"Ulluco."

"What's that in English?"

Irini grinned. "Oo-yooo-co."

"Ah. What's it taste like?"

"Smooth, like velvety walnuts."

María-Luz said she hoped I was enjoying my stay, and headed toward the shed.

"So here it is." Irini had shifted to English. She swept her pole a semicircle.

"Pepe the farmer. How long's he been doing this?"

"Last August we celebrated the fourth anniversary of the birth of the idea. Pepe's idea. The farm is three years old."

Conceived the summer I left. I felt centuries away. And Pepe should be showing me all this. "You've heard nothing new?"

"Of Pepe? No." She took my arm, a light pleasant pressure.

Was she coming on to me? Few Mexican woman would be so forward. But Irini wasn't Mexican. European— I leapt to an association: she had a rich father in Hamburg, and he was dying. Why didn't she go to Germany? Because of Pepe? Cosmic-woman and agro-man. Then what did she want with me? Even if she thought Pepe was dead, she wouldn't, so quickly—

She stuck the bamboo pole into the ground. It anchored us. She turned me to her. "But I know Pepe. He's not harmed, yet."

"How can you say that?"

"I feel it."

"Feel what?"

"His breath. A kind of equilibrium. As he moves."

"Irini—"

"In my breathing. When I sit, very still."

"That's bullshit." Harsher than I'd meant. But she seemed to be trivializing whatever had happened to Pepe.

She let go my arm. "If he were dead, I'd know this."

Jaime knew his friend Teófilo was dead. Cosmic trees, witches' spells, thrusting. "How?"

She looked me full in the face. "I'd know." Her eyes seemed to plead, believe this.

Okay, first I'd take her tour. Then time to get serious. Check out the Telecable office. Talk to Pepe's campaign people. "I hope you're right." Track down Teófilo's Leica. Do something. Those damn green eyes. I pointed to the mounds and ditches. "What's all this?"

"Ah. Pepe saw them like this here, overgrown. Without water of course. He wondered, were they burial mounds? Here since Moctezuma's day? He spoke to Daniél Chávez in Guadalajara, Daniél the archeologist. He came, he— Pepe hasn't told you anything of this?"

"No. No." Implying I didn't know Pepe well at all. Maybe I didn't— A sudden sense: I am being watched, as from a great distance. I looked around to survey the mounds. What could they hide?

"Daniél saw they were agricultural mounds. Like the Inca mounds, in the Andes. Ours are less large, you can see, a metre above the water. The ditches are a metre deep." We crossed a ditch on a wooden ramp to another mound. "When Daniél came they were much eroded."

"How's it all work?"

"Irrigation." She pointed to the river. "And when it's dry the ditches hold water." She stuck the bamboo into the ditch, scraped the bottom, brought it up dripping ruddy mud. "The algae and bacteria down there, they die, and the deposit becomes fertilizer, very rich. And the ditches hold the heat. Even on cool nights the roots are working. Growing happens very fast."

"Clever."

"Normal." Irini smiled, pleased with herself. Or with Pepe, or with the mounds. Or all three. "The Hinojosa family owned the land along the river. They grazed a few sheep. To grow anything here, they knew, you needed to bring in machines and flatten the land. This was too expensive for them. But Felicio told them he wanted to buy the land. And the Hinojosas decided to gull the old doctor, so they ask three times the worth of the land. They bargained, and got nearly twice. But Felicito says it's now worth ten times what he paid. The Hinojosas hate Felicio, and Pepe more." She pointed to some thick green leaves. "You see here?"

"What is it?"

"Potatoes. On one mound-hectare we grow nearly forty tonnes. On a flat hectare they produce three tonnes or so."

"No. Come on."

"Of course. Everything is water. Or comes from water. We draw water from the river."

"Even when it's this low?"

"Pepe built the entry passages upstream." She smiled. "Like the Aztec engineers who designed it, before the Conquest."

Okay, I was impressed.

She showed me oca, a tuber with an acid taste looking like a short wrinkly turnip. "Felicio calls it a potato that makes its own sour cream." I saw naranjillas, tomato-like with a yellow-orange outside, pulpy-green inside. "The juice is even better than apricot nectar." She sounded like a brochure. She took my arm.

Again the sharp feel of someone's eyes. I glanced about. Nobody. I must be feeling jumpy, I thought. Very unlike me to worry about being seen by anyone.

"Do you know, there are twenty thousand edible plants in the world? Three thousand have been used as food. Today only thirty-five or forty kinds feed the people on the earth. 'Produce of the devil!' the priests of the Conquistadores called most of the vegetables and fruit of the new world. 'Destroy them!' But the potato survived, as feed for slaves. On the boats the sailors ate potatoes. In Europe they said the potato caused syphilis, and leprosy. But both afflictions preceded the Conquest." She took my arm. "Imagine all the tastes we still can try."

A sudden pleasing idea.

And a yet stronger sense of being watched. I shook my head and closed my eyes. And saw a ghost of Alaine, observing us.

"For these plants the chinampas system is very good."

"Sorry?" I felt myself shiver.

"Chinampas. This kind of agriculture. As it was done till the Europeans introduced the ox and plow. All those shallow furrows. The water runs off and the soil with it."

Now it was Irini who seemed far away. Shallow furrows, I made myself think. No, I'd never considered shallow furrows. Shallow furrows. A man and a plow, an ox-team, generations of machine plows—as basic to my naive sense of farming as seeds and fertilizer. "Smart." Shallow furrows.

"It's a special place."

"I understand."

"No." The green of her eyes was less dramatic now, more in place here in the garden. "You don't." She turned, held on, and looked at me, from eye to eye. "In some places you feel the layers of civilization. From the past to now."

I felt her arm quiver where our shirt sleeves touched. I forced my attention onto her words, away from her arm's pressure.

"The vegetable world isn't permanent, it renews itself." Her voice became a whisper set against the river murmur.

"The first shoots. Fertilization, growth, ripening, harvest, decay, death. The new shoots. Annual. Also, historical." We walked.

"Seasons." For a moment this so obvious category took on a scope to encompass all else.

"Seasons, larger cycles. Agronomists know some of them, a few. But lots of cycles are invisible. To a generation, even to a family of two-three-four generations. Mostly invisible to me."

We reached the pickup. "Do I hear a 'but'?"

"Not invisible to Pepe." She let loose my arm. She looked at me again, her eyes nearly soft. "Agriculture is more than a profane skill. There are large powers, like the force in a seed, or from rain. Sunshine. And in the Jardín these powers connect to those in the ground. Pepe understands this."

She'd gone a bit breathless again. I realized my sense of being watched had dissolved.

She glanced across the mounds. "The cycles can't be taken for granted. They break." She smiled, her lips tight. "But sometimes we can remake them."

I almost believed she could, she and Pepe, in this world of theirs. I groped for some of the ground she'd shifted out from under me. "Look, I've got to buy some stuff before the comida. Oh, you coming to Felicio's?"

"Of course." She raised her eyebrows. "With you."

My nape, then my scalp, warmed.

She smile-frowned at me. "I'll take you to town."

We got in the truck. "Okay, it's impressive. The quantity of potatoes—"

"And quality. A perfect boiled potato is wonderful."

I wanted to glance her way, to study her face, her hair. I needed another track. "This Daniél Chávez, he's a good friend of Pepe?"

"Yes."

Then my mouth ran ahead of my savvy: "And was Teófilo Através a friend, too?"

She glanced my way, her eyes a hard glint.

I explained about Jaime, the Leica, Através' photo-essay on church architecture. "Jaime is afraid Teófilo is dead."

She nodded slowly. "I think Pepe fears this also."

"Is it dangerous, to write about Michoacán churches?"

"Depends on the stories you tell."

"Ah. What stories?"

"For example, the story of a stained glass Adoration. For the south window." She honked at a burro on the road. "A non-existent window."

"Sorry?" I turned. Now I could look at her.

"There were tales of tax fraud. The mayor was involved, the last one, Naranjo. Some say Teófilo Através saw a big story. He took many pictures of the cathedral."

Her lips, in profile, opened and closed.

"He believed the fraud also involved the old bishop. Our police chief, too."

"Rubén?"

"So some say. You see, the bishop wanted to retire. In seven years in town he'd added to his glory only twenty kilos worth of belly and buttocks. But if an admirer commissioned a renowned Morelia glazier to produce an Adoration, much spiritual glory would flow to the bishop. But no one admired the bishop so the holy man had to fake an anonymous bene- factor. For this he needed cash, and entered the scheme." A dark smile. "The mayor decreed an increase in taxes. For schools, and fixing roads. Some said new taxes was Rubén's idea, others that he was paid for his silence. Half the money would go for the roads. And the rest? A part for the bishop's Adoration." She sighed. "Através researched this. And one day Através was gone."

"Did you know him?"

She nodded. "Not well. I met him at Felicio's."

"Is there a link between his disappearance, and Pepe's?"

She accelerated around an empty stake truck. "Doubtful."

"But you talked with Através?"

Another nod. "He was interested in the Purepecha Indians."

"For an article?"

She shrugged. "I've worked with the Purepechas, a little. They understand plants." We passed the razor-wire fence. She pointed. "There. The site of our textile maquiladora."

"Here?" I glimpsed the river beyond. "The river above the garden?"

"Naturally. Your potato will come complete with its own bleaches and solvents. It won't need washing."

An ironic bitterness there. As if she were trying to guard herself from a large loss. I liked her for it. "Can't you make them build it somewhere else?"

"Upstream from Michoácuaro? Who'd drink the water? It has to be on the river, textiles have to be washed."

"Below the garden then."

"But," a grim smile, "this land, it's Avéspare property."

I turned to face her again. "Luís's family's land?"

"Emilia's own. She bought it. Years back." She glanced at me. Our eyes held… She concentrated on the road. "She's wealthy. From her father." Irini's shoulders shivered.

We climbed upward to Michoácuaro. Ahead, a slow-moving truck. She said, "The Purepechas believe time is multiple. The past isn't gone, it's only driven underground."

"Where?"

She shook her head. Black hair stroked her cheeks. "All past times exert their influence. But they surface every day. Giants hold us in their grasp. And the old stories. The sickness too."

We caught up to the truck. The air turned rancid—

TWELVE

"Manure." Irini rolled her window up. "Pigs."
I breathed shallow. The road curved up the side of the hill. I tried to distract myself from the stink by telling Irini about the rally, its anger and violence. The stink permeated the car.

"I didn't know." She concentrated on the truck. "I was at the Jardín."

I held my lips tight shut. The stink sludged in through my nose. I gave up and told her about the fall of the statue. The stink creamed my eyes.

"Abelardo's gone?" Then, the road hidden by a curve, she swung into the oncoming lane. I grabbed the door handle. She roared by the truck and lurched back into her lane. "Good riddance."

"You knew there was nothing coming." I unwound my fingers from the handle.

"Sure." She turned in toward town. She seemed about to say more, didn't, and stopped at the plaza. She leaned, kissed my cheek, pulled back slowly. "I'll come for you at three."

I got out, waved goodbye. She drove off. I could feel the press of her lips. My oh my.

No sign of the TV people. I bought more straw ornaments and some chocolate bonbons. The coffin seller sat on his curb so I wished him a very good Navidad. He stared through me. I walked up the hill. The day had grown hot. Five hours till Irini picked me up. I felt a tight twang, happy but uneasy.

Vera was scrubbing a window with wet newspaper. "Hello." She ignored me. "Doesn't the ink smear?"

"This is how we clean glass here." She rubbed harder.

A mighty foul mood. "You have the key to the Telecable office, Vera?"

She spun to face me. "Don Abelardo won't be the last to fall."

I smiled. "What other statues are there?"

She glared. "Be careful, señor." She turned to the window. "I'll bring the key."

"Gracias." What was with her? In the casita I unpacked the presents. Insignificant. Sweat prickled my back. I drank some water and rinsed the glass. In the bathroom I splashed water over my eyes and cheeks. Water. For washing, drinking. The river by the Jardín, for irrigation. Water makes glass germ-free again, for re-use. I am surely one of the few who boils water in Michoácuaro. Even so it tastes soft and smooth, sweet, like passing banks of clover.

I sat on the veranda. Ernie came out, he didn't see me. On his shoulder, the black and white cat. He held it with one hand. It nestled into the side of his neck. He stroked it, then set it down. It rolled onto its back and he rubbed its belly.

A knock. Vera, with the key. "And Flaco found this at the gate." She handed me an envelope with my name on it, big block letters. "Why are you going to the Telecable?"

I tried to sound like a dubbed U.S. cop show on her TV: "Maybe Pepe left a clue."

Her eyes went wide. "You'll be very careful?"

"What's to be afraid of at the office?"

"Pepe went there." She shook her head in little jerks. "Please, Señor Jorge, don't disappear." She turned and was gone.

I opened the envelope. Cliché of clichés, cut from a newspaper: "Leave *MICHOÁCUARO* or *you* DEAD." Silly. Scary? A little. Sent by Stocky and Tall? Someone figured me for knowing something I didn't. Or able to do something I couldn't. That worried me, yes.

So I packed up a straw candle and a star for Constanza but headed first for the Oficina de Telecable de Michoácuaro on a small side road several hundred metres up the hill. Pepe, to local delight and dismay, had brought to town, by way of parabolic disk, images of the distant world. He sold memberships with monthly payments and cable by the metre. He did well. But Laura next door, the maestro's criada, feared the cable. The work of the devil, she would say. But, Pepe pointed out, she herself watched television all the time. No, Laura cried, her television pictures come through the air, this is normal. Pictures passing along a wire? Unnatural. Please, señor, you must be very careful. Or the wire will possess you, strangle you, slice through your throat.

I walked the route Pepe must have taken the night he disappeared. The sun was hot but I felt a shiver. Had Pepe been stopped? Where? At the Telecable I unlocked and glanced in. No one, of course. An old desk, two chairs, a filing cabinet, a coffee maker, a mirror on the wall. High ceilings. I pulled out a cabinet drawer. Files of accounts. A section on arrears, some more than two years behind, but not cut off; yes, that was Pepe. He was coming here for a book, Vera said. On one wall, shelves. No books. A half dozen coffee cups in a plastic bag. Otherwise bare. Had Pepe really been coming here? In the trash, three empty beer cans and a paper cup. I took it out. A lipstick smear. What woman had been here? Irini? When? Why?

I relocked and headed on up to Constanza's house. She lived alone, her four children married—three sons gone north, the married daughter's house two streets over, her five grandkids Constanza's great joy. Her own place, cement blocks and aluminum siding, was built for her by Agostín her brother, an illegal working for years as a gardener in Oregon. I met him once. He'd gotten his papers some time before, he'd filed for the amnesty. Illegal, yes, but he'd been in the U.S. so long… He received his immigrant status. Soon he can apply for citizenship. He started his own nursery outside Portland and made good money. Regularly he sent Constanza money. "Much money in Portland," he'd said to me, "good business. New people, from California. In California are too many people. They love flowers. People from California, they spend a lot of money for flowers." He laughed and laughed, crazy Californians and their flowers. Constanza's husband went north also, in 1979. The children were two, three, five and six; they stayed with her. He sent her twenty-five dollars three times in the first seven months. She's not heard from him since.

I knocked. Through the glass I saw Constanza walking toward the door, drying her hands on her apron. She recognized me, dashed the last four metres, tore the door open and gave me an abrazo to make a wrestler proud.

She knew I was coming, Vera is her niece and every detail is exchanged. They're close as mother and daughter; once I thought they were. Constanza too is short and broad, cropped curly black hair whiter now, her smile a display of silver-capped teeth. "You look well, Constanza."

"My thanks to the Lord."

"And what's new?"

"Señor Jorge—" She stopped, sharp. "Nada."

"Something wrong?"

"Ai, come to the kitchen. Agua fresca? Una coca?" She laughed, now enjoying herself. "One of my famous martinis?"

Constanza's martinis: señor, please, today I will make your martini. I was much touched. She mixed carefully, not asking for advice. She handed me the glass. I toasted her. She smiled with pleasure. I sipped— The liquid spurted out, spraying her dress. She'd mixed the gin with tequila. "Coke is perfect," I said.

She poured me a glassful. We sat at the table. She wouldn't meet my eye. "May the Lord help me, señor. There's something I must say." She scooted away imaginary crumbs.

"Yes?"

"Always when I would come to your house you asked me, 'What's new?'"

I nodded.

"This isn't a good question, señor. What is new is not good."

"I don't understand."

She thought a moment, and nodded. "Here, in my barrio, two things are important. Health, and work."

"Yes?" Yes, I was beginning to see…

"The Holy Jesus sends us good health, this is normal. If something is new, then I'm not healthy. Work, to have work, this is normal. If Our Lord lets me work in my house, or in your house, or in the field, this is good. But no work means no money. You see?"

What's new. Our ideology of progress, imbedded in a figure of speech. "Constanza, I apologize."

She smiled, accepting. "In Vera's house, Don Pepe is gone. That's new." She shook her head. "Do you think, will Our Lord send him back to us?"

Constanza's repeated reliance on Her Lord had bothered me, likely as long as my What's new? had annoyed her. She was competent to handle a dozen jobs. In another world she could have been an accomplished businesswoman. But right now, for a moment, I got irritated. With no sense of possible consequences. "Constanza. I think your reliance on Our Lord to find Pepe isn't necessary, okay. Or from what I've seen, even Jefe Rubén or the judiciales. Do you understand? I could run this investigation better than—" I shrugged. The words hung between us.

"I thank our Blessed Virgin you've come, señor. I know she sent you."

"Constanza!"

She nodded. "I'll pray for you all the same. And you will find him."

No avoiding celestial support. "Thank you." I gave her the straw ornaments. "I had a nice shawl for you, but on the bus, my suitcase got lost—" I shrugged again. My basic statement of incompetence.

"Gracias. You are good to me." Her eyes welled.

We talked about her brother and sons up north, her daughter here at home. She mentioned Ali Cran but veered away. Her concern for Pepe. How lovely little Alicia was.

I wanted to know about Ali Cran and Vera. "You're pleased these days with Ali Cran?"

She seemed to blush. "Our Alicito has become— strange."

"Oh?"

She whisked some flecks from her apron. "Last year. He cut the horns from ten dead cows and filled them with manure and buried the horns. In the spring he dug them up, señor, he spread the filth on his land!"

Peculiar, except I've heard of similar practices among organic farmers in New England and Ontario. "Strange, yes."

She looked relieved. "But—his harvest is bigger, they say. Señor? Can he have made—made a pact?"

"A pact?"

"With the Evil One. Bishop Delcoz believes this of Ali Cran." She shivered. "And—of Don Pepe too."

"You believe the bishop?"

"He came to Michoácuaro to help us." She sat back, as if to see me better. "From Hermosillo. His parish there, it was a drug-filled barrio. Doctors, businessmen, important people." She considered her words. "Teachers also. Students. He cured their disease."

"And here?"

She looked at me, a challenge. "He cleansed the police."

"You mean Rubén?"

She nodded. "Señora Bárbara is a devout disciple. And Rubén is at mass every Sunday."

"Amazing." So Felicio wasn't joking. "Ha!"

"It's not for laughing, when sin is banished from the law."

Devout law enforcement. First-rate gossip from Constanza who listened widely and sometimes made up a few connections so spread more than she'd heard. And Rubén's own version?

We chatted some more, and I left. For Constanza, Pepe would come back with the help of the Lord. Though her faith in his being alive buoyed me, a rash of impotence spread under my skin. And the cut-up newspaper note added a stab of fear to my uselessness.

I wanted people around. Irini. Up the hill, her enclave closer than Pepe's— No, that would have to wait. Back at the casita I wrapped some straw stars and candles for Vera, chocolates for Alicia, and walked a hundred-fifty metres to their house. All cement, it sat by the canyon rim. Its facade, four metres wide, shared common walls with the neighbours.

I called, "Vera?" and heard, "Sí, pase." A dark hallway. To the right, a bedroom. Three double beds, two against the far wall, one by the door. Pepe had told me that Vera and Alicia share one bed with Vera's sister Cristina. Their parents sleep in another. Three brothers nine to seventeen have the third. In there too was the television, on now: a cartoon superhero throws a villain by his hair across a field.

I found Vera in the kitchen, Alicia on her grandmama Marta's lap, two of the brothers, a table, a stove, a faucet but no sink, the water draining down a hole in the floor. And a two-foot tinfoil Christmas tree. From Pepe's home to Vera's, a hundred-fifty metres, is a leap from the First to the Third World.

Marta greeted me with deference, the boys with great shyness, Vera and Alicia amiably. I told them about the stolen suitcase. Sympathy for me, no regrets for what they weren't getting, real pleasure from the ornaments. The boys hung them on the little tree, overpowering it.

The younger boy Cecilito, his timidity dissolved, grabbed my hand and drew me out back. They were raising a pig for market, I had to see it. The railed pen stood at the very lip of the canyon. In it paced the porker. "Over fifty kilos," said Cecilito. "Nearing the knife." Beside the pen, the outhouse. It drained down the canyon wall to the arroyo and the river. So close to the edge I was hit by sudden vertigo. I held on to a rail and crouched, as to better see the pig. Think about something, anything, far away—

Cecilito pointed out the black splotch on the pig's right ham and the snot in its nose. I stared. And pulled back.

In the shade of the house sat a terrarium, wood-framed, glass sides, some fine screening on top. I bent to look. Sand, rocks, leaves. And scorpions, a dozen or more.

Alicia knelt beside me. "You like them, Tío Jorge?" On home turf she was unintimidated.

"Handsome animals." Best behind glass.

She giggled. And, as I suddenly knew she would, removed the screen.

I stepped back a foot—between rim of canyon and scorpion box. Her family, silent, watched. She leaned over the terrarium lengthways, shading it with her upper body.

"Careful."

A moment of dark angelic smile. Then concentration. Her hand moved so slowly I had no sense of motion. A high-pitched whistle, barely audible. She reached for a solitary alacrán. He looked powerful. Again the whistle. The other beasts retreated. She set her hand on the sand. The scorpion sidled her way, an arachnid lope. His pincers touched her fingers.

"Alicia…"

He climbed onto the pads of her index and middle fingers, checked out this addition to his environment, and ambled over to her palm. He poked around with his pincers, stroking at bits of dead skin. Slow as before, she raised her hand. I was mesmerized.

The alacrán came level with the top of the glass, over, out. Toward me. Closer than arm's length. I had faith in her. None in myself. She took my wrist and drew it to the scorpion. I complied, palm up— But beneath hers. I let her bring our hands to maybe eight inches from my eyes. The alacrán's pincers explored for mites, or dirt, arched tail flexing like a body-builder's biceps. Graceful, built for self-protection. An insect like any other. The sole of my shoe was powerful too.

Alicia drew her hand away. It took forever, a minute, two, to return the alacrán to its home. She replaced the screen. The two boys, her uncles, gazed at her. I'd bet they didn't tease her much.

I caught Vera's eye. She smiled a little and looked to her hands. I said to Alicia, "You're very brave."

"They tickle my fingers." She giggled again, and glanced up to Vera. Vera beamed such love and pride at her daughter. Alicia ran over to the hallway, through, and out the front.

Alicia, a señorita with rare control. Ali Cran's daughter.

THIRTEEN

At two I showered and put on a formal open-collared white short-sleeved Mexican shirt and tan slacks, and felt okay. Then I caught myself checking out my image in the mirror. My moustache looked too thin. My hair was too grey. Wasn't I too old to worry about the company of a lovely woman? I felt foolish. Still, I wrapped the Scotch for Felicio in festive paper.

Irini drove in. Mention the note? Maybe when she brought me back.

We headed down the hill, saying little. I felt strangely shy. And Irini's own silence? She in a loose bare-armed white dress looked cool and fresh. A wispy thought breathed, Reach over, touch her shoulder, so smooth— Except I had a sudden strange sense, I knew more about Irini than I knew I knew. And a more familiar voice said, Act your age.

At the plaza the merry-go-round went round and round. At Rubén's office his deputies sweated in the heat. I felt a touch of sympathy. The judiciales at the palacio watched us drive by.

Irini said, "This afternoon we won't speak about Pepe."

How could we not? "Why not?"

"Felicito finds it distressing."

"Ah." Or was Irini herself now upset? Of course we'd talk about Pepe. Maybe even brainstorm.

Felicio Ortíz lives halfway up Cerro Gordo, literally Fat
Hill, a jut of sierra some five kilometres long. Cerro also
means backbone, and the hill did have a ridged look, a line
of primitive vertebrae. The truck suffered the spines as we
twisted over rocky outcroppings. I marvelled that Felicio's
VW could negotiate this road day after day. We turned up a
narrow track, better cared for, to his house. He called us up
to the veranda.

The view looked down the lush green valley toward
town. On the far side I made out Pepe's compound and the
blue pool next door. Felicio in white shirt, bright red apron,
white pants, and black boots, embraced us. "Single malt!
Jorge, the devil's own delivery man!" He apologized to Irini
in Spanish: "We'll be three only. The Delgatos won't come,
her mother isn't well."

Irini's face seemed to say, So why do we need this big-
deal comida?

Felicio said, "What will you drink? The scotch is for my
solitary evenings. Margaritas are mixed. I need to add ice."

We said yes to margaritas.

His look at me half-shared a secret. He grinned, and
clucked his tongue. "Ai, Jorge."

"What?"

"We'll drink to it all." He shook his head and left.

"What's with Felicio?"

Irini shook her head. "No idea." She leaned over the rail.
"Remarkable, no?" She spoke to the valley. "We're here, and
that's important. But we're so far from everywhere else."

I stepped beside her, following her gaze. "A good thing?"

Her elbow, cool and smooth, touched my forearm. Her
green satin eyes locked with mine. "What do you think?"

I smiled, tiny. "Hello, Irini." All I could figure to say.

A small nod. "Hello." An even tinier smile— She drew
away, folded her arms, stared some more across the valley.

Then I asked, "Irini, you and Pepe, are you together?"

No movement. "Does it make a difference to say we're not?"

I felt a strong tug; not toward her, not away. "I'm not sure." She smiled. I said, "I think it does."

Felicio came back, too soon. The drinks brimmed cool. He raised his glass and said in English, "To the great Professor Jorge who has sworn to find Don Pepe because the fool Rubén and the filthy judiciales are incompetent." He drank.

I said, "I beg your pardon?"

"But Jorge, it's all over Michoácuaro, your oath."

"What're you talking about?"

"That you'll find Pepe without Our Lord's help."

"Oh for godsake, Felicio—"

"Ah! So you do in fact need heavenly assistance," Felicio roared. "You know, I've heard undeniable but very different versions of your boast from four friends, two patients and one enemy."

"Damn her."

Irini's head shook. "Who?"

"That fffff—fool Constanza.

"Yes, Leticia Rodriguez from the Lion's Club explained it to me, you booked your flight long before Pepe disappeared. You knew you'd be needed. You have second sight."

"Is this supposed to be funny?"

"Very serious, Jorge. Migro Cardo claims you'd take such an oath only if you knew where Pepe was. Another friend declares you're the kidnapper yourself, how much ransom do you want? Anyway you won't get half that."

Irini glared at me. "What is all this?"

No way for Irini to escape the subject of Pepe. Why had she wanted to? I described to her my chat with Constanza. Felicio laughed harder.

Irini sipped. "It isn't funny, Felicio."

"But we have to laugh in difficult times, no?" He seemed not at all distressed. "To laugh well, to eat well. To drink to

Pepe's safe return." He raised his glass. "I've prepared a chicken he would enjoy. You too, Jorge. Double-stuffed, belly and neck, in the proper British way." For Felicio all English-speaking peoples belonged to the same gastronomic race.

Irini seemed worried again—more, disturbed; but for specific reasons not apparent to me. "It's a dangerous development," she said.

"Silly maybe. But where's the danger?"

She shrugged. "Maybe for you." Her mouth twitched.

Tell them about the note? "Look, I'm fine, right? Nobody's going to cause me any trouble, okay? I'm fine. I believe this." Another Flaco, a Nicandro, another macho act; hiding fear? Maybe that was it... Or maybe, that note—? As if it told me something about Irini that I had known before arriving here. What?

A second margarita and all our edges softened. I tasted nuñas, popping beans, some red, some black-spotted. "You heat them in oil," said the señora of the garden. "They open, they spread their wings like tiny butterflies." With salt they tasted like roast peanuts, but less heavy.

I told Felicio about Ernie beating Blaze. He shook his head. "You know, Ernesto inherited this dog. His name was Blaise. Poor beast. Blaise Pascal the philosopher-dog." He shrugged. "Now only his legs bend in the wind."

Irini talked about a younger Blaze who chased squirrels through the undergrowth. Felicio told us about a squirrel that would break into his kitchen, steal soft fruit—overripe zapotes, mangoes. It would carry them to his bedroom and hide them under his pillow.

Irini told a story too: Ernie, paranoid about burglars, always locked the house. At two one morning he was certain he heard robbers outside. He leapt from the bed, grabbed his machete, checked the windows. All tight. "You should know," she stressed, "Ernesto sleeps in the buff. But he can be violent in any state of dress." A windy night. Likely he'd heard branches rubbing, maybe snapping. He went out. The door blew shut. He tried to get in but everything, all the windows, the three doors, were locked. Irini smiled. "Maybe he was out there, shrieking my name. So unfortunate, such a strong wind, it must have drowned him out." He didn't come back to bed. Maybe he'd located the robbers, maybe he was teaching them the lesson they deserved. In the morning, beside the door, there was Don Ernesto. A fetus-ball, hugging his machete for warmth.

The story gave me a little insight into Irini's role in Ernie's life. It depressed me.

A buzz from the kitchen. "The chicken has prepared itself." Felicio went to get it.

We sat and didn't talk. She lay her hand on mine. I smiled at her, and she at me.

Felicio called, "A little help, please!"

Delicious food, German wine, stories. Vegetables from the Jardín: arracacha, tasting of celery and roast chestnuts with a dash of young cabbage. Instead of potato, the oca, with Felicio's joke, "Oca! Sour cream built in." We toasted Pepe's health many times. Wherever he was, he'd laugh with us when he came back. Then suddenly the toasts felt like sacrilege: I saw the doctor's face as a mask, and Irini's lightness as distant, cool and tight with strain.

Felicio's mask-mouth curved up. "Jorge the atheist researcher follows the clues to Pepe!" He chuckled. "Search and locate, but without the Baby Jesus!" A story to be told for many seasons. But with what as an ending?

He cleared the table. He poured Fúndador brandy into large goblets. I told them about meeting Emilia Avéspare.

"Why'd you go there?" Irini's eyes bored into me.

My control broke a little. "I'm worried about Pepe, damn it!" I shoved my chair back. "We figured I should go, Felicio and I."

"We're all worried." Her glare held. "But you don't know what you're doing."

I said, "Do you?"

She leaned toward me. "More than you."

"And you? Why aren't you searching, making phone calls to people Pepe knows, see if anybody's heard anything, I don't know what else, trying to find him?" She took a sip and didn't answer. Well, damn her. I shook my head. Dead end. Shift. "Is the factory going to get built?"

She sipped her Fúndador. "It's for Emilia to decide."

"Why's she waiting?"

"Because, for finished goods, U.S. buyers pay the frontier price."

"They have to ship the goods up there?"

She nodded. "Add the price of transportation, suddenly the sweatshirt or shorts are too expensive. Even when they pay way below minimum wage." A bitter little laugh.

"So Avéspare needs a subsidy. From the PRI."

Felicio grinned. "Hear how Jorge grasps the situation!"

Irini said, "But first EspórConMex needs peace in town."

"Who?"

"The factory's parent corporation. But a factory in a Mexican wild west full of shootings, kidnapping?"

"Emilia knows." Felicio belched. "She's lived in the U.S."

"She's no fool." Irini dared me to disagree.

"If you knew her story, Jorge, you might even admire her."

I sat back. Suspicion to understanding to praise. From down the valley we heard a murmur of thunder.

Irini said, "I'll take the dishes to the sink."

Felicio folded his hands. "If you must play the woman."

Whereupon my developing sense of Irini fell off the balcony: she jumped at Felicio, tickled him ribs and armpits, he giggled, squealed, didn't fight back the whole ten-fifteen seconds.

"I don't play." She stood back, fists on hips. "I am all the things I do." She stacked plates and swept out to the kitchen.

Felicio wiped his eyes. "You see. Clever, and frivolous."

I needed to get up, follow and— What? Help wash dishes? Somewhere, far off, maybe that too. Not now. "Tell me about the admirable Avéspare."

"Ah. In Monterrey, you see, Emilia wins a beauty contest. She is fifteen, sixteen. Imagine Emilia, long legs, a lovely bosom— A man from Texas, a Mexican, he sees her picture in the paper. He has the biggest used car dealership in San Antonio. He falls in love with the picture. He woos her, he wins her. He brings her to San Antonio."

"Where her English comes from?"

"Jorge, one can live forever in San Antonio and speak only Spanish. No, she marries to enter the beautiful world of the United States. But he wants twelve radiant children. So she divorces him. Her father, prominent in the Church, rejects her. She leaves with nothing, goes to Philadelphia, of all places. Her dream is to be an English-speaking beauty. She will learn English as it is spoken. An insurance office by day, a bar at night. The two Americas, she told me many years later."

"How'd she end up here?"

"You see, she returns to Mexico City with her new English. She works. She is still lovely but no longer a young belle, she is nineteen, twenty. She meets the lawyer Luís Avéspare, she marries him. Their three children are born in Michoácuaro, Luís comes from here. Ten weeks before each birth he brings Emilia here. Four times. One child dies at birth. Now Emilia's father embraces his daughter, the mother of his grandchildren. He leaves her his money. But Luís becomes very ill, a carcinoma. His doctor says Luís will die very soon. Luís at thirty-six wants to die in Michoácuaro. They return. He doesn't die. The x-rays read by Dr. Ortíz say Luís should be dead. When he goes at fifty-four it's a heart attack, one moment laughing, the next a corpse." Felicio shook his head. "So it happens."

Irini had come back. "He lived so long with the cancer Emilia thought he was immortal. When he died she was devastated."

"You knew her well?"

"Through Ernie. He's worked for EspórConMex most of his life. Michoácuaro would be perfect for the factory, Luís believed. He brought Ernie here." She turned. "I'll get coffee."

We watched her go. The sky above us had gone grey. A couple of kilometres to the south all stayed blue. Soon Irini came back. "I'll drink this with you. Then I have to go."

I raised my cup. "A wonderful meal, Doctor Ortíz. Thank you." I sipped. "Now about gardens and the maquiladora plant—"

"The questing Jorge never rests!"

"This factory. Could it be built somewhere else?"

Irini nodded. "Villasucita is a possibility, and Marapécuaro. Mostly those."

"Maybe somebody from there grabbed Pepe. To create unrest here. Pepe stays gone, they sign the papers, a factory is built somewhere else." Drops of rain splattered the patio.

"You don't know Michoácuaro." Irini sipped coffee.

"Instruct me."

I felt her gaze search my brain. "If Pepe isn't found for three weeks, five, it gets quiet again. And Michoácuaro forgets. Even someone like Pepe."

Felicio shook his head. "Not over the years."

"Over the decades, maybe not. Over the years, yes." She turned to Felicio. "Remember Através the newsman? Jorge and I spoke of him this morning. In Michoácuaro, he's forgotten."

"Sure, he wasn't from here." Felicio nodded. "Poor fat Teófilo. A funny man, Jorge. He sat where you sit. We laughed and told stories the whole afternoon, the six of us. Pepe and he. Ali Cran also. Hot country stories, very personal stories. Stories about ghosts, monsters. You remember, Irini?"

She nodded, distant.

"You explained about the Purepechas, their idea of history."

I closed my eyes and for the minute she explained I saw them all:

A History of the World

Irini the señora of the garden says to Teófilo the large unkempt journalist: "If you speak to the Purepechas about their history, if they come to trust you, you'll learn about the large cycles."

Teófilo waits.

"There are five ages. The age of the giants. The age of the stories. The Conquest which they call the age of sickness. The age of their personal ancestors. And the present."

Teófilo grins. "A quaint version of our own history."

"No. For the Purepechas all the ages exist together. The earlier times live on. Under the ground, buried. But active. They move us, they limit us. Literally. Right now."

"The past in the present."

"There's only the present."

Teófilo asks, "And what do they believe will come next?"

A sad smile. "Some say now is the last age."

Felicio giggled. "And we talked about you too, Jorge." He raised his brows. "Ali Cran said, you know him, five ages in the world like five ages in each of us. Pepe argued like always so Ali Cran proved there were even five ages in a gringo he knew! He imitated you so well, we laughed very hard." The memory brought a layer of old laughter out of Felicio.

None from me. Irini was smiling. "What's so funny?"

Tears in Felicio's eyes. "If you don't see—" More laughter. "I can't help you."

I turned to Irini. "I don't get it."

She gave me a muted smile. "I guess you had to be here."

I sipped brandy. I saw, distant, my tombstone: Held By Humours He Never Grasped. "And Teófilo, what did he say?"

Another small laugh. "That he adored his señora, Carmen. Distant, but a pretty hen."

"So nobody knows what happened. Where he disappeared to."

"Uruapan? A cave in tierra caliente? A dungeon of the judiciales?" Felicio shrugged. "He's dead, you believe? So do I."

Irini shook her head. "His disappearance is a silent fact. The kind of silence that is necessary to bring the maquiladora here."

"Are you saying Emilia and company may have killed him?"

Irini shrugged. "Who can know? Journalists find their necessary enemies."

In her bitterness she sounded more like Jaime Léon than I could have ever imagined. The rain still fell, large drops. A connection there, disconnected, but it made sense—a flash of this notion, a splash from that tangent. As if a bit of clarity had appeared, close to hand. Could I be oblique, too? "Pepe went to the Telecable for a book."

Irini nodded.

"I didn't see any books there. I found three beer bottles. And a coffee cup. Lipstick stains on it."

Irini coloured lightly. "My cup, probably."

"When were you there?"

Immediate answer: "Three days before he disappeared. He was processing his billings."

"You drank from a paper cup?"

"There's no running water there."

"Anybody else there with you?"

She squinted. "No. Why're you asking?"

"The beer bottles."

Another light shake. "I don't know."

"Did Rubén look around in the Telecable office? And Pepe's study?"

"Of course." Felicio rubbed his eyes. "But Rubén misunderstands Pepe when they speak of the weather. If Pepe left a note, 'I'm standing naked in the plaza,' Rubén wouldn't be able to find him."

And I, right there, hadn't searched in the study. "I'll check out his notes later tonight."

Irini said, "The house will be locked."

"We'll break in." Felicio grinned. "I always wanted to commit a burglary."

To me Irini said, "I'll come with you, tomorrow morning. Vera can let us in. Pepe doesn't like anyone in his files." She turned to Felicio. "I thank you for a fine meal." She bussed his cheek. "The gentlemen will wash the dishes.

"Wait." I got up. "I'll go with you."

"And leave Felicio with this mess?" She smiled, too sweet. "I wouldn't hear of it. Felicito will drive you back." And she left.

Felicio called, "Goodbye, my dear."

I was dismissed. Her car drove away. Felicio was drunk. Felicito would not drive me back. He went to the bathroom. The rain had stopped. I'd been sure we'd leave together, spend the evening together, perhaps the night. I'd figured her for thinking the same; guess not. My full stomach pushed against my disturbingly empty chest. Maybe I wasn't that old.

Damn her anyway. What, have a two week affair with a woman I'd never see again? Forget it. Pepe was the only issue.

Consider the hypotheses. This one: Pepe is dead. Why? Who would want this? Someone or some group I didn't know about? How could I figure this? No, instead, someone I do know. Avéspare? Irini? Felicio? Rubén? Vera? not Vera.

Or did one of them know Pepe was dead and had put up a brave front? Why? Ridiculous. Or maybe not responsible but covering up his death?

Or try it this way. Pepe is alive. This free-floating cliché that a politico or journalist who vanishes is by definition dead, this blurs other kinds of thinking. But if he is alive— Then what?

My thinking had gone ajumble. I blamed it on the wine. Later I'd restart all hypotheses.

Felicio returned. "When all is weighed, I like Irini."

Me too. "Why?"

"Often, she has good sense. Pepe's kind of sense."

"When I asked were they lovers, you said he was too smart."

He sat. "There's a freedom in Pepe. It can be his doom, but so the man is. Irini?" He shook his head. "Irini comes with two qualities. She's a—kind of primitive communist. The earth and its fruits are for all humankind, we're part of the universal strategy, blah blah, a naive form of the Gaia thesis. Itself not a complex world view." He shut his eyes. "On the one hand."

I waited. "You sleeping?"

"I seek words. Yes, the second quality. Irini believes in the privacy of property. She will for example allow no intrusion of el Jardín de los Viejos. It's hers. Like her truck. She lets no one drive it. If someone else touches it, it falls apart." His eyes opened. "She believes this."

"At the Jardín I honked the horn."

"And you still have your hand? I'm amazed."

I couldn't recall even irritation from her.

"The worst is with a man. Like the Chilango, a perfect human. He insulted her in public, perhaps in private he beat her. It didn't matter, he was hers, no one could speak against him. Then it was over and he was scum. She had an affair with a young man, twenty-three. He was the most clever, the handsomest and so on. No other woman must speak with him. Ownership."

"Got it."

"And Pepe? She respects him, very much. Also she likes him. Perhaps they have fucked. But a couple?" He shrugged. "I don't think so." He grinned. "You interested?"

"I don't enjoy being owned." I smiled back. Could Irini ever own me?

"It's true." He nodded. But he was thinking elsewhere. Then he smiled, wide like a child. "Time for our detection?"

"Irini said wait till tomorrow."

"Isn't it better to search sooner?" Ready and rarin', our Felicito.

The low sun, shining sideways between the ground and a jagged cloud layer, struck the clouds from below with sooty fire. Felicio's shirt glowed golden. I nodded. "After sunset."

"You're the expert." We sat and gazed across the valley in silence. The sun went quickly, the dark took over. We washed and dried the dishes. We went back out. The night, still warm…

"What was Irini's life before the Chilango, do you know?"

"Ah." He reflected on this. "Another Fúndador?"

"Will it help our investigation?"

"By providing the clarity we need."

"I'll drive."

He chuckled, and poured. "I know very little. The father is German. He married her mother, a Spaniard, after the war. Irini was educated I think in convent schools. She was married for a time, in Seville. The marriage ended and she came to Mexico." He sipped his brandy.

It had itched but hadn't risen to the surface. Come to Michoácuaro and one and one don't fit together anymore. Still, I wouldn't jump to absolute conclusions. "Are there other German expatriate women in Michoácuaro?"

"Irini isn't enough for you?"

My laugh came from both corners of my mouth. Not up front.

"Shall we break and enter?"

FOURTEEN

I braked at the entry. Pepe's gates stood open. Hadn't I closed them? I took Felicio's flashlight, got out, let my eyes get used to the dark. A slit of moon. Leave Michoácuaro or you dead… No Tall or Stocky, no truck. My head throbbed, the same arc, back again. I flashed the lamp. On the driveway, tire tracks—since the rain a vehicle had come in, and backed out. I drove in, avoiding the tracks. "See that, Felicio? Someone's just been here."

"The seed of crime is a bitter fruit!"

All down his slick hillside Felicio had proven his sobriety by quoting—misquoting—semi-appropriate lines from radio shows his children and he used to listen to in the fifties in Houston to learn English. Skidding down bald rock: "More sinuous than a locomotive—" Passing a campesino on a white burro, eerie in the pale light: "What news for the Lone Jorge and his faithful sidekick Felicito?" And eying the judiciales at Marranando's house: "Pure evil eats at the hearts of men!"

"Stay here," I said. In the casita I grabbed some newspaper. I covered a segment of the tire track and held the paper down with four stones. In the morning I'd sketch the tread. "Okay, let's go."

At the kitchen door I found my key— And had the sense, clear as noon, of another presence in the compound. I put a finger to my lips.

"What?"

Silence. Nerves? I shook my head and held up the key.

"What's that?" Felicio was fascinated.

"Skeleton key," I muttered. "We researchers never leave the office without one." I rubbed it between thumb and forefinger.

"What're you doing?"

"Warming it." I slid it into the lock, and turned. To Felicio's delight, the door opened.

He whispered, "Twang your magic turnkey, Jorge!"

"Shhh!" We were inside. "Now, the stairs."

"I'll get the lights."

"No!"

"But Pepe's guest has to see what he's doing, yes?"

Sure. My damned headache inflated. I just wanted to lie down now, close my eyes— But now, up we went to the crow's-nest. Felicio held the railing with care; over the next decade he'd have to slow down. Lights. In the entry office, the normal chaos.

Felicio said, "What are we looking for?"

"Damned if I know. An agenda. A list of projects."

"Usually Pepe is very ordered." He lifted a messy pile of papers. "Look at this." He shook his head. "Detection is exhausting." He yawned. "And not very exciting."

"Sit. I'll look." What would Pepe have written down? No order to anything here. I should have waited for Irini. How well did she know him, and his life?

Felicio said, "I believe Pepe kept a journal."

"A notebook? Loose-leaf? Spiral? What colour cover? Where'd he go to write in it? Did he carry it with him?"

Felicio tittered. "The godless investigator in overdrive." He headed for the back room. "His old notes are here, with his files." He pushed the door open. "Oh-oh-oh. Jorge!"

I squeezed by. In front the shelves stood neat but on the right, books, pamphlets, and a couple of file cartons lay scat-

tered on the floor—letters and clippings spilled about, notebooks sprawled open. "What's missing?"

Felicio shook his head. "No idea."

Some files dealt with the Telecable, others the Jardín; several were journals of events in Michoácuaro. The latest held
entries till June, Pepe's decision to run for presidente municipal. July to now was either gone or unwritten. "Felicio?" I
found him flat on the couch, eyes wide open, a collapsed pile
of books under him. "You okay?"

He stared at me, his focus askew. "I'll spend the night
here." He closed his eyes.

"Good idea." Great idea. "Take the guest bedroom."

He nodded, eyes still closed. "Give me two minutes."

I searched for notes, letters, anything recent. Nada. I gave
up. "Felicio?" His eyes stayed closed. No, Felicio might wear
a mask but he couldn't act. "Doctor Ortíz! Time to deliver
Señora Avéspare's baby!"

A cherubic smile. "So round, so firm, so fully packed. So
free, free and easy... on the..."

Only a hundred fifteen pounds but all dead weight, so I
left him. And more rain on the roof—damn! In the kitchen,
my head pounding, I found plastic bags. The tracks beside the
newspaper had washed to a blur but beneath they stayed
clear. I replaced the paper with plastic.

The alcohol in my blood needed some cooling and the
rain refreshed me. What the hell. Felicio's keys were in the
ignition. I turned up the hill and drove to Irini's gate.
Locked. I climbed up to look in. All dark. Then I felt dizzy. I
closed my eyes, waited... Go. I pulled myself to the top, my
stomach twisted, I dropped over. I jarred my knee. My
penalty was darkness in Irini's place. No truck. To the Jardín?
Tomorrow, tomorrow. At the gate-top, eyes closed, protecting
my knees, I dropped. And felt a pinch in my left hip.

I drove back slowly. The lock on Pepe's gate wasn't
forced. I closed up. In the kitchen I left a note for Vera,

Felicio is upstairs. I called Rubén's office to report the break-in. No one. Call him at home? Tomorrow would do. I returned to the casita, weary. Only 9:15. Too early for sleep.

I sat in the dark room. Not moving helped. Then I realized: someone broke into Pepe's office between the two rainstorms this evening, looking for something. Till then they hadn't found it. Evidence Pepe was alive?

The note-writer wanted me gone. With Constanza's story around town there'd be some pissed-off people. Blanco, wondering what I knew. Stocky and Tall. Avéspare and her Toni. Rubén, thinking I'd insulted him, smarting? Who was the note-writer?

A knock on the door. I sneaked a look. The beggar lady. How'd she get in, the witches' passage? I opened. "Señora. Felíz Navidad."

"Please. You can help me. I'm hungry. What can you give me?" Same apron, same bags, same rebozo low on her brow.

"I have a few mangos, would you like some?"

"Sí."

"And a beer. Would you like a glass?"

"Sí."

"Or in the bottle?"

"Sí."

"Okay." I brought her a bottle and the mangos.

She opened her bag and set the beer and fruit on top of parcels wrapped in plastic. "Muchas gracias, señor, gracias."

"Did you buy tortillas with the money I gave you?"

"Dílar."

"What's that?"

She stuck out one hand. The fingers and back of her hand looked like a small ahuehuete trunk. "For the rheumatism."

With such hands to carry bags— "You need more medicine?"

"Don't eat the tortillas María makes. They're not clean."

I used to go to María's just around the corner, but Germina's tortillas three blocks away did taste better. "Okay. Thanks." I rubbed my forehead. "Señora, may I ask you—?"

She squinted at me. "Your head hurts. You have amoebas."

"Yes, a headache. But no amoebas."

"Sí. Amoebas."

People get various amoebic diseases here, from bad water. Amoebas cause digestive mysteries not curable by penicillin. They enter the bloodstream, reach the brain, bring on strokes. The source of strange aches is instantly recognized: amoebas. But it takes months to develop amoebic symptoms. I said, "I don't think—"

She interrupted, speaking softly. "I must give you a message."

"From?"

"You will not see him again. You have his greetings."

"Who, señora?" I felt a chill. "Don Pepe?"

"Him. Your sweeper."

Moisés de Jesús, the first person I met in Michoácuaro. The first to speak with fear about the statue of Abelardo Núñez. "Where is he, señora?"

"He has gone resting."

I nodded. "I thank you." As Moisés de Jesús had wanted.

In 1985-86, Moisés de Jesús was my sweeper. Soon he died. After his death he became my self-appointed mentor. Saying this sounds bizarre. It leaps across any line of credible reality, from what seems normal over to an inexplicable way of thinking. But years ago, with M. de J. leading, I stepped across that line. Now, back here, I felt his absence. "Señora, please, tell me about him."

"The neck, blood from the neck, too soon..." She turned, and strode toward the gate.

Neck? "Señora! One minute!" I slipped my sandals on and ran after her. Lightning bugs. No beggar lady. I listened.

"Señora?" Not so much as a swish through wet grass. Too weird. Too much to deal with tonight.

I poured a beer. I toasted Moisés de Jesús. The lightness in my head was melancholy, a soft loss. I'd accepted the beggar lady's message so easily. I went to bed and searched for Irini's eyes, her grin. They wouldn't stay. Maybe I'd dream... I woke to the war-cry, the splash. The Chilango at his ritual, all energy. I slept again till mid-morning.

I showered. On the driveway the VW was gone. As were my plastic and rocks. The tire tracks were swept away. The godless researcher oversleeps.

At the casa I found Vera. A chilly "Buenos días" from her. She snapped at Alicia for something I hadn't seen. She glared at me. "Were you all drunk?"

"What do you mean?"

"Mud everywhere, shoe marks, Señor Pepe's room such a mess."

"Vera—the marks. Where?"

Alicia sat on Vera's lap. Her alacrán bravado wasn't around.

"I washed everything."

"Damn it!" I glowered at her. "Show me where they were."

My anger seemed to drain away her irritation. She took me to the living room. "Here." Pepe's bedroom. "Here." The guest room, the pantry, upstairs. "Everywhere."

"Does anyone else, anyone, have the key to this house?"

She shook her head, and thought. "Three keys. Mine. Don Pepe's. And one extra. Now yours."

"What about the outside gate?"

"Also. Three keys."

And lock-picking equipment? Rubén. The judiciales. Avéspare's Toni? And many people I didn't know. "Damn it!"

Tears filled Vera's eyes. Alicia hid her face in her mother's neck. "Please. Tell Alicia to go out and play."

Alicia looked up. Her mouth seemed to breathe, Will you be all right, Mamá? Vera nodded. Alicia ran outside.

"Please, thank Alicia for showing me her scorpions." I forced a smile. "Is it Ali Cran who thinks I'm in danger?"

She stared at me. "He told you this?"

"No, Vera. He told you." As I started to say this, it was a guess. Then immediately I knew I was right.

She looked flustered.

"When? After Pepe disappeared?"

She shook her head, too quickly. She dried her face but her eyes neared flowing over. "Some say—you should go away. You, Televisa. Others, that you'll bring Don Pepe back. But maybe they'll try to—to make you—disappear also."

"I'll be careful." I patted her shoulder. "And in two weeks I'll be gone. What people think doesn't matter to me."

"Señor, it matters to us. We must remain here."

Stupid. "Of course. I'm sorry." Sure they had to live with whatever I did here. Damn stupid.

She smiled sadly, and nodded.

Speak to Rubén. Then with Irini about Pepe's notebooks.

I walked down the hill. Smiles, "Buenos días, señor." Giggles from four boys. A blatant averted glance. I was visible. Had I in some blind way already harmed Pepe? Blundering in like any norteamericano. The cluster of deputies parted as I walked up. Naked-chest and one in a tee-shirt saying in English ONLY DOPES USE DOPE took longer but also pulled back.

At his desk, Rubén. Across sat Ernie, boots on desk, face glowing with delight. "Hey Hoar-hay!" Heavy fake-gringo accent.

Rubén smiled, minimally. "Good morning, Jorge."

"Rubén. You have to know something." I nodded toward Ernie. "First, Constanza's tongue quotes what was never spoken."

"What? You don't believe, as they say—" Ernie roared with laughter. "Rubén the capon raises his squawk at the hens 'cause he can't raise anything else?" He got up and clapped Rubén on the shoulder. "Bet you know how to treat a hen, amigo." More laughter. "Hoar-hay. Tell Rubén about the witch's laser!"

"Ernesto. We are searching for a missing man."

"You won't find him, jefe." He tapped Rubén's hand. "He's gone."

I felt Rubén's instinct: floor him. But the jefe's censors were strong. Ernie left. It didn't take an Ali Cran to read the last minutes. I sat, feet flat on the floor.

Rubén said, "So things are."

"Look, Rubén. Constanza invented all this."

"A story changes in the telling. And my job is more difficult." His face was grey. "You know, yesterday in Ojo a campesino told one of my deputies that I, Rubén Reyes, kidnapped Pepe. Why? Because Legarto on his Telecable wondered why I did not arrest our ex-mayor for his crimes." He shook his head.

"Who's Naked-Chest-and-Vest?" I gestured outside. "He thinks he's tough."

"Pincho Rodriguez." Rubén half-smiled. "He likes the pun."

Un pincho is a prickle, or thorn. But it's near to pinche, meaning something like lousy, or miserable; just short of shitty. As, That pinche Ernie. And it sounds like Pancho. "Witty fellow."

"If we had enough streets he'd be street-smart."

I showed Rubén the newsprint note. "Think it's serious?"

He studied it. "The words are from different newspapers. At least four." He nodded. "Cut with a knife, not scissors." He examined it again and smiled. "If someone wants you to go away, it is so you won't help find Pepe. This means Pepe is still somewhere, alive."

Or so I wouldn't find his corpse. But Rubén's optimism helped. I told him about the break-in, calling his office, getting no answer.

"Jaquito was in charge." He shrugged. "Who the hell commits a crime on Navidad?"

I let that pass. "A question, my friend. Any news about the journalist's camera?"

"I searched my files. No record of a camera." He shook his head. "Sorry."

Long gone, as I'd figured. "Thanks." I started to leave. "Look, what do you know about the town's beggar ladies?"

"Lots of them around. Give them nothing."

"A rebozo around her head, a checkered apron, three bags—one red, two purple."

"Maybe Lucinda. She used to be a regular guest at the jail. Too much truly bad tequila." A tight laugh, no humour.

Rubén was making an important macho distinction. Bad tequila is served at every cantina, every fiesta in tierra caliente, normal to drink it. Any man drinks it. Often with warm Coca-Cola. But only certain women will drink truly bad tequila. "What do you know about her?"

"Not much. She came long ago, she squatted at a shack the other side of the graveyard, top of the cliff. She lived there so long, who would kick her out?" He shrugged. "She's no problem now."

"Why not?"

"Ah. She collected many things in the shack, bricks, bottles, old clothes, paper. Then there was a fire, it went on for hours, all that junk. It all burned to the ground. She must have been boozed unconscious. For a kilometre around it smelled of burned meat."

An unsettling place, Michoácuaro. Rubén says Lucinda is dead. I accept this, with that speed. Why didn't I say, Are we talking about the same person?

"What about her?" Rubén stood and strapped his gun-belt on.

"I saw someone who—looked like her."

Rubén nodded. "Too many beggar women in town."

I made an effort and said, "Times are hard." We walked out. Pincho and Tee-shirt, Puño Filo by name, stepped back.

Rubén, off to investigate the break-in, offered me a ride. I had to go further, meet Irini— But first I needed to sit in the plaza. To reflect on Lucinda the dead beggar lady.

FIFTEEN

I see Pepe standing by the rim of the fountain. He cups his
hands, takes some water, drinks. He looks my way. Hello,
Jorge.

What are you doing?

Drinking.

You'll get amoebas.

He laughs.

I opened my eyes. No one by the fountain. But a palpable
fear that when I next met up with Pepe he'd be as dead as
Lucinda. Blood hammered at my temples.

I stood. About Lucinda no conclusions but the three
obvious: someone else, not Lucinda, died in the fire; or my
beggar lady wasn't Lucinda; or a dead beggar lady was talking to me. Which meant I'd gone a bit crazy. Wouldn't be the
first time.

Confusion drove me from the plaza. I treated myself to a
taxi up the hill to Irini's compound. The space felt more lush
than I remembered, a tangled spread of green and flowers;
around Pepe's grand casa tranquility reigned, here excess.

Beside Irini's truck, a blue Nissan. Next to the Nissan,
Tough Toni. He stepped toward me. "Señor."

"Sí?"

"If you bring harm to Señora Emilia, I'll kill you."

I said in English, "Fuck off, friend." The sound of my words made me feel feisty. Shivers of fear didn't hit till I reached the front door. I stood still in a very weak box of silence.

Beyond the door, voices not quite shouting. Carefully, I knocked.

The voices stopped. Irini opened. I said, "Hi."

Her face went through annoyance, relief, bad-timing, gratitude. She smiled. "Welcome."

"I'm interrupting."

"Naturally. And a good thing too. Come in."

The little house, a square, was built around a central peak. Support beams radiated three-hundred-sixty degrees. I entered the living-room/dining-area/kitchen half. Facing me, her wide purple skirt spread across two-thirds of a couch, sat Emilia Avéspare. "Buenos días, señora."

She nodded. No return wish for a quality day. A coffee cup in front of her was half full. Or half finished.

I spoke Spanish. "Sorry to disturb. I can come back."

Avéspare said, "We're done."

"Of course, señora." I sat. "And why do I meet you here?"

Emilia glanced at Irini.

Irini said, "Emilia wants me to persuade Pepe, when"—she glanced at Avéspare—"he returns, to sell her the Jardín land."

When. Was Emilia playing her game both ways? Sincerely concerned, or pretending? "Why do you want the land, señora?"

"Señor Professor, don't be obtuse. Vegetables can grow anywhere. For the factory there is only one possible loca-tion."

Irini shook her head. "Aside from Emilia's awful timing—" Irini stopped, affecting to retain a cool I didn't for a moment assume she'd lose. "No, I could never advise Pepe to sell."

"But you find the offer generous, yes?"

"Generous?" A small bitter laugh from Irini. "In its way."

I turned to her. "What way is that?"

But Avéspare answered: "The amount, of course." A weary sigh. "Señor. EspórConMex will buy this property at a substantial profit to the owners. Enough for a piece of land four times as large. Enough left over to buy two tractors."

"Tractors." From Irini, a bile-green smile.

"And kilometres of irrigation pipe. Michoácuaro needs jobs, señor. From the factory. From vegetables." Emilia bent toward me, her look indeed pleading. "I beg you. For our community, convince Irini and Felicio Ortíz."

"But won't you build the factory anyway?"

She sniffed. "Of course. But Legarto, alive, is still foolish. I foresee years of litigation. If he's dead the doctor will carry on for Pepe. We have to resolve our difficulties now."

Maybe the factory's outflow was in fact controllable. Maybe the town-city of Michoácuaro would do well with two thriving operations. Maybe I didn't hear that musical-comedy line of futility, Farmboys 'n' cowhands kin live together—

Irini stared at Emilia a long time, objectively maybe ten seconds, then turned to me. "This bank of the river was chosen by the Aztecs. Worlds meet here. You feel this."

Again Avéspare sniffed, dramatically now.

But Irini showed Emilia a smile so gentle it shocked me. "True, other parts of Michoacán can be farmed with ditches and mounds. The Jardín will be their model."

Emilia's face held still. "Then you do concede—"

"Señora." Irini's smile faded. "Luís, Ernesto, they began this factory idea, but they're gone from our lives. It's the wrong kind of industry for here." She turned to me. "No offer to buy the Jardín is discussable. The land wouldn't let us."

Avéspare's eyes looked ahead, without focus. She drew her skirt to her sides and stood. She was tall, a handsome woman. Traces of a splendour that once won a beauty contest remained, proud bosom, slender waist. "We shall see." She walked out.

I watched Toni open the Nissan door. Toni. Stocky and Tall. The note-writer. A week ago no one had threatened me. Not even Gottfried Sommers. The car drove away. "You were gentle with her."

"She's determined. But I think not wicked."

I wondered. A measured force, Irini. "Irini. Can we talk?"

She glanced sideways at me. "Stay for comida. A drink?"

Only a twinge of headache now. "Agua fresca, thanks." I sat.

The near side of her mouth smiled. She was wearing loose white pants and an unbuttoned blue shirt tied at the waist, over a tank top. Breeziness suited her. And I was smitten. In the kitchen, beyond the counter that cut the room in two, she sliced two limes in half, squeezed each into a glass, added refrigerator water. She said, "Do we go to Pepe's study?"

"Too late. Somebody else got there first."

She nodded. She brought the glasses back. "Of course."

Damn her.

There's a trait in some people that I call The Naturally Principle. In everyday speech it works like this: I make a minor discovery, I say, "Mmm. They brew great coffee here." The response is, "Of course." Or, in the idiom of the Principle, "Yes, naturally." The person I'm talking to has known this for years. It can't be otherwise, it's always been that way. The entire structure of the universe, fully grasped, verifies this detail as factual; like a wise parent addressing a simple child, my interlocutor understood all this long before I in my clumsy fashion stumble onto it. Irini Farolla, devotee of the Naturally Principle. The green eyes are, of course, part of it.

Another explanation for Irini's lack of surprise: she'd committed the burglary herself. I sipped agua fresca. Why, how? Looking for? According to Vera, she had no key. She didn't strike me as a pick-lock. Nor as a cat-burglar, despite the eyes. My suspicion lost substance.

Except, damn it, innocence stays pure only so long as it utterly disallows suspicion. Hardly likely that Irini broke into Pepe's study but till now I'd not considered the possibility. Thinking otherwise, considering non-overt options, are some more tools of my trade. I felt suddenly inept—a carpenter who's left his hammer behind, a researcher leaving too many doubts up north.

So between her "Of course" and my response I travelled, faster than light, home for my tool kit and back. "What d'you mean, of course?"

She shook her head. "We joked, right? how Rubén is blind. So anything important in Pepe's study still had to be there."

Right. "We lost the chance."

Then she shuddered.

"What's the matter?"

She looked over at me. Those damn green eyes. "Suddenly I feel his safety less clearly."

"You're a strange woman, Irini."

"No. But, till now I haven't—questioned his return."

"And?" Was she shifting ground here? Or had my sense of doubt gone into overdrive?

"Something just changed." She seemed far off. "As you arrived, I was afraid of Emilia. This is new. Before, she'd be— subtle. She'd play twenty games at once. Games of possibility. With many people." A new shudder. "Slowly. Everything moved slow. And her games brought power to Luís." She sighed. "Today the intricacy was gone. Only the shrewdness remains. You see?"

"I didn't know her before."

"She played games. She spun webs that lasted a long time. But she wasn't any assassin spider. Those she caught, she toyed with them. She wouldn't kidnap Pepe, for example. Let alone kill him. The game would end." Her glance seemed to search for Pepe. It didn't find him.

My spider sense of Emilia. "Pepe was in the web?"

"Everybody who knows her is." An ironic smile. "Now the strands are stiffer. She offered to buy the garden. But with threats. Three years ago, four, she'd never have threatened."

"What threats?"

"Accidentally the factory could dump tons of dye. Contaminate the vegetables."

"So break her web."

"She's spinning like she's got nothing to lose." Irini smiled. "Her American education recalled?" She went back to the kitchen. "She buys what she likes. Even, who." She took a bag from the freezer. "You like chicken? You don't have a choice."

"Yes." Irini's shifts were a code I still had to crack.

She ran water over the bag. "I'm no longer in her web. Oh, maybe at its edge, where it's weak. I've freed myself from webs a couple of times. I won't allow a third one." That hard glance again, eyes searching my face, boring into my chest. "Maybe Emilia too has freed herself."

"From?"

"From? Domineering men."

"Domineering?" Irini wasn't talking about Emilia, but about herself. Again I spoke without thinking. "Men like your father in Hamburg?"

Her face bleached. She leaned on the counter, her eyes frightened. "Goddamn you!" The water ran on. "You're one of them!" Fear rose to fury. "How can you?!"

"I don't know your father. I've never met him."

"Then what the hell!" Her eyes crossed my face, they screamed, Betrayal!

I took her hand, a most natural thing to do. The hand was soft, dead. I sat with her on the couch. I told her about the phone call, a man desperate for his daughter to visit him. I explained I had only made the connection now, I wasn't here to do Sommers' work, but I had to tell her about his phone call.

She listened hard. "Let him die quickly." She withdrew her hand and hugged herself. "The world will be a better place."

My hand felt empty, my throat tight. Losing what I didn't have yet— "Irini…"

"Gottfried Sommers." She whispered the words. "A true professional. Compared to him, Emilia Avéspare is an angel."

"You don't have his name."

She shrugged, impassive. "Legally I'm Irini Sommers Farolla. My mother was Carmen Farolla. As bad a name as Gottfried Sommers." She shook her head. "In some ways, worse."

"Why?"

"I don't talk about it."

I nodded. "But you'll tell me."

She thought. She stood, turned off the water, sat as before. And rested her hand on mine.

During the war, in the underground, it was Gottfried Sommers's job to kill Nazis. The man called himself Der weisse Schneider, The White Tailor. Or more specifically, the white cutter. He worked with knives. He claimed he'd eliminated thirty-seven Nazis.

War exists, it demands these things.

But listen, said Irini Sommers Farolla: Gottfried kills a Nazi. The SS round up women, children, and shoot them. But he is a patriot. He ignores reprisals. More people are killed to avenge cut-up Nazis.

After the war the Americans rewarded him. For his courage. What does he want?

"A hotel."

"Why?"

"So I won't ever again sleep in the cold." A comedian! He made money, he bought more hotels. He forced owners to sell cheap, with threats he backed up. "The owners were Nazis in the war. There's no difference." He enjoyed killing them, this time financially. His hotels are white, The White Citadel in Munich, The White Stag in Hamburg, and so on. Carmen Farolla's idea.

Carmen and Gottfried met in Spain. Her father owned land. The old man always said, "Be above politics. Be with the strongest." Irini, an accident, went to the best schools. She hated the holidays.

Carmen and Gottfried grew very rich, many hotels on the Costa Brava, the Costa del Sol.

Irini received a telegram, Carmen is dying. Ernie said, "It's easy to hate a parent but you have to respect death." She believes all he wanted was to meet her father. They went to Spain.

Irini said goodbye to her mother. Carmen died the next day. Ernie and Gottfried adore each other. Ernesto beside Gottfried was so like him Irini had to wonder, Is this why I chose Ernie? It made her sick. She vomited for two days. At the funeral she puked on her mother's grave. Carmen's friends said, In the end little Irini showed her true feelings for her mother.

Irini agrees.

Carmen had left Irini some money. She lives on the interest.

"And you returned here?"

"Yes."

"Both of you?" Irini with Ernie—

"Ernesto wanted to stay. Gottfried had business ideas for him, prospects. But he came back with me. He knows I am his access to Gottfried's inheritance." A bitter little laugh. "I was furious. With myself I mean. A few weeks later I left him."

Her hand squeezed tight on mine. My throat relaxed a little. "I think your father wants to make his peace with you."

"He doesn't make peace, he scares people stiff." She took my fingers. "He has his thugs but mostly he's intimidating, in person." She shook her head. "Maybe not now. If he's sick."

I took a chance: a Gottfried imitation: "There will be difficulties created, mein Herr."

She shuddered. "That's him."

"He sent me money. It's in the bank waiting to be returned, Five thousand dollars."

"To talk to me? He got you cheap." She shook her head. "In some ways I am my parents' daughter. I'm not brave but to them I can be vicious." She squeezed my fingers hard and with a bleak grin found my eyes.

"He never even told me your name."

She nodded. "His tactics. It makes his minion participate in the work, it gets you involved. Till it becomes your own project."

And so I opened a new bank account. "What if he leaves you his money?"

"I don't want it."

"Because it's dirty."

"Carmen's money is dirty. It lets me live." Her grip relaxed. "Maybe the living cleans it."

"Use it for the Jardín."

"If there's really money, sure. If not," a head-shake, "I'm no further behind."

"Still—" There was many a sick cause a hotel fortune could support.

She smiled suddenly, warm and delighted. "So. He telephoned you."

I nodded. "He'd read my book. A chance in a million."

Her eyes gleamed. "Not chance at all."

I laughed. "He hires good investigators then."

"No." She brought her other hand to mine. "The same force that brought you here."

"Right. Pepe's inauguration."

"Yes, to see old friends, to be warm in December. And more. We don't always see the whole pattern. But about forces there are only two possibilities, right?"

"Tell me."

"Patterns inside patterns inside patterns. Everything has its place."

"Or?"

"Or—" she took two of my fingers in her right hand, two in her left, and squeezed, "not."

"And if not?"

"Then everything's an accident, the silly luck of contact, no forces at all."

"I'd say we make some patterns and fall into others. We call them habits."

"What, like sunrise? The seasons? Like the shape of affection for friends? Menstruation? Reverence for wisdom? Generations?" She smiled, so sweet.

That know-it-all smile; a subdivision of the Naturally-Principle. "Well, affection, reverence, I don't know—"

"How immense is love between a man and a woman?"

A spring morning with Alaine… "Biggest thing in one's private world."

"Thank you. And for two people from distant parts of the globe to meet, and be together because they feel that draw?"

"Chance."

"Never."

"How, never?"

"The place one's in, the time, they're part of the cycles of your life." Smoky green eyes probed my eyes. "We, for example, we meet. For whatever purpose."

"To find Pepe. For example."

"You came here because you needed to. And because you're a friend of Pepe's."

"I didn't have to come." The back of my head pulsed, lightly. The smoke cleared, the green went deep, if I fell in, good to fall in— "I—almost didn't."

"But you're here." She slid over to close beside me, our upper arms touching. "You're here, I'm here. A most unusual thing." She put one hand to my cheek, then around, high on the back of my neck, softly as to caress the headache away. "Yet, normal." She brought my face toward hers, her mouth touched mine. We stayed like that, her lips firm, sunny.

I wanted to pull her to me, around me, blend with her. But—

She drew back. Her smile was delicate. "Been out of circulation a long time?"

Somehow that made me giggle.

"Who knows what can be, without trying." Her little grin.

"I'm sorry. I'm not—"

"You asked me, are Pepe and I a unit. It's not in Pepe's makeup to be part of a unit. I was, seven years. Before Ernesto. Ernie and I were a unit. Yes," she nodded as she saw my frown. "But Pepe and I, we're very good friends." She stood. "And you?" Her eyebrows went up once, and dropped again. The small smile. "We'll see." She turned. "The chicken needs me."

She went to work at the chopping block. Onions. Ullucas. I came over and stood across from her, looking at her fingers, her knife. I was being a large-scale ass. "Could I have a beer?" She pointed to the fridge. "Want half?" She shook her head. I opened one and sipped.

She disjointed the chicken. I watched.

She looked up. "I've disliked myself, you know, for always wanting a man. With Pepe I decided we could be friends.

Partners. He respected this." She stared at the chopping block. "But I've wondered, am I right?" She shook her head. "I'm the Señora of the Garden. Full time."

A lovely woman. Wise and— Felicio said, banal. Wrong. I set my beer down, came to her side, watched her fingers at work. She turned to me, eyes again exploring. She wiped her hands. I touched her hair. Our faces came together, our lips. Her arms came around me. I felt a great joy. Craving. A tactile fear, unnamed. Our mouths explored, we held each other, we held on a long time.

She moved back first. "Soon." She stroked my lips.

I nodded. "This takes some getting used to again."

"Wade in the stream."

I didn't want to but figured I'd better. I went out. I rolled up my pants and let water gurgle over my feet. It hushed the blood. I touched my lip and felt the pressure of Irini's mouth. Her fingers. A long old time, yes. And was new time starting here?

Over by the waterfall, a stone statue, a Chac-Mool. The water god first of the Mayas, later the Aztecs. He sat with feet on the ground, bent at the knees, back lying on a stool-like support, head looking my way. The sun hit his forehead. "Good afternoon." I sat on the ground by him. The shadow on his right eye gave it the concentration of a hunter closing on his prey, ready for a kill. On his head, a crown of stone reeds. On his belly, held in his hands, a bowl for water. Lying on the bowl, a stick maybe a metre long. An offering? I picked it up. "Tell me, Señor Mool, about Irini. Irini and me." A ways behind me, children's voices. A car engine, its hum. The beer made me sleepy. "I like her very much." I closed my eyes.

I see Alaine. Not her ghost, she herself. Inside my head, I know this, but she's also out there, beyond me. She looks at me; not, as Irini does, probing. Eyes without movement. Lips with no smile or scowl. She's never looked at me from so neutral a face. I say, Alaine… The sound of the name moves toward what I see. The sound meets the face. With slow motility the form of her face dissolves. To curves, to flecks, to nothing. I say, aloud, "Alaine—"

I opened my eyes. The Chac-Mool has her face! Then his own, in frozen stone. I shuddered, I sat a while. I flicked dead leaves into the stream. They floated off. Another leaf—I recoiled. A scorpion, tail curved, ready to lash. I brought the stick close. The alacrán struck, a tap. I could crush the thing, dangerous, little kids around. But it was too alive. I offered it the stick again. It took hold and climbed on. I carried it gingerly to the compound wall and whipped it over.

"Very good."

I spun about. A mid-size man, arms folded. Alejandro Cruz Ocampo, known as Ali Cran, so dubbed for his early affinity with another alacrán. "Amigo!"

"Jorgito." He unfolded his arms and gave me a warm abrazo.

"What are you doing here?"

"Maybe our friend," he pointed to the wall, "called me." Over forty, outwardly not aged. Squinted eyes, the moustache maybe a centimetre droopier, face middlish dark. Still slim. Much-washed jeans clean, pointed brown boots shiny under dust. "You've grown older, Jorge. Do the years bring you insight?"

"I've learned a few things, yes. Some adapted from here."

He nodded. "You come back to our world, for more knowledge."

"I came to spend some time with Pepe, and you, and Felicio—"

His eyes narrowed. "But Pepe is gone."

His words seemed soft as apathy, the avoidance side of mañana. "Damn you, Alicito!"

He took my arm. "Come. I want to greet Irini."

SIXTEEN

No sense from Irini, as we sat, if she had expected Ali Cran. I wanted very much to talk with him, yes. But alone. At the same time I wanted to be alone with Irini.

She served bite-size chunks of pan-fried chicken, a carrot/pea/ulluca salad dressed in mayonnaise and sprinkled with diced onions and jalapeñas, and chayotes in honey. No comment from either of them about Pepe. A fear as deep-repressed as in Flaco and Nicandro? Her chat with Ali Cran sounded like a conversation begun hours earlier. I was outside their time.

In Michoácuaro I'd often seen time measured with little benefit of clock or calendar. Invite people to a meal, no telling when they'll arrive. Plan a drink, project a picnic, but daily living gets in the way. Non-arrival can mean a broken axle, a cow calving, a new lover, a hangover so ragged it has to be drunk into submission.

For example, when I lived here five years ago, a touted storyteller, a friend of Ali Cran, accepted an invitation for supper at my house. I worked hard on the meal. He was late; he was later; he didn't show up. As promised I'd chilled a pitcher of martinis. I was furious. In the morning I gave the food to Constanza for her daughter's family. He showed up in the evening, some convoluted story about a cousin who'd been shot in the buttock. The guest was here but, sorry, no

food in the house. Have I finished the martinis? No— He
found yesterday's limp tortillas, some peppers, tomatoes,
onions: a superior pan of chiliquilas. We ate, talked, drank till
three in the morning.

Or the masks on Ali Cran's living room wall in Dos
Arroyos—the cherubs, Malo, Nahuatl ritual masks. A tiger
face, fierce, with rabbit ears, made of tin and leather, from the
area now called Honduras, the north. How old is it? Old.
How does Alicito know? The man he has it from said:
Venerated in many pre-hunt rites. Age, measured by use.

And by spirit content: The mask has much spirit, it's
played a central role in the hunting ceremony, it's very
old.

I'd been listening to Irini and Ali Cran with half a brain
and missed their transition—if there was one. Maybe because
they spoke a very quick Spanish. The price naranjillas were
bringing in Kyoto. Shipping cherimoyas via Guadalajara
rather than Mexico City. This year's crop, Ali Cran would
again adjoin its sale to the Jardín's.

It was three hours on horseback from the distant rancho
to the road. I asked, "That much produce—how do you get
it out?"

"But, by helicopter."

It seemed a colonel in the Federal Narcotics Expedi-
tionary Force is indebted to Ali Cran. On account of the
colonel's erotic bent—his machine demands he show it con-
stant use. Slave to this animus he complies as best he can, this
señora, that maiden; a whore when necessary but since in
today's society many juices flow free his charm is normally
sufficient. Still, at times his consort carries the onus of
informed kin—an envious husband, an old-fashioned
brother. And the colonel, though vigilant, screws up as well
as in.

So Ali Cran has plucked the colonel from a number of
stews, each a story in itself: "The Cactus Kiss," "Two

Scorpions in the Taco," "Velvet Virgins"—not innocent damsels, rather a painting on sheen-cloth depicting Mary Mother of Grace and a friend, their unction compromised.

In appreciation the colonel contrives, at cherimoya harvest, to receive a strategic piece of intelligence of, say, a large marijuana field, location previously unknown. Immediate action! He flies his chopper over tierra caliente. At Lomas Secas the cherimoyas wait in crates, the crates bagged in tarps. Three trips, four dangling bags at a time, the crop deposited gently at the Jardín de los Viejos, and a chunk of the favour is paid off.

Lamentably the intelligence tip has proven less successful. Only a tiny field deep in tierra caliente, not one of those vast operations everyone knows of but is unsure in which precise valley... Still, the little field is now ashes.

I laughed, as he expected me to. Irini asked about old Blaze.

"No more beatings that I've seen." I told Ali Cran the story.

He mused. "Maybe each time Ernesto beats the dog, we break a car window. After the windows, we slash tires."

"It wouldn't help."

"We release the dog. It heads for the hills, it becomes rabid, it comes back to bite Ernie."

I shook my head. "He'd be too scared to run away."

Ali Cran shrugged. "He has to want to live. To hunt and screw."

But old Blaze had forgotten such urges. Unlike, it hit me, me. Hunt and screw was maybe coarse... I felt awkward, and shifted gears. "Irini, that statue out there, the Chac-Mool, you put it there?"

Her gaze looked through the wall. "It brought me here."

"How?" The many forces of Irini's universe.

"I could live here, or on Avenida Benito Juárez."

"Why those two?"

She raised her eyebrows. "In both I'd be safe. On the roof next to Migro Cardo's shop there's a ten-foot Tezcatlipoca."

Ali Cran turned her way. "You're serious?"

"He's up there, arms folded, protecting the barrio."

Tezcatlipoca. If memory served me right, he would be the god of providence, prestige, wealth. As well as discord and anarchy, and the patron of witches.

"Fly your helicopter over the town." Her superior smile. "You'll see at least two Tlaloc statues. I know five more Chac-Mools."

"Pagan gods? Your bishop hasn't torn them down?"

Ali Cran chortled. "Delcoz walks a narrow road."

"Ah," I said. How to get Alicito to leave. Shift my leg. Scratch my arm.

"Between what he wants, and what he can get." Ali Cran stretched, and stood. "In Hermosillo he made mistakes."

I stood up too. "Drugs, I heard."

He nodded. "It began there. Most wanted it to end there. You see, in Hermosillo, Father Delcoz took on sacrilege, corruption, gambling and, most dangerous, debauchery and philandering. The chairman of the Church fund-raising drive, a certain Señor Solda, prominent kitchen appliance dealer, was married to Agata, an invalid, a wasting disease, fourteen years in bed, full care. For eleven years he has also been the lover of and beloved by Matilda Díaz, a widow. Six months from Delcoz's arrival the parish is transformed, a pious community. Or nearly. Delcoz learns about Solda and Matilda. Solda must forget Matilda. Scourge the traces of her finger's touch from his skin! Devote himself solely to the Church. But Solda loved Matilda. He tried compromise. He offered bribes, truly large donations. Delcoz was incorruptible. The battle went public, people took sides, families divided. The archbishop of Sonora stepped in. Delcoz for his many good works is promoted to bishop. He leaves his beloved parish. Middle-class pleasures return to Hermosillo. And Michoácuaro has a new bishop."

I almost spoke Felicio's phrase, So it happens. But instead I asked, "Is he purifying Michoácuaro as well?"

"Don't you feel cleaner, Jorge?"

"I never felt dirty."

"Good. Because for our holy Delcoz only the larger scouring counts. Now he lays a base among the influential." Ali Cran laughed. "He even rode out to Lomas Secas. On a burro."

Irini smiled. "He paid a toll for crossing private land."

"He came without cash. But his vestment makes an adequate groundsheet for my sacks of fertilizer."

"You sent him back naked?"

"So much devout intricate underwear—" He shook his head. "Designed to save young men from too much self-inquiry."

Irini stood. "Coffee?"

Ali Cran shook his head. "I have to go."

"I'll take some coffee," I said.

He said, "Jorge, you want a ride to the casita."

I looked toward Irini. No glance back, no indication I should stay. "Okay, later I'll come back."

"Good." A little smile now from Irini. Sorry, or ironic?

We thanked her for comida. Ali Cran's high-axle Jeep was nearly new. Cherimoyas must pay well. I climbed in.

"I won't take you back right away."

"I didn't think so."

He turned the Jeep uphill. "Tell me of your life in the north, Jorge."

I'd imagined the black starry sky of Lomas Secas, and long stories. Instead I gave him headlines. "But it's more complicated," I said. "It'll take a few evening tequilas."

He pulled off at a lookout. Michoácuaro lay below. I felt the pull of small vertigo. "You'll come to Lomas Secas in the New Year. Now, what have you done since your arrival?"

Pepe not at the airport. The missing suitcase. Breaking and entering with Felicio. Avéspare, Rubén. Vera and her daughter Alicia? He didn't respond. "And Lucinda the beggar lady..." which produced a scowl. The newsprint note. Nothing said regarding Irini.

He leaned back, staring ahead. "Pepe always says, Jorge sees us on our own terms."

"Pepe idealizes." But Pepe in the present tense felt good.

"Things that should be strange, you accept."

"Maybe I'm naive."

He smirked. "Also, you're the champion of a thousand fearful campesinos. And for many superstitious Michoácuarans."

"What're you talking about?"

"The Núñez statue, Jorge. Be naive, but not falsely. It's always been feared. The story of your bravery lives on."

"That's absurd." He was referring to that incident from years ago, when I spoke on television about a ghost living in the statue.

"Then Pepe disappears. A crisis. Who arrives when he's most needed? Don Jorge. You've been transformed by people who watch Mexican telenovelas, and animated superheroes."

"Don't make me ridiculous."

"Listen to me. Factories from the north bring jobs. The hero from the north will find Pepe, he'll return order to us."

"The town gossip wags her tongue."

"Grasp the situation. Constanza is—" a laugh, "your prophet. She recounts your words."

"Not mine."

"Of course not. But for a century the statue has aimed a pistol across the plaza. Then the superhero arrives in Michoácuaro and the statue falls. The tale will live for decades: 'The Statue Assassin.' A coincidence?"

"A dumb extraordinary coincidence."

"But the ordinary reduces us, the ordinary is corrupt. We accept the ordinary crimes of our ex-mayor Basilio. Every mayor before him was corrupt. We survive by cynicism, by craft."

"Like your borrowed helicopter."

He laughed, tart. "Each technology invents its ironies."

"Listen. Why aren't you looking for Pepe? I'd kinda like to spend some time with Pepe. An alive Pepe. Before I have to leave."

"In Michoácuaro they say, A day without irony fills my life with lead. Pull down a statue? Because a crowd yells it's shooting at them? Perfect."

"Look, I was there, I saw—"

"You were in the plaza as Abelardo fell? Coincidence becomes cause, cause is proof."

I slumped back in the seat. "This is ridiculous, Alicito."

The sun slid toward the horizon. Ali Cran sucked in his cheeks and started the motor. "You find Irini attractive."

"She is attractive."

"Not in the abstract." We rolled across potholed ground. "Keep searching for Pepe in your way, Jorge. You see what we don't." He laughed. "I have to help a friend find a bed."

I turned to him and awoke the ache in my head. "Chaba?"

He drove unspeaking for maybe a minute. "You arrive. You know of Chaba's search. You've met Lucinda." He sighed. "Possibly you'll bring Pepe back."

"Good luck." I heard Jaime León's bitter laughter. We rode in silence. The sun had set. He could drop me at the casita. I'd walk up to Irini. "Alicito, have cherimoyas made you rich?"

He chuckled. "What more can an old man hope for?"

We stopped in front of Pepe's open gates. A large automobile sat in the driveway. Ali Cran scowled. To cover the worry in his eyes? "Coming in?"

"Yes. Chaba's waiting with Vera." He parked behind the car, blocking it. "Judiciales."

"Why?"

"To flirt with Vera?" A half-smile. "Or to arrest you."

"For?"

"Your growing reputation."

"Stop it!"

Ali Cran, ignoring me, got out and led the way. In the kitchen, Vera and two judiciales. In the corner, Chaba. With much deference he shook my hand. "Chaba," I said. "Did you find your bed?"

"I know where it sits, señor. Alicito will go with me."

"Sí, Chaba. If it's there, we'll have it soon."

Vera gave Ali Cran a little smile. He kissed her cheek.

The judiciales sat at the kitchen table. One had a dark face, thin eyes, a thick moustache. The other wore reflecting sunglasses. In their early twenties, two kids inside mean black shirts. Each wore, on his belt, a pistol; a distracting ornament. I forced my voice low. "Buenas noches." Not buenas tardes, too late for business calls. I had a reputation? Might as well use it.

Moustache rose. "I am Sergeant Gorjarro, señor. You will come with us."

You will come— I waited, for fear of squeaking. Then: "Why?"

"Lieutenant Blanco will talk with you."

"About?"

"He'll tell you, señor." He stepped toward me. Dark-glasses stood.

Ali Cran stepped between us. "No, señores."

Gorjarro snapped something I didn't understand. Ali Cran yapped back in hot country slang. I caught Rubén's name. Dark-glasses barked instead of speaking and it would've been funny if his hand hadn't rested on his pistol. Ali Cran was equal parts authority and mockery. I stood, arms folded, playing Chaba's role for me. Prominent men don't get involved in squabbles.

Then Vera shoved the bristles of a broom into Gorjarro's belly, so surprising him he only stared. She tapped Ali Cran on the chest with the broom's handle. "Out of my kitchen!" Dark-glasses grabbed Gorjarro's arm and pulled him out the door.

I said, "What did you tell—?"

Ali Cran held up a finger. Suddenly a horn, blasting. Ali Cran smiled, and went outside. An engine started, gears engaged. A second motor, a backfire, a squeal of tires. A roar. Silence. Ali Cran didn't come back. Fear in Vera's eyes. I went outside to look.

He was returning from the gate. "They forgot to close up." Worry remained in his voice.

"And what did you three agree on?"

"Tourists bring foreign currency. It enriches our nation."

"I have to bribe them?" I heard Gottfried Sommers: You will come with us.

Back inside, Ali Cran noted that Lieutenant Blanco would be mighty angry. So Vera must spend the night in the casa, for her safety and mine. Chaba said he'd inform her mother. The main gate should remain locked. Alicito would call in the morning.

"Look, this isn't necessary—" I had to see Irini.

"These muchachos are serious, and dangerous."

Chaba agreed. I encouraged him in his odyssey. He dipped his head and stood tall. "You are brave, Señor Jorge."

"I hope your bed's really there."

A grin. "It will be. May you go with Our Lord, señor."

Vera took Ali Cran's arm. The three walked out together.

And that's the way it is, another day that alters and illuminates our times. And I am here. I come from a later media generation than Doctor Ortíz.

Vera returned alone. "The gate is locked, señor."

Not the witches' passage, and all the walls were scaleable. I tried to call Irini. No answer.

Vera fed me soup, beans, tortillas. Mangos and mandarinas. Back in the casita I sat on the veranda. A small moon whitened trees, walls, and me. Blaze whined. I watched him pull himself to his feet, three of the four, and hobble toward the pool. He raised his head and howled. The wail broke on the upturn.

I went in, tried to read, couldn't concentrate. I wrote a message to Gottfried Sommers for faxing: I have contacted your daughter Irini. She will remain in Michoácuaro. I lay down.

What the hell did they think I could see that they here didn't? Maybe they found my northern rationality so strange, so illogical in Michoácuaro terms, they'd infused it with some kind of heroic hope? Trouble, trouble.

I closed my eyes. I felt the touch of her lips, a warm sweet press, on mine… My light went out. I jumped up. Someone darkening the compound? I stepped onto the veranda. The Chilango's lights were out too. Down the valley, no lights. Okay, not just me.

In bed I stared at the ceiling. I fell half-asleep. Semi-woke to the sound of fireworks… sniping… backfiring… explosions… I woke and slept a half-dozen times.

And woke fully. I lay on my side, eyes closed. Felt the itch of a stare. Heard nothing. I felt myself observed. Tall and Stocky? I lay motionless. Yes, steps. Thieves? Let them steal what they wanted. Gottfried Sommers, come to threaten: You will take another ten thousand—

A light tread approached my bed. My left eyelids separated. Small moonlight. A blur of shape. Three feet away, a face in the shadow of a hat. Nose, cheeks, mouth covered. A gleam of eyes staring at me; we waited… He stepped close, arm up, it came down, I grabbed, missed, a fist smashed my side. I think I gasped. I turned, face in pillow, couldn't see him. His mouth beside my ear, his hand holding me down by the neck, a raspy voice, "Leave Michoácuaro. Believe what you read." I tried to answer, no words nothing, needed breath for breathing— A shuffle. I half-turned my head. A new glint. Prominent Academic Stabbed To Death In Michoácuaro Casita. Fool Deserved His Fate, Police Chief Says.

The voice had said, Leave. I couldn't leave if I was dead. Sure I could. Metal touched my lower lip, pressed, side of a blade. "Go home."

Say, Yes. The blade turned, flicked, away. The arm went up, slammed down at my kidney— On my side I doubled over.

Slowly the pain went dull. My cheek lay in wet. I lifted my head gingerly, touched my lip. Blood. Thick-sticky. I pulled myself to sitting. Flicked the light. No power. Stood, found the flash. To the bathroom. Shone the beam into the mirror. Yeaghgh… Chin, cheek, all blood. I washed my face and around the lip. A couple of stitches would help. No, not deep. Do lips mend quickly? I folded ice into a washcloth, put the package in plastic and held it to my mouth.

Vera! I pulled myself across the compound. I felt no other presence. In the casa, Vera slept. My leaving was the lip-slicer's focus. Believe what you read. The note-sender, his eyes—

My pillow had soaked up most of the blood. The sheet was only tinged. Sorry, Vera, I tripped in the dark and bit my lip.

I lay down again. Someone wanting me gone so badly, did it prove Pepe really was alive? No, I was grasping at the thinnest straws. What did they think I might do, that they tried to scare me away? I'd done nothing since being here. Why was someone afraid of me?

Sleep arrived, tatters of it came, drifted away, came back— The morning "Aiee-ayyeeee-aahhhh!" and its splash. More ragged sleep. Lucinda in the swimming pool, skirt and apron drag her under, Pepe jumps in to save her, can't swim— I dreamed I was dreaming this dream. I said, Enough! and sat up. Which woke me.

My lip around the cut was puffy but the clot looked solid. No kissing for a while. More ice. A beautiful morning, the air limpio, flowers luminous, all that chlorophyll gleaming and triumphant. Vera sat, her elbows drawn in so tight she seemed Alicia's size. "Buenos días."

"Señor, your lip!" I told her about my fall. She looked frightened but reached for a small bowl. "Spread this on your lip."

"What is it?"

"It heals Alicia. When she cuts herself. From the cactus."

I pasted some green creamy gunk on my lip. Vera again drew herself in. She was elsewhere. "And what's the matter?"

For a moment, a contained face. Then her eyes filled with water.

"What, Vera?"

She blew her nose. "Ali Cran called. The judiciales, you know? at that house, Marranando's. He was killed, the one there. Here. He was cruel but why should he be dead?"

"Hold on. Who's dead?"

"The one with the sunglasses last night. There." She pointed to the next chair. "He was shot. Now they'll come again for you. And what will happen to Don Pepe, will he still come back?"

The details took a while. The sunglassed judicial, name of Roberto Cazabe, had received a message: at the rear of the cathedral he would learn significant facts about Pepe Legarto. A few minutes later, around eleven-thirty, all the lights in town went out. Then shots, the whole town heard them. They found Cazabe behind the cathedral sprawled in his blood. Seven bullets in his chest. A calibre used neither by the judiciales nor the police.

Further information: The killer was very tall, at least two metres. A woman had killed Cazabe. Three men did the shooting. The killer was one of Rubén's deputies. The gringo had hired the murderer. Ali Cran was seen in town, clearly he was responsible.

Even the stupidest cop would have to come and question me. So? Pay a call on Blanco.

I sipped coffee at the side of my mouth. The phone rang. Irini? No, Rubén the hi-tech jefe, speaking from his car phone. He'd buzzed at the gate, no answer, were we all right?

I asked Vera, "Isn't the bell working?"

"I took out the fuse."

I went out to open. Rubén drove in. "Your lip?"

"A present from the note-sender." I told him about my visitor. "I think he cares."

"This is serious. Be very careful." His investigation into my note was moving slowly, very few newspapers from the last weeks still available. His deputies resented playing paper-boy—except for Pincho, detecting turned him on. "We need to speak, Jorge."

Yes we did. "Coffee in the casa, privacy in the casita."

He pointed to the casita. "Not even instant?"

Inside, I poured water into the kettle. "You look terrible, Rubén."

"Sleep deprivation." He wiped his face with a handker-chief. "Bárbara and I were speaking. Come to comida at our home."

"Very kind." A breakthrough? Rubén knew many men well, he drank and ate with them but rarely at his home. "Thank you."

"Tomorrow."

I knew Bárbara from a party at Pepe's five years ago. I learned about the price of feeding her animals, four large dogs and a flexible cat population. "Do you know, to feed them it's a hundred thousand pesos a month."

Back then, about a hundred dollars. "A lot of money."

"But naturally." Written in the heavens. "For my babies." But she had the grace to say, "It's embarrassing also."

"In what way, señora?"

"When I pay more for the meat for the animals than what my maids and gardener make?"

Right now Rubén looked worn out. "You have heard, there will be a new election for presidente municipale."

"What? When?"

He nodded. "Called by the PRI and the MMM together. Each think, because of the present furor, they will win."

"But without candidates?"

"Pepe and Marranando, in absentia."

"Crazy."

"Of course. And so, Jorge, you'll do me a favour. Yes?"

"If I can."

"Anyone asks why I'm here now, it's to invite you to my home."

"That's the truth." But what was the favour?

"These judiciales, one of theirs was killed. They can be brutal. Don't provoke them."

"Why would I?"

"Your simple presence, Jorge." Explaining as to a five-year-old.

He irked me now. "Would they harm me?" I was tough. "In the street?"

"They can remove you from the street. You'd miss your plane home."

I didn't need more high drama; unlike my intruder. "Come on, I'm a foreigner. Some high PRI type would have their balls."

"There can be accidents."

"With TV cameras in town?"

"Today I saw no Televisa trucks. Only thirty vehicles of the judiciales. They've closed the bank, the Oficina de Rentas. They occupy the office of the presidente." He searched my face. "A favour."

The last of Rubén's power, gone. "What can I do?"

"I need to find Pepe. Or his corpse."

"Rubén, you know I want to help—"

"Of course, I know, you'll find him in your own time. Look. Pepe and I aren't good friends. But compared to these ones here now he's my brother. I'd kill to bring him back."

A prepared speech.

"I trust you, Jorge. Look, all I have, all my houses, I've borrowed against them to bring EspórConMex here. So people can live well. If the judiciales stay, the Americans will take their factory somewhere else. That's the end for the town." His head shook, weary. "And for me."

It felt both sad and a relief knowing whatever the crisis, Rubén remained himself. A day without irony fills my life with lead. So I made sympathetic noises. He, taking my meagre words as a sign, seemed to wind down. "Ah, Jorge. We wait for you to pull the Pepe-rabbit from your sombrero. Before the election."

I did not like the role I was being cast in.

SEVENTEEN

Below the veranda a grey-mottled hen pecked at seeds and bugs. Ernie's little cat stalked the hen. The hen turned, saw the cat, the hen's head went high. The cat froze. The hen stepped toward the cat. The cat's fur bristled. The hen's neck leaned forward, her beak opened, out came the curse: Squaaawwwk! The cat's feet loosed their springs and it fled. The hen caw-clucked and ran-flew ten metres down the garden. Blaze at the house corner slept and wheezed.

Mid-morning, hot already and my head ached dully. A part of me cursed, Damn it, take the Jeep. Head to the hills!

But which of three hundred and sixty tangents to follow? Stop. Start again. Up north I was a steward, upkeep my duty. Here—

Back to the beginning. Pepe says he's going out. He's abducted. Dead? Not killed between home and office. No ransom note, no responsibility claimed. A more basic question. Pepe is my friend, but he has older and closer friends here. They are doing nothing to find him. Why not? Should this be telling me something? What? That they don't know where to look, how to carry out a search? Or, that they don't care? I couldn't get myself to believe this.

Okay. Pepe left either voluntarily or involuntarily. If the first, then not with his Jeep, it's right there on the drive. Rubén has investigated; no one saw Pepe leave by bus. So:

someone took Pepe away. Who? Where? By what mode of transport?

Okay, he left involuntarily. Violently? In a violent act the most likely suspect is a person one knows.

To start with the least likely, Felicio. But why Felicio? Pepe was no enemy. Felicio had bought the land for El Jardín for Pepe. Tough old hombre, breaking and entering for the sport. But coercing Pepe at gunpoint? With three grizzled machete-wielding campesinos from tierra caliente? I couldn't see it.

Irini? Why her? She wants the garden for herself? She abducts him? By herself? With whom as a helper? She's holding him somewhere, kidnapped. Or she's killed him. If either, she's a great actor.

I see him then, clear as day. A sidewalk cafe, glassed in. Two women, another man. Pepe tells a story, the whole of Michoacán is searching for him. He laughs. The cafe is in Amsterdam. He sips wine. The day is sunny and cold. The image dissolves. The woman beside him, short straight black hair, small face, hand on his arm, fades last. And what was all that about?

Okay, maybe Vera. Why? How could she make him disappear? Maybe she cast a spell on him, some voodoo, now he's a zombie. She knows the hill-trails. On foot she leads him, his mind empty, around the outskirts of Michoácuaro to a waiting car. From there— After, she fakes her fear? She wouldn't know how.

Ali Cran could take a squad of judiciales down to tierra caliente and make them vanish. But only out of spite, or for the sport. Still, Pepe is his friend. Not a political friend. Except in the politics of food production. What motive?

Delcoz. Why? For the bishop Pepe is the devil, the corrupter of Michoácuaro, the vile fruits of his garden, the evils of cable television. How would he spirit Pepe away? And would he? Delcoz needed to be seen destroying Pepe, a personal victory over Pepe; but Pepe could vanish for reasons having nothing to do with Delcoz. Did I need to pay the man a visit?

Rubén. No, he needs Pepe back. For peace in Michoácuaro, or whatever else would get rid of the judiciales and reinstate his authority.

Avéspare. But she too wants concord, for Rubén's economic reasons and her own political ones. Pepe, dead or alive.

Too many potential possibilities. And too many not very real possibilities. Hidden causes, too many unknown people. But why the Amsterdam cafe? Because it rang of Jaime's sense of romance? Or some political reason I hadn't fathomed yet.

Clucking madly, a hen tore across the grass. In full pursuit was a rooster, shiny brown feathers and a tattered comb. She kept five-six metres ahead of him. They vanished behind some acacias, squawk-squawk-squawk-*squaaaawk*! and reappeared, he as fast as she. She reached the witches' passage, leapt, and through. The rooster sprang— Beside the hen a second rooster, he mottled grey. The brown pursuer landed, slapped to a halt, veered, meandered off: Don't mind me, folks, just passin' by.

So, in the teeth of Rubén's warning and Lip-slicer's demand, I allowed myself a moment of silliness and created the post-Felicio maxim, Nothing sleuthed, nothing truthed. Feeble armour. Not that I needed truth but I couldn't stand around doing nothing. I called Irini. No answer. I told Vera I was going to the plaza. A minor attempt to restrain me: You are hopeless—

I put some of her gunk on my lip and headed down the hill. At the centre large black sedans, a couple of dozen, shone like gangs of roaches on a kitchen floor. The Televisa truck had been joined by two minivans and a hatchback, same logo on their doors.

At Teléfonos de México I sent my fax to Gottfried Sommers. 18,000 pesos. U.S.$6.00.

Impressive too were the gents in black shirts and jeans patrolling in twos, one with a heavy-duty rifle, the other an Uzi. Six pairs on the plaza alone. Was Lip-slicer among them?

A knot of people stood in front of the palacio municipal. Eliseo, half-asleep, guarded the bank, its door chained and locked, shades drawn. His rifle looked antediluvian alongside the judiciales' vogue weaponry. "Eliseo. How are you?"

His head yanked up. "Señor! I'm—yes, I'm frightened. It's not a good time." He stared at my lip. "Very bad."

"Is there news? The man who was killed?"

His rifle pointed at the palacio municipal. "There he is."

"Who?"

"The dead judicial. His coffin."

By the group of people. "Cazabe? His body's on display?"

Eliseo nodded.

"In the heat?"

Eliseo giggled. "Come here. Under the portico it's cool." I did. "They say," his voice fell, "Cazabe was seconded from Mexico City. Just for the Legarto case."

If so, the federal government was involved, dressed up in a state judicial police uniform. Emilia and Rubén would be squirming. But that young kid, seconded? "No word about his killer?"

Eliseo shook his head. "They say a Seng Twelve killed him."

"What's that?"

"They say it's of Chinese manufacture."

"Here?" For the armaments industry, buyers everywhere.

"From the shipment the governor sent to the jefe, they say."

Bad news. "And what does Rubén say?"

Eliseo shrugged. "Quién sabe?"

Had Rubén known this They-say version of things when he came calling? "Keep your head down, Eliseo."

"You'll see." He nodded. "Terrible things will happen."

I walked over to the knot of people. Two men crossed themselves and glanced away. By the coffin, steel blue with metallic edging, a small Mexican flag draped over, stood four judiciales, one at each corner, black shirt, tie, jeans. They cradled their rifles. An old man stroked the flag, nodded, moved on. Yesterday the corpse inside was a young man. He represented many things I despise. Today his one chance at life is over.

A voice behind me said, in English, "Excuse me. You're the professor?"

I turned. "Who're you?" A pert young woman, cropped brown hair, a shoulder pack.

"Betsy Picard, *TIME* magazine." She looked the age of most undergraduates I teach. "Can I talk to you?"

"About what?" I started walking.

She waved her hand. "All this. You knew Pepe Nitido."

"Pepe Legarto. Nitido is the add-on matronimic."

"Oh yeah, I always do that. My feminism coming out."

The core of machismo, a man's father's name. Mexico could be tough on Ms. Picard. "Pepe's a friend."

"Present tense? You think he's still alive."

The black-white dead-alive terms. I discovered my senses knew only that Pepe was not here. "Maybe he's in Amsterdam."

"Come on. Guy wants to be mayor, he'll stick around. 'Less somebody's offed him."

"Maybe." Musta' been a demon editor at her college paper.

"So?" her hand swept over the plaza. "What d'you think?"

What I want to think: Pepe and his black-haired signora, divorcée, soft lips, sipping wine at the Café Lauscher.

Tomorrow they leave for her Tuscan palazzo. I said, "This too will pass." I felt old, I'd seen it all. "Bit of a flare-up. Nothing serious." As soon as I spoke I disliked myself for trivializing Pepe's disappearance.

"The dead cop?"

"Likely unconnected to Pepe." I did not want to be quoted in a U.S. periodical.

She nodded, her first non-pushy gesture.

I glanced about. Four judiciales. Eight eyes on us.

"Listen, d'you know where Legarto-Nitido is and you're not telling these guys?"

"If I did, why should I tell you?"

"Because I want the story." She grinned.

I liked her better for the grin, an American thank you.

"Some say you're good at figuring things out. Some say you could sit down with Nitido right now, drink a tequila with him."

"That's what some say, is it?"

"Like—" she looked at me, her head at a slant. "Like Crusader Rabbit."

I laughed. She didn't know Pepe was the rabbit in the hat.

"I minored in TV history." She pointed to the rubble of the statue. "They say you being here got it smashed."

"Better check your sources before printing that."

She nodded, too serious. "I have a dozen people who swear you yelled out, 'Pull it down, pull it down!'"

"Echoes of bad tequila the day after."

"You don't feel in danger yourself?"

I was from up north and safe, right? But Lip-slicer refocused my perspective. On the third hand, he could have killed me. So he didn't want me dead. Yet. "Tell you what, Betsy Picard. I'll meet you tomorrow, here in the plaza about this time. Anything I learn, I'll let you know. If I don't show, contact my embassy."

"Put that in writing."

"Sure."

She found her pad. I wrote out a dramatic little note. "Thanks."

"De nada, señorita. See you tomorrow."

She grinned. "Take care." She headed for the press trucks.

I felt cheered; two weary partisans facing the unknown. I walked over to Rubén's office. Pincho stared beyond me. "El jefe isn't here."

"Tell him to call me." I turned and left.

Some inner voice of mine said, Take a taxi up the hill, spend the day with the señora. In whatever garden. My normal voice said, This isn't why you're here. Maybe it is, said a new voice.

I made my way to Marranando's house, now base for Blanco and the judiciales. Sounded like a sixties salsa-rock band. Half a dozen men guarded the place. At the entry to the courtyard an ancient Sten gun was mounted on a stand. Okay, I'd visit the lieutenant later. On by Migro Cardo's blacksmith shop, shut tight. No people, cars, burros. I was alone. I shivered. One of the legends about Ali Cran ascribes a tail to him; it grows, it has to be clipped regularly. The shearer in these accounts is Migro Cardo the blacksmith.

I stood across the street and looked up. A bad angle. I moved on. Yes, as Irini claimed, a statue. I saw it waist-up, a huge idol. She'd said Tezcatlipoca; could be.

A quiet car stopped. Black. Two black-shirted gents got out. One carried a rifle. The other saluted, all polite. "You will come with us, señor."

I remained formal. "My apologies. I have no time."

He said, "Ah, what is time?" A philosopher, or in my panic I misheard. He took my elbow and with a crunching grip led me to the car.

"Where're we going?"

"Into the car." He smiled, dry.

Something in my brain shrugged and I got in. He slid in beside me and closed the door. The car was air-conditioned, a clammy cool. I shivered again, this time with cause.

The other judicial U-turned and at Marranando's house headed down the passageway. Two men dragged the Sten gun to one side.

In the courtyard three men and their weapons lounged about. Flowerpots sat under the overhang. Geraniums in the shade? Bad gardening. A tall man opened the car, led me to a door at the back and knocked. We heard, "Sí!" and entered.

At a table, making notes, a phone to his ear, a cigarette at the edge of his mouth, sat Lieutenant Blanco in a light shirt and tie. He gestured to a chair. I sat. My guide left. The room felt out of balance. A night table held the phone base. A mattress stood on end against the wall, the frame leaning against it. Chaba's bed? Now he could marry. I grinned. Blanco, noting this, scowled. My heart boomed away.

After "Sí sí" half a dozen times, "Gracias" twice and "Adiós" at last, he put the phone down, looked at me, and nodded.

I nodded back. I too could do mime.

"We meet again."

"Tell me why I'm here." As low a voice as I could manage.

He raised his eyebrows. Softly: "My man didn't explain?"

His eyelids blinked constantly. "Nothing."

"Imbecile." Blanco shook his head. "I wish to exchange views with you, señor."

I stole the initiative. "You didn't want to visit me?"

"Capitán Oscúreo wished me to be your host."

"Yet you offer me nothing to drink?"

"Forgive me, señor. I'm not in private quarters."

"You're poorly equipped."

"Alas, yes."

Our sheen of politeness glassed my panic in. I felt giddy enough to stand. "Then let's resume our chat on my veranda."

"Sit, señor." The same softness, a new edge.

"Come this evening. I'll expect you." I started off.

"Sit!"

He was standing. Strapped to his belt, the pistol. Not, I decided, a fashion accessory. I sat. "What do you want, Señor Blanco?" I forced out a dab of weariness, my cool disguise.

"Lieutenant Blanco, señor." He spoke gently. "They say you know where Legarto is." Curious eyes, they blinked constantly.

I tried to conjure up Pepe in Amsterdam. "No idea."

"Then why do many people in Michoácuaro concur on this?"

"People believe funny things."

His turn to nod. He stubbed the cigarette. "Only yesterday, the cantina halfway to Ojo, you know it?"

I nodded. A dark little adobe shack. Even Rubén who would drink anywhere found the place unnerving.

"Just there, one of my men heard two campesinos crediting the policía judicial with the strangest practices." He shook his head: such alien moments. "Señor, you are a doctor of philosophy yes? In your philosophy, you explore other ways of thinking."

No fool, this Blanco. "Of course." He saw through me.

"Then imagine this. Tomorrow Legarto gets off the bus, he is with us again. What do you envisage?"

I noted Blanco's face. Flat mouth. Eyelids blink, blink. "Many would be happy." I felt Blanco's drift. "Others, upset."

He nodded. "A renewed anger. Blameless people hurt. How in the cantina the campesinos dreaded this, that the innocent should suffer." He smiled. "But as philosophers we must ask, who is without blame? Perhaps I'll accept your invitation. We shall pass a pleasant hour considering this question."

"You'll be welcome. But," I gathered my bravado, "if your friends aren't of an epistemological state of mind, please come alone."

"It would be best, señor, for a month, maybe longer, who can know? for Pepe Legarto to remain away. I urge you to consider the wisdom of what I say." Blanco stood. "We must avoid chaos, bloodshed."

I forced myself to remain sitting.

"That's all, señor."

"Among philosophers, Lieutenant, can there ever be a closure to discourse?"

"Unfortunately now I am very busy."

I forced my tone to flat. "A final question, then." Flying on adrenalin.

He leaned across the table, staring through blinking lids. "I'm at your service."

My heart bashed at my ribs. "Forgive my directness. Are you holding Legarto in a detention centre? Or anywhere else?"

On his face, mock sorrow. "How can you think this, señor?" His little sadness whispered: Pepe is not my prisoner, I wish he were.

I thought, he's not faking. Or did he want me to think, incorrectly, that he wasn't faking? "Gracias." His civility was a surprise—in other circumstances a pleasant one. But right now it just barely masked the brutality beneath the surface. Adrenalin moved me to and out the door.

"Señor. Till you return north, do not leave Michoácuaro."

"I have no plans to." I stepped into the courtyard. Slow, do not run. Or fall. I felt the stares. I passed the Sten gun and floated out. My feet were rubber, my legs balsam. Hips of paste. I thought my soles flat to the ground, one ahead, next, the other. By the bank—

"Señor! Gracias a Dios!"

I glanced Elisco's way, nodded, walked on. Across the plaza. Many eyes. For the coffin seller my third-sweetest grin, "Not today, feller." Don't leave Michoácuaro. Up the hill. I felt heavy; heavier. Pepe's gate. Locked. But the key slid into my hand, into the lock, the door swung open, I was in.

The casita lay miles ahead. I sat on the ground. Stay in Michoácuaro. Leave Michoácuaro. The forces of fear ought to get together on this.

Flaco found me watching the grasses grow. "Señor?"

Slow, slow. I turned to face him. "It's a hot day."

He grinned. "Hot also for judiciales. Very brave, señor."

Word had reached here already?

"Señor." His blind eyes stared down at me. "There's a problem."

I couldn't handle it. "What is it?"

"The Chilango house. The masetas with the geraniums. Some have vanished."

"Walked away by themselves?" My funny joke.

Flaco only shrugged. No accusations.

I stood up. Reached the casita. In. To the bed—

Blaze stares down a deep hole, I pull him away, something down there, what? He draws me across the hole to a small river, running black. I follow it downstream to a lake. A boat, and I row. Green water, deep. The boat floats on the green. The boat is heavy and hard to steer. I'm rowing Alaine across the lake. I can't see the far side. She wears a lacy white dress and carries a blue parasol, open against the sun. Her face is grey. Then a dock or gate, and clouds of bugs. Blaze whines, whines—

Blaze's whining woke me. I dragged myself out to the veranda. Ernie's truck stood by off the terrace, a dozen geranium masetas in the bed. He loaded another. Blaze yowled a whimper.

I had to. I slipped through the witches' gate. "Hola."

"Hey Hoar-hay, give me a hand." In English: "Hey, that's a helluva lip! She give you a love bite?" He roared a laugh.

"I tripped. What're you doing?"

"Getting organized. Before that bastard Pepe comes back." He lifted another maseta, grunting as he went.

"I thought you thought he was dead."

"Him, his ghost, all the same. He said I was trying to steal his house, you know that? I'm real angry and I'm not gonna retreat. Except I've got to be in Mexico City and I'm not saying to anybody I'm going. Except you. I trust you."

"Look, Ernie—"

"He charged me with not paying rent. Well he can't 'cause I haven't paid a centavo since I moved in. So he tries to get rid of me. Ha! they're gonna have to carry me out. He wants to destroy my life? I'll make him bleed." Ernie fairly tingled with laughter. "He can take me to court about pay-ing the rent but I haven't paid the rent so he's out of luck."

I had to be missing something.

"Fuck, this place was a mess. Huge leaks, had to be plugged. The blind one's brother did it, Nicandro, cost a for-tune. He cheated me. And in the bathroom, the rug, ever hear of a rug on a bathroom floor? I tiled it. A dozen improvements. Listen, I don't blame you telling Irini I beat the dog. It needed beating, fucker attacked my cat, shat in the house. I trust you, you told the truth to that bastard Rubén about the lock. And I'll beat that shit-dog anytime it snaps at me."

"Listen, next time—"

"No problem, Hoar-hay. And I'll tell you something, I'm going to lock the doors and windows. You tell Rubén there's valuables in here, my mother's jewellery she left me, beauti-ful stuff. I'll be travelling to bring the factory here, word'll get around, I know that. Somebody, likely Rubén himself, he'll break in and steal everything. I mean that bastard Pepe's stuff, 'cause I won't leave anything of my own of value. And listen, you're my friend, anyone breaks in, let them take it, the stove, the refrigerator. Don't interfere."

"Yeah?"

"Yeah, 'cause I'm taking my mother's jewellery. Don't protect that bastard's stove, it's not worth it. And take care of yourself, you hear?" He got in the truck, the bed half full of masetas, drove out his gate and up the hill.

EIGHTEEN

The known enemies: Lip-slicer, Tall and Stocky, Blanco the blinker, Note-sender, Toni. Or, for reasons unconnected to Pepe, Gottfried Sommers? And the unknown and unsuspected enemies.

Five o'clock shadows climbed the crags of Cerro Gordo. The sun's glow rose above the rock. Unseen light beamed over the horizon on to eternal space, reducing little Michoácuaro to handleable proportions. And me to a little precision: what didn't link up? Tall and Stocky were too clumsy to be Blanco's men. And too artless to be Lip-slicer. Nor was Lip-slicer Blanco's man: "Stay" and "Leave" contradicted each other. Or did they? Nothing added up. Maybe I should find a different kind of arithmetic.

At the casa I found Vera with a small woman. I called Irini again; again no answer; at the Jardín? Vera introduced me to her friend Laura, ex-criada for the maestro next door. Laura reached a dark hand to me, avoided my eye, and whispered, "Mucho gusto." A tiny brown nut of a woman, maybe forty-five, maybe seventy, quick eyes or just brimful with nervousness, no teeth, ultra-shy, she sat silent in the corner. A fearful witch?

Vera gave me some thick soup. My lip was healing well but I sipped with care. She then gave me a scolding designed for those of her betters who act out of line with their station. "It's wrong, Señor Jorge, to let the judiciales take you."

"But I'm here."

"But it's dangerous. Do you know, people say they're not afraid. But suddenly everyone has a compadre in Ojo de Agua, in Morelia, they must visit there for the New Year."

"I hope Pepe's friends don't leave. He needs their votes."

She shook her head. "You mustn't search for him tonight."

"Vera, I promise."

Laura gave me a thin smile. "Don't go out tonight."

Laura gave me the creeps. Vera gave me the flashlight. I asked, "Did Pepe have a flash the night he disappeared?"

She considered that. "Yes, I think so."

A flashlight. The road to his office. The Telecable. Tall and Stocky, grabbing him on the way? They'd be up to it.

"Señor. I forgot. There's a package for you." She located a shoe-box tied with string and handed it to me.

My name on it. A package bomb? "Who's it from?"

"Señor Avéspare brought it."

"Thank you." Laura's glance flicked from me to the package. I left. A waxing moon. The stars gave off plenty of light. I locked the casita door, the door to the patio, and opened the box. Wrapped in soft paper, a camera. Yes, a Leica III-f. Not brought by Toni. A note: "Señor. Please return this to its owner. Forgive its misappropriation. The person responsible has been dealt with. Ignacio Avéspare."

Dealt with. I was in the señora's debt. I rubbed more gunk on my lip. Jaime would be pleased. But what had happened to Teófilo Através?

Why did Blanco pick me up? To deliver a message: Legarto, stay away. Dubious. To show Michoácuaro I functioned here by sanction of the judiciales? Perhaps. I lay down and closed my eyes.

Irini and I. I have extended my stay. We are together at the ocean after Pepe is found. Irini and I. Long talks over dinners in small Mexico City restaurants. In small restaurants at home. Irini and I. We make love— Well. This was a new way of thinking…

Another voice: Irini joining you in the frozen north? The madame of what snow-pea garden? Collecting Cree fruits and berries? Or: stay in Michoácuaro, become assistant gardener, fertilizer detail? Or: you both write long letters, a month back and forth, letters of sweet agonized yearning? Be serious.

And Irini's voice: Who knows what can be, without trying?

Around, by, past, over…

The howl of a worn-out dog. Poor old Blaze. Three yips, more howling. I got up to look. I slid the veranda door lock open and pushed. Stuck. I examined it. Nothing obvious blocking it. Stuck fast. Curious. More whines, and yipping. I couldn't see Blaze, the angle of the side window cut him off. An aggressive bark, the strongest yet. I put on shorts and shirt, key into the lock, turned— It wouldn't budge either. As if its mechanism were detached. Two unopenable doors. Blaze yowled, feebly. I tried the door again. I kicked at it. If I believed in witchcraft I'd know who was responsible. I turned the handle; bastard wouldn't budge. At the back of my head, pain jagged.

Why was it stuck? The mechanism was out of kilter. Why? Something had moved internally. How? The house had shifted, a little earthquake. But I'd felt no quake, the door's alignment was smooth and straight. Okay, something inside had worn out, a little metal fatigue. I suddenly heard Felicio: Use your skeleton key, señor professor!

Two jammed locks. One disbeliever in sorcery. No way out. Shout for Vera? But she wouldn't hear me. Wait till tomorrow? She wouldn't expect me. I'd be here till comida.

Blaze whined, sad but sweet, as to a friend.

Witchcraft. How long does a spell last? Can you jinx a lock? keep it hexed? How to undo hoodoo, or nurse a curse? Stop it.

I tried the door again, pulling gently. Harder. No. Turned the key. No. Yanked. No. If I broke the glass, reached outside, worked the key— Time for that. Door to the veranda. No.

Headache back full force. I lay down. I'd figure this out. I closed my eyes. Better…

No. I'd go to sleep. On the positive side, I was safe from Lip-slicer. I switched the light off. A long howl from Blaze. The moon filled the windows yellow-blue. I'd napped in the afternoon, sleep wouldn't come, the night was young…

Bouncing on a silver stream, a large green ball, tapping hollow. I woke. The taps came from the door. I sat up, slipped into my dressing gown and flicked the light on. "Vera?" No answer. At the door: "Who is it?"

Three knocks, hollow like from a steel drum, me inside the barrel. Three more knocks: Blanco and his judiciales? I edged around to the window. One person out there, small, head covered in a dark cloth—Lucinda the maybe dead beggar lady.

I said, "I can't get the door open, señora." I pulled the latch. Stuck tight.

Three hard beats, seven short light ones. And again.

"Sorry, I'm telling you—"

The latch pulled back. She stood in the doorway, red bag in one hand, two purple bags in the other. "I'm very poor. Please, you can help me. I'm hungry. What can you give me?" The Lucinda who opened obstructed doors at night, that Lucinda.

"I've got a few things. Oh—and thank you." I checked the door from outside. The latch worked perfectly. Inside, same thing. I closed the door. Opened it. "Wait a minute."

My headache pounded again. At the veranda door I drew that latch. Of course it opened.

Has the beggar lady ever wondered, does the man in the dressing gown come here to live so he can open and close doors? Now she knows. I said, "Would you like a beer? Some cookies? I'm in your debt."

"Perfume."

I shrugged. "Sorry, I don't have perfume. What else—"

"Perfume."

Perfume right now or she'd lock the casita up tight. My aftershave! "A minute." I found the green bottle. She smelled it, nodded, dabbed some on her hand and ran it over her forehead. She near to smiled.

I grinned; and winced and pressed at the back of my head.

She said, "Amoebas."

"No, no—"

She looked up at me, right temple, right eye to left eye, left temple. "It hurts."

"Not so bad today." But now it was.

"The pain is terrible."

"How'd you know?"

She said nothing.

"I mean, that my head was hurting?"

"Coconuts."

"Excuse me?"

"Coconut milk. Seven coconuts. Milk coco. Not meat coco."

"I don't understand."

"In the evening, cut one open. Stand it in the shell in the night air. In the morning, drink it. Seven mornings."

"Oh. Thank you."

"The spiders. The king." She nodded twice. "Under the tarpaulin."

"King?"

"He's alone. Cherimoyas are best with milk. He counts, up, down." She reopened the aftershave, and dabbed more on her face. "Good," she muttered. The lingering gaze.

"Something else?" I opened the door below the sink. "Look, I've got sugar, and honey." I pulled out a bag. "Like some?"

She stared. "Salt."

"Sugar. Really." I undid the bag and gave her a pinch.

"Sugar." She tasted it. "You are in danger."

"Why?"

"It isn't salt. You're my friend. It's dangerous. You're his friend. Gracias, señor. Go with God. And with much care." She screwed the aftershave tight, dropped it into her red bag, backed out the door, turned, went.

I let her go. I closed the door— Slapped the latch open. The lock worked fine.

From Lucinda's burnt shack they pulled the body out, so much charred flesh, and buried it a hundred metres to the east. Clearly Rubén just assumed the body was Lucinda.

I locked the veranda door. Two naps had done me out of sleepiness. I read a long time, at one-thirty put out the lights. Sleep again drifted in, took me…

A terrible clanging, bong and strike and echo back and bong clang bonging bong, the world my steeple, no escape.

I wadded toilet paper in my ears. Buried my head under the pillow. Bells slammed, no escape-kape-kay-kay-kay—

After three they ended. The hush was stark. The stream's murmur exaggerated the silent roar. A rooster insisted he'd seen first light. I rolled into muddled sleep. I woke briefly to Ernie's pre-dawn splash, chunks of water flew through the air and spattered on sandy soil, dry dry everything dry. I woke to a revving engine next door. I showered. At the edge of my mind, near-tangible clarity; a bit of shaping could make it real… It wouldn't come. I applied more gunk to my lip. Healing well. Clever Vera. I made coffee, stood on my veranda, sipped.

The water in the pool lay flat. Greening up. Ernie would leave. His gardener would empty the pool, scrub it down with chlorine. With Ernie gone could Pepe reclaim his property?

I see Pepe raise a glass and toast me: Glad you came? Someone puts a bowl of fruit on the table; a woman, I almost recognize her. A deck of cards, face up, king of diamonds. A shack, a lean-to. A tarp shades us from the sun. The distant air too is clean beyond clarity. Snatches, snatches. Pepe should be in Amsterdam. The pool was green. Solitaire, shade from the tarpaulin— Enough. I called Rubén's office.

"Jorge! I hear you had an interview with Lieutenant Blanco. But all is well? Or I would have interceded."

"My friend, now I need a favour."

"You have only to ask."

"Can the jefe find a trailer for two horses?"

Five seconds of silence. "Jorge, why do you ask this?"

"To borrow it."

More silence. "And you'd take this trailer—where?"

"Then you have one."

"Possibly I could find one. Old, no good for bad roads."

"I'll go to Lomas Secas. Tomorrow, early. For one day."

I almost heard him nod. "I'll see what can be done."

"Thank you." He told me to come to his office. From there we'd go to his home. I liked Rubén. Despite his self-important airs.

Vera was sorting laundry. I told her about my project.

"Don't go to Lomas Secas, señor. It isn't safe."

"Vera. Don't make me into a prisoner."

"Prisoner?"

"My locked door. What did you do to it?"

"I, señor?"

"You. The witch of locks."

"Señor. You sound like Don Ernesto." She paired up socks.

Men's socks. "Are those Pepe's?"

"Of course."

"Why are you washing them now?"

"Because they're dirty."

"But Pepe hasn't been here over a week."

"So he hasn't needed them."

"And the locked door?"

She shrugged. And flattened the sock pairs.

I shook my head. "I'll be with Rubén for comida."

She nodded and sprinkled water over a man's dress shirt.

I asked to take Pepe's Jeep. She found me the keys. I got directions to the MMM office. I still wanted to speak to Simón. First I called and reached Irini. "Thanks again for lunch. I've tried to reach you. Been at the Jardín?"

She said, "A lot."

"I'd like to see you. Soon."

"Of course." She thought for a moment. "It can't be today. Or tomorrow. The morning after?"

"I could come over now—"

"In two days. We'll have time."

Today with Rubén, tomorrow Ali Cran. "I'll think of you."

She laughed, near-merry. "As I've been thinking of you?"

"Hope so." Two days. Almost soon. And beyond soon?

I stepped out into sunlight. Flaco with the flat of his hand traced the contours of a bush of small white roses. A wilted bloom, and he deadheaded it. I walked over to him. "Buenos días, Flaco. Can your brother guide me tomorrow to Lomas Secas?"

His lips tightened. "I'll tell him, Señor Jorge. Then he has to."

Flaco's hesitation brought my headache ticking back. "A good man, Nicandro."

"Sometimes, yes."

"Always, if he does what you say."

Flaco smiled. "He does what I say because in his head he's not so very smart. His wisdom is, he knows this."

"You're a fine psychologist, Flaco."

"With my bad eyes, señor, I must hear what people think."

Certainly. "Can he get us a couple of horses, do you know?"

Again his discomfort. "I believe so, señor."

In the casita I took an aspirin. It didn't help much.

NINETEEN

On my way to the plaza a couple of jeeps squawked propaganda for the election. Posters plastered to their doors told which absent candidate, Marranando, Legarto, each backed. I double-parked. Coming out of the cathedral was a procession, maybe a hundred men in their twenties and thirties and a few old women, led by the flag-draped casket. The group moved toward a hearse. Shouts, Pepe's name, the noise became a chant, "Pepe Legarto asesino! Pepe Legarto asesino!" Pepe the assassin.

At the hearse eight judiciales set the coffin on a stand, keeping people back. The crowd, slow to respond, shouted louder: "Pepe Legarto asesino!" The judiciales drew their pistols. The crowd scrambled back, the slogan went ragged and died out. The eight stood at attention, raised the pistols and fired five unsynchronized rounds into the air. It terrified the pigeons.

They re-holstered, slid the coffin into the hearse, closed the door, and saluted. The hearse drove along the plaza, reached the road for Morelia, turned and was gone. But for certain not forgotten.

At my elbow: "Nice show of authority." Ms. Betsy *Time*.

"Hi. When did they start with the chant?"

"This morning."

"Scary business."

She nodded. "So what's new? What did you learn?"

"Nothing new. So nothing bad is new."

"Okay, I guess." She looked about. "But it's a good thing you showed. Word is you had a chat with the head jefe." She pronounced it hay-fay.

"No. With Blanco."

"That's him."

"No, there's some superior. Name of—Oscúreo?" Then I got it. Dark, white: bad cop, good cop. A wit, our Blanco.

Betsy's head shook. "Never heard of him."

I described my talk with Blanco; for Betsy, so much local colour. "Tomorrow I'm going away for a day or so."

Her eyebrows rose. "A lead?"

"Seeing a friend on a ranch."

"Wish I could get out of here. Enjoy."

On to find Simón. An old building and a sign, MMM HQ. One side of the roof had fallen in, replaced by a makeshift covering in blue. I stopped the Jeep and stared at blue tarpaulin.

Half a dozen desks, twice as many people. Phones buzzed, a Gestettner cranked out propaganda. Simón? Out. Someone recognized me as Pepe's friend and brought me a glass of tea. I'd find Pepe soon, they said so. Did they believe it? Or had they already lain him with Teófilo; in whatever grave. I tried to discourage their attempt to turn me into a potential hero. Yes, I'd come back to speak with Simón.

My friendly headache twinged, on the right side just above my ear. I tried to think it away. That didn't work. I sat in the Jeep and closed my eyes. Too much noise here— maybe I should go back to Pepe's, lie down, drain the ache from my head—

The midday sun baked the Jeep's seats dry. There was something else I wanted to do, and time for it. The Jeep climbed up to the City of the Dead; it lay behind white-washed walls. Some graves were covered with shiny plastic flowers, others with desiccated real ones. I drove by and looked for the remains of Lucinda's house. I found nothing. I must've remembered Rubén's description of the place badly. Which irritated me, and didn't help my headache—it now proscribed an arc from above my left ear to above my right, beating a rhythm as it bounced back and forth. I closed my eyes and let the headrest support the weight of my skull…

I must have sat there five minutes or so. Might as well head back. Eyes open—all as before. Okay, maybe drive a little farther, around a couple more bends? Why not. Start the Jeep, and drive on. A dip in the road, then a sharp curve, an open area. More scrub, nothing obvious except a small shack. Maybe her house had been here—scrub retakes the terrain quickly. At the shack they might know where Lucinda had lived.

It's built of rough boards, the spaces in between stuffed with rags and newspaper. A hairy piglet tugs at its cord, a couple of chickens scratch in the sandy soil. On one side, a chaos of barbed wire only a snake could negotiate. On the other, many things: auto batteries bleeding dried acid, loose bricks with clinging cement, unpaired shoes from high heels to huaraches, many wooden cartons. By the wall two alcatraz lilies and geraniums in paint cans, cheering the place.

The door, ajar—four raw boards nailed to slats. "Buenas tardes?" No sound. Go in and look? Push the door open. A low dark room, a dirt floor. A cot and rumpled blanket. Next to it, crammed full, dozens of plastic bags. To the left, floor to ceiling, piles of newspapers. On a shelf some bottles, toilet water, aftershave. A green one, like mine. All empty. "Hola!" No response.

On the rear wall, a filthy poster: Maximilian, Emperor of Mexico, a mid-nineteenth-century anomaly. A king of sorts?

Out behind, a space defined with the remains of fencing, about twenty metres square. A kind of torpor rising from the earth. The air is tight and fat. At the very back, no fence because it was the cliff edge, a tiny outbuilding a metre and a half wide and as high, its walls weathered boards. The roof and front, green tarpaulin! Between me and it, more stuff—collapsed cardboard boxes, car door handles, broken toy cars, hubcaps, lengths of rubber hosing. But organized: plastic doll parts with plastic doll parts, brown bottles with brown bottles and clear with clear, a corner of machine gears. Rust and weeds, yet order. My headache, ticking away. The thick air is rank.

Watch for scorpions and broken glass. Here, so near the cliff, unstable ground, approach the building with care. The stench and a dim buzz-whir, they're in there. Pull back the tarp— A surging stink, alive and solid. Rotten fruit, black vegetables, ancient chunks of bread, all coated with flies, beetles, grubs, many crawling beasts. A compost pile? Drop the damn tarp! At the rim, staring down, hypnotized… rocky protrusions, the stream deep green, its draw— No! Back! Back to the shack. Sweeter air now, compared to the decay under the tarp. Back. Shallow breathing, all the way back to the shack.

The shack is here, Lucinda lives in the shack. The shack burned down, Lucinda died in the fire. Only one statement can be true. Both statements are true. Or: neither is true. Or: am I the final arbiter of what is so? Is Rubén? Often Rubén and I don't see the same thing. But in this instance, this Lucinda, this December, how can I know what is in fact true?

A rustle behind me, a voice: "Sí?"

I turn. Lucinda stands facing me. "Señora. Buenas tardes."

"Can I help you? What can I give you? I have so very little."

"Excuse me for walking in—" I back into her bedroom. She stays with me. My head pounds, pounds. I press the back of my head. The air is hollow, so is my head. I need sound, I point to the papers. "You must, uh, read a lot."

She stares at me. "Coconuts."

"What?"

"Seven."

"Yes. Seven. Thank you." She, somber, watches me. I step out the front, walk do not run to the Jeep. I sit in the Jeep and close my eyes. And what is this about? I breathe deeply. Wonderful clear air. I let it wind me down...

I started the Jeep and drove away without looking back, notions of pillars of salt tickling my brain. That white powdery stuff under my sink, hardly a pillar—? Kings, spiders, tarpaulin. Her shack was there, her burned-down shack. Maybe it hadn't burned. Or was rebuilt. And no one knew? I'd been inside. I didn't know what to think.

Back in town I parked near the market. The rational town sparked, alive in daylight. Walls and lampposts plastered with handbills, Vote Marranando for Tomorrow's Michoácuaro! Vote for Pepe! Vote PRI for security! Vote MMM! Vote Vote Vote Vote Vote Vote Vote Vote Vote Vote Vote Vote Vote Vote Vote Vote Vote Vote Vote Vote Vote Vote Vote Vote Vote Vote Vote Vote Vote Vote Vote Vote Vote. The word looked very silly.

At Gertrudis's stall I bought five gladioli for Vera: Sorry for getting angry. "Gertrudis, where can I buy coconuts, the ones with liquid?"

She told me which shop. "But why coco de leche?"

"I may have amoebas." I touched my head. A dull ache.

"Coconut milk for amoebas? Where'd you get that idea?"

I smiled, thinning my lips. "A famous gringo cure."

"Loco."

In the shop the coconuts lay on the floor beside a case filled with telephone answering machines, portable typewriters, blenders. Clearly mid-tech coconuts—back off, alleged amoebas! I lugged the coconuts to the Jeep and lay them on the back seat. If Lip-slicer was watching, would he think I was staying on?

Close to comida; Nicandro might be home. I found him in front of a new little house, red brick and painted cement blocks. I asked about the horses.

"I've spoken with Flaco," he said. "There's no problem."

"I'll bring the trailer this evening."

He nodded. Despite his words he looked testy, even anxious.

At the plaza, several official vehicles but only a pair of judiciales. Three old men by the fountain. In front of Rubén's office, one deputy. I went in. "Where is everybody?"

"You're early," Rubén said.

"I can come back."

"Let's go."

"I've got Pepe's Jeep."

"Drive around to the back and follow me."

"What's going on?"

He scowled. "Some say one of my deputies killed the judicial. Others say it was a feud, the dead man forced himself on somebody's sister. Yet others say Pepe did it."

"That's crazy."

"Sure. But people say what they believe they know. Come on."

I drove around and followed him, four blocks west of the plaza. Before the 1910 Revolution his house had been a convent. Then three separate owners had let it lapse into further disrepair. Rubén bought it in 1978 for, as usual, back taxes.

We sat in wicker rocking chairs under the portico. At his side, a two-way radio. He had modernized rather than restored the convent but it retained its old bones, including an elegant inner courtyard overwhelmed with flowers, an extravagance of colour.

"What'll you drink? Mercedes!" Rubén patted the radio. "I have to stay in contact."

Movement behind some copa de oro trees across the court; coming toward us, Bárbara and Bishop Delcoz, she in a white blouse and a white skirt, his gown severe black. Rubén stood. Delcoz nodded. He held out his hand, knuckles up; on his middle finger a thick gold ring with a bulky deep red stone. Rubén dropped to one knee, took the fingers, leaned forward, kissed the stone.

I was astounded.

Rubén straightened, looked my way, and introduced us.

I said, "Mucho gusto."

The bishop gave my hand a solid shake. He was about my age, maybe half a foot taller, thin ruddy hair. "A pleasure to meet you, sir." He smiled. "I know much of you." He spoke English.

I said, also in English, "And I of you."

He laughed. "Yes, in small cities they discuss the new arrivals, no?"

I was unprepared for the civility. "You've been here for some time."

"Time? Time is the espacio we come to know each other in, yes? I've learned much, in my time here." Again a smile. "You have helped me."

"I?" I searched for a man who threatens his flock with hell-fire. I didn't see him. The bishop's eyes were actually dancing.

"Your book. It teaches me." He chuckled. "In two ways."

Suddenly something lethal in his pleasure. "I'm delighted."

"My archbishop gave it to me. 'This norteamericano has seen traps,' he said. 'Learn from him.' I pray I have, sir."

"I hope some day you can tell me what these traps are."

"I hope so, too."

I shook my head. "Two ways, you said?"

He smiled again, now with little of his merry mirth. "From how you write, I have learned about you."

"And the value of such knowledge is—?"

"It's good to know much about human nature, no?"

A chill calm to him now. "Sometimes too much knowledge can subvert action."

"Not for me." He stared at the space above my eyes.

I nodded. "I believe you."

He turned to Rubén. "You weren't at mass." He spoke Spanish.

Rubén refused the bishop's eyes. "It's a difficult time."

"As difficult as eternity without salvation?"

"I'll make amends."

"Do." Delcoz stared at him for five silent seconds, then turned to Bárbara. "I have to go." He walked away, Bárbara behind him.

I said, "I'd like a large tequila añejo, please."

Rubén glanced at me, and smiled weakly. "Me too." He left.

I sat. Flowers everywhere. The colours felt arbitrary, anarchic. Not a dog or cat in sight. Not even a criada. All replaced for love of a bishop? Poor bastard Rubén.

He came back. Nine-year-old Mercedes and Lazarito age seven carried drinks, guacamole, tortilla chips, salted jicama. I chatted with the kids for a few minutes. They left. "A man with great power, our Delcoz." Rubén stared into his already empty glass.

Bárbara and Lazarito lugged out a table which Mercedes promptly set. For two, Rubén and myself, Bárbara would join us later. Comida was an adequate veal stew and potatoes. Rubén believed he'd found three of the five words from the newsprint threat-note in two local papers. "This narrows our suspects to thirty thousand Michoácuarans." He scowled.

We spoke of earlier days. Rubén made his way through a quarter litre of tequila. The children cleared. Flan for dessert. And Rubén's new relation to the church, what was this?

"Bárbara admires Delcoz." He spat a laugh. "Very much."

"Why?"

He waved his arm wide. "He brings us peace. We all wish for peace in our souls, no?"

"What does he bring you?"

"Solace? Does he bring me solace?" A sad chortle. "The pathway to solace."

"And what's that?"

Rubén's smile stayed. "Confession."

"Come on."

"You see, I know I am in some way special in the world. This isn't the sin of pride. I've confessed this to Delcoz."

"I don't understand."

"Shall I confess to you, also?" He seemed very drunk. He sipped more tequila. "You can tell no one, you mustn't betray a confession." Another nod, agreeing with himself.

"Well?"

"I have, Jorge, a capacity for accumulation. I collect houses. Buying, having, this gives me integrity. My capacity makes me special." His speech stayed bright and clear.

"Go on."

"I've learned what I was meant for." He sipped tequila. "Wealth." And confessed: "Made by producing goods."

All paths lead to the textile factory. "EspórConMex?"

"You've got some money? Invest with us. With our profits we'll afford the best hotels and restaurants in Rio, in Miami—"

"Rubén, be careful. Lots of new enterprises fail quickly."

"For EspórConMex, we have the best market research. No, this is safe." He smiled darkly. "As soon as peace comes here."

"And if Pepe returns, will he support the factory?"

Rubén shrugged. "A political man must reside in the polis."

Michoácuaro, breeding ground for religio-metaphysical cops. Shareholding cops. "Why will you make so much money?"

"Simple economics." He poured more tequila.

Glad my small investments sat elsewhere. "How?"

"Wages here will be lower."

"Go on."

"Cheaper to live in Michoácuaro than Matamoros."

Hundreds of campesinos, thirty dollars for a forty-eight-hour week. If Rubén thought he had a townful of crime and mayhem now— No. He'd resign as police chief. Live in one of his other houses, the hacienda on the hill, a country gentleman. Crime would be somebody else's problem.

"Projects I invest in, usually they shatter." I grinned at him. "Like the Abelardo statue."

"That was something. You know, I was standing beside it."

"See where the shot came from?"

"It had to be high up."

"Like, the roof of the Avéspare house."

He leaned forward. "What're you saying, Jorge?"

"The señora's Toni was up top there."

Rubén sat up straight. "You saw him shoot?"

"No."

"But he was there." He sat back, and nodded.

"He had at least a pistol. Under his coat."

Rubén waved that away. "Always." He laughed a little. "Emilia is pleased with him. I think, pleased big."

"Big?"

"She is, they say, a woman with strong needs."

"And Toni?"

"He has no money, he does what he has to." A dirty chortle. "I wouldn't want his job."

Emilia had sent the Leica by Ignacio, not Toni. A couple of pieces, fitting together? Who knows what can be, without trying. "Does Toni guard her, say, against reporters?"

"What reporters?"

I showed him the palms of my hands: empty. "Televisa?"

"I'm sure."

"Teófilo Através?"

Rubén's cheek sucked in. Seconds and seconds of silence. He downed the rest of his tequila. He wiped his mouth. "Why're you asking about him again?"

"His camera's been found. I have it. He won't need it."

"Why not?"

"Dead journalists don't take pictures."

He refilled his glass. "He's dead, you say?" Half the bottle was gone.

Shots in the dark. "You know this." Hitting targets.

"What can I know?"

"About the death of a reporter. Tell me."

"I can't speak about this."

"Confession, Rubén. Solace." And some tequila…

He stared at me. "What I tell you, it's between us."

"I promise."

"An accident. A tragic tragic accident."

I nodded.

"He was—talking. He believed we held him against his will."

"Did you?"

"I— No."

"Go on."

Rubén's head shook. "He dived through a window. I caught his leg, I pulled him back. His chin caught the glass. He cut his throat, the large artery. Stupid. He bled to death in minutes. Nothing to do."

"You were alone?"

"The others had left."

"Who?"

He shook his head. "I was supposed to release him after an hour."

"And your conversation with him?"

"To convince him, he must not publish any story that brought shame to Michoácuaro."

"And he disappeared. And his death was covered up."

"Why broadcast an accident to all Mexico?"

"Hell, Rubén. Kidnapping, maybe murder. How'd you get involved? With whom?" Though now I could guess.

He sat straight. "Don't worry. It was an accident. Brought on by itself. Or I'd surely have told you nothing."

Up north I could push to make Teófilo Através' death public. Here, how to interfere? Time spent with Rubén is flirtation with a different morality; one can get hurt, bodily, ethically. In an accident brought on by itself. And when I was gone, however I left, they'd all still live here.

"Brought on by itself."

He found my glance and held it. "No problem, Jorge." He shrugged. "Bárbara will join us, she likes speaking with you. We'll have a Fúndador." He called her. "She likes that too."

He didn't need to add, Don't mention Através. Através was men's business.

A couple of minutes and she came from the house, a round woman looking shaky on high heels. I complimented her flowers. We mourned the tensions in Michoácuaro. "So difficult for Rubén," she said. "But he receives guidance from Bishop Delcoz."

"You're the bishop's good friend, señora?"

"I've helped in his work, a little." She blushed modestly.

"That must be satisfying. And how have you helped?"

Rubén chuckled. "She's clever."

Bárbara beamed, this time toward her husband. "I've introduced him to many people. He's won their hearts."

I nodded. "He's a man of power and charisma, yes."

"But too much power is dangerous." She gave a demure nod.

Rubén said, "What she means, she's taught him to be a diplomat. His authority is always there. But now, harder to see."

In Rubén's voice, a deep pride: one soused chief of police, one pious reborn lady. We chatted. I raised my Fúndador. "Your good health, my friends." We drank. "I have to go."

"We'll get the trailer, the trailer." Rubén stood.

I wished her well. She would pray for God to keep me well.

She took Rubén's hand and whispered. He drew her face to his and kissed her on the mouth, gently. She stepped back, again a blush, dropped his hand and bade us godspeed.

In the Jeep, Rubén saw my coconuts. "So gringos are part monkey!" He laughed, hard.

We drove off. I felt something shift in our friendship. In part, because of his subjugation by Delcoz. Much more, the Através death. And partly his produced fondness for his wife; couples newly displaying affection make me uneasy. His attempted joke irritated me way beyond the tease.

We arrived at a fenced lot, drove in, rear-end to trailer. He hooked it on, we left. At Nicandro's corral the two of them unhooked the trailer. We drove off, back to Rubén's house.

Over the whine of tires his phone rang, an intrusive sound. He jerked forward. "Sí?" His face darkened. "Sí, Enrique." He nodded. "Sí sí sí." He hung up. "Jorge. Stop the car."

I pulled over to the side. I was sweating. "What?"

"My friend Captain Malasombra. In Morelia."

"Yes? What?"

"He thinks he's found Pepe. A body, in a ditch, south of the city."

I gagged— "They're sure?"

"The right build. On his wrist a watch like Pepe's, an expensive watch. Whoever killed the man left it. The—the face is burned, Jorge. With acid. The skin on the fingers too. Enrique can't be certain, they'll get the records of Pepe's teeth from his dentist."

My throat opened. I jumped from the Jeep, breathed—
Gagged, vomited, veal potato bile— I held tight to the Jeep.

Rubén set his hand on my shoulder. "Malasombra will
let me know. Meanwhile say nothing. False information is
dangerous. Jorge, this kind of murder—it's a favoured form
of assassination by the judiciales."

I rubbed my head. "Come on." I'd had enough of Rubén.
Of the whole day. I felt empty, empty— I dropped him at his
place. At the casita I forced myself to unload the coconuts
and left them on the veranda. I locked the doors. I could not
let myself believe the body in Morelia was Pepe. I could not.

I should call Irini, I thought, tell her all this. I didn't.

TWENTY

I slept badly. I lay awake staring into the dark. I could tell Nicandro I'd visit Ali Cran some other day. Why not now, señor? To await news. Of? A friend who's now acid-burnt toast.

The woman, Lucinda, apparently burned. And her house. But she's alive. And if Lucinda is alive— No, it must have been someone else who was burned.

If the body in the ditch was Pepe I couldn't help him, he was dead this morning, he'd be dead tomorrow. If the body wasn't Pepe, nothing had changed. And that was the assumption I had to work with. As to danger: to Pepe, if he was dead, what danger? And to me, from Blanco? Surely Lomas Secas is a suburb of Michoácuaro?

Ernie's yell, and the splash. I dressed, made some instant coffee, drank it and left.

Nicandro, waiting by his front door, greeted me with a tight smile. Rosebushes along the plastered facade promised red, yellow, and pink blooms as soon as sunlight touched them.

Our mounts were already in the trailer, one a bony dun gelding, the other a faded brown sway-bellied mare—drab and time-beaten, appropriate to my sorry search. Good high axles on the Jeep. Nicandro drove.

I glanced back toward Michoácuaro. Maybe eighty metres behind us, a dark sedan. I touched Nicandro's arm

and pointed over my shoulder. As if we could be over-
heard.

He nodded. "They've been with us since the bottom of
town."

I didn't want to cause him trouble. "Look, we can stop. If
they ask I'll play the tourist, a little horseback riding—"

"You must decide, señor."

Did I really need to talk with Ali Cran? Three kilometres,
four. At the adobe restaurant we turned. So did they. "Still
there."

"Shall I stop?" He concentrated on potholes.

The sedan kept pace, its springs jouncing hard. On the
passenger side a man leaned out, a pistol in his hand. Bastards!
Try to stop me, will they? "Keep driving and fuck 'em."

Nicandro grinned and swerved around an outcrop. We
bounced over ridges. The poor horses. A gully, a sharp rise, a
drop, a level stretch. *You will leave, we have to stay.* Nicandro
roared ahead. At the rise the sedan twisted, bottomed out,
stopped, and hung on the ridge. A door opened, a man raised
a pistol— "Nicandro!"

"Hold tight."

"The horses!"

"We're more important!" He accelerated. We rounded a
curve left. Ahead, another stone ridge. We slowed to a crawl.
Nicandro wound the Jeep about and crossed the ridge at a
diagonal. Somehow the trailer followed. Down a slope,
around a curve. We slowed, and stopped. "Stay low, see what
you can. I'll check the horses."

"Okay."

"The motor will run for one minute. Then I'll turn it
off."

Creeping along in scrub I drifted back past the second
ridge. The Jeep motor roared, muted, died. Silence, as if we
were far ahead. Pre-dawn bird twitter and a bit of breeze.
Maybe a hundred metres back I saw one judicial kneeling by

the side of the sedan, staring under; the other was peeing against the embankment. The first stood and shook his head.

I clambered back. "Yep, they're stuck."

Nicandro patted the horses. They seemed too old to get het up about much. He touched the carrier frame, right side. A clean bullet hole. "Rubén will wonder." A frown. "Let's go."

A couple of kilometres from Dos Arroyos we pulled into the small grove. Nicandro unloaded the horses. "Are you afraid of judiciales, Nicandro?"

"They don't concern me."

"What then?"

He shook his head.

"You're worried. What's the problem?"

"What we do." He tightened the cinch on the brown mare. It pulled up some of her sagging belly, a girdle on a fat lady. "Alicito doesn't know we're coming."

In that instant I felt going to Lomas Secas was the most important thing I could do. "Nicandro. The responsibility is mine."

"Sí, señor." He seemed as weighted down as before.

We rode toward a little notch. The sun rose. Suddenly the air was warm. Every bush on the hilly horizon stood in relief, brown against pale blue. A haze of smoke rose high, dirty purple, cane stubble burning to clear the land for a new year of cane.

Nicandro stared ahead and kept the pace slow. To shift his thinking I complimented him on his house. "You built it yourself?"

A nod. "I bought only the land. Seven hectares."

"You saved a long time to get it." I was impressed.

"I had built another house. I sold it."

"And it was like this one?"

He laughed. "Very different. In Nogales."

"But aren't you from Michoacán?"

"Sí. But at the frontier, I worked. And I built my house."

"You were in Nogales long?"

"Eight years, señor. Eight."

We passed through a field of dry corn stalks, and by some unplowed land. Little shoots of green showed in the shade of boulders. "And the factory where you worked, how was it?"

"Very clean, señor." He shook his head. "Many were not."

"What did you do?"

"We made parts for refrigerators. Here, when I was fifteen, I learned electricity." He concentrated. "The Nogales factory sold to many American companies, Japanese companies." He grinned. "Do you know, what is the difference between the electric system of a Japanese refrigerator and an American refrigerator?"

"What?"

"Nothing!" He guffawed.

"Like gringo automobiles, and those from Japan."

He nodded. We had a small conspiracy. "I helped my neighbours with wiring. I earned enough to build a house. Tight from dust. Ai, the dust. In a desert, why build a city there? Except it's also the frontier. Where the road passes." He shook his head. "A strange thing."

"What?"

"A road." He gestured ahead to the trail, worn clear. "Roads aren't natural, señor."

"No?" Our horses took us slowly on. "How so?"

"Villages are natural, for people. People walk. Horses, burros, they walk. Feet walk. Down there—" He gestured vaguely ahead to the Sierra Madre, three hundred kilometres between us and the Pacific. "Villages. And trails, like this."

"For people to travel, no? Like roads, for cars to travel."

He shook his head. "When I was in Nogales I went on the road from Nogales to Tucson, a very wide American road. But on it, one car, two. They need only little roads there."

"It's different."

"Do you know, señor, how long Michoácuaro existed before it was Michoácuaro, before the Conquest?"

"No."

"Many centuries. Many people lived here. And the road from Morelia? Forty years old." He shrugged.

"Without roads, you might not have gone to Nogales to work."

"To work in Nogales, señor, it wasn't natural."

I laughed. Round one to him. "Your wife was with you?"

"Of course. I needed her."

Nicandro and his wife, struggling together to improve their lot. An Amero-Mexican dream. "And when did you come back?"

"Nine years ago."

"Any children, Nicandro?"

He smiled. "Nine."

"In your house, do you have room for that many?"

"There'd always be room for more."

"Nine isn't a good enough number?"

"Good, bad, my wife can't make more. The doctor did it."

A round to the doctor. "Maybe it's for the best."

He shook his head. "It's a waste."

"What is?"

"To use her."

"Use her?"

"To fuck her. She's worthless now."

"Hombre, there's more to it all than having kids." Man-to-man talk in tierra caliente. "Her pleasure, yours."

"For pleasure there's always a woman at the Domicilio." He grinned. "The bishop doesn't like the Hotel Domicilio."

"And your wife's pleasure?"

"She has no pleasure." He shook his head. "She lies flat and prays."

"Was she always like this?"

"In the beginning—" His brow wrinkled. "Slow. She said, I should be slow."

"And?"

"I'm a man, señor."

Oh hell.

"I don't use her now." Nicandro's mood had improved. "It's better."

Mexico, home to a hundred million by the new millennium. Home to poverty for a long time. We rode in silence, I now sore in the tail. We passed through a little barranca, wide enough for one horse at a time. In the valley below, eye-shocking contrast: Lomas Secas. The bright green of banana trees. A duller green, likely avocados. Another I didn't recognize, the cherimoyas? The pond, larger than I recalled, used to be filled with carp.

The ranch house sat narrow and low. A veranda ran along the side facing us. In the corral, four horses. Beside it stood two stacks of railing. Nicandro grinned. "I'll work today." He pointed to the rails. Six barking dogs leapt about us. But our horses were too old for fear, or they'd seen many dogs. Nicandro spoke sternly. The dogs backed off and glared mainly at me.

On the veranda stood Gitana, arms folded. "Welcome."

"Ali Cran invited me. He said after the beginning of the year. But—" I found her eyes. "I felt I should come earlier."

She smiled. No warmth. "I'm pleased you did." Anger directed my way, but somehow not at me.

I followed her into the house. Little had changed. In the kitchen, shelves of bottles filled with dried herbs and plants, Gitana's curative flora. She asked me to sit. I chose the armchair. The pillow felt kind to my rump. The air felt very wrong. "Ali Cran isn't here either? Again?"

"He rushes into the twenty-first century."

A strange answer. "Does that transform Lomas Secas into an oasis?"

"It produces well. The water draws birds." She nodded at me. "People, also."

"Soon you'll have to flee." We were speaking in codes.

"We do."

"To?"

"Rancho Verde." An anger in her, but held in.

Green Ranch. "A third ranch?"

"You like the name? There's no water." She shook her head. "And no people."

I understood, at last. "A place to carry out experiments." And I felt used. And deeply angry. Worse than being told nothing about El Jardín de los Viejos. "Agricultural experiments."

The cold smile again. "These are important."

"Political experiments."

She shrugged.

"You know, the town is close to violence. Maybe to anarchy."

"Anarchy is a human creation." She spoke as if quoting. "It's made, it can be unmade." She sounded imperious.

Which only fired my outrage. "And why Rancho Verde?"

"You'll ask Ali Cran these questions."

What, wait till we got there? "For pitysake, Gitana."

"He said you'd get here sooner or later."

"I was here days ago!"

She gazed at me.

"Come on, Gitana. Why?" What was I to them anyway?

"Let's go." She stood, grabbed a small satchel and a straw hat, and headed for the door. I followed.

The foreman, Antonio, whistled twice. Four horses came running. Antonio spoke to them. Two turned and loped off, toward Nicandro. With him was a man, bent away. He looked familiar.

Antonio shook my hand. "Que milagro, señor!" I agreed. He threw a saddle onto a roan. Gitana saddled the other, a chestnut. The horse nuzzled her neck. She whispered in his ear, strapped her bag and a skin of water to the saddle, and mounted.

So did I. "What's her name?"

Antonio grinned. "Boba, señor." He tied my case on, and another water-skin. "Short for Bobalicón. But she's gentle."

Meaning, nitwit. But she looked way more muscular than what had brought me here. She demanded all my attention, a good thing because being toyed with made me uncommonly angry. Naturally my headache was back.

Gitana called to Antonio, "A sombrero for Señor Jorge!" He brought me a wide straw hat held in place by a chinstrap.

"How far is this Rancho Verde?"

"Not very."

"Gitana, I've been on a horse all morning."

"Less than two hours." She slapped her horse's flanks with her heels. Horse and rider darted forward.

I lagged behind the next while, three lengths, ten lengths, four lengths, according to the terrain. Exercising hadn't prepared me for chafing thighs. Rock, sand, dried-out brush, so waterless, what could bloom here? Thirty kilometres from Michoácuaro, had any winter rain come down on this land? My thighs squeezed Boba's flanks and she sped up alongside Gitana. I asked.

"Yes, we've had rain. But it dries quickly. If a seed breaks its shell and sprouts, the next day the sun burns it dry."

"In the wet months does much grow here?"

She nodded. "Five days of rain and it blushes with green."

An hour of rises and dips. Dry, dry. In the distance, a dark spot. It grew. It took on contours. A couple of square shapes. Green bushes! Two figures. Gitana urged her horse on. Boba kept pace. I drew to a halt and dismounted into Pepe's grinning abrazo.

TWENTY-ONE

P epe said, in English, "Is no secret safe, my friend, when
you're prowling around?"

No shock. I'd had two hours to prepare. But renewed
anger, yes. And down in my gut a flush of relief. A gift from
the grave. I'd never accepted he was dead. Well, maybe a bit
of the time. I was furious. I held him at arm's length. Lost,
and reclaimed. A good good friend. A son of a bitch. Huge
relief. I wanted to throttle him. "How could you do this?"

"Welcome to Rancho Verde," said Ali Cran.

Another miserable bastard. "What the hell are you two
doing?"

Pepe waved his arm. "You like my hideaway?"

"You know what's going on in Michoácuaro?"

"You see what's happening here?"

I stared where his finger pointed. Green plants. "What?"

Ali Cran said, "Dwarf creosote trees. Their roots can go
down thirty-forty metres."

"This is insane, Pepe!"

Gitana said, "Would you like some water?"

I sighed. "Please." She seemed calm now. Conned into
going along with this scheme, and hating it?

The shelter was built of rough boards to a height of two
metres, about four metres square. Orange tarps stretched
across the top for a roof, and extended out two metres, an

awning. They could drop to enclose the front. Inside stood a table, two chairs, a cot, a box on end, plastic barrels of water. And vats and tubs filled with the sandy soil of tierra caliente. Ten metres away, a shed, also with a tarpaulin roof, more vats, more tubs. On the table, two plates, two knives, two glasses, three notebooks and a package of playing cards. While Michoácuaro smoldered. Was this the vision of Lucinda the beggar lady? Or had she been talking about her shack?

Pepe followed my exploring glances. "Our experiments," he explained.

Some tubs were covered in loose plastic, some held green plants. More tubs outside, more tiny shoots. Gitana gave me a glass of tepid water. I said to Pepe, in English, "My better guess had you at the Café Lauscher, in Amsterdam."

Pepe said in Spanish. "And what convinced you I was here?"

I picked up the pack and turned it over. The king of clubs. Silly. "I saw you here." I heard Ali Cran chortle.

Pepe said, "After you arrived, or still in the north?"

"Damn it, Pepe! What the hell are you doing?"

"But, research."

"In Michoácuaro. And with Michoácuarans."

Pepe said, "Sit down, Jorge. Here."

I did. He sat on the crate. For this I'd come down here: outrage at a friend, some vats in tierra caliente, a sore butt. "Has Ali Cran told you what's happening in town?"

"I'm glad I'm not there."

"Pepe, a man's been killed."

"Not because of me, amigo. The judicial died for private reasons. The rape of a young girl. Revenge was necessary."

"Murder still avenges rape?"

"Of course." But his shoulders sagged, heavy.

"Damn it, Pepe! Where are you living?"

"A man makes his choice, he rapes." Ali Cran spoke softly. "Another man chooses also, how this rape is paid for."

Gitana said, "And she, the girl?"

"She desired his death." Pepe's face had aged ten years.

"But they blame you, Pepe. Or Rubén, or Ali Cran."

"Not you, Jorge?" Ali Cran, at my shoulder. "Then there's no danger yet."

"Goddamn you! Listen to me. It's not one death, a whole town will get hurt—"

"When there's change," Gitana said, "many suffer." Sympathy; but within the inevitable.

"You're not there, you haven't felt the tension in the plaza."

"A good thing Pepe's here, then."

Pepe glanced from Ali Cran to me. "Tell us, Jorge, what is to be done?" He grinned.

"Come back. Now."

"I will. On the right day."

"You people are incredible. You design a crisis, Pepe walks back into town, you think they'll proclaim you Señor Saviour?"

Gitana said, "Before, what did you mean, you saw Pepe."

"Just that." I jerked around. "Here. Playing solitaire."

Ali Cran took the knife from his belt and tested its point with the pad of his thumb. He said, "And in Amsterdam."

"Yes." Pepe, solemn. "I'm often in two places at once."

"Ai, Pepe." Ali Cran shook his head sagely. "With the Telecable, all is possible. Two, three, a hundred places—"

"Stop it! Pepe. Why'd you disappear?"

They explain: the votes for mayor are counted. Pepe truly believes this time the PRI will concede defeat. In Morelia, Marranando is pronounced the winner by a slim margin. Yes, Pepe fought a good fight.

Pepe's campaign manager Simón, after screaming his outrage, seeks legal redress. He appeals to the Bureau of

Elections, he raises an outcry in the media. He remains furious.

Ali Cran says, "Now we have to destroy the Michoácuaro PRI."

Pepe sums up his bitterness with an exaggeration: "While we're at it, let's smash them in all of Michoacán."

Ali Cran rejects Pepe's anger. "Of course."

The PRI's control over the police, the bureaucracy, the non-governmental infrastructure is near-complete. Pepe knows this.

Alicito says, "They say you lost. What choices do we have?"

They agree, attacking the post-electoral process will get them nowhere. Simón is nowhere.

Except maybe the media. Television, the international press, they're hungry for An Event. An Event with Much Drama.

Two days after the Morelia ruling Ali Cran says, "Let's undermine Marronando's victory."

"How?"

"We create a vacuum."

Pepe agrees to disappear. Kidnapped, killed? His presence wiped away. By agencies and actions unknown. If people care, if a crisis occurs, if the newspeople take it on, it could lead to a recount, a new election. If no one cares, Pepe will have a month at Rancho Verde; hot country research. What's to be lost, right? They become The Alliance for Constructive Chaos.

Who else needs to know about The Alliance?

Gitana? The trail to Rancho Verde passes through Lomas Secas. Gitana, included, believes the project worth the attempt. But she is afraid. For Pepe, for all of them.

Irini. Through the Jardín, Pepe and she are part of each other. She'll sense Pepe is alive. Pepe finds this uncanny. She's in.

Jorge? Disagreement. Pepe believes it unfair to bring him from so far and tell him nothing. Ali Cran insists Jorge in Michoácuaro must act as he's remembered, the naive gringo who could utter the belief of the naive Mexican, that there was a dead man living in the statue. The naive gringo who was brave enough to speak of this. If Jorge knows Pepe is hiding he'll act unnaturally in the eyes of Michoácuaro.

Simón? Gitana knows Simón is self-aggrandizing, even devious. Yes, in the campaign he did work twenty hours a day on behalf of Pepe. Finally not to be trusted. Ali Cran agrees.

Felicio? Doctor Ortíz tells every story he knows. And some he doesn't. He's out.

Vera? Pepe missing will cause her pain. But without the pain her aunt Constanza would discern the truth. Vera's pain is a price to be paid.

Rubén? Not an issue, can't be trusted.

Pepe tells Vera he's going for a book at the Telecable office. She insists he doesn't need a book. He goes anyway. At the office Irini finishes her coffee. They drive off to the little grove by the trail. Pepe and Ali Cran ride on to Lomas Secas, and to Rancho Verde.

Jorge arrives in Michoácuaro.

Ali Cran cleaned his thumbnail with the knife point. "Pepe's genius, my essential planning."

I turned. "I thought only agro-business was important."

"What's good for my ranchos is good for Michoácuaro, no?"

"That's shameful." Gitana spoke softly.

"You see, my ranchos produce wealth. This is enjoyable. But to create a national crisis, even an international incident to make my Mexico a bit more democratic, this is an experiment worth undertaking."

Pepe said, "It was, we saw this, the moment to force a confrontation. We believe Michoácuaro is ready." He smiled without cheer. "One makes a choice, yes?"

"You sound less than convinced."

Pepe rubbed dirt from his fingers. "Two things have to happen. The Jardín, you've seen it? Remarkable what those Aztecs knew. The town has to secure the permanence of the Jardín. For this I must take office."

Pepe as pivot, as icon of power, didn't seem natural to the man I used to know. "And the second?"

"The maquiladora has to be stopped."

"Hubris, Pepe?"

"A campaign promise." He shrugged. "Maybe that's the same thing."

"So you disappeared. And if they'd reimposed Marranando?"

"I'd have returned on inauguration day and challenged him."

"It stinks. When you create mass demonstrations that can only turn violent, you're fucking around with people's lives."

"We don't fuck!" Ali Cran held his knife by the blade. "You want to fight and not get filthy? Don't be naive, Jorge." He shaved a hair of nail from his left thumb. "How easy to live a good life. Clean gringo morals. Drop into Michoácuaro every few years, give us natives a lesson in ethics."

"And playing Michoácuaro roulette, that's ethical?"

Gitana shook her head. "Today Ali Cran is right."

"Dumb crazy dangerous macho ethics."

Ali Cran glared at his knife. "Is it sane for dye vats to poison a river for ten thousand campesinos?"

"It's a fucked deal, Alicito. All of it. Who are you really worried about, the campesinos or yourself? Your garden?"

Pepe put his hand on my forearm. "Jorge. For me to disappear, it wasn't a noble choice. But better than continue to let the Michoácuaro PRI govern illegally."

"So you disappeared. Doubt-free."

"Many doubts. For example, you. We spoke of telling you, before you came. We feared you'd stay home."

Irini is against informing this Jorge about The Alliance. He arrives, she meets him. His concern for Pepe, her sense he could understand the intents of The Alliance, now lead her to believe he'd be more valuable if they told him everything. She concedes she's attracted to Jorge. Pepe finds this humorous.

Gitana is opposed. Michoácuarans must see Jorge's presence as a force to be reckoned with—that he can act in ways that are different enough to help them overcome a too natural fear of judicial firepower.

Ali Cran trusts both Irini's second analysis, and Gitana's. Pepe says, "Let Jorge decide."

Ali Cran agrees to bringing Jorge out here. "But without telling him why. Because, if he chooses not to come and knows what is happening here, it could be disastrous. To us and him."

Ali Cran sends tall Romero and stocky Ricardo to bring Jorge to Rancho Verde. Jorge eludes them, because they weren't expecting him to resist.

Irini still wants to tell Jorge. Now the others reject this. Let Jorge be seen in Michoácuaro, searching for Pepe.

And how will I respond to Irini now? Thank you, Irini? I said in English, "Thanks a bunch, amigo."

Pepe lifted the plastic off a vat. "These onions, they've survived a week on one litre of water, they're growing." Another vat: "Potatoes. See the little green leaves? Healthy."

Gitana brought me a mug of water. "Gracias." Air-warm, but delicious. "Not good enough, Pepe. You diddle with experiments and Michoácuaro waits to explode."

"Yes, but what is the real bomb? The factory, of course."

"But right now you're the fuse."

"And for the moment we control the matches. The governor sent the judiciales, no? He wants this factory. But many voted for me when I explained its dangers."

Ali Cran said, "Pepe was eloquent."

The pack of cards caught my eye. I played a high trump. "And what about another spark in this keg of Michoácuaro dynamite? The death of the journalist Teófilo Através."

A silence of some seconds. Pepe said, "Why do you believe this Através to be dead?"

Play it all the way: "Because I too witnessed his death."

Ali Cran said, "You've seen a great deal."

I shook my head. "I believe his death to have been an accident."

"What accident?" Gitana, hands on her lap, stared at them.

"His throat got cut. A pane of glass. He died quickly."

No one spoke for maybe half a minute.

Gitana glared at me. "Who told you this?"

I presented my hands, palms out, and shrugged. "Rubén?"

I gave her my wannest smile. "Can you imagine Rubén telling me such a thing?"

Ali Cran said, "You've mastered one or two lessons, Jorge."

"Two or three."

Pepe nodded. "Teófilo is back there." He pointed vaguely toward Michoácuaro. "Rubén came to me, he explained." He leaned forward. "Emilia had gone to meet Teófilo. Also Toni Estracho, Rubén Reyes Ponce, and my tenant Ernesto were there. At the meeting she threatened Através. She said he must not write the story, ever. If he did, he would die."

I said, "About tax scandals, the old mayor, the fat bishop."

Ali Cran sniggered. Gitana's eyes were watering.

"And where are we if a journalist's death is just brushed aside?"

"They didn't plan to harm Teófilo." Pepe thought a moment. "I believe that. But, they said, if he wrote this story, every day he'd have to wonder, Do I die today? An empty threat, maybe. So Teófilo dove through the closed window, the glass cut his throat. Rubén came to me. What should he do? I—consulted." He glanced toward Ali Cran. "We wanted to throw the blame on Emilia. But we couldn't figure how."

I truly did not want to hear this from Pepe.

"What else? Blame Rubén, punish him? You see, I believe Rubén's version." He shook his head. "We buried Teófilo."

I said in English, "You hid the body."

Now he nodded. "And what would you have done?"

What indeed. I said nothing.

"We could have left him. He'd be found. And the discovery of the body would be reported to Rubén." He smiled. "Rubén would have to investigate."

"Where'd you bury him?"

Pepe chuckled. With a wave of his hand he introduced the new narrator, Ali Cran. "Tell him."

"We gave him a Christian burial." Ali Cran spoke solemnly. "He's lying on top of María de Lourdes Disporatedo Suarez."

Gitana smiled.

"Where?"

"Where he won't be found. In the cemetery."

Ali Cran nodded. "He'll lie there as long as the Disporatedo family pays for the plot."

"At least his own family should know he's dead."

"Pepe made inquiries. Através wasn't married."

"His parents? His mistress? Friends? Come on, Pepe."

"Again, we were faced with a terrible choice. We decided for Michoácuaro."

A solid wall. "What did Rubén tell Avéspare?"

"The truth." Ali Cran grinned. "Teófilo was on a pil-grimage. To Lourdes."

I suddenly heard myself laugh.

Pepe Legarto playing with the fate of the town. Ali Cran the dissembler. Gitana, scheming along with them. Rubén, acting in the line of other duties. My friends in Michoácuaro.

Ali Cran said, "Hungry, Jorge?"

"Pepe." I stood up. "Come back now."

From beside the cot Ali Cran took a paper bag. Inside, some small scaly brown-green fruit. He cut one open. It looked like custard with black seeds. With a spoon he scooped out a heap of the flesh, and handed it to me. "Taste."

"What?"

"A fine cherimoya. Have you tried it?"

"This is stupid—"

"Try."

Lip to palate, creamy sweet. Like banana and papaya, hinting of pineapple. Vanilla. A touch of coconut. "Not bad."

Pepe said, "Cherimoyas alone could revitalize Michoá-cuaro. But single crops are foolish."

I took another scoop. "This fruit, some potatoes grown on mounds, and the town's crawling with judiciales."

"Many potatoes. I'm pleased you've been to El Jardín."

"Pepe, listen to me. The Morelia police, they found a corpse. They think it's you."

"Maybe they're right," said Ali Cran. "At times they are."

Pepe laughed. "Will they say it's not, before the elec-tion?"

"What's your decision, Jorge?" Another bleak Alicito smile. "You're with us now. Going to turn against us?"

With them. Under the same tarpaulin. "Pepe. Make a choice. I'm leaving."

He shook his head. The little smile, ironic, gentle.

Gitana and I rode off. Much, much had slipped away. Who was this Pepe? And Irini. Shapes in my mind whirred,

whirred some more. The sun was high, my butt sore, nothing was whole. Gitana and I stayed silent all the way back.

At the corral Nicandro and another man, Señor Tall, saddled our dumpy horses. If I'd gone with them that night? I mounted, and nodded to Tall. He returned the nod, polite.

We started off. The dogs set up a howling, as if bewitched. My sweeper Moisés de Jesús believed dogs yowl at a full moon because it tells them they owe their souls to their human masters. Despising the truth, the dogs howl in anger. The baying of the rancho dogs turned funereal, filled with sorrow. Nicandro led us through the narrow barranca and the howl of dogs was gone.

Teófilo in the grave. Pepe in hiding. I tried to evaluate, but keeping my thighs from rubbing too hard against the horse's flanks took all my concentration.

The sun was a width from the horizon when we reached the Jeep. "No judiciales?"

Nicandro shook his head. "They've reported to their lieutenant, surely."

The road back was clear. At Nicandro's house we unhooked the trailer. Tomorrow I'd take it over to Rubén. And Nicandro? "Nicandro, about the judiciales. Will you be okay?"

He thought about it. "I'll say we went out hunting." He smiled. "It's almost the truth."

I left. At the plaza Pepe's recorded voice blasted through a loudspeaker. It promised a hundred new agricultural jobs. The coffin seller, waiting in the dusk, stared at me as I drove by. Up past Ernesto's gates— I slammed on the brakes. A heap of something in front of the Chilango's driveway. I rolled backwards. Pulled on the emergency brake, got out.

The heap was Blaze. Flies buzzed at his ears, in his nose, along the gash of dry blood from neck to shoulder. Through flies, glazey eyeballs stared at me.

Shit bastard Ernie.

TWENTY-TWO

I locked Pepe's gates, leaned against the Jeep and did nothing. First time in thirteen hours. Rage at Ernie drained into loathing. My head ached, my rear was sore, my thighs itched with burn. Fireflies sparked tiny messages.

What, return and expect to find people as they were before? Naive. For Pepe, Ali Cran, Gitana, all of them, hiding Teófilo Através' body in a cemetery made sense.

Rubén the cop deals with corruption and status, his law the place where the one meets the other. Gitana the herbalist finds the body inhabited by death and life, her role to discourage the former, enhance the latter. Irini, not from here, practises her fraud and guile more softly than the rest. Ali Cran persists in his tricky ways: when there's life there's betrayal. And Pepe? Educated in Europe and North America, participant in high-tech communities, reviving forgotten farming procedures. Asserting murder balances rape, playing out a lethal charade to keep a factory from destroying a river. Pepe remains a Michoácuaran.

And I the eccentric, all outraged about an old dog. I'd thought I understood Michoácuaro, just a little. Wrong.

I locked the Jeep. Very un-Michoácuaran of me. In the kitchen I poured a beer. On the veranda and beyond, a spooky lack of sound, Blaze's absence hanging thick in the foliage. I stared at seven coconuts. Incapable of helping an old dog but I'd bought into a coconut cure. Why not? What's there to lose?

I found a sharp knife. It took only a minute for the coco's skin, fibery green, to dull the blade. The machete. With care I hacked off shell. Drops of liquid bled out. Most stayed inside. I widened the hole. In the open air, as instructed, I balanced the fruit upright and covered it with a napkin.

I had wound down. I went to bed. Snatches of dreams followed me the night long. My friends were my nemesis. Pepe, Ali Cran, Gitana. Irini too.

And Alaine. Out of place in this Mexican town… But sharp in central detail, muted at her sides. Neither smile nor frown, not neutral, not helping. She says, Yes. What? I try to ask this but make no sound. Her words form: Of course. Alaine, I whisper. She can't hear. The best I can do. And she: Now you will. I watch as she weakens, and fades. I cry out, I love you. I hear my words, I loved you.

Ernie's war-cry. The splash. My pillow was wet. From the pool, I thought at first. Sweat.

Go back to tierra caliente, convince Pepe to come back. First find Irini.

Over at the big house Vera gave me a subdued smile. Alicia in a corner nursed a doll. "Vera, could you make me breakfast?"

"Sí, señor." She brightened. I called Irini. No answer. Where the hell was she? Vera and I spoke of what she'd cook the day Pepe returned.

Now I ate her excellent huevos rancheros, high bright orange yolks. "Excellent eggs, Vera." My lip felt better, healing well. Because of Vera's green gunk.

Vera had relaxed. "You heard the shooting last night?"

"Nothing. Was someone hurt?"

"They say the fountain in the plaza was red with blood." More, more. "Whose?"

"It was terrible to see, they say."

"Anybody reported wounded or dead?"

She shook her head. "I'm very frightened, señor."

And she looked scared. "Vera, Pepe will return soon."

She nodded faintly. "If it's God's will."

I sighed. I said I'd ask Rubén about the fountain. The gate opened, a vehicle drove in.

Vera went to the window. "Señora Irini."

Good. "Why wasn't the gate locked?"

"She called, señor. To say she was coming."

No one tells me anything. I got up. "Before she leaves, please ask her to come over."

"But she's here to see you." A hint of grin.

"Of course." I went out. I felt her eyes on my back.

"Oh hello," Irini said.

"Hello yourself. Come with me." I heard her behind me. I went out to the veranda.

She saw the coconuts. With a smile she rubbed her cheek.

I leaned on the rail. "Your friend Ernesto killed Blaze."

She nodded. "An old dog. Sad."

"He bashed his head in. You saw him, outside Ernie's gate?"

"No." She sat beside the open coconut.

I watched her. "You should've told me about Rancho Verde."

She stroked the coconut shell. "You have amoebas?"

"I'd have played along."

She looked into the coconut. "I've heard about this cure." She looked at me. "Long ago, visiting my parents in Morocco."

"Damn it, Irini—" I went in, found a tumbler, came back. Poured the liquid. Two-thirds full. One small fly. I plucked it out.

"Ever had coconut milk?"

"No." Suddenly I could trace where Irini had been, her pattern of disquiet over the last days. I sensed her confused loyalties and my anger dried away. I forgave her, knowing forgiveness wasn't the issue. I wanted to hold her, stroke her hair, kiss her eyelids. Be with her days long. Instead I said, "What's the difference between a milk and a meat coconut?"

"The milk are younger." She smiled. She was reading me. "In the north you get mostly meat coconuts. Easier to ship."

I said, "I saw Pepe yesterday."

"I knew you'd find him," she said.

I sipped. Diluted, like watery honey. A hint of cherimoya. I got it down. "You could've saved me a lot of anguish."

She shook her head. "I agreed to secrecy without thinking I'd ever want to tell you."

I shook my head. Too late to be part of their planning. "Tell me something." Not too late for everything. "At Felicio's, you figured we might guess."

She touched my hand lightly, "Pepe says you watch, you listen and understand."

"You came to Christmas dinner to guide our talk."

"I did my best." A chuckle.

The power of small laughs. "You left, you broke in, you stole Pepe's notebook."

She stepped close. Her head hung down in dramatic penance. She told me she knew Pepe made no notes about disappearing. She drove to the casa, she has Pepe's keys. How to signal to Jorge, search out Ali Cran at Lomas Secas.

She realized her car in the compound was a mistake. She backed out, parked up the hill, returned to Pepe's office. But Jorge and Felicio drove in, too soon. She panicked. Make the office look burglarized! She tips over some files. They unlock the veranda door. She slides out the back, waits till they're inside, keeps to the shadows, slips away.

I set the palm of my hand on her hip, the other hand on her cheek.

She smiled, drew tight against me and raised her head. Her eyes were that sweet warm green. "What they're doing, I know it's necessary. But it scares me."

"You went back and forth to Rancho Verde."

"I brought what Pepe needed." Her arms held tight around my waist. "And what do you think of the new rancho?"

"The botany?"

"Ali Cran sees into the earth." Her glance went out across the valley. "He listens to the sand and the soil. He hears the flow of water."

"And soon Rancho Verde will be green." I let my hand slide down her soft hair. "He'll be rich, he and Pepe."

She shook her head. "Pepe trains people to use their land to grow what grows best. Alicito has two ranches. He uses what Pepe learns."

"They remain friends."

She nodded. "Only, their goals are different." Lightly she kissed my mouth. "If the Jardín succeeds, Michoácuaro will be richer. Pepe wants this, very much. Alicito sees how a piece of land can be transformed, according to its promise."

"While Pepe sees what used to be there?"

"Of course. Without Pepe, Ali Cran wouldn't ever have heard of, say, arracachas. Let alone know how to grow them." She lay her hand on my cheek, smiled, and with one finger traced my lip to the wound. "For him a seed is a child. He listens, he brings it to the best soil."

"He chats with baby arracachas"

She sniffed a laugh. "The Aztecs didn't discover all the secrets." She brought her face to mine. A long kiss from warm lips, slow-moving taut.

I opened my eyes. Two outsize white butterflies swirling loops over her head flirted across the garden. "What'll you do?"

"Weeds grow. If Pepe's there or not."

We held each other, we kissed. Minutes had no existence. I felt safe from the past and free of the future. We kissed, we talked, we began learning, we searched with hands and tongues and small words—

"Señor!" At the door, Vera. A quick kiss. We went to open. "Señor!" Her face was awash, her breath came short.

"What's happened?"

"Oh señora!" She collapsed against Irini's chest.

Irini held her. "Vera, what?"

Vera wiped her cheeks, her nose. "They've found him—"

Irini caught my eye. "Who, Vera? Señor Pepe?"

A hoarse breath. "He—his—his body, they found it."

The body near Morelia. "I'll call Rubén." Or could it really be Pepe? Had I led the judiciales to Rancho Verde? At the house I dialed. Busy.

Irini found brandy, poured a glass, made Vera sip. "Laura called to tell her about Pepe." She added in English, "A good sign. Laura's the queen of misinformation."

Vera's eyes were glazed. I dialed again. Still busy. "I'll find Rubén."

"Call us." A quiver now at the edge of her mouth.

Her pickup blocked the Jeep, the keys inside. I drove it out. Blaze's corpse was gone.

At the plaza I parked. And felt afraid. People stood about, small still groups. I walked by the sandbags to Rubén's office. No electioneering. No *Time* magazine. No one moved. The plaza felt new, I was an intruder, a bug, crushable. If I stood still. I strode to Rubén's door. Guarded by Pincho, Dopes-do-dope tee-shirt Puño Filo, two others.

"El jefe is waiting for me."

Pincho smirked. "He's gone."

"He'll have your balls when he hears—"

"We must all be careful for our balls, señor."

I backed off. Kept moving, across the plaza. Felt heads turn my way. And knew where I was: in the grown-up version of

Alicia's terrarium, the plaza a pit filled with all manner of scorpions: Uzi-bearers, lip-slicers, note-writers. In front of the bank
stood Eliseo. Three steps up, to his side; not high above the pit
but safer. Inside the bank, three tellers and no customers.

"Eliseo. What's happened?"

He shook his head. "As you see, nothing."

"Someone said a body was found. Maybe Don Pepe."

"I haven't heard this."

"What about blood in the fountain?"

He frowned. "Some say three men, they were in the
Higo Negro cantina, very drunk. One has a pestilence. They
say he thought pissing blood into the fountain would be
funny."

"This happened?"

"Three drunks? marching into the plaza? the judiciales
don't see them?" He shrugged.

"And the blood?"

"By the fountain," he whispered, "are drops of crimson.
But blood dries brown, not like polish for a lady's nails."

I nodded. "Thank you, Eliseo. Be careful."

"If God permits it, Señor Jorge."

Back through the pit. At Rubén's office who should step
out but the jefe himself. I called. Rubén, Puño Filo, Pincho
and two others headed my way.

"Good to see you, Jorge. And what of my trailer?"

Damn. "This afternoon, okay?"

A grim smile. "Who knows when I'll need it."

"They say a body's been found. Maybe Pepe's."

"The one near Morelia, you know about this."

"No others?"

"How many do you want?"

My active entry into The Alliance for Constructive
Chaos: "Do they know, was it Pepe?"

"The dentist is on a holiday in Miami. The investigation
continues."

"But meanwhile people are talking about this Morelia corpse."

"Yes." He nodded. "You think it's Pepe?"

"I pray it's not. But how could I know?"

"What in fact do you know?"

I looked him square in the eye. "Not a thing, Rubén."

"Why do I not believe you." He shook his head, weary.

I scanned the plaza. A man was walking sharply toward us. "And here?"

A blurt of disgust. "The governor has decreed tomorrow's election is illegal. It won't happen. And Marranando has disappeared from the hospital."

I said, "Who'll keep people from voting, the judiciales?"

The man reached us, Simón, Pepe's campaign manager. He nodded to me. Tears in his eyes. He addressed Rubén: "Pepe's dead, yes?"

"Why do you say this?"

"For the love of God! You've got the report!"

I said, "What report?"

Simón glared. "Near Morelia they found a body, burned. A man, wearing the Helvex watch I've seen on Pepe many times."

Rubén said, "It's being investigated, Simón."

"Two people told me, Rubén! In hours everybody'll know. We need a statement. We've got to mourn his death in a controlled way. A ceremony. To avert a greater tragedy."

"We've got no confirmation."

"Pepe is dead! Will you explain this to the town?" His voice quivered. "Or pay the price."

"I'm waiting for verification. It's that simple."

"Listen to me, brother Rubén. Simple is, the town is full of Pepe's supporters. Simple is, if they believe he was murdered by the judiciales, when night comes we'll have a riot. Or before. And the judiciales will have an excuse to avenge their dead associate. They'll come in with guns."

I said, "But if the Morelia body isn't Pepe?"

"The watch is Pepe's, Señor."

"Or stolen from him? Was it one of a kind? Often even fine watches are mass produced."

"Your doubt is reasonable. But Pepe's friends will still assume the judiciales have murdered him."

Rubén's tight face said, To a mob of campesinos, the judiciales and the police are one. "I have to use your telephone. Take me past your courageous deputies."

Rubén led me in.

Simón grabbed his elbow. "Resolve this, Rubén."

I called Irini. No conclusive evidence the corpse was Pepe. She repeated this and I heard Vera crying. In English I described the mood at the plaza. "It's deadly serious."

"Come back now," she said.

Back to Irini's pickup. In the driver's seat, Lieutenant Blanco. I said, "Lieutenant. This truck's owner doesn't like others at the wheel."

"Get in, señor." He gazed ahead. "We will speak."

I stood still.

He turned. His voice growled. "Get-in-the-truck."

I got in.

"Did I explain, you will remain in Michoácuaro?"

"I'm right here."

"Ah. And tierra caliente?"

"Tierra caliente. But that's part of greater Michoácuaro."

"Do not mock, señor. These are dangerous times." His scowl chilled me. "Do-you-understand?"

"I apologize, Lieutenant, for causing an inconvenience."

He opened the door, and glanced my way. "Next time my men will not aim for a trailer." He stepped out and walked away.

I didn't say, And leave my acid-burnt body in a ditch? Blanco knew this wasn't Pepe.

Pepe's gate was open. Behind the Jeep, the blue Nissan. I parked. The Nissan's appendage Toni sat behind the wheel.

Our eyes met, and held. Eyes I knew. High above my face. The flick of the knife on my lip. I touched my lip. It felt tender. Toni's day would come.

I was overwhelmed by a desire to turn to the casita, to sleep, to awaken at a better time. But I went the other way.

TWENTY-THREE

In Pepe's living room sat Emilia Avéspare, Ignacio Avéspare, Ernesto Montemayor. And Irini, who gave me a tiny eyebrow-raise. Young Avéspare and Ernie stood, and shook my hand.

"Señor."

"Señor."

"Señor."

"Señor." I nodded at Avéspare-madre: "Señora. I thank you for the camera."

"Señor." She nodded. "And now there is little time left to avoid violence."

"I agree." I didn't see Vera. Off casting powerful spells, draining anger from the town? Young Ignacio chewed gum. Emilia wore a white blouse; her skirt, dark blue, spread wide from her waist. Ernie wore a necktie so it had to be a serious meeting. "What will you do?"

"It's what you must do, señor. Either prove Pepe Legarto is dead, or alive."

"Wait a minute—"

"If you prove him dead, your sorrow will silence the city. We will accept your mourning.

"Señora, how can I do that?" To trace the pathways from yesterday, from last week, maybe that's possible. To trace cobbled stories as they contaminate each other and produce exaggeration and myth, that can't be done.

"My son will sponsor the mass. Bishop Delcoz will con-vince Michoácuaro much would be lost from violence."

"And if Pepe's alive?"

She said, "Don Ernesto?"

Ernie got up. He spoke to me in Spanish. "We know each other as neighbours, señor. Our acquaintance is my pleasure. Despite differences in conduct and philosophy, we remain on the best terms." Confirming Irini's sense of his formal power, even charisma. In Spanish.

Ignacio concentrated on the floor tiles.

"If Pepe returns, EspórConMex and El Jardín de los Viejos can live happily side by side."

"I don't understand. How?" I heard Ernie, but felt Emilia drawing me in close enough for the Chilango's words to spin their deal. Why, finally, did they need me for anything here?

Ernie smiled at Irini, two strangers, one transaction. "Señora Farolla. Between EspórConMex and the Jardín the question is one of clean water, yes?"

"Lots of problems, Ernesto." She mouthed his name with apathy. The lines in the green of her eyes shot out disdain.

"If the Jardín water is clean, you'll have no objection."

"The factory will bleed poison. It's in its nature."

Ernie's smile was infinitely cordial. "I've negotiated with the Department of Commerce. We all want to improve the quality of life in Michoácuaro. The government will present the Jardín with a Lavewasser Scrubber with a capacity of one hundred twenty thousand litres. This insures clean water to the Jardín, forever."

I glanced at Irini. "A what scrubber?"

"A monster filter, made in Denmark." She looked as if she'd been end-run.

"What happens to water that's not filtered?"

"It flows away." Ernie smiled.

"Filthy, downstream."

"Of no concern to you."

I said in English, "You're something, Ernie."

Ignacio Avéspare, palms together, hands hanging, leaned forward. "The filter comes only if proof of Legarto's state arrives in Michoácuaro. Alive, or dead." A whisper.

I shook my head. "If he's not alive, the garden's dead anyway."

"You'll do what you can, señor." No request; a prediction.

My estimate of young Avéspare's macho level rose a couple of notches. "How do I find Pepe when others have failed?" For effect I threw in, "As they failed to find Teófilo Através."

That stopped our chat. No one looked my way. Till Ignacio said, "Your reputation, señor. We hope you'll take time to—concentrate. Or however you practise your profession. For the sake of our city." A forced smile. "As a favour to my mother."

"And for the sake of your investments."

Emilia Avéspare leaned toward me. "You are not a generous man, señor. Your range of what is valuable is narrow."

"You make large accusations, señora."

"You have no sympathy for our people. But you don't need to, you come from a wealthy nation. That wealth, it provides you with a profession—"

"At which, señora, I work rather hard."

"I'm sure of it. But such professions, they exist because a high level of wealth allows them to be practised. You can have a great education system, señor, a great medical system, only by paying your teachers and your doctors well. They're paid either from private money, or from public money which was private money before it became tax revenue. That money, all of it, was made, señor. Made, as in making a profit. And from it, paying taxes."

I had the weird sense that young Avéspare, hands again together as in prayer, was now guiding his mother's words.

"To make profits, señor, people put money into a project. They risk this money— No, please, hear me out. Some
projects are safe, some less so. Local projects, let's say.
Sometimes, for the good of one's community, one must
invest in local projects. My son and I, señor, we wish to help
our community prosper. We do this as we know best,
through the city's economy. You come here, señor, you enjoy
our hospitality. What do you contribute? Don't condemn our
efforts here." Emilia Avéspare sat back. "We live here."

Impressive. Beyond her web, behind the smoke, a clear
vision; more than avarice? "I support your desire, señora, to
help Michoácuaro prosper. I mean this, despite the irony
which sometimes rises in me. But coming from afar I see
what you cannot. So I fear for you. Chemically poisoned
water will destroy the lives of campesinos downstream. And
the health of your city as well. The creation of North
American wealth has contaminated our lakes and rivers.
Contamination has produced disease. Now we have to clean
up our water systems. At great cost. Don't make our mistakes." A simple speech, I thought. Likely not good for
much.

"Señor. There are certain perfections we cannot afford.
EspórConMex will come into existence and evolve only if it
supports itself." She drew her skirt close, as if consolidating
her authority. "The government will provide a Lavewasser
Scrubber. Then our two enterprises can live side by side. The
effort must now be yours. Use the talents of your profession.
See Pepe Legarto wherever he is. If he's dead, tell us where,
and how. If he's alive, bring him home." She stood. "Uncertainty allows violence. This is your responsibility."

Ignacio and Ernie got up also. Ernie said, in English, "Do
it, ol' buddy."

"Thank you for the visit, señora, señores." My responsibility?

We watched the car pull out. The engine died away.

I took Irini's hand. She squeezed my fingers. She said, "They're right. Pepe's got to come back. It's the moment."

"Yep." Pepe back would give him municipal clout. But Pepe back would provide the calm for bringing EspórConMex its subsidies. Pepe back would highlight the irony of convergence. No way around it, he had to come back. And since timing was all, now was way better than later. This time we'd have to convince him. Not we; Irini. "But if I leave, the judiciales will know. This time they'll be ready, and follow me to Pepe."

She'd go. Four hours to Rancho Verde, longer back in the dark. Near midnight before he arrived. No choice. She bussed my cheek, the kiss of a friend. "We meet here? Or my house."

A flash of insight, simple stock-in-trade for my profession: "At Felicio's. Out of town."

She considered this. She agreed.

"Your thoughts are elsewhere, Irini."

"Some of them." She squeezed my fingers.

"Tempted by that scrubber?"

She glared. "Of course." She kissed me hard on the mouth and I came back in kind. Then she turned and was gone.

I stepped outside. My Mexican love affair. At the casita I hacked open a new coconut. What might happen before I drank it.

Down below, my side of the fence, a lost lady chicken, a brown one. She clucked at the metal, no way through. She marched up, down. Suddenly on the other side, a rustle, a brown rooster. He saw her. One of his ladies? He there, she here, no way through. He too paraded along the fence, down, back. And found the passage. He doodle-dooed away. She ran to the sound, spotted the passage, fluttered through. He mounted her, one-two-three, and they went their separate ways. Thank you señora. And you, señor.

Someone at the door. I opened. Jefe Reyes, eyes red, scowling. "What's going on, amigo?"

He brushed me aside though there was plenty of room. His radio crackled. He sat. "The whisky you brought, you have a bottle at least as good for Pepe. I need a drink."

I found Pepe's Chivas and poured it.

He sipped. And smiled. "No, my single malt was better."

"Okay, what's up?"

He looked at his watch. "At sunset, our disaster." He shook his head. "Two rallies. Simultaneous, on the plaza."

"Shit. What rallies?"

"The MMM called the first. They say I'm hiding the fact that Pepe's dead."

"Word does get around."

He frowned. "And I'm told Simón's now saying this all over town: that he holds Delcoz to blame for Pepe's death. Because Delcoz built up an atmosphere of hate by preaching lies about Pepe till someone killed him."

"Damn stupid of Simón."

"Poison. But they say Delcoz is—concerned. So," his head shook, "there'll be a counter-rally, called by a few decent citizens. You've heard of Ramus Dei?"

I nodded. Rubén, eavesdropping on Bárbara's phone calls? "Does the bishop go along?"

"Sure. His chance to scald the town's soul a whole lot more." Rubén's grim little smile twitched. "The mob burns down the Hotel Domicilio, the Telecable station, the cantinas. The Jardín. And of course the Movimiento por un Michoácuaro Moderno. All that modernization stuff."

"And the judiciales?"

"They'll kill to keep order." A bitter laugh. "And after, the MMM will blame the judiciales and me. And the judiciales, they'll all get drunk to celebrate and shoot more people."

"And you, my friend? What can you do?"

He shrugged. "I've spoken with Emilia. The PRI is telling people to stay home. A few will listen." He shook his head. "Not the MMM or those with Delcoz."

"And you can't stop it? Seize control?"

"Against Blanco?" He gave a bitter little laugh. "People already say I refuse to find Pepe's killer. Or I protect his killer. Or I've brought the judiciales here. Maybe I killed Pepe myself, strangled him. For my bishop."

"That's nuts."

"Yes." His smile was sad now. "I fear for my town." He leaned toward me. "So—today is the day I must have your help, hombre."

Him too. "But what can I do?"

"Make a statement. Don Jorge who knows us so well."

"Stop it."

"Tell them the corpse isn't Pepe."

"Why don't you say that?"

"They wouldn't believe me." He stared at the ground. "Anyway there's no evidence. But you could say, No, it's not Pepe. And Pepe will come back."

"Will he?"

"How the fuck should I know!"

"I don't get it. How does saying Pepe isn't dead stop the rallies?"

"We stop Simón's rally. And Delcoz has nothing to attack."

It had a looney logic to it. I jangled between silly bravado and fear. Happy Holidays, Don Jorge!

We talked, and drank. Me too, three-four-five whiskies. It wasn't my place to participate here, the gringo from northern lands has nothing to teach here; but Rubén and whisky overcame my doubt and my scruples. We had to keep the sparks from reaching tinder, stop the rally from flaring out of control. And not get burned in the process. Soak the kindling beforehand, dampen the ground. Create some metaphoric downpour. Knowing Pepe really was alive helped.

As people headed to the plaza, we'd saturate the streets with my message and dispel both the Pepe partisans and the Delcoz congregation before they became fired into rampage.

I worked out some phrases. Rubén corrected my Spanish. We'd ride in Pepe's Jeep. Rubén telephoned Pincho. "Bring a loudspeaker system up to Don Pepe's house. What's happening on the plaza?" He listened, he nodded. "Okay." He put the phone down.

"What's he say?"

"They're setting up the stage with the big speakers." A worried scowl. "It'll be a battle of the amplifiers."

Pincho and another deputy arrived and clamped the speaker to the Jeep's roll bar. Rubén poured more Chivas. I said, "We should be sober."

"Jorge. At our moment of dying, wouldn't it break the heart to recall this bottle of gold standing here, half full?"

I raised my glass. "To our long-range health."

"We will survive." We drank. "Or go down in flames."

I thought of Irini. One last kiss, her firm sweet lips. Yes, I was capable of romantic drivel. We drank again. I thought, To you... Rubén finished his. But he only had to drive. "Rubén, maybe you shouldn't drive."

"Whisky makes the steady hand."

For him this was true. "I mean, maybe people won't listen if you're sitting next to me."

He considered that. "No. I have to protect you."

We'd left even loco logic behind, so I didn't argue. In truth, he'd do his best for us. Which might be pretty good. If it worked, our greater glory would reflect on him.

We drove off. The cathedral bells started to toll. Ha! The signal for our intervention. Dozens of men, walking into town. I wanted the Jeep windows closed. Rubén insisted mine be wide open, Michoácuaro had to see who was speaking.

"They'll know me by my accent."

"They need to look at your face."

That bothersome thought kept burbling: the face of North American imperialism, vintage 1990. Like many of my predecessors, I rejected that label. I was here to bring peace, and civilization, and so on. I tossed the thought aside.

Down through files of men, toward the pit. A few women. The corner, the turn. Coffin seller sat on his curb. "Start?"

Rubén shrugged. "Sure." I flicked on the amplifier. A whine of feedback filled the air. Skullface whirled, his hat slipped, his hand whipped out to grab it. He'd actually moved.

Hundreds of white shirts filled the plaza, a kind of informal communion. The clanking tune of the merry-go-round gave melody to tolling bells and human buzz. I adjusted a couple of knobs. Here we go.

I spoke into the mike. I explained, my voice echoing off walls, I was a friend of Pepe Legarto, a friend of Michoácuaro, a friend of calm and of civic responsibility. They might have seen me on television years ago, speaking of the statue of Abelardo Núñez. Repeated. Repeated.

We passed by the Avéspare house, our amplifier on maximum. Groups of people under the arcades, by the fountain, stared at the Jeep. What was the mood?

No Betsy *Time*, no Televisa trucks. Worrying, worrying. The cathedral blocked the sun, its shadows long. The bells seemed to toll faster, as if to drown me out.

I went on, "I lived here, my friends, for a year. After the great earthquake. The cathedral clock had stopped at 7:19. My whole time here it said 7:19. It was a year of peace, for me, for you, peace and friendship. I've returned to Michoácuaro. My friend Pepe Legarto needed me. Even from far away I knew he needed me." To drink tequila with, argue with, not for this bullshit. "He is not dead. He'll be with you soon." Repeat. More. Repeat. I realized I was getting heady on the bullshit. "He'll be—"

Sploosh on the windshield. A great gob of red, a very ripe tomato. Rubén held our pace.

Go for it. All the way: "He'll be back tomorrow. Midday tomorrow." Rubén glanced my way. We hadn't discussed announcing a time for Pepe's return. In for a centavo, in for a peso. "I see him, he salutes you, you the peaceful citizens of Michoácuaro." Rubén looked really worried now.

We drove downhill from the plaza, face on to the hundreds approaching. Rubén glared. I started again: "I am a friend of Pepe Legarto, a friend of Michoácuaro—"

We turned a corner. Many people. The bells rang out. I asked the crowd to stay away, great danger lay at the plaza. I improvised: Forces from beyond Michoácuaro are among us, alacranes with guns. Keep your children indoors. I see Pepe at this moment, toasting the safety of his town. I lapsed into my prepared speech, "Pepe needed me, I returned to—ughgh!"

My neck. I wiped away very rotten avocado flesh and a hard slimy pit. I stifled a blast of curses. Glop dribbled down under my shirt.

I saw a woman grab a man's arm but he strode away. I saw several women holding children, men beside them, standing in place. I saw deaf Gertrudis, as we drove by she grabbed the Jeep's window frame and walked with us, "It's good you do this." I squeezed her forearm, she let go. How could she know what I was saying? I felt a counterfeit high—so much manipulation, so fake. An egg splattered on the windshield.

We turned the corner. Blanco stood in the entryway of the Marranando house, hands on hips, watching. I cut the bit about dangerous outside forces but left in Pepe's return, what the hell. Hi there, Lieutenant, as you requested I'm still in town.

Up one street and down another, to the centre, away, back. On the plaza, loudspeakers screeched out a tape of mariachi guitars. But people were listening to me—likely they'd heard the mariachis a thousand times, and we were the new act. A small crowd did gather, but nowhere near as large as the horde that toppled the statue. Our scam might be working.

Sunset. Around the square, around again. Mariachi blare. Twilight. I should have taped my message, my voice muscles ached. Around, around, around.

A black panel truck screeched to a stop ten metres in front of us. Rubén braked hard. A figure leapt from the truck, then two more holding stubby dark things. Rubén drew his pistol—

Outside my window, Betsy *Time*. Pointing a microphone at my face. Two men with her, Mexican reporters, more mikes. Great.

She spoke a stilted Spanish, complete with peninsular lisp. "Theñor! What'th going on? What'th happening to the rally?'

I turned off our sound system. Mariachis wailed, bells crashed. "You nearly missed the excitement."

They'd gone to Morelia to follow the charred body story. The double rally was announced and they rushed back. Was it true the gringo had announced visions of Pepe Legarto?

"Yes yes." Me, humble. "That's what I announced, it's true."

She said, her English hard, "Are you shitting me?"

The Mexico City reporters grinned.

I spoke a prim professorial English: "You watch your tongue, young lady." I raised my eyebrows. "And what you write."

She promised, a worthless gesture. Out went my words, out into the universe.

I saw it all, as it would be seen: A man disappears into the void; this is small news. He's murdered; headlines, large then small. But disappearance, death and resurrection? What a story! A gringo eyewitness is quoted, then featured. Ever deeper into the muck of glory.

I repeated my message for half a dozen reporters and a couple of cameramen: Yes Pepe's been held against his will. No I don't know by whom. Yes he's safe now, in hiding, but tomorrow at noon... More, more. Adrenalin gushed, my tongue ran on, I gilded the bougainvillea. Yes sometimes I see into the future, I knew Pepe would be among us soon. Yes this aptitude came from my research—

The mariachis stopped. And the bells. Wonderful silence.

More reporters arrived. "Tomorrow Pepe Legarto will answer your questions." I nodded to Rubén. He eased the Jeep by the black truck. The reporters followed. He speeded up and we drove past the statue rubble. At the platform a couple of men were unplugging sound equipment. We turned left, and up the hill. Neither of us spoke, no adrenalin left for words. I unlocked, Rubén drove in. I opened his door. "Come on, I know about another bottle."

He got out. "Jorge, truly you have balls."

"Lucky I can look into the future, no?" I winked. And felt ashamed of this hero self, that infernal Crusader Rabbit bringing truth and americano justice to the unwashed masses. Neither verity nor fairness here, just a lot of street theatre, psychodrama for the masses. Including scamming Rubén.

"You truly had me believing you." He scratched his nose. "I've lost a litre of water in the last hour, and not because I pissed my pants." He giggled. "Yes, let's drink Pepe's whisky."

We sat in the kitchen. Under my shirt dry avocado glop itched. I mixed martinis. Rubén claimed to esteem my martinis. We drank to health, and health once more. "Pepe will be back."

"Such luck would be more than luck."

I shrugged.

"Jorge, I owe you very much." He looked at me with great intensity. "It's good you and I rode in the Jeep." He nodded. "Whatever you need, if it's in my power, I'll give you." He closed his eyes, as for an oath. "So long as I live."

"Happy to have helped."

"One of my houses, rent-free, whenever you wish. Bárbara will cook for you, your favourite foods. In the cellar of the prison, confiscated from a very dangerous criminal, is some fine peyote, it's yours. At the Hotel Domicilio are two new whores, both very clean."

Okay, he'd made the offer. Why not? "You mean anything, truly?"

A huge sweep of his hand.

I raised my glass. "Your health." We drank. "Before these media people leave town, will you call a press conference? To announce you've discovered the body of Teófilo Através."

"Jorge!"

"We'll create a story. For his family and friends it's important to know he's dead. You'll report where he's buried."

He looked at me sideways. "And this is?"

"But in the cemetery, no? On top of María de Lourdes."

"Alicito told you." He grinned, sheepish. "He promised silence."

"So Ali Cran knew? Interesting. But why should Ali Cran tell me about Teófilo?"

"Then how did you know?"

"But I have great skills, no?" Adrenalin and Scotch spoke for me and I let my grin grow. "I look forward, I see Pepe tomorrow at noon in the plaza. I look backward, I see two, three people dig into the grave of Señora Lourdes. They deposit Teófilo's corpse in her embrace."

His warmth was gone. His chin hung to his chest. His eyes watched me as if despite weariness he dared not look away.

"Well?"

He rubbed his forehead with the fingers of both hands. "Such an announcement, in truth it may not be in my power." He shook his head. "But if you truly do conjure Pepe back, yes I'll try to arrange it." He sighed. "If Pepe returns, perhaps it will be in my power." His nod showed great fatigue.

We drank. The phone rang. A reporter from *El Universál.* I spoke briefly, felt as weary as Rubén looked, and hung up. It rang again. *Proceso.* I spoke, I cut the connection in mid-sentence. Three minutes later, another ring. "Rubén. I'm going to sleep." I got up.

He nodded, and followed. He was far away. The phone again, it rang and rang. He manoeuvred his car around the Jeep and backed out the gate. I closed up. He didn't wave.

TWENTY-FOUR

I couldn't wait till midnight doing nothing. I couldn't drink any more. I didn't dare nap for fear of not waking up. San Jorge Gringo, saviour of Michoácuaro, had to stay alert.

Across the valley, spots of light. One was Felicio's home. I yearned for an hour of talking English. I hacked open a coconut and set it out. The phone at Pepe's kept on ringing.

I got in the Jeep, the loudspeaker still attached. Damn gate! My next present for Pepe, an electronic gate opener.

I passed a judicial sedan, dark and still. The speaker-display screamed a silent, Here I am! I stopped, soberly so soberly detached the damn thing, stored it in back and drove on, temperate as an old horse. By a street lamp another judicial vehicle waited. One of its soldiers sat on the hood, on his lap a rifle. Another passed him a bottle. They didn't scare me, not much—

Since we clever researchers don't like being detected I drove beyond the turn for Felicio's, slowed, cut my brights, rounded a couple of curves, pulled off, killed the motor, got out and peed. Nobody following. I felt good about that. In the on-coming distance a truck groaned and down-shifted. Its engine died. Silence. A weak glow of light. I walked up a hundred metres, another curve— A roadblock: car across the highway, figures outlined in the truck's lights. Humbled, I hustled back. I heard the truck start up, got the Jeep going, U-turned too wide and slipped into a shallow ditch, pulled

out, drove, cut off at Felicio's road; thirty metres in I killed
the motor. The truck passed. Parking lights on. The Jeep
wound up around boulders surely grown here since
Navidad. Felicio's lamps shone bright. My relief felt greater
than I'd have expected.

"Jorge! Glad you made it."

"Waiting for me?"

"I sensed you might come."

Him too.

He fluttered about. A drink? No thanks. Hungry? Not
really. Oaxaca cheese, crusty bread, a creamy avocado, tomatoes off the vine?

"It's not necessary." But he was gone. And back, with
fresh coriander too. And pepino dulce, from El Jardín de los
Viejos. He said in Spanish, "You'll have a beer with me?"

I wouldn't insist on English. "Felicio, I have a surprise."

He nodded.

"Pepe is returning." Depending on roadblocks.

He nodded harder.

Had Irini stopped by? "Pepe's been with Ali Cran." I told
him about Rancho Verde.

When I stopped, he said, "Of course."

"Did you know this already?"

"If Ali Cran had told me, later the story would be part
mine. Ali Cran share a story?" His smile crackled. "But I felt
it could happen so. Thank you for telling me. Why?"

"You'll be their host for the night."

"As it should be." His pleasure smothered any concern.

I helped him make up beds. Felicito's revenge: Ali Cran
sharing the twin-bedded room with Pepe, who snored. For
me, the couch. "If you leave and the judiciales find you, at the
very least they'll castrate you."

I lay down. My part was done. In half-sleep I addressed a
crowd of thousands: what wonders we'll bring to Michoácuaro—two, three, fifty gardens! I was Ali Cran's financial

advisor, Rubén was made archbishop. A gunfight erupted, Delcoz against Pincho, Pepe grabbed me, Jorge, Jorge, "Jorge!" I opened my eyes. Pepe. And Ali Cran and Irini. And Felicio, grinning.

In sleep my headache had come back. I needed more coconuts. I detailed my evening performance. Laughter. "How'd you get through the roadblocks?"

"What roadblocks?" More laughter.

Irini said, "Alicito knows all the dirt tracks."

Pepe said, "The escape routes of his prodigal youth."

We plotted Pepe's return. It pulled me right back in. Ali Cran said, "We'll lead from strength. You, Jorge, with Pepe. At the head of the crowd."

"No." Enough was enough was enough.

Pepe said, "Yesterday's gringo, today returned with the rescued kidnapped presidente municipal? We'll have boundless coverage."

"I'm finished playing hero for the media, it's that simple. It's politically wrong."

"Your help is vital, Jorge," Pepe said. "You convinced them, you and Rubén. They want to see you again."

Ali Cran said, "When you leave here, you lose nothing. But we must regain our town."

That argument again. Nothing to say back. Let tomorrow do its worst.

I slept across a rocky night. I opened my eyes. Eight-fifteen. At the back of my head, throbs of steady ache. I groaned, heard Felicio bustling and sat up. I remembered the plan of the day and fell back on the pillow.

Felicio appeared, a glass of orange juice in hand. "For strength, a little vodka in it?"

"Oh god. I need a shower."

"Of course. And wash your hair. To confront the world press." He chuckled. "Come along." The sky was flat grey. The others were laughing while they talked and ate.

The hot shower felt good. Fifteen minutes later I joined them. Felicio's coffee helped. They had agreed on Pepe's story for the crowd. At Pepe's side, Jorge in jeans, a safari jacket—

"In what?"

Pepe was delighted. "Jorge the great anthropologist back from jungles with the prize: Me."

From hero to clown. I argued. To no avail.

In Irini's pickup I scrunched on the floor, a blanket over me. We entered town along back streets. She turned a corner. "The plaza," she whispered. "Crawling with judiciales."

"What're they doing?"

"Wait." We drove. "There. The Rent Collection office." We slowed. "People vote there. It's closed. Four judiciales."

"Armed?"

"Heavily." We slowed, stopped. "They're searching the truck in front of us. Sshh."

She pulled up. I heard her chatting. We started again, slowly. "What happened?"

"I smiled." Faster. "He let me by." I felt the angle of the hill. "Oh boy—"

"What?"

She slowed. "Past your gate, it's another roadblock. Don't move." She stopped, unlocked, opened, drove in, "Stay there," shut and locked the gate, returned.

"Can I sit?"

"No. Here comes Vera."

"What happened?"

"They watched."

Vera reached the truck. "Señora—"

"Hola, Vera. Anyone inside the house?"

"No. When I came, yes. The judicial lieutenant, Blanco. He searched the house, and the casita." Vera giggled. "The Chilango house too, Señor Ernesto was very angry."

"Vera, don't speak on the phone, okay? They can listen in." To me, Irini said, "Okay."

I straightened up and got out. Vera glared at Irini, then at me. "Is all this what you have done, señor?"

I said, "Didn't I promise Don Pepe would come back today?"

"Truly? And he's well? And alive?"

I nodded.

"Oh, señor!" She grabbed my hand and kissed my knuckles.

I eased away. "Vera, you must tell no one. Not even Laura."

Vera giggled with relief and went to the casa with Irini.

Once more into the scorpion pit. On my veranda I stared at the waiting coconut, turned my back on it and leaned against the railing. Heavy low clouds.

"Great going, Hoar-hay! He really gonna be back by noon?"

Damn! I waved, whirled, and whisked back in. He was too idiotically delighted. I had nothing better to do so I drank my thin coconut milk.

Irini brought the safari jacket. I frowned. "Ridiculous."

She bussed my cheek. In a sleeveless yellow dress she looked the perfect companion to a reappearing candidate for mayor. Where had the dress come from? She hadn't gone home—

In her hand, a thing. "What's that?"

Her eyes gleamed, a lovely canary-green. "A hat, of course." Australian, outback, left brim clipped to crown. "Put it on."

In for a centavo. Far away, a thunderclap. I glanced in the mirror. A hatted ass stared back at me. Eleven-thirty.

"Vera's preparing a large comida." Irini put her arms around my neck and drew my face to hers. "After, we can escape up the hill." She kissed me, tight warm lips. "Thank you."

Is there ever a precise moment when things end, things start? Great white anthropologist Jorge steps from the plane and into the world of others. Everything is now contaminated. Vera: He will go away again. The price to pay for being, oneself, transformed.

In the future we will all do many things. Right now we had to evade a hundred judiciales and get to Rubén's office. "How will they sneak Pepe in?"

"But Doctor Ortíz has many emergencies, in town also."

"But naturally." I got down on the van floor.

She drove out the gate. "Hang on."

"What?" We barrelled toward the centre. "What is it?"

"The judiciales are signalling— Too bad I didn't see them." We turned a corner. "Okay, sit up."

I slouched, the blanket about my head. On the plaza, on the sidewalks, crowds of people. The palacio municipal, the main polling station, was chained closed. Still, a festive mood. A dozen media trucks, the eyes of the world. Judiciales everywhere, pairs in cars, pairs on foot.

In front of Rubén's office stood seven deputies and by the curb Pepe's Jeep—canopy off, cab open, loudspeaker re-attached. Ali Cran behind the wheel chatted to reporters. We drove around back. Felicio's VW. Que milagro. A roll of thunder. Irini knocked, twice long, twice short, twice long. The door opened a crack. Rubén, seeing me, shook his head and let us in. I put on my hat. A relief of laughter from Felicio and Pepe. More than a dash of hysteria around. I took the hat off.

Felicio's boots glowed black, his snowy pants and shirt shone white. Irini looked light in her yellow dress. Pepe wore a white formal shirt and jeans; pinned to his collar, a red carnation. Rubén in full uniform, tie included, reached out his hand. "Congratulations, Jorge." I took it, we gave each other a solemn abrazo. He was a friend again; scamming again.

Irini said, "Let's start."

I looked at Rubén. "You too."

"We'll clear the way." He opened the front door and barked an order I didn't understand.

Pepe grabbed me by the elbow. And we went out. On my side, Puño Filo thrust an arm against forming crowds. Pincho on Pepe's far side held his pistol at the ready. Other deputies protected our backs. Up above, more heavy clouds. The merry-go-round bleated its tune.

At the Jeep a dozen media types leapt toward us, microphones brandished, shouting questions. Rubén's men did in fact keep them off, even knocked one reporter down. To Betsy Picard, holding back, I called, "Later!" She nodded. We clambered into the Jeep, Ali Cran at the wheel, I in front as well, Pepe between us sitting high on my seat back. In the rear, Doctor Felicio Ortíz and Señora Irini Farolla.

We drove around the plaza, around and around. Pepe made his speech, "Compañeros and compañeras, Michoácuaro is our town again!" Massive cheers. We were a one car parade. The judiciales watched. Cheers, louder cheers. Alicito beat out rhythms on the horn, punctuating Pepe's spiel. Then from Pepe a new line: "Tomorrow, my friends, we shall all meet here at the plaza, tomorrow at mid-day. I'll take the oath of office. From tomorrow I shall be your mayor!"

Mighty cheers. I stared at him. Stupid. I shouted in English, "Pepe, for pity's sake!" The ante upped. Beyond any level we could sensibly play.

He covered the mike. He grinned. He spoke English also: "We'll argue later."

Ali Cran's smile was for himself alone.

The cheers doubled, tripled. And multiplied again as Pepe repeated his announcement.

Ali Cran was right, no way to fight and stay clean. In my jacket I felt sweaty from a jungle I'd never explored. Irini scowled. El doctorcito waved, imbibing the town's pleasure. Beneath dense clouds, the jubilation on Michoácuaro's faces came to us as a roar. I traced it back to fear.

The weightless rhetoric pouring from Pepe amazed me. The town loved him. I feared for him, then. As presidente municipal he could become a lesser man.

Platitudes, circles, cheers, circles. We met the press. Pepe Legarto: "I was blindfolded the moment they took me. They injected me, I was unconscious. They moved me three times. I was alone. At the final place, a little adobe beyond Ojo de Agua, my norteamericano friend walked in. There I was, tied to my chair. They'd abandoned me. I hadn't eaten for two days."

A few heavy raindrops. My turn: "Two days ago I saw the future. I recognized a little square, not far from Michoácuaro. I saw a road, an adobe house. I made out Pepe, tied to a chair. I knew where to go. I found him, I hid him, I brought him back." A deflating sensation, lying to the local/national/ world press. Commandeering. Inane. My choice. For Michoácuaro.

One question gave me pause. Betsy Picard: "How'd you get by the roadblocks?"

I smiled, kindly as I could. "If I can see beyond Ojo and into tomorrow, should roadblocks pose a problem?"

Amazingly they all wrote it down, a logical response.

It can be mocked now, this second sight business. But I'm no longer certain: Did I see, two days before arriving at Rancho Verde, an image of Pepe under that awning, playing solitaire? Of course in Amsterdam too, with the dark-haired signora.

We returned to the casa, Pepe, Felicio, Irini, I. Simón, jubilant through residual anger, joined us. A dozen campaign workers arrived. Rubén was late. We called his home and left word with Bárbara, this celebration needed el jefe. Ali Cran had disappeared as we spoke to the press.

Constanza, Vera and Laura had prepared guajalote con mole.

"In so little time? Impossible!"

"Magic,"Vera said. Then admitted it was all defrosted, the turkey, peppery mole sauce. Freezers too are magic. Good, she was laughing again. The room, the whole casa, felt almost at ease, approaching balance.

The phone rang and rang. Vera told everyone, No interviews. But one time she handed it to Pepe. "The governor." We grew quiet. Pepe listened. We heard, twice, "Sí." And then, "No, no. It's impossible." And a minute later, "I can't do this." The conversation ended. He turned to us. "The governor isn't pleased."

Silence. Simón asked, "And?"

"Tomorrow when I take the oath of office, I'll make him even more unhappy."

Whoops and cheers, laughter, dreadful jokes from Ali Cran at last arrived with Gitana. Under the laughter I felt a nervous unease. And suddenly I feared for Pepe, a large dread.

Acute pain stabbed at the back of my head, and I felt dizzy. Too much tequila already? Stupid, the party was just prelude to going off with Irini… A new kind of vertigo, no precipice needed. I stood still, anchoring my feet. The room itself, the celebration, was all out of balance.

The carnation hung from Pepe's collar, upside-down and wilted; too symbolic even for Michoácuaro. "We have to talk."

"But aren't we talking as we speak?" He spoke English.

I led him to his veranda. Outside, my sense of disbalance eased. "Pepe, challenging the governor, that's mad."

His sad smile. "Of course. But what weapon is more powerful than a bit of madness?"

"Come on, federal law, public opinion, you have to—"

"Jorge." He shook his head. "Public opinion is manufactured, fabricated. Even I can make public opinion." His eyes sparkled. "Come, let's drink."

"They'll kill you."

"They'll try, whatever I do." He took my arm.

"I can't let you."

He laughed. "You've got two possibilities. Be my friend, or the friend of the governor."

"Or avoid the choice by leaving." Again that disbalance…

"From Michoácuaro? But leaving changes nothing. You'll carry the town with you."

"So being your friend is the only option."

He put his arm over my shoulder. "From the day we met."

We rejoined the party. Pepe's great idea was to try the seven-year-old Bordeaux he'd brought back from a conference years ago, twelve bottles. "Save the San Ángel for Rubén Reyes Ponce! He won't know the difference." Laughter in every corner.

I remembered Rubén's need to finish off the Chivas. I poured myself two fingers of the single malt. The glass felt unnaturally heavy.

The phone kept ringing. The closest drinker answered. Felicio announced himself prime storyteller of the afternoon. For once Ali Cran didn't argue.

The torrent came at last, lightning, an instant thunderclash. The telephone rang again. Felicio drank to the storm: "May it knock out the telephone lines!" Pepe's glass went up for the dozenth time, with the same toast: "To all my friends!" And talk, stories, laughter.

In one of the few dips in volume the phone rang twice, so clear. Vera took it. I still see several of us watching her, she presses the phone against her bosom, she stumbles—

Irini reached her first. "Vera! What?"

"Jefe Rubén— They say he's been stabbed, he's dying—"

TWENTY-FIVE

Rubén had been slashed many times, apparently by his deputy Puño Filo. But, with blood pouring from his wounds, Rubén had shot Filo dead.

I was the least drunk. "I'm driving." Pepe acceded and got in. Felicio scrambled into the back. The rain had stopped.

Knowing Rubén wasn't dead, just dying, I felt a bit better. The old bastard had been wounded before, half a dozen times. Pepe urged me to speed up. No worry, Felicio insisted, Rubén couldn't die, he had to curse Pepe at least once more.

Rubén's room was guarded by Pincho and two others. Three newsmen waited. Bárbara at the bedside held Rubén's hand. First Pepe embraced her, then Felicio. She shook my hand. Her tears flowed. "They say his chances are— He's— it's critical."

Pepe said, "He'll make it, Bárbara. He's very tough."

She nodded, searching for conviction.

Felicio's eyes, staring at Rubén's pallor, handed down a more dubious judgment. But Felicio was drunk.

A young surgeon joined us. Rubén had been stabbed nine times. Three of the wounds should have been fatal, two to the lungs and a curving abdominal one. But Rubén had survived surgery; if his heart held out, if there were no infections— The surgeon was guardedly optimistic.

"Should we wait?" Pepe's question asked, Will Rubén wake? And if so, will it be our final chance to speak with him?

"If you like." The surgeon sighed. "Returning to consciousness, seeing friends, sometimes the body manufactures strength." He smiled weakly. "We don't know why."

Bárbara sat with Rubén.

We found coffee, thin brown ink. I sipped with my eyes closed. Beside me, a voice, tentative, "Señor Jorge?"

Vera's cousin. "Chaba. How goes it?"

"For me, señor, very well." He nodded. "But for el jefe?"

Sure, Chaba was an orderly here. "We have to wait."

"With the help of the Lord." He crossed himself. "And with your help, señor, I've come closer to my father's bed."

"What did I do?"

"You said about the sugar, it wasn't salt. With the honey."

Chaba, at last around the bend? "That makes a difference?"

He gazed at me kindly. "Forgive me, but salt and honey, they preserve you from harm. From the evil eye." He thought for a moment. "Salt is the blood of Our Saviour, honey— honey—"

"The honey and salt, the sugar, they were for me?"

"Quién sabe, señor. But—sugar cannot protect you." He shook his head. "You must be blessed in many ways."

"So what was the sugar doing there?"

"My bed, I believe, was in the casita. The Chilango, I'll find out." A vigorous nod. "Someone traded my bed for the sugar." His head shook. "There's very little salt in tierra caliente, it's very valuable." He touched my arm. "I hope you haven't used the sugar. I'll have to return it. For the bed."

"No no, it's all still there."

"Thank you. I'll pray for jefe Rubén, señor. May you go with God." He squeezed my hand, and withdrew.

Could Ernie really have substituted sugar for salt? But what did he want with Chaba's father's bed? And how could I believe any of this made sense?

Betsy Picard arrived. I gave her an interview. She sounded satisfied. She'd be staying till tomorrow, after Legarto Nitido was sworn in as presidente. She and the others spoke to Pepe. And to Felicio who gave them his own version of reality. Close enough to our official truth.

A flurry at Rubén's room, two nurses, the doctor. We gathered by the door. At last the doctor let us in. Rubén's eyes looked beyond Bárbara. A flicker of a grin. "Pepe. Jorge."

We bent over him. Pepe said, "You're going to live, amigo."

"Sure, Pepe." He winced. "Jorge. You like—stories. I have two—little stories—for you."

Behind me Felicio said, "Rubén, it can wait. Rest."

"Two." His eyelids dropped shut. "Jorge—"

I sat, my face inches from his. "Slowly."

"First. The jefe goes to—Emilia." His eyes opened. "Early—earlier. He tells her, he said he must tell—the press, about Teófilo. Only that Teófilo is in the grave, only—" He stopped, he breathed, two-three-four times, shallow.

I nodded.

Rubén opened his mouth. With his upper teeth he wetted his lower lip. I took the washcloth, wiped his cheeks, and his chin. "Mmm," he said. "Emilia isn't happy…"

"It really upset her, then?"

"Bad pub-publi— Bad. But the jefe says— His conscience, in the new year he—" He breathed again, a lot of energy for a shallow drag of air. His whisper came thin. "His conscience. She doesn't—she can't believe. She says, 'Who has you—by the balls.' Emilia is—not stupid." He closed his eyes.

I touched Rubén's shoulder. "Rubén, save your energy."

"Not— Not smart either." He opened his eyes.

I nodded. "But you can tell me later."

"She says, 'When will you do this, clear your—your conscience.' El jefe says, 'Tomorrow, the new year.'" Rubén wanted to laugh. He knew it would hurt. "Start—clean."

I turned. The others had gone. Good. Bárbara needn't hear about Rubén's misdeeds.

"She calls—later. She says the jefe is right, make clear— Teó— Teó— His death. She says, we should meet— Not her house, Ig— Her son was there. Go to the Palacio Muni— Back door."

"Slowly, amigo."

Rubén's eyes were wide white ovals around brown circles with tiny black cores. "She has—key. PRI key." His eyes begged, Now I know, why didn't I then? "The jefe comes— late. Goes—up, Puño there, and Toni, only—" With his eyes he damned himself: so unprofessional. "A sur—prise, yes Jorge? Not—ready. Toni, Emilia's—whore. And el jefe. Puño stabs hi-him— Quick. Sha-sh-sharp. Toni shoots Puño, silencer— Bleeding, but el jefe sees... Toni kicks—him, laughs—" A tickle of a smile.

"Rubén, Pepe has to hear this. About Toni."

"Only—only a story, Jorge."

I nodded.

"My phone. Press— Office." A high smile now, with great effort. "Pincho—co-co-comes." He shuddered.

"Rubén, rest."

The edges of Rubén's lips, trying to smile, twitched. "Lots of time—to rest. The other story. Emilia and—Teófilo the—" He suddenly coughed, silent. His eyes closed.

"Rubén—"

Now the hint of a smile. "A—moment."

"Easy, amigo."

"Jorge, get Av-avé— Emilia. Get—" He closed his eyes.

"We will." I wiped his face again. Avéspare had to be out of her mind. Or panicked? Or thinking clearly. On Rubén, dead, she could unload all the dirt, Teófilo and more. Few would believe she'd ordered Rubén's murder.

"Jorge." His eyes opened, a slit. "Get Bá-bár-bárba—"

"I'll find her. Lie quiet." A crisp brown face gone grey and soft. I went out. Bárbara sat, staring down. On one side Pepe, on the floor Lazarito, on her other side Mercedes, her hand lying on top of her mother's two. "He'd like you to go in."

Bárbara nodded, and stood. A child on each hand. "Did he tell you a good story?"

"Very good."

Her eyes overflowed. "Often he says about a story—'I wonder, would Jorge would like this one.'"

"He has remarkable stories."

She wiped her cheeks. "Yes." She led her kids to the room.

Pepe got up. "What did he say?"

I told him, in capsule.

Felicio joined us. "If Rubén makes it through the night he has a chance."

Back at the casa the celebration had dissolved, to restart after the inaugural. Felicio drove home. Wine ached in my joints, I felt high on coffee and flattened by the day.

Pepe said, "Shall we talk with Emilia Avéspare?"

"Now?"

"With Rubén alive she'll be more receiving, no?"

"What do we ask her?"

Pepe, his glance jaunty, said, "We ask what she and her Toni know about the attempted assassination of Rubén."

In the Jeep I thought only a little about Toni and his pistol. Litres of adrenalin cascaded through me.

At the plaza, many judiciales, ever ready, and a couple of TV trucks. We parked between them and the Avéspare residence. I walked back to the rear of a truck and knocked. A reporter Pepe had spoken with at the hospital invited us in, they had a bridge game going, and beer and tequila. Betsy Picard said, "What's new with Ponce?"

"Rubén Reyes is resting." And to the Chilango cameramen Pepe said, "Look, one of you, could you shoot some video of us, really obvious? There, at that house. If we're not out in thirty minutes, come knocking. With all your equipment."

Betsy, speaking English: "What's up?"

"You'll be the first to know," I said.

They followed. Pepe knocked. Silence. A second knock. A third. A light over our heads. The door opened a couple of centimetres. Ignacio. "Yes?"

Pepe said, "We have to talk to Señora Avéspare."

"She's not here."

"May we come in?"

He thought about it, then opened the door. We entered. No Nissan. He led us around the bougainvillea to the back. He offered coffee. We declined.

"What can I tell you?"

Pepe said, "Señor Avéspare, where is Emilia?"

"She's gone away."

I said, "Where to?"

"She said she'd spend this New Year at Los Puertos. On the coast. Her—chauffeur Toni would drive her there."

Pepe spoke softly. "And they left, when?"

"Late in the afternoon."

"They'll travel through the night?"

"So it seems."

"She set up this trip a while ago?"

He smiled, weary. "She doesn't share her plans with me."

"Her going to Los Puertos, when did she tell you?"

"I found her note this evening."

"She has an apartment at Los Puertos?"

"No."

Pepe nodded and got up. "Thank you, señor. If she contacts you, please say I have to meet with her."

"I think I won't be speaking with her. I think, from now on, you'll be speaking with me." He turned to me. "You need not, señor, feel concern about Toni. You have my apologies."

Ignacio was growing up.

He led us through the bougainvillea garden to the door. A convincing stride. We bade him goodnight. "So Mamá has eloped."

Pepe smiled darkly. "To arrive at Los Puertos at four on New Year's morning with no apartment, this isn't very clever. Emilia is clever."

Betsy and two men crossed from the plaza. "What was all that about?"

"We wanted to talk with Señora Avéspare but she wasn't there." About what? "Plans for her factory. See you tomorrow." The plaza bristled with judiciales. We headed back to Pepe's.

I was giddy-weary. Was the maquiladora dead? I wanted to drive around and around Michoácuaro singing through the loudspeaker, Emilia and Toni, where are you hi-i-ding? Gone. Would her passion for Toni compensate for all she'd left behind in Michoácuaro?

Passion, still possible for us older folk. Where passion leads, maybe love can follow.

No extra cars in the drive. A relief. I said to Pepe, "Glad you're back, hombre."

"We'll have some good evenings. Buenas noches, Jorge."

I walked to the casita. Fireflies by the score, tiny points of glow. I reminded myself to hack open a coconut. At the corner of the casita a shadow moved. I froze.

"Señor!" A figure— "It's Eliseo." He glanced about. "Could we speak? Inside."

"Does the night have ears?"

He nodded. "Many, señor."

We sat at the kitchen counter. He accepted a beer. He looked very worried. I said, "Tell me, what's happening?"

"The judiciales are around every corner. In the cracks in the sidewalk. It's very quiet."

"Good." I was too tired for chat.

He looked about. "A fine casita." He admired it. "One could live here, with a family."

"It's a little small."

"Yes." He nodded. "My family and I, the house we live in, it's small." Another nod. "Smaller than this."

"Yes." What did he want—

"It's not a good time, señor."

"It'll improve, I'm sure." When he left. I could open my coconut. Get the machete— In the deep distance I heard the gate swing wide. A vehicle drove through, and stopped.

"A terrible thing, to stab the jefe." His head shook. "But Filo is dead. That's good."

"If he'd lived he could say why he did this."

"What isn't good, the other still walks in our streets."

"What other?"

Eliseo leaned my way, eyes hard. "The one who entered the Palacio Municipal with Filo."

"Who?"

More softly: "The one who drives Señora Emilia."

I leaned toward him. "Did you see him, this Toni?" I too was whispering.

He dropped his eyes. His head shook pure negative.

"Then how do you know?"

He gave me a weak smile. "They say this was—"

I grabbed his shoulder. "Not 'They say.' Who told you!"

He pulled away. I'd hurt his dignity. "I must not tell."

"Eliseo. If we want to arrest Toni, we need proof."

He sat straight, recovering status. "You don't need legal proof to kill that one."

"Let me talk to whoever told you this."

"She saw Toni and Filo enter the Palacio before the jefe. She's afraid, señor. But she sees everything. She knew I would tell you." He nodded. "You understand, señor."

I was pretty sure I did. "Eliseo, it'd be better—"

A knock on the door. "Jorge?"

"Yes?" This night would never end. Pepe came in.

He saw Eliseo. "We each have visitors."

"Eliseo, I've got to give your information to the new presidente municipal." Eliseo nodded. I told Pepe.

Pepe thanked Eliseo. We led him to the gate. Past Rubén Reyes Ponce's official car. Eliseo left.

"Okay. And who's with you?"

"Pincho. He swears Filo told him Rubén was a menace to Michoácuaro. And Pincho should figure whose side he was on."

"Dramatic."

"Pincho says he told Filo to go to hell. They'd had a lot of tequila."

"Sounds likely."

Pepe shrugged. "I'm tired, Jorge. But Pincho notes, correctly, that Rubén has no assistant. Only deputies. Pincho fears the judiciales will take full control. He wants me to make him acting jefe."

"By what authority?"

"Yes, precisely."

"You can do it tomorrow at twelve-thirty."

"He believes the police should be in charge of security, before and during the inauguration."

"Makes sense."

We went to the casa. Pincho too looked weary, and less cocky. Pepe said, "My friend has spoken with Rubén Reyes. The jefe has asked you to be acting jefe for two weeks, or until jefe Reyes returns to his duties."

A sudden energy in Pincho's shoulders lifted him from the chair. All five and a half feet of him stood tall and broad. He snapped his hand to his forehead, saluting me.

I nodded and raised three flat fingers to my brow with the indifference of one who makes such appointments daily. "Keep the peace, Pincho." I reached out my hand.

He shook it, deferential and equal in the same instant, and left. What had I done now? Pepe and I sat and drank for an hour; and another.

Church bells clanged, wild. Pepe's brow wrinkled, he rose, went to the phone and called the hospital. He spoke, nodded, put the phone down. "No change in Rubén." He listened to the bells. "They're saying, tomorrow is here."

I looked at my watch. "Happy New Year, Pepe."

"And to you, Jorge."

We finished our drinks. Pepe walked with me back to the casita. Fireflies sparked. Inside, I locked. I cut open my coconut. I went to bed.

Booze and coffee fought a renewed Mexican Revolution in my blood, gut to skull. Judiciales battled deputies, Blanco toppled Marranando's statue, Felicio swung his sword. I tossed, I drew the sheet tight around me. My bed felt out of all balance.

At its proper moment: "Ayayaaaayeeeee-aaahh!" Blood-thirsty.

I waited. No splash.

TWENTY-SIX

Pants on, the door— Locked! I yanked. The key—? In my pocket. Calm. I slid it into the lock, and turned. It opened like any door.

A sharp pre-dawn sky. No one by the pool. Around at the passage I pulled the wires wide. To the pool. Moans. A rooster crowed. At the edge I looked. A whimper. Oh my.

The stairs were dry, the pool empty. Nine feet below, Ernie, naked, lay flat, his chin on the cement, staring ahead, little croaky sounds coming from his mouth. His skin was grey. His right arm bent backward at the elbow, an impossible angle.

I'd been imagining a cannonball. How could he have splatted in that position?

From below the horizon a beam of light struck a low cloud and angled down on Ernie. He wasn't alone. Moving spots. Many. It couldn't have been more than a second but it felt way longer than it's now taking me to write this sentence for my brain to recognize the telltale shapes: scorpions. A bare pool, a naked man. Lots and lots of scorpions.

I stood frozen. Several of the beasts had found Ernie. More headed his way. I saw two dark spots on his right leg, three on his back, one at the elbow's curious angle, another by the crack of his ass. Ernie shouldn't be afraid, they attack only when cornered. Except here even distant soldiers were marching to battle, Don Ernesto their bounty.

Another rooster crowed. A flutter of hens.

Ernie gasped, "Eeeh. Aiieee." And, "Yeeehh. Ih. Ihh." He watched their approach. "Eeeeehhh," he whispered.

I shouted, "Hang on!" How could I help. A voice, English with a Michoácuaro accent, spoke to me: Help? Why? I watched.

Ernie sobbed to an alacrán two inches from his nose, "Eheheheheh—"

Get them away? Go down. Barefoot? No no. Then? Watch some more...

"Eeee-iieeeeee—!"

Ernie's eyes were closed. An alacrán sat on his cheek, as still as silence. No rush.

A sliver of sun crept over the flat of the hill and touched the side of the pool. So limpio, the air. In the clear light a deep-toned rooster crowed. My paralysis broke. "I'll get help!"

At the witches' passage, a chicken. I kicked it aside. Shoes. A jacket. I ran to the big house. "Pepe!" I banged on the door. Get alcohol, raw tequila. Or tranquilizers, slow down the venom. "Pepe!" I banged again.

He was dressed. He saw me through the glass. "It's open."

I slid it wide. "You got tranquilizers?"

"Looks like you need a fistful."

I explained. He offered a tiny smile. "Demerol? Or Valium?"

"Better bring both."

Gumboots. Brooms. I put on the boots. We were hurrying, not rushing, Pepe and I.

Poolside. Below, cavorting, fluttering, ten chickens and three roosters were pecking away. A breakfast treat—juicy scorpions. Fowl with horny legs, bony beaks, no fear.

We stepped down the stairs. Feathers, venom, and Ernie. He'd turned himself over. So his back wasn't broken. "Eeeyaa. Eeehhhh. Eee." His brown belly hosted a couple of alacranes. A rooster pecked at an alacrán lodged between his great and second toe. A hen pecked at his testicles—a robust alacrán hiding there, trophy-size. We sent the hen scurrying and brushed Ernie off. Yelps, whimpers. We turned him to his side. He screamed. One advantage of being naked: hard for scorpions to hide.

One crawled out of his hair.

I used the broom to sweep the scorpions away. Pepe said, "You'll be safe soon, Don Ernesto."

He wheezed some more. I swept. He wailed. Pepe loped to the house for a phone.

I swept some more. The sun shone on Ernie's skin. Sweat poured from his face, and belly. I saw multiple puncture wounds. All around us now, down in the pool, hens and roosters gorged themselves on a wondrous breakfast. What happened to scorpion venom in their crops? Ernie groaned. My mind wandered. To Avéspare and Toni. Rubén. To Irini. Irini, Alaine. Irini.

Pepe returned, with a blanket. The zest was gone from his gait. He covered Ernie. He lifted Ernie's right eyelid, he looked at the eyeball. "We should raise his feet." We did.

"What did the hospital say?"

"This. And to cover him. Till the ambulance gets here."

"Should we open his gate?"

"It was ajar."

We watched chickens devour scorpions.

Pepe said, "Jorge."

"Hmm?"

"Rubén died."

I suppose I'd known. Yet the tumult of yesterday and these past minutes... "Shit." In the distance, a siren. We'd given the fear of death so little space to perform, how could he have died? Emilia Avéspare and Teófilo Através, my dumb demand for public awareness of Teófilo's death, my contribution to Rubén's murder. My tongue tasted of bile. "Pepe, I'm sorry. I am so so sorry."

Pepe said, "He was a part of Michoácuaro."

The siren grew from weak to piercing. An ambulance stood in the driveway. A couple of men, a stretcher.

I went back to the casita. Pepe was due at MMM HQ, final preparations, his acceptance speech to be approved by Simón. I had to join him there to ride in the motorcade.

No further word from the governor. Maybe he'd backed down, maybe the inauguration would go ahead without incident. Sure.

I sat alone on the veranda and drank my coconut milk. I was getting used to it. No headache this morning.

Poor bastard Rubén, truly gone. I'd never hear his second story, Emilia and Teófilo…

I felt nothing for Ernie. Anyone might have drained the pool. Only Ali Cran could arrange for scorpions.

I saw into the future, an infusion into the lore. Did you hear about the Chilango? They say… Important that the storyteller know, and include, the sounds coming from Don Ernesto's throat. And, recalling those little wails, speak kindly of Blaze. Who knew about Blaze? I suddenly realized one of my responsibilities during the next week: a training course. After I left, those storytelling duties would fall to my deputy, Doctor Ortíz.

The week I would give to mourning for Rubén.

Near to eleven. Would Irini call or come by, offer me a ride to the motorcade? I walked over to the casa. In the kitchen Alicia sat against the far wall, the remains of a yellow mango in her hand. Its juice smeared down her white dress and glazed across her cheeks. The glaze was cut through with tears.

"Hey, little one. What's the matter?"

She turned her face to the corner.

I knelt beside her. "Alicia? You all right?"

She squirmed her forehead into the angle.

"Want another mango?"

She nodded against the walls.

In the refrigerator I found a juicy one. I turned, and caught her glancing at me. Her nose dove back into the corner. "You can't have it till you turn around."

She pointed to a pocket in her dress. "Put it there."

"Mangos are only for girls who talk to other people."

"I won't talk to other people."

"Why not?"

No answer.

"Who do you want to talk to?"

She sniffed. "My alacranes."

Of course. "Oh little one, of course. I'm sorry."

She turned. She was weeping but she grabbed the mango fast as a chicken snaps a scorpion. "Not—your fault."

"No one's fault."

"My mamá's fault." She sniffed a drip back up her nose. "And that mean Laura."

"But, why blame them?"

She sniffed, stood, bit into the mango, turned and ran from the house.

I poured some coffee, sat and sipped. I got up, found some eggs. Did Ali Cran have pits of scorpions around town? I broke an egg into a bowl—

"I can do that, señor."

"Vera!" I was caught, cooking in her kitchen.

She took the eggs.

I sat. "Alicia's upset." No response. "About her alacranes." I waited. "She blames you. And Laura."

No smile. "Because it's our fault." Pride in her voice.

"What did you do?"

"You'll have two eggs." No question. "We cast a spell on the Chilango."

"A spell. What now?"

"Very forceful. Very dangerous."

"Why?"

"Because it was strong."

"But why'd you cast it?"

"He stole the maestro's masetas, yes? Laura gave ten of them to the maestro. They belong to the house. We waited too long, he took some away. A strong spell was necessary." She shook her head, her concern harsh. "Something went wrong."

"What?"

"I don't know." With arms folded she stared by me, a professional mulling a quandary.

"Vera?"

Her name brought her back. "Sí, señor. Some chorizo?"

"How did you do it, the spell you cast?"

She shrugged. "As I learned."

"Can you tell me?" She looked unsure, as if I'd asked too much. "Or is it a secret?"

She shook her head. "No secret. We—projected the spell."

"What was it, what you projected?"

"I don't understand."

"Did you, for example, project masetas to drop on his head?"

She laughed. "A simple pure thought. Nothing more."

"A pure thought?"

"Yes. As, he should dream it. For every maseta he took, an alacrán should wait for him. On the veranda."

"And sting him?"

"Oh no. Only, so he doesn't meet more alacranes, he should bring the masetas back. And cover the alacranes with the pots. The alacranes would be happy, and Don Ernesto too."

"Did Laura want Don Ernesto to be happy?"

Her eyes opened wide, her hand leapt to her mouth. She whispered through her fingers, "Laura!" She shook her head. "Gracias, señor." She made my eggs, and hummed to herself.

Proving you can't trust a vengeful witch, not even your best friend.

Fine eggs and beans. The phone rang. Vera answered. "Señor Legarto is not here." She looked at me. "One moment."

I mouthed, Who?

She covered the mouthpiece and whispered, "Morelia."

I felt a chill. I took the phone. "Yes?"

"Señor, Lieutenant Ángel. We have recovered your suitcase."

"Wonderful!"

"The case is full. Presents, señor?"

"Yes. Where was it?"

"Heróica Villasucito. The jefe of the station has tried all week to locate the owner. At last he contacted my office."

"I'll come tomorrow."

"It's not necessary. My captain will bring it. I am told Michoácuaro has suffered a tragedy. My condolences."

"Word travels fast."

"About misfortune, yes."

We agreed on a fifty-thousand-peso reward for the man who located the suitcase, about twenty dollars. "Lieutenant, my thanks." And a superb New Year to the citizens of Villasucito.

No call from Irini so I called her. No answer.

At the plaza the platform was again in place. Red, gold and green bunting decorated the stage, the lampposts, some vehicles. Battered speakers crackled test sounds. Half a dozen judiciales stood watching. Media crews were setting up. At MMM HQ Pepe and Simón were deep in discussion. I said, "Everything okay?"

Pepe grinned. "They say the inauguration might be opposed." His cheer was overdone.

"The governor?"

"Blanco. He may keep it from happening."

"He has the right?"

Simón folded his arms. "The governor has sent a decree, they say."

"They say? And no one's sure?"

Pepe looked at Simón. Simón shook his head and checked his watch. "It's getting late."

"Anyone spoken to Blanco?"

From Pepe a half-ironic smile. "Gringos are so pragmatic."

"Pepe, what the hell are you doing!" But he was back in conversation with Simón. I left.

The faceoff was on now, Pepe with Simón here, over there Blanco and his judiciales. In between, town-people and campesinos; violence fodder. I hurried to Marranando's house. A couple of vehicles, four men in the drive, the Sten gun in place. I marched in. Three judiciales became a barrier three hundred kilos thick. I blurted my celebrated ploy, "Lieutenant Blanco will have your balls if you don't let me through." They weren't intimidated. Likely their balls rested in Blanco's pocket already. One went to speak with the lieutenant. He came back and flicked his head toward Blanco's door. A different kind of intimidation. I knocked.

"Enter." I opened and went in. Blanco looked up, and blinked. "Yes?"

Only one question. "Will you try to stop the inauguration?"

Blanco massaged the bridge of his nose, scratched his chin, examined his fingers. "PRI and MMM have been informed."

"Of?"

"Hombre—" He blinked. "The governor has appointed an interim presidente municipal, Licencio Oswaldo Ocampo from Pátzcuaro, to serve till tranquility is restored and he calls a new election."

"Lieutenant. They plan to defy the governor."

"So I understand." He spoke softly. "They will fail."

But surely Pepe understood this. "When did you inform them?"

"Both parties were enlightened at eight this morning." He stared at me.

I had nothing to say. "This is crazy."

Blink. He nodded. Blink. "When people act unlawfully, craziness often follows."

"Some of your own men could get hurt."

"Automatic weapons against machetes? No no." A quick secure shake of his head. "But if so—" A shrug, a blink.

"You may be hurt too."

"One of the risks." A serene nod. "But today, I don't think so."

I stared at him a moment, then got up and left. The barrier parted, I was out. Damn! Up the road I saw five vehicles led by Pepe's Jeep, loudspeaker attached, Simón urging all Michoácuaro to the plaza. The parade crept along and people cheered. In the third vehicle, Irini's truck, a bedful of campaign workers led chants, and the crowd yelled back. Irini waved to me. I jumped into the cab. "Irini, it's bad." I told her what Blanco had said.

"No one can stop this, this time." She pointed to the massing people. "Look."

I dropped down, ran forward, jumped up on the Jeep's running board, passenger side. "Pepe!" He was driving. Under the roar of Simón's miked voice he ignored me and waved to his fellow Michoácuarans. By the platform a media mob swarmed him, and hundreds of townspeople. I couldn't get around to the other side. "Simón!" He turned. "I talked to Blanco!"

Simón gestured to the crowds. "But here is the Popular Will."

And where was the Law? Law was saying, This is wrong. Law made by suborned politicians. Law executed by a

President of the Nation as dye-vats pour into the rivers of the heartland. Law enforced by legal thugs. Law, wrongheaded. Law. Not the whim of Lieutenant Blanco.

The crowd hoisted Pepe to the stage. Thousands of men and women, many many kids. Cries of "Pepe! Pepe!" Applause. Stamping of feet. Then I too was pulled up. I stared out. Thousands, thousands— A buzz from the right of the platform. Weapons cleared a path, four men with automatic rifles. Then Blanco, and more rifles. "Señor Pepe Legarto?"

"Yes."

"We meet at last. The governor of Michoacán welcomes your safe return. But this inauguration is illegal. By his order it will not be held. An interim presidente municipal will manage the affairs of Michoácuaro till new elections can take place."

Simón set himself in front of Pepe. "Four-fifths of Michoácuaro says Legarto will be sworn today."

"Don't test me, señor."

"Don't let yourself look ridiculous, señor." Simón snapped his fingers. Two dozen men separated themselves from the crowd, pushed people back, and formed a row of white shirts. On the belt of each, an automatic pistol. At their centre, Pincho, arms folded, pistol in hand. Simón smiled. "Please, Lieutenant. Leave the platform."

In silence men and women, with and without children, looked to the side streets.

Pepe's mouth twitched. "Simón. Stop. I'll win the next election."

"Yes. After you serve the term you were elected for."

"No. I believe the Lieutenant is serious."

"So do we." Simón nodded toward Pincho. "The law of Michoácuaro demands the inauguration of Pepe Legarto."

"You force me to act, señor." Blanco gazed across the plaza, eyes steady, not a blink now. He raised his hand and swept it high over the crowd as to the heavens. On four sides—the roof of the palacio municipal, the bank roof, the Avéspare roof, a half-dozen more—many armed judiciales. A plaza full of people saw them. No one moved. Blanco nodded to Pepe, and swept his arm once more. The judiciales pointed their rifles skyward and fired two rounds.

Screams. The crowd broke, the edges loosened, screams, stampedes down the side streets. Some fell, some picked up others. In three minutes the plaza pit was near to bare. Pepe, Simón, myself, half a dozen others, Blanco and his four men remained on the platform. Pincho, three deputies, and Irini stood silent below. Judiciales on the rooftops. Blanco's boys herded us from the stage. And that was that.

Pepe, suddenly much older, smiled sadly. "Lots of time to drink together now, amigo."

TWENTY-SEVEN

Time to drink, to talk and think. Michoácuaro, peaceful. On the rooftops, under the porticoes, shifts of judiciales came and went. Life on the plaza, overseen by them literally, meant no public life. Three old men on a bench is a general meeting and foot patrols break it up. Four kids and a dog is potential for insurrection; pairs of judiciales take infantile pleasure in scaring the kids home.

I gave Pepe the lock from Ernie's gate. He ran his fingers along the cut. He shook his head and smiled. "Laura does good work."

I visited Bárbara and paid my condolences. But the domestic Rubén wasn't a man I'd known. I mourned him with Pepe. He told me stories about Rubén. We drank to Rubén.

I confronted my role in his murder. "If I hadn't pushed him about Através—"

"If he hadn't warned Emilia, if he hadn't agreed to threaten Teófilo, hadn't been chief of police, hadn't been greedy."

"Sure, he'd have died some other way. Some day far off."

"And who else played a part?" Pepe's little smile. "Say, myself. If Rubén hadn't come to me about Teófilo, if I hadn't advised him. Or Delcoz, if he hadn't charmed Bárbara and subverted Rubén through her—"

"Sure. But still I played my part."

"Then mourn. Here, and later up north." He smiled. "Maybe he'll enjoy being mourned in the snow."

I continued my foolish coconut cure. The tension level in town decreased. So did my headaches. All very strange. But very good.

The only public event allowed was Rubén's funeral. Blanco decreed it would be held on January sixth, the Day of the Three Kings. Clever; time to let anger cool, and on this day of giving presents the town's focus would be on its children. Only the bishop would speak; Bárbara wanted this. I hoped Skull-face had Rubén well-iced. Pincho came every day to report to Pepe. Pepe told Pincho such a meeting had no meaning. Pincho persisted.

Irini and I spent many days together, and three nights.

One afternoon she mentioned Gottfried Sommers. "You know, with his last breath he will hate you."

I could imagine it. I hadn't even tried to convince his daughter to visit him. "I guess so."

She handed me a sealed envelope. "I've written him."

"Saying?"

"That I won't see him. That I hope he isn't in great pain in his last days. That you spent a lot of time with me, you urged me to see him."

"But I didn't."

"Oh yes. With the strongest argument, that I could use his money for the Jardín. For many gardens like it." She kissed me. "Please send it. I don't want any contact with him."

I took the letter.

Our first night together, though we'd planned it well— dinner at her home, talking, we'd see what would happen— I was anxious. I drank a quick tequila before arriving. It didn't help. I knocked. My heart bashed harder. She opened the door. I went in. We kissed lightly. Friends.

She poured two glasses of wine. "To you." We sipped and set our glasses down. My blood pounded. She kissed me, and I her. We held each other, stepped into each other, our kiss went on— She pulled her head back and grinned. "You're almost as nervous as me."

"How do you know?"

"My heart's drowning out yours."

We laughed, we lingered in the advantage of the other's pleasure, we found each other's depth for the first time. Oh it was lovely, grand, easy at last. We lay still together and talked into the night, and later began again.

The second time our simplicity was gone, the vacuum of its absence replaced by a desire so huge Irini said later she didn't remember any like it. And who was I, where had I been, to disagree? A good friend, she said, not a sexual partner she felt it important to add, would have called our unholy profusion The Night of the Tiger.

The third night was, I'd say, sweet. Soon the señora would return to her Jardín, the anthropologist to his classroom. We clung to each other and held back from any finish for a long long while. When it came with the slowness and certainty of the rising sun I sensed I could love a woman again, Irini had shown me this. I cherished her for it.

We lay side by side, awake, silent till she said, "Ernie's gone away. Forever. Thank you."

Over the days I felt Pepe's fear for Michoácuaro ebbing. It looked like Avéspare had really skipped town. The likelihood of a factory faded. After all her hype she'd left her city behind. The Jardín's chance for survival multiplied.

Lieutenant Ángel traced the Nissan to the Morelia airport. Emilia Avéspare and a man had flown to Mexico City. From there they'd disappeared. Irini said they were "playing Pepe."

Pepe disagreed. "It's different. She's chosen to be a woman, with a man."

The Day of the Three Kings dawned clear. A burly cop from Morelia, Enrique Malasombra, arrived at Pepe's at ten with my suitcase. I gave him coffee. We spoke of Rubén. Captain Malasombra had known him for thirty-two years. I checked the suitcase. All the presents were there.

"And please give my thanks again to Lieutenant Ángel. The very best New Year's wishes to him and his wife—is it Marilita?"

Malasombra squinted, not understanding. But then he nodded. "Ah, Marilita. No, the marriage was annulled. Years ago."

"Annulled?"

"Of course. She was barren."

Later in the morning we gathered at the cathedral, Pepe and I, Irini with us, and Felicio. Contingents of police came from around the state, from Mexico City, Monterrey, and Vera Cruz, as far off as San Diego and Minneapolis. Rubén must have gone to lots of conferences.

Before being lowered into the earth, Rubén was submerged in holy vapour as Delcoz's sacraments and a porridge of ritual held off any quick eternity. I hoped Bárbara was finding some balm in it all. The bishop harangued us for half an hour: our sins had led to the premature death of Rubén Reyes Ponce. Iniquitous and pernicious beings such as we could hope for heaven only by scouring our souls of venality, wickedness, pagan acts, sensuality, blasphemy, infamy, mockery, hell-broth, and all the many sewers that flesh descends to.

I didn't walk out. It's not every day that I'm accused of so many remarkable sins.

Irini and Felicio left immediately after, they'd had enough. The rest of us trudged up to the graveyard behind a horse-drawn hearse, Bárbara wanting a funeral with every tradition in place. More ceremonial torment, now under a burning sun. They lowered the jefe into the ground. Pepe paid his condolences to Bárbara. I said, "He was a good friend, señora."

"Yes." Bárbara nodded. "A good man."

Suddenly Delcoz stood beside Bárbara. "You are leaving soon, señor."

"I must."

"Michoácuaro will be a better place when you are gone."

"For Michoácuaro I have lasting love. In some ways it's my home."

"But in a few days you leave." A cold smile. "While we remain, for many years."

I searched his eyes. Hard, grey, gleeful wrath. Poor Bárbara. I left them together.

I wanted to walk a bit. I said this to Pepe.

"It's too hot, Jorge. Come, we'll have a cold beer."

No, I'd join him later. They headed back to town in twos and threes. I found a tree and crouched in its shade. I pondered Rubén's sorrow: somewhere a bottle of good whisky remained half drunk, and he would never finish it. Out of nowhere, tears came. I let them flow. I felt far from the graveyard, far from Michoácuaro. Delcoz was right, they were all right, I belonged elsewhere. I cried for Rubén, and for the town's loss.

One site I needed to see, the grave holding María de Lourdes and Teófilo Através. I went searching. The plots lay irregular and it took me half an hour. A simple stone: María de Lourdes Disporatedo Suarez, Servant of the Church, Joyous Daughter of Agustín and Catalina.

Joined in death with Teófilo. Ali Cran's waggery. I felt better for standing there.

A final duty. My eyes itched. My headache, remarkably, was completely gone. A thank you, however silent, was in order. I made my way to the far end of the cemetery and Lucinda's shack. It wasn't there.

A week ago— The sun bore down. I stared. Maybe the woman wasn't Lucinda. But the hut had stood right here.

I shuffled about among weeds and bushes. I raised little dusty sand whorls. My eyes burned. I found some cement blocks crumbling back to powder, and charcoaled wood dried by sun and wind. A fire, a corpse. From trash to dust. I forced myself, I walked to the cliff drop-off. Slowly, slowly. A touch of vertigo. Here had been the tarp-covered compost heap. Dust.

No sense, no sense. I walked back and squatted on the hot decaying cement. I let my head hang down, my eyelids drooped—

Rubén says, Jorge, you could not have seen her.

I say, She unlocked my door.

He says, I have six alternate explanations.

I refuse to listen. Rubén, I'll open my eyes and you'll be gone.

He laughs. You were never logical, Jorge. Open, closed, you can't see me.

I believe he wants me to look. I open my eyes. He stands five metres away, down the road, holding a bottle. It's not possible.

He's squinting. You really see me?

I nod.

What am I wearing.

A white shirt. Your uniform pants. The brown tie.

May I be damned.

Assuredly. Unless you repudiate Bishop Delcoz.

He laughs. Ai, Jorge.

The bottle, is it tequila?

He nods. It tastes sharp now. Not like back on your side.

Rubén. Tell me. With Lucinda, did you do an autopsy? Was it really Lucinda?

He shrugs. There are many old beggar women. Too many. He smiles a little, and shakes his head. Time to go, Jorge.

Wait—

He walks with a normal step yet moves from the cemetery at great speed, no way catch him. No sense trying.

I was tired and hot. Had I seen the hut, spoken to her? In the clarity of my memory there was no doubt.

I said nothing to Pepe about chatting with Rubén. I did urge him to speak with Gertrudis, she'd seen who entered the palacio municipal with Puño Filo. And I insisted he write out, typewriter was fine, no signature, how to find Teófilo Através. He agreed. I pushed for an explanation of how Teófilo got there. This Pepe wouldn't do.

I gave my refound presents. The cashmere shawl for Constanza, its softness, brought on literal tears, and a damp hug. For Felicio, a book on Chinese cuisine. He flipped through it. "It stirs my imagination," he said, "and my stomach." I left with him a coffee-table book, large pictures of insects, for Ali Cran and Gitana; I wasn't up to more hours on horseback. The pocket calculator I gave to Rubén's kids, ingratiating myself with Bárbara; yes, she said, he'd finished the single malt I'd brought him. Vera and her family received the brand-name shirts graciously, but not with more enthusiasm than they had the chocolates and the straw ornaments. For Alicia, a panda bear.

Pepe got the MacDonald novels. His present for me was a copy of that book I saw in his library, *La Condesa de Michoácuaro*. Her face gloomed from the cover. A romance? "No, Jorge. History. Though they say the story's true. You'll enjoy it."

A day before leaving I invited Pepe, Irini, Felicio, Ali Cran and Gitana for comida at Las Rosas, the restaurant on the road to Morelia. Irini had said she'd be late. Gitana sent an abrazo with Alicito; one of her horses was foaling.

The place was Felicio's choice. "Here they understand how to treat an old doctor."

"Which is?"

He opened a menu and handed it to me. "Read."

Framed in roses drawn in yellow and red, a statement: "By medical recommendation, we counsel you to have your food with wine. Drinking wine makes one euphoric and talkative, the perfect state of humankind."

Correct.

We ordered, to start, a bottle of tequila reposada for the table. Ali Cran told a story about a blind sculptor and his painter wife who'd lived in Michoácuaro. For twenty-two years the town heard the husband accuse the wife of poisoning him; she charged him with unending infidelity. Finally, at seventy-three, she left him and went to Pátzcuaro, he too profligate to live with. Two weeks later she died in her sleep. The sculptor, free at last, bought a bottle of good whisky, then visited two friends, drank a third of the bottle with each, returned home in exultant stupor and crashed to the ground with a massive coronary. An hour later he rejoined his wife. They've been battling ever since.

Pepe, no more drunk than the rest of us, got up and told a long story he'd heard from Rubén about Michoácuaro in the time before they sprayed trees with chemicals, back when vultures still stole mangos out of the trees. And he acted all the parts:

A campesino is plagued by a monster. One night he tracks the thing down, he kills it. But the monster turns out to be his neighbour's donkey. The campesino, horrified, buries the donkey. But the donkey comes back to life, it haunts the campesino, the neighbour, the town. Pepe played the monster haunting us all. Pepe shot the monster. Pepe buried the monster, he played the vultures, he played the monster's legs.

They laughed, they couldn't stop they laughed so hard. I laughed too but with diminished laughter. Rubén's story from beyond the grave: I had dreamed this weeks ago. Their laughter chilled me.

So it was a relief when Felicio began a sad story about an ill copa de ora tree. Its owner decided to cut it down, wood for his wife's tortilla fire. But one morning a single bud appeared. It bloomed, a fine golden trumpet, it hung in the wind—

Irini scraped back a chair. "Pour me a large glass of that tequila."

Pepe did. She sipped, then chugged half of it down.

Felicio patted her hand. "As your medical advisor I suggest no more than two of those a day." He waited. "Tell us."

She breathed in deep, and exhaled. "EspórConMex is coming to Michoácuaro." She nodded at our stunned faces. "Ignacio Avéspare and his PRI friends. The Interior Minister approved the subsidy for transportation, from here to the frontier. There's no mistake. I called the Ministry myself, I actually got through."

Pepe poured himself a glass as large as Irini's. He sat back, shook his head, stared at her.

We finished two bottles of tequila that afternoon. No private goodbye to Irini, only a very drunken abrazo like with the others.

The drive to Morelia and flight to Mexico City next morning ranks among the most dreadful journeys of my life. Jaime couldn't pick me up. I found a cab. The driver got lost. A twenty-minute trip took an hour. Jaime's wife Luisa who knows a great deal about the wracks and agonies of the body, put me to bed.

I felt better next day. But now Luisa was ill, her spleen, or maybe her pancreas. I gave Jaime the Leica. He was elated. And the typed data about Teófilo. "I found it slipped under my door the day I left." No, no idea who brought it. No, I hadn't shown it to Pepe.

Jaime was devastated for hours. But he'd already mourned his friend, this was only confirmation. Next morning he was cheery as a magpie chomping a butterfly. "We must hear the truth, even when it's painful." His eyebrows rose. "And it'll be a fine scoop for me."

On the flight home I did decide what to do with Gottfried Sommers' five thousand dollars. At least this part of his cash would go to the Jardín de los Viejos. Except whatever it cost for Irini to buy and have installed an automatic gate opener for Pepe. Though, on reflection, I figured he'd turn it down.

An excerpt from

THE CONDESA OF M.

by George Szanto

Book three of
The Conquests of Mexico trilogy

Available in trade paperback
Spring 2005

ONE

We banked sharply to the left. "The lights are really close," Kiki said.

I leaned her way as far as my seat belt allowed. Bright yellow dots lined the boulevards below. "Yep." The air looked smog-free. This was not my memory of Mexico City.

Rissa's eyes concentrated on her reading, thin lines of type to keep her oblivious of turbulence, descent, and a terror that tons of steel might not settle safely on hard black tarmac.

"Look, that big building, I can see people!"

I felt Rissa cringe. In truth, I'm not great on landings either. I put my hand on Kiki's shoulder—in case she became frightened. She grinned, a cheeky flash to her grey-green eyes, and twisted back to the window. Her thick ruddy curls blocked my view. I reached for Rissa's hand but she held tight to the manuscript. And in minutes with no help from any of us the plane landed, a thud, a bounce, a rolling roar, and we slowed to human speed.

This was our honeymoon trip, more than four months late. We'd been married at Rissa's family's cottage by the lake, where her father lies buried and her mother's ground waits. Rissa's cousin, the photographer for the regional weekly, took our official pictures. Two made it into the paper, one of me and Rissa, one of Rissa and her daughter-bridesmaid, Kiki, now going on nine—not, she insisted, still eight. We

sent tear sheet copies, with a covering note, to people who
hadn't been able to attend. "At eleven in the morning of
August 23, 1993, on the shores of Lake St. Francis..."

The plane rolled to its gate and stopped. Rissa's wan
smile was an improvement. My own least favourite part of
the trip had started. The air control system closed down. Kiki
slung her back-pack, Brave Bear's head sticking out, over one
shoulder, tuned into her Walkman and sang along as sound-
less as the tape, her bush of hair bobbing in silent rhythm.
Our carry-on bags included the padded case protecting my
solstice present from Rissa, a super-light laptop with colour
screen. A special gift: I'd just finished a ten-year project, a
long book about victims.

I'm nervous going through any Customs, more so in this
instance because being in Mexico wasn't just honeymoon-
innocent. Early in October I'd had a call from Véronique
Poitier who was, this year, Chair of the Writers-in-Prison
Committee for our local branch of PEN, the international
organization of playwrights, poets, editors, novelists. "I have a
case for you."

As if she owned it. "What case?" I'd been giving a little
time to this—support for writers jailed for their beliefs, and
the attempt to get them released. Mostly it's tedious work,
postcard campaigns, organizing rallies at consulates, writing
to embassies, to leaders in the prisoners' countries.

"It's a coincidence. That town you once wrote about,
Mechomicho something?"

"Michoácuaro."

"Yes, there. The government's tortured and jailed a
writer. Calls himself Mono Loro."

"Rings no bells." But a memory did itch.

"You'll know people who know him. He's been found
guilty of attacking a bank. Does that mean he robbed the
bank?"

"I don't know—"

"Call some people, see what you can find out for me."

"Véronique—" Damn! Except, fair enough, I could make a couple of calls. "Tell me about him."

"Come down and read the file."

She's been talking to me like that, hard-nosed and dominant, for a couple of years. Before, for a summer, we had a fling, casual on both sides I thought. I drifted away and maybe that hurt her. I asked, she never said. But she'd already brought me onto the PEN committee.

Now, walking into the terminal, I felt my knowledge of the Mono Loro case was written all over my too-warm jacket. As visible as bringing my computer into Mexico. Which isn't illegal, just complicated. A friend had checked at the Mexican consulate: on entry I'd have to leave a deposit, three times the machine's cost, repaid on departure when I showed I'd not sold it. Nine thousand dollars? No way.

We waited twenty minutes in one of seven immigration lines with arrivees from Rio, Amsterdam, Tokyo. We got visas, good for a month. The luggage carousel stood silent.

Véronique's file had provided me with few solid facts about Mono Loro—pseudonym for Padre Joaquín Chuscadón, a Catholic priest. PEN lawyers had examined the documents: money was allegedly taken but Mono Loro was never charged with theft. So the writer-priest "attacked" the bank, but not for money? Some kind of symbolic action? No information in the file.

I knew the bank. I even knew the bank's president, an s.o.b. named Oscar Porchero. Nobody'd ever proven him dishonest but unsavoury he was. The file noted that Chuscadón's lawyer argued his client had been indicted mainly because he'd helped campesinos fight governmental privatization of communal lands. The writer-priest was sentenced to nine years in Zacazontitlán prison, a known hellhole.

Looking through a list of works by Mono Loro—literally, Monkey Parrot—I realized where I'd seen his name before. I'd even read a book of his, *La Condesa de Michoácuaro*, a novelization of a legend about an eighteenth-century noble-woman accused of blasphemy. "A local tale for your flight home," my friend Pepe had said when he'd given me the book. A coincidence? Pepe claims there are none. I'd scanned the novel on the plane, later forgot about it. So I searched out the book in my library and read the first few pages.

Since the week of her birth, María Victoria Cervantes y Gazoponda had received from her father the Conde of Michoácuaro presents both fine and delighting. The slender gold chain and narrow cross for her christening. Many trinkets and dolls. The portrait of the little Green Virgin. Teresa, as maid and companion. Gowns cut in Madrid's latest fashion—which was to say, Versailles'—to elaborate the charms of her lean figure. And a flower garden, and perfumes, and the palomino stallion Ballano who lent her the wind's freedom. Most prized were the books, books by the hundreds, sources of thought and solace, shipped to the rancho from distant presses. The conde knew little of the contents of these books. Of what concern to him, no harm in books, if they pleased María Victoria she must have as many books as she wished.

Her most important gift came from Teresa. At first blood she brought María Victoria to the lagoon in the volcano's cone, to take part in the movement of the waters.

The years passed. Her father gave María Victoria time. Still, she must wed. At the rancho, Santa Rita de Taratzingán, the edge of tierra caliente, she had met all the marriageable men of the region; none pleased her. As did no one over the two half-years, seasons of balls, teas, fiestas, soirées, spent with Mercedes her aunt in Mexico City, four days from the rancho.

Two seasons, five proposals, none accepted. Her father, Tía Mercedes at his side, spoke to her. "My child, you must choose."

"Between The Boor and The Fat One? Between Stammer and Limp? Or Don Pulque-Breath, or Lieutenant No-Soul?"

"Victoria." Tía Mercedes' smile weighed down the air. "You're nearly seventeen. Do you plan to become a spinster?"

María Victoria, a bit too tall, a touch too slight, her nose bent a degree to the left, her chestnut hair too waved for the fashion, shook her head. Marriage was inevitable, she being the only child of the Conde de Michoácuaro; property must have its continuity. Why, why had her mother the sainted tiny beautiful Josefina, second condesa of Michoácuaro, died giving her birth? Why had her father never remarried and conceived a son? Answers would be found only in the balanced mind of God. Meanwhile, duty to the land and its people, the hacienda and its outbuildings, the grand house on the tree-lined avenue in the City of Mexico, these would be hers; but must not be hers alone. "I will marry. One day." A boast, she knew. They would not let her wait. "When I'm ready."

"What, pine for love? Don't be a fool." Agostín turned to his sister. "Mercedes, you've let her hear too much gossip."

For Mercedes, gossip, the sharper the better, lent the season some intrigue. But she passed on none of the stories; facing her second half-century, she'd come to realize her contemporaries were not her friends. A tall thin woman, she believed she could see great distances. She raised her eyebrows to her brother. "My mouth is closed to gossip."

"Then too many false amorous stories."

María Victoria interrupted: "Papa, I'm not interested in love."

"In what, then?"

She shrugged. "I don't know." Though in part she did. "I would like to return to Santa Rita." Where the ceremony at the volcano's waters awaited her.

"To marry a simpleton from the provinces? One of those de la Nigrucinos? My child—"

"Never." She chuckled.

Mercedes and Agostín conferred. It had to be a gachupín, imported stock from Spain, pure blood. In the new world he would manage and enlarge the fortune of the family. There were such young men; one would come. Mercedes must write to Madrid, to distant cousins and acquaintances. Information would cross the water, Agostín and Mercedes would choose, make the offer, in months it would be settled.

Gonzalo, third son of María Victoria's mother's sister's husband's second cousin, once an army officer with no taste for distant wars, at thirty-two a mercantile administrator of proven ability, came from Toledo to Santa Rita for María Victoria. A fine couple, all agreed—she near as tall as he, and slender, her grey eyes sparkling; he a time-weathered man, a sharp nose, curling hair already grey, angular cheekbones rising to gentle eyes.

She feared his arrival. Weeks of turmoil: to be linked a lifetime to this stranger. But her fear mattered only to her. They were wed, María Victoria and Gonzalo.

In the first days she came to respect him; in weeks to care for him, cherish him; and soon to love him with all in her soul that was alive. For years she took full pleasure from his esteem and desire, he her orbit, she his focus. Pleasure, and more: generous Gonzalo, Gonzalo as indulgence, Gonzalo her best friend.

Why would such a story be offensive to Mexican authorities? And why would a priest write it?

A few days after I read Mono Loro's file, a letter arrived from another Michoácuaran, Dr. Felicio Ortíz. Jorge married! Wonderful! I must come for the holiday time and bring the two beautiful women whose photos he saw before him, clever of me to wed and instantly produce such a pretty daughter. He'd spoken with Pepe, Pepe had remodelled the casita—a bedroom below the veranda, perfect for lovely señoritas. Felicio was writing because Pepe had gone away to climb rocks, his crazy new passion.

Last time I'd seen Felicito, then ninety, his mind had been clear as the best tequila. I showed Rissa the letter. Felicio had written in English and she was charmed. "A wonderful idea. Let's go to Mexico and call it our honeymoon."

I couldn't have hoped for better, but felt a touch troubled. Rissa was well aware of my love for Michoacán. Since we'd been together she sometimes claimed she wanted to do something or other because she knew I'd like to. I adored her for this but it worried me—if it didn't give her some pleasure, later there could be resentment. Often I held my tongue. Now I spoke up.

"No." She shook her head. "Michoácuaro is part of you so I want it as part of me too."

"Okay." I gave her a small thank-you grin. Her big smile back made me feel she knew something she wasn't saying.

A week later Véronique on the phone interrupted our dinner. "I hear you've decided on Mexico for your honeymoon."

"Who told you that?"

"My sources." Her haughty smile sped down the line. "Listen, the Mexican writer's on a hunger strike, his sister wrote us. You have to go see him."

"Look, I'm in the middle of dinner—"

My not saying no flatly was the needed wedge for Véronique. "See the lawyer first, bring him money for an appeal." And, she insisted, I had to track down the Governor of Michoacán: impress on him that, argument from the global village, the eyes of the world were on him; that, high moral argument, jailing Mono Loro had struck a deadly blow at human rights and the freedom of expression in Mexico; that, argument from economic rationale, since our nations were about to be united in a new trade pact, any unilateral betrayal of justice could not be tolerated. In short, Mono Loro must be released.

"Look, it is after all my honeymoon—"

"A couple of hours out of your honeymoon for an innocent prisoner? To say the world hasn't forgotten him? Come on."

I agreed to take down five hundred dollars. To now I hadn't mentioned any of this to Rissa. Crime and violence aside, she isn't a fan of priests of any sort. And despite grudging respect for Véronique's work, Rissa clearly disliked the woman. A pinch of jealousy? Distrust, said Rissa.

A feeling I shared, but not for Rissa's reasons. I'd met Rissa through her daughter, by the side of a public swimming pool. Kiki, then seven, came up to me: "Why's the water green?" We talked and I took an instant liking to her, a bright ever-curious kid. Suddenly a commotion; she grabbed my wrist, "That's my mom!" She pointed. I had a quick image of a slender woman; up on the high board a brown tank-suit, a bounce, a double flip, and she cut the water cleanly. She surfaced. Two dozen hands applauded. Kiki introduced us.

The daughter quickly became my friend. And suddenly I was in love with Rissa. Once, taking Kiki to a so-called kids' movie, we ran into Véronique. In silence she glowered at Kiki—in fury? Or with rancour, as though my no longer being with Véronique was Kiki's fault. Though I know that up north such things don't exist, it still felt as if she were laying an evil eye on Kiki. So, yes, distrust of Véronique, foolish but present. I didn't tell Rissa about the incident. And I organized my time at the PEN office for when Véronique wouldn't be there.

When I got back to the dinner table, Rissa asked, "Who was that?"

I told her Véronique's request, mentioning neither priest nor bank attack. Rissa nodded and spoke to Kiki about homework. I could feel her cool. Violence upset her, she claimed. Except she dealt with it every day where she worked, HalfHouse, herself on the line. Only last month a frenzied ex-husband had taken a baseball bat to the fridge, screaming at Rissa, "The hellfire of Our Lord will burn to the ground this house of Satan!" and dragged his ex-wife away.

Getting ready for bed, Rissa said, "Did you have to say you'd do this?"

I shrugged.

She sat beside me, her hand on mine. "Why?"

I stroked her fingers. "I'm with the woman I love, and the novelist-priest's in jail alone."

"Priest?" Her lips went flat.

Rissa believes religions around the world are to blame for the worst excesses—political, military, and domestic—that human beings can wreak on each other. She even has doubts about liberation theology. Mostly I don't disagree but she's virulent in her condemnation—any priest in jail is one fewer priest to worry about. Still, I explained.

She nodded, without looking at me.

By the time I'd finished my ablutions she was asleep. Was her irritation more because of the priest, or because Véronique was the instigator here?

So I called Pepe. Rissa, Kiki and I would first spend a few days in Mexico City. I'd phone from there about our arrival. He gave me bad news about Felicio, a small stroke. El doctorcito was recovering but still weak. I realized that I was deeply upset; now we really had to go. I forced myself to ask Pepe what he knew about the Mono Loro case. Less than he should; the trial had been shifted to Morelia, his cable company didn't cover it. But he'd learn what he could, and try to find more of what the novelist-priest had written and send it to me.

I bought our tickets and reserved a room at a Mexico City hotel I knew. The Mono Loro material arrived—some poetry xeroxed from newsprint satirizing the Church, and a pamphlet written under his real name, Joaquín Chuscadón. Most copies of this had apparently been seized before they could be distributed. It dealt with a breakaway religious community. "La Nueva Belén: El Rosario o el fuego"— The New Bethlehem: The Rosary or the Flames. No doubt a warm and whimsical read.

It was mainly the condesa story that fascinated me. I was translating some of it, partly to reclaim my fading Spanish, partly to give Rissa a sense of life as it may have been in the colonial towns we'd visit. Mono Loro drew his heroine as a proponent of the natural superiority of women, a minor but persistent current in eighteenth-century rationalism.